Text Classics

PETER RYAN was born at home in Glen Iris, Melbourne, in 1923. His parents worked at the recently created Repatriation Commission. Ryan attended Malvern Grammar with the aid of scholarships and, after matriculating, was a clerk at Commonwealth Railways and the Crown Law Department.

In 1941 he enlisted voluntarily in the army, completed Basic Training and was sent on active service to Port Moresby with an Anti-Aircraft Searchlight Company, part of Moresby's base defences. For his intelligence work he received the Military Medal and was mentioned in dispatches.

After returning to Australia, Ryan taught at Duntroon and joined the Directorate of Research and Civil Affairs, then was a labourer in a bush sawmill. He gained a degree in history while managing a publishing firm. After working for a decade in advertising and public relations, he turned to journalism.

Fear Drive My Feet, Ryan's acclaimed account of his wartime service, was published in 1959 and has mostly been in print ever since. Sir Edward 'Weary' Dunlop commended it in a foreword to the 1992 edition.

In 1962 Ryan was appointed director of Melbourne University Press, a position he held until 1988. For the following fifteen years he was secretary to the Supreme Court of Victoria's Board of Examiners.

Ryan was a long-time *Age* contributor and since 1994 has written a monthly column for *Quadrant*. His other books include *Brief Lives* (2004) and a memoir, *Final Proof* (2010).

Peter Ryan and his wife, Davey, live in Melbourne.

PETER PIERCE is adjunct research professor in the School of Journalism, Australian and Indigenous Studies at Monash University. He is the editor of *The Cambridge History of Australian Literature*, the co-editor of *Vietnam Days: Australia and the Impact of Vietnam* and *Clubbing of the Gunfire: 101 Australian War Poems*, and the author of *The Country of Lost Children: An Australian Anxiety* and *Australian Melodramas: Thomas Keneally's Fiction*. His reviews appear regularly in Australian newspapers.

ALSO BY PETER RYAN

Encyclopaedia of Papua and New Guinea (editor)
Black Bonanza: A Landslide of Gold
Lines of Fire: Manning Clark and Other Writings
Brief Lives
Final Proof: Memoirs of a Publisher
It Strikes Me: Collected Essays 1994–2010

Fear Drive My Feet
Peter Ryan

Text Publishing Melbourne Australia

The Text Publishing Company acknowledges the Traditional Owners of the country on which we work, the Wurundjeri people of the Kulin Nation, and pays respect to their Elders past and present.

textclassics.com.au
textpublishing.com.au

The Text Publishing Company
Wurundjeri Country, Level 6, Royal Bank Chambers, 287 Collins Street, Melbourne, Victoria 3000 Australia

First published by Angus & Robertson 1959
This edition published by The Text Publishing Company 2015
Reprinted 2021

Cover design by WH Chong
Original page design by Duffy & Snellgrove

Printed in Australia by Griffin Press, an Accredited ISO AS/NZS 14001:2004 Environmental Management System printer

Primary print ISBN: 9781925240054
Ebook ISBN: 9781925095876
Author: Ryan, Peter, 1923–
Title: Fear drive my feet / by Peter Ryan ; introduced by Peter Pierce
Series: Text classics.
Dewey Number: 940.548194

This book is printed on paper certified against the Forest Stewardship Council® Standards. Griffin Press holds FSC chain-of-custody certification SGSHK-COC-005088. FSC promotes environmentally responsible, socially beneficial and economically viable management of the world's forests.

CONTENTS

Across the River;
Into the Mountains
by Peter Pierce

AUSTRALIA'S campaigns in New Guinea from 1942 to 1945, which eventually defeated the Japanese, generated remarkable poems by the RAAF pilot David Campbell— 'Men in Green', 'Pedrina'—and some of Kenneth Slessor's most vivid war correspondence (or what survived his bitter battles with censors). James McAuley, who served there, would experience religious conversion and write of this when he returned after the war. A clutch of novels— tales of Japs and the Jungle, sometimes infected by racial animus—were written by veterans. The best known of these used to be T. A. G. Hungerford's *The Ridge and the River* (1952), *The Last Blue Sea* (1959) by 'David Forrest' and, from the same year, Norman Bartlett's *Island Victory*. John Hepworth's novel *The Long Green Shore* emerged in 1995, after decades of lying in wait. Yet the most distinguished and enduring of all the writing about this war that took place so close to Australia was the youthful memoir—completed when the author was twenty-one, and dealing with events of a couple of years earlier—*Fear Drive My Feet*.

As Peter Ryan recounts in the Preface to the 2001 edition, his book was written 'when the travels of 1942 and 1943 were like the day before yesterday'. Repatriated from New Guinea, he had what he called 'a soft job' teaching Tok Pisin, the pidgin English used in New Guinea, to cadet patrol officers. In the unadorned, compelling style that emerged fully formed in *Fear Drive My Feet*, Ryan reflected that 'very few soldiers of eighteen would have been sent out alone and untrained to operate for months as best they could behind Japanese lines; that few indeed would have passed their nineteenth and twentieth birthdays engaged in such a pursuit.' He wondered, with no affected modesty, 'Might this be an interesting topic?'

Public judgment, emphatically in agreement, had to wait until Ida Leeson, the former Mitchell Librarian and a guest of Ryan's in 1958, read the manuscript without his knowledge. Ten days later, Angus & Robertson agreed to publish a book that Leeson and the firm's esteemed editor, Beatrice Davis, surely guessed would become a classic of Australian literature of war. It was published the following year.

In his preface, Ryan recalls thinking during his time in New Guinea of how—if he survived exhaustion, solitude, exposure, disease, mortal peril—he would never travel anywhere again. Hunted for a week by Japanese soldiers with tracker dogs, he 'sought refuge by climbing a stupendous dry cascade of huge boulders, as it ascended ever higher up a mountainside'. For weeks at a stretch, he would try to sleep 'with the lively expectation of being dead by dawn'. Thus it was, he declared at seventy-seven, 'I have never been to England, Europe or America, and have never wanted to go.' However, since the end of the war he has returned twenty-eight times to the country of his exciting and enervating trials; edited and published the *Encyclopaedia of Papua and New Guinea* (1972), while he was director of Melbourne University Press; and written *Black Bonanza* (1991), an account of the Mount Kare gold rush; besides wisely and humorously counselling many travellers to Australia's nearest, if scantly known, neighbour.

Fear Drive My Feet is a strange and striking account of an education, a non-fiction *Bildungsroman*. For Ryan, this does not involve the distractions of schooling or first love, a literal or sentimental education, but service with Kanga Force, whose 'fantastic campaign of patrolling and harassing the enemy from behind both Lae and Salamaua' he salutes. The courageous motley band that he joins was formed in April 1942, when the New Guinea Volunteer Rifles were supplemented by Independent Companies of the Australian Imperial Force. Its objective is to screen Japanese movements west across New Guinea. Reconnaissance has to be as close (and hence as dangerous) as possible. In one of the pivotal moments of his narrative, the young Warrant Officer Ryan crosses the Markham River and begins his adventures in 'the savage country of the Lae–Salamaua area'. To the east are thousands of Japanese troops; to the north, the Saruwaged Mountains, 'so high that you can't see the tops for clouds'. And here he is, 'sent wandering through the jungles of the largest island on earth with one partly trained police recruit'.

Yet he is not altogether unprepared. In the Boy Scouts he had been an enthusiastic participant in bushcraft, map-reading, prismatic-compass work, first aid (particularly wound dressing) and hygiene. Nor is he without some knowledge of New Guinea. Ryan's father, Ted, fought there in the Great War, taking part in the capture of Rabaul and rising to lieutenant in the military government of Australia's new ex-German territories. He may have settled there for good, except that severe malaria forced his return to Australia. The family home in Glen Iris, in Melbourne's eastern suburbs, was full of New Guinea artefacts, mementoes and photographs. Moreover, Ryan's father taught him to speak Tok Pisin, a deal of which he remembered when his assignment began and its use was essential.

Vital to his operations, intelligence gathering and survival is sustaining bonds with not only those natives employed to assist him (for whom he holds deep respect and affection) but the people of remote villages and perhaps doubtful loyalty, on whom he depends for supplies. In exchange for fresh food, Ryan can offer 'Trade tobacco, sheets of newspaper [for rolling cigarettes], coarse salt, and New Guinea shilling-pieces! Strange currency, I thought.' The authors of *The Oxford Companion to Australian Military History* wryly agree. The New Guinea campaign, they write, was 'fought on a logistic shoestring'. Burdened with his miscellaneous cargo (even that begrudged by the 'base bludgers' away from the front line, whom he has cause to execrate), Ryan heads north: 'In this line of mountains, like gates in a wall, were the dark gashes of the valleys of the three main tributary streams on the north side of the Markham—the Leron, the Irumu, and the Erap.' This is a visceral but also an expressionistic journey—into a landscape of terror and exhilaration.

Ryan moves through country rocked by earth tremors, roamed by shit-eating pigs, within earshot of Allied bombs falling on the Japanese base at Lae, though it is days' trek distant. His little party sometimes presses on through deep fog: 'it was unnerving to walk into the valley as the unseen stream roared below, or to make what seemed to be an endless ascent into space.' All the time, as the tension steadily increases, the enemy remains unseen, if present in rumour. Are they sticking to the coast or 'now warily extending patrols up the valleys'?

In the climactic sequence of *Fear Drive My Feet*, Ryan is sent back into action in the company of Captain Les Howlett, an experienced New Guinea patrol officer. Once again the Markham has to be traversed: 'All the hazards of a sea voyage were to be had in a trip across this incredible stream—reefs, islands, currents, waves, and sand-banks— any one of which might have wrecked us.' This ordeal convinces Ryan that the Markham is the very 'boundary of creation'.

Now there are clear signs of a Japanese presence and native collaboration: a new rest-house has been built, and bridges constructed across streams. It seems to Ryan that the villagers 'were concealing what they knew: either lying to us or keeping silent'. He discovers that the Japanese know of the hazardous trip that he made to seek information from Chinese prisoners outside Lae, and there is now a price on his head, dead or alive—two cases of meat and five Australian pounds. This is mentioned stoically, but in good humour.

Ryan's youthful spirit is tested relentlessly: he has to judge whom to trust, what path to follow, where danger might lie. Few narratives of growing up involve ordeals so arduous, whether monotonous or deadly. Ryan knows the measure of what is taken from him: 'All sense of adventure and excitement had long since vanished from this patrol, leaving behind an empty flatness that was only one degree removed from despair.'

Plagued by 'headaches, faintness, giddiness and attacks of nose-bleeding', Ryan and Howlett return over the mountains to the village of Chivasing, where they are betrayed by the natives and ambushed by the Japanese. Howlett is shot; Ryan survives by burying himself 'deep in the mud of a place where the pigs used to wallow, with only my nose showing'. He can hear the Japanese calling out to each other,

> and their feet sucking and squelching in the mud as they searched. I could not see, so I did not know exactly how close they were, but I could feel in my ears the pressure of their feet as they squeezed through the mud. It occurred to me that this was probably an occasion on which one might pray, and indeed was about to start a prayer. Then something stopped me. I said to myself so fiercely

that I seemed to be shouting under the mud,
'To Hell with God! If I get out of this bloody mess,
I'll do it by myself!'

Later, at the Bulolo base, Ryan is berated by a stock figure of military bureaucracy: 'Don't you realise it's a crime in the Army to lose your pay book?' While a battle is fought nearby, Ryan recuperates before being flown to the coast, over 'the land which had soaked up the sweat of two years'. He reflects on man's bravery, on patience and endurance, and hopes it will also be learned that 'wars and calamities of nature are not the only occasions when such qualities are needed'.

The book concludes with this prose of noble plainness, but its story and the manner of its telling have resonated for more than fifty years. Richly realised are aims modestly stated: the depiction of war, but 'on the smallest possible scale', and 'what happened to one man—what he did, and how he felt about it'. *Fear Drive My Feet* is informed by Ryan's admiration for the Roman emperor and philosopher Marcus Aurelius, to whose counsel for the control of fear, 'cease to be whirled around', he paid special notice when under aerial bombardment.

The book has two telling epigraphs. One is Erasmus's remark that 'in the Military Service, there is a busy kind of Time-Wasting.' This speaks to the long periods of inaction that the book describes—waiting in lonely bush camps to go into action, recovering from malaria and the broken bones caused by falls, at the mercy of intermittent orders and supplies. The second epigraph is from Job, 18.11: 'Terrors shall make him afraid on every side, and shall drive him to his feet.' The facing and surmounting of those terrors, mental and physical, is the matter of Peter Ryan's book—the finest Australian memoir of war.

Fear Drive My Feet

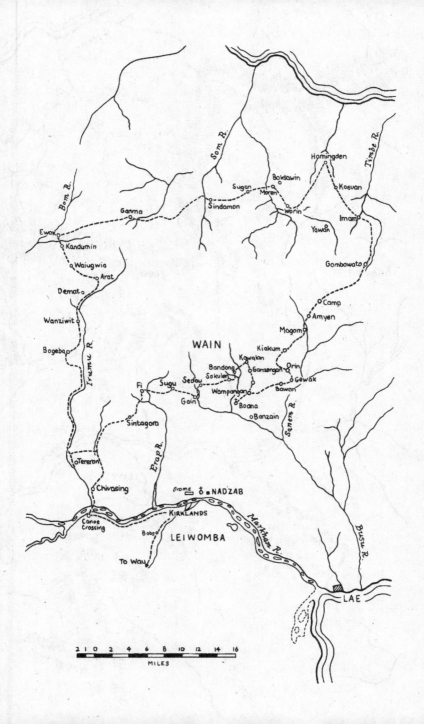

Sio

Kwama R.

CROMWELL RA

RA

RA

Masaweng R.

Yumeng R.

Kua R.

Bulum R.

MOMALILI

Zupong R.

FINSCHHAFEN

Buso R.

Bulu R.

Buhem R.

Mape R.

SCALE OF MILES

0   5   10   15   20   25

PREFACE

I WROTE THIS book at the age of twenty-one, when the travels of 1942 and 1943 were like the day before yesterday. Any small uncertainty – a precise date, the name of a village headman – could be settled from dog-eared notebooks, or the tattered sheets of old patrol reports. Flicked over in pursuit of some such bald fact, these crumbling documents gave off the musty smell of paper which had begun its decay in the mildews of the tropics. Many years passed before I understood: this haunting odour, in silent eloquence, had been speaking to me just as clearly as the written sentences now fading on the pages. Truly, a trace of Proust lurks in the least of us.

During 1944 and 1945 I had a soft job in an Army school in the grounds of the Royal Military College, Duntroon, teaching New Guinea pidgin English (Tok Pisin) to cadet patrol officers. Those nights not spent in the mild dissipations of the Mess were for reading or writing in one's room – a narrow cell furnished with a bed, a table and a chair, all of monastic austerity. My window opened outwards towards Mount Pleasant where, just a hundred yards away, was the tomb of General Bridges, killed on Gallipoli as commander of our first A.I.F. Now he lay there at peace, beneath his immense bronze funerary sword.

The notion of actually *writing a book* seemed preposterous, when it first crossed my mind one frosty night. I had left school at sixteen for a dull job in the Victorian public service, from which I enlisted shortly before Japan entered the war in late 1941. What possible qualification had I for authorship?

At school, my English and History master, Gordon Connell, had been a teacher of genius. (He had, a few years earlier, taught our famous architect and writer, Robin Boyd.) From 'Cactus' Connell I had learnt, at least, not even to start writing unless there was something interesting to say; and if there was, to say it simply. He also infected me with (no one has ever put it better than Gibbon) 'that early and invincible love of reading which I would not exchange for the treasure of India'.

It struck me that very few soldiers of eighteen would have been sent out alone and untrained to operate for months as best they could behind Japanese lines; that few indeed would have passed their nineteenth and twentieth birthdays engaged in such a pursuit. Might this be an interesting topic?

In the quiet nights of Canberra, a small and rather nervous manuscript built up. The hard decisions for the greenhorn author were what to leave out, for a great deal had happened besides the story told in the pages of this book: the sinking in Port Moresby harbour of the *Macdhui*, the ship which carried me from Australia; numberless enemy aerial bombardments; the later escape, by a matter of minutes, from sinking by a Japanese submarine in the Gulf of Papua; the taxing walk right across New Guinea over the notorious Bulldog Track; running supply lines of native carriers to our troops operating behind Salamaua. This was all too much for my untried skill to tackle, and all too much for the patience of readers. I decided to focus on a series of intelligence patrols all carried out in the general region of the Markham River, which enters the sea near the then great Japanese base at Lae.

Between 1945 and 1950, three different publishing

firms read this amateur manuscript. Two said they were keen to publish, but were eventually thwarted by post-war publishing problems, chiefly the world shortage of paper. So the manuscript was tossed into a cupboard at home and would still be there, but for an extraordinary chance.

In 1958, in Melbourne, we had briefly as a house guest that wonderful woman Ida Leeson, Mitchell Librarian from 1932 to 1946. When the poet James McAuley was once asked to define the meaning of the noun 'secret', he replied that a secret was 'something very carefully hidden so that it could be discovered by Ida Leeson'.

Doubtless trawling our cupboards for any secret which might lie there awaiting her, she found my abandoned script and, without my knowledge, read it. She announced that she was taking it back with her to Sydney, to discuss it with Angus & Robertson. Ten days later came the exciting telegram: 'Angus & Robertson will publish stop love Ida'.

So I was to be an author! Just like that! A&R's superb chief editor Beatrice Davis excised scores of absurdly superfluous commas, but made no changes of substance. Not a word has been altered since. *Fear Drive My Feet* appeared in hardback in November 1959, and Lance-Corporal Kari (promoted now to resplendent Sergeant-Major) came down from Port Moresby for the launching. All the reviewers were very kind, Douglas Stewart of the *Bulletin* devoting to the book the whole of his prestigious Red Page.

Gwyn James, manager of Melbourne University Press, took it up for his new series of Melbourne Paperbacks in 1960, and it was twice more (in a different format) issued by MUP (1974 and 1985). Then in 1991, Penguin Books chose it for inclusion in their Australian War Classics series, with a Foreword by 'Weary' Dunlop. It has thus been in and out of print, but usually available ever since 1959.

It amazes and delights me that so plain and unembroidered a tale of one man's travels sixty years ago still finds its readers. But when asked, as sometimes happens, 'How do I feel about it all now?' it is hard to find an answer.

There is certainly 'no memory for pain' in the ordinary

sense; the torn feet, the ribs broken from falls, the intensifying bouts of depressing malaria – all that vanished years ago. But several curious things still linger with perfect clarity.

There were for example, two separate days – only two – when I felt that I was on the very brink of madness from loneliness and strain. A stern self-lecture on the virtues of the stiff upper lip seemed to do the trick – perhaps *just* in time.

There was a day on which, at the end of a week of being hunted by the Japanese (said now to be assisted by tracker dogs) I sought refuge by climbing a stupendous dry cascade of huge boulders, as it ascended ever higher up a mountainside. At about 10,000 feet I sat down to rest a while, and from a sudden recollection of a school geography lesson, realized that this chaotic wasteland of random-strewn rocks was the moraine left behind in the retreat of an ancient glacier. Altitude and exhaustion play hallucinatory tricks, but a great voice seemed to boom in my ear: 'This is the end of the Earth! This is the end of the Earth! You've reached the end of the Earth!' I remember my answer exactly. I said: 'If ever I get out of this, I'll never travel anywhere again.' This was not in any sense intended as a vow, yet it was what happened. Now seventy-seven, I have never been to England, Europe or America, and have never wanted to go.

At times, every night for weeks at a stretch, when the Japanese were close, I lay down to sleep with the lively expectation of being dead by dawn. Certainly this frightened me, but I had learned by then that tranquility can be preserved even in the midst of terror: mostly I slept as sweetly as if I had been in bed in my mother's house.

Well…all these are idle memories of a war long won – or perhaps lost. But most of all, looking back, my main feeling is of gratitude. Dispatching an eighteen-year-old on such a job as mine was heartless and irresponsible. And yet it was the best thing that ever happened to me: I got the chance to discover what I could do, and I am grateful.

P.R. October 2000

'And in the Military Service, there is a
busy kind of Time-Wasting.'

ERASMUS OF ROTTERDAM (1466–1536)
The Education of a Christian Prince

'Terrors shall make him afraid on every side,
and shall drive him to his feet.'

The Book of Job, 18.11

INTRODUCTION

THIS BOOK is completely factual. The events it describes happened, and the people mentioned in it lived – or still live. It treats its subject – war – on the smallest possible scale. It does not aspire to chronicle the clash of armies; it does not attempt to describe the engagements of so much as a platoon. It tells what happened to one man – what he did, and how he felt about it.

However, it will be helpful to the reader to have some knowledge of the background against which the story takes place; to supply that necessary glimpse of the wider picture is the purpose of this short introduction.

New Guinea represented the most southerly extent of Japan's all-conquering Pacific offensive of 1941–2. And it was in New Guinea – at Milne Bay – that the Australians inflicted the first land defeat on Japan. The campaign in the world's largest island therefore embraced both the nadir of our fortunes and the turning of the tide in our favour. New Guinea was also the stern schoolroom in which we learnt the tactics and techniques – for example, jungle warfare – which led us finally to victory in 1945.

The events described in the following chapters deal chiefly with the period of our unrelieved defeats, when the character of the war in New Guinea was most curious and interesting.

The Japanese took Rabaul in January 1942 after heroic, but hopeless resistance, from the Australian garrison. In March they occupied the important north-coast towns of Lae and Salamaua. There was no resistance. What could a few dozen men of the New Guinea Volunteer Rifles do against the Japanese who swarmed in thousands from their landing-craft? In much the same way the Japs helped themselves at their leisure to the greater part of the north coast. They made an assault on Port Moresby itself which came very near to success.

There is real fascination in this early period of hopeless inferiority in numbers and equipment.

When the Japanese landed at Lae and Salamaua the few New Guinea Volunteer Rifles men retreated to hideouts in the bush or fell back on the township of Wau in the mountainous goldfields inland. The N.G.V.R. had been civilian residents of New Guinea – gold-miners, planters, government officials. They were joined by a single Australian commando unit, the 5th Independent Company, and the two units were grouped under the name Kanga Force, with its headquarters in Wau. In parties of a few men they conducted a fantastic campaign of patrolling and harassing the enemy from behind both Lae and Salamaua. Everywhere they were outnumbered hundreds to one, and their communications spread out over a hundred miles of tracks.

In the Lae sector they had to face all the text-book conditions of jungle fighting – dense growth, swamps, malaria, steamy heat, crocodile-infested rivers, and so on. In the Salamaua area the main problems were mountainous terrain – probably as rough as any in the world – dense rainforests, cold and damp.

The enemy was strong enough to have taken Wau, with its important airfield, any time he chose, but the aggressive activity of our patrols bluffed him for a whole year and kept Wau in our hands. All this time Kanga Force was short of supplies. There were no transport aircraft to fly in material from Port Moresby or Australia. Stores therefore had to be carried round the south coast from Port Moresby to the mouth of the Lakekamu River by steamer. There they were transhipped to pinnaces and moved up the Lakekamu to Terapo, where they were transferred into whaleboats and canoes for a two-day journey upriver to Bulldog. At Bulldog all stores were made up into fifty-pound 'boy-loads' and sent off to Wau on the backs of carriers, nearly seven days' walk over mountains heart-breaking in their height and steepness. To reach our troops in the Lae forward area another four days' carry was needed.

In sober truth this was probably one of the most extraordinary lines of communication in military history.

Somehow Kanga Force held on, patrolling, harassing, watching enemy movements. Elsewhere on the north side of the island, behind Finschhafen, Madang, and Wewak, the position was even worse. There was no regular military force in the rear of the enemy. Our only contact was from small special parties, often one white man and a few trusted natives. They lived – often in conditions of frightful privation and danger – in the jungles and mountains behind the enemy's coastal bases. At last, in January 1943, the Japanese decided to make an assault on Wau. Reinforced by a fleet which had landed troops early in the same month, they set out from Salamaua and very nearly achieved their objective.

Our air transport position was now good, but the 17th Australian Brigade, ready to rush to Wau to stem the advance, was held up in Port Moresby by bad weather. When they arrived in Wau their planes landed among Japanese fire on the aerodrome. But they saved Wau and pushed the Japanese back to Salamaua. Within the next seven months, combined land and sea operations with the Americans gave us back Lae and Salamaua. There was much hard fighting still ahead in New Guinea – two more years of it – but after Wau the issue was never really in doubt.

The whole character of the war had now changed. Superbly trained, supplied, and equipped, our troops attacked an enemy who, though fanatical and tough, was increasingly embarrassed by ever-weakening communications as our offensive by land, air, and sea mounted all over the Pacific. Gone was the day of the lonely white man maintaining single-handed contact with the enemy. By the end of 1943 we went where we pleased, and we went in force.

This book describes some of the adventures which befell one man in the struggles of 1942 and 1943 in the savage country of the Lae-Salamaua area.

I

I SAT DOWN on a shaded boulder, head bent, sweat running in a chain of drops off my nose and chin; they fell with a slight pat-pat-pat onto the sodden legs of dirty green short trousers. The rushing water lapped my feet and filled my boots. I wriggled my toes round inside them, luxuriating in the cool sensation. When I stamped my feet little geysers of water shot out of the boots and up my shins; that was cool and pleasant too.

Near at hand, the thin wail of mosquitoes. All over my back, through the sweat-soaked shirt that clung to the skin, I felt the jabbing of their red-hot needles. It was no use slapping – it only made you hotter, and made no difference to the mosquitoes.

In the distance, the deeper, though faint, hum of aircraft engines. Where? Madang? Lae? 'What's it matter, anyhow? They're too far away to do me any harm,' was my vague thought.

Wail of mosquitoes, hum of aircraft engines, roar of swirling water, and the constant pat-pat-pat of dripping sweat. 'There's the whole orchestra,' I thought. 'There goes the non-stop background music for God knows how many months to come. Let's see just what sort of a mess I'm in, anyway.'

I ticked the facts off on my fingers as I called them out aloud. It isn't necessarily the length of time you've been alone that sets you thinking out loud – if the aloneness is sufficiently intense you start doing it in half a day. The facts came out in a sort of verbal column, like an inventory or shopping-list:

'I'm eighteen years old, and I've been in New Guinea a couple of months.

'A day's walk to the east is Lae, and some thousands of Japanese troops.

'North, a few hours ahead of me, is the Markham River, and somewhere nearby in the jungle is Bob's, the camp from which a few hopelessly outnumbered Australian commandos are carrying on the war against the Japs.

'Across the Markham, just visible through the trees from where I sit, are the Saruwaged mountains, so high that you can't see the tops for clouds; among those incredible blue ranges, somewhere or other in an area of roughly three thousand square miles, is another lone Australian, Jock McLeod.

'Object of my journey: to find Jock and place myself under his orders in his dual job of "governing" some tens of thousands of natives and watching the activities of our Japanese enemy.'

By this time I felt a lot happier. It was reassuring to hear a voice, even one's own. Secondly, I seemed able to marshal my facts pretty well. That indicated that I was sane as well as alive. Napoleon himself, I thought complacently, would have made his appreciation of the situation in much the same way.

His purpose clearly stated, obviously Napoleon's next step would have been a consideration of resources and ways and means. Again the verbal list:

'Resources: Reputedly a fortnight's rations, but really only enough to last a hungry man about a week.

'No compass.

'No maps.

'One old rifle with a damaged foresight.

'A thirty-year-old revolver with ten rounds of ammunition.

'Bottomless, unbounded ignorance of the country.

'Only the slightest acquaintance with pidgin English, the language needed to converse with the natives.

'For assistance, one keen but emotionally unstable native police-boy, whose home is hundreds of miles away and whose ignorance of this part of the country is paralleled only by my own.'

I realized that my verbal listing had turned almost imperceptibly into a sort of double-entry bookkeeping, and that every item so far had fallen on the debit side.

'All right,' I thought, 'let's fill in the credit side of the ledger.'

There was a pretty long silence.

'Well, I'm damned if I'm going to walk all the way back to Wau just to admit I couldn't find Jock,' I said at last, a little louder than before, and hastily ruled off the ledger. Even at that stage it seemed as if a lot of entries in those accounts might be written in red.

It never occurred to me that I'd been given a pretty slim chance of survival by my superior, the district officer who had sent me on this errand. Nobody thought it very strange then, least of all myself, to send someone into that country without such basic necessities as food, maps, and compass. When you are eighteen the fact that quite stupid people can play chuck-ha'penny with your life doesn't seem too unjust. This is partly because the thrill of the adventure is more dangerously intoxicating than liquor, and you aren't too closely in touch with reality. You stride down the jungle trail full of confidence, a pioneer, a new David Livingstone; you feel exactly like your favourite hero from the *Boy's Own Paper*.

The hangover from this kind of binge is unpleasant. It arrives not when you understand clearly the danger you have been in but when you see how useless your whole mission was, how futile and purposeless your death would have been, and, above all, when your sober but aching eye discerns that nobody whose business it might have been took the least trouble to see that you got even a reasonable chance of living.

But these are afterthoughts, and no such shadows clouded my purpose that hot afternoon in 1942 as I rested in the shade.

Five natives squatted in another patch of shadow, a few yards downstream. They were armed with leafy twigs, which they flicked across their shoulders at the clouds of mosquitoes that hummed round their shiny brown backs. Four were carriers whom I had borrowed in Wau to carry my bedroll, my rations, and my few odds and ends of personal possessions. They wore only lap-laps – strips of ragged and faded red cloth tied in a knot about their middles. As they sat on their heels patiently suffering the mosquitoes' assaults, they talked quietly in pidgin English and passed from hand to hand a fat twelve-inch-long cigarette which one of them had rolled out of black twist tobacco and a sheet of newspaper.

The fifth native was Achenmeri, my so-called police-boy. In peacetime, patrol officers working in the bush had found the assistance of several well-trained members of the native constabulary invaluable; now, in time of war, they were indispensable. Yet here was I sent wandering through the jungles of the largest island on earth with one partly trained police recruit!

I studied him carefully as he sat there smoking. His dark-brown face was thin and parrot-like, almost as if his head had been squashed flat between two boards. His body was as skinny as a skeleton. No matter how much he ate, he looked half-starved. His upper arms were adorned by keloid scars in the shape of grotesque formalized faces with gaping mouths. They were the result of wounds inflicted as part of a ritual that was a common practice in the Sepik River country, where his home village was. The fact that he had become a constable of police tickled Achenmeri's vanity enormously. He was particularly proud of his uniform – khaki shorts, shining brass-buckled belt, and khaki peaked cap with a gleaming badge. The cap, which perched precariously on top of his woolly hair, he was in the habit of removing, to turn self-consciously round and round in his hands, lost in silent admiration of a piece of property so magnificent and carrying with it such prestige. As his fingers were never too clean, the new cap was little more than a greasy rag before we had been on the track many days. The rifle, too, added to his already vast conceit. All day long he fondled and patted it, and he spent every spare second rubbing off imaginary specks of rust. I discovered that he had never fired a shot out of it, and was really rather scared by the weapon. He knew which end the bullet might be expected to emerge from – wasn't there a hole there for the purpose? – but little else. His anxiety to display his devotion to duty was pathetic. My slightest order was the signal for shuffling and stamping, for saluting and slapping of the rifle-butt, and his dark eyes would roll wildly as he hissed, 'Yessir!

Yessir! Yessir!' He might have been a good musical-comedy figure, but was hardly a source of comfort and inspiration to a young greenhorn on his first patrol into territory that was wild and largely unexplored as well as being controlled in all its approaches by the Japanese.

A faint breeze just stirred the green foliage that grew like a wall on either side of the river. From the sun I guessed that it was about three o'clock. The meagre information I had been given suggested that we should reach Bob's camp shortly before dark on this the third day. It was time we moved on.

'Achenmeri!' I called.

Instantly there was a scuttering of pebbles and a fumbling as he sprang to attention and saluted.

'Yessir!'

'Talkim four-fella you-me walkabout now.'

The other four grinned to each other at my halting order in pidgin English. Natives, and white men who had mastered the language, spoke so rapidly that the words seemed to pour forth in an almost incomprehensible torrent. I was trying desperately to acquire fluency, and listened keenly to every word the boys said, though understanding but a small part of it. One of the few useful tips I had been given by the district officer was that pidgin was a real language with rules and grammar of its own, and must be learnt as such. He was one of the best pidgin speakers in the Territory himself, and emphasized that it was not merely a matter of bastardizing English by throwing in a few 'fellas' and 'belongs'. He pointed out that many Europeans who had lived for years in New Guinea had never realized this fact, and their ability to converse with natives easily and accurately was limited accordingly.

The carriers were standing up now, stretching their back muscles before lifting their loads. The proprietor of the long cigarette put the six-inch remnant behind his ear, and in a few moments we set off single file along the narrow muddy track, my iron patrol-box swinging from side to side, lashed to a pole which two boys carried on their shoulders between them.

For most of its length the track followed a stream called the Wampit, which was a tributary of the Markham River. Bob's, I had been told, was almost on the banks of the Wampit, and not far from the junction of that stream with the Markham. It was hidden in thick jungle, but one of the carriers said he had been there before and could guide us to it.

As we walked, the country became lower and flatter, and the track increasingly muddy. The heat, too, grew more and more oppressive. It was the sort of heat one sometimes finds in big laundries or in other places where there are large quantities of boiling water. Though we were now almost down to sea-level, and the heat and humidity could not have got much worse, I nevertheless had the strange feeling of going ever downward into an inferno.

At last, a little after five o'clock, with the Wampit on our right hand, the carriers stopped at a dried-up, rocky little watercourse that crossed the path; they pointed up it to the left.

'Master, lookim,' they said. 'Road belong place belong all master.'

I could see no 'road'. The boulder-strewn gully showed no footprints. The only track seemed to lie straight ahead. But they assured me that the path led to the Markham River, and they struck off confidently up the watercourse. After a few minutes' scrambling over the stones, I saw Bob's there in front of us.

I shall describe this jungle camp carefully, since for me its atmosphere, its people, and its life sum up one important phase of the infinitely varied, infinitely monotonous activity called war.

The place was named after its founder, Bob Griffiths, who had built it at the time of the Japanese invasion. He was a member of the New Guinea Volunteer Rifles, a tiny local militia of a few hundred, the only force to meet the assault of many thousands of Japanese. In fact, so few men had we that all the Australian posts at that time were called only by some familiar name – Bob's, Mac's, Kirkland's, and so on. Nobody asked who Bob or Mac might be – they were known to all.

From where our little party halted, at the foot of an enormous ficus-tree, I could see that the camp consisted of a dozen or so rough huts thatched with sago-palm fronds, and left without walls for the sake of coolness. They were not in a clearing, but sprawled about in the thickest forest. So intent had their builders been on concealment from the air that the huts themselves had taken on the impress of the builders' desires, and had a furtive look about them, almost as if they knew they were supposed to be hiding.

The tall trees, with their tangled superstructure of creepers, quite blotted out the sun, and I knew that even at midday the place would have the appearance of being in a green-tinted twilight. Now, towards dusk, it seemed infinitely sombre and forbidding. The ground was damp and spongy, and a vague smell of decay pervaded everything. The jungle tolerated this man-made excrescence, it seemed, confident that in a little while it would be swallowed up without a trace.

Everything in this little settlement was damp. Clothes and blankets soon acquired a clammy feeling that was impossible to remove, for one dared not sun them in a patch of grassland not far away, lest they be spotted by the Japanese reconnaissance planes that often flew low overhead. Blowflies buzzed lazily everywhere, and every couple of days the blankets were fly-blown.

No breeze stirred the air. The smoke from the cooking fires hung motionless in a blue haze among the trees, and over the whole area hung a fearful silence, too vast to be broken noticeably by the voices of the forty or fifty men who comprised the garrison. Even the rattle of gunfire was subdued by this uneasy quiet.

Gaunt, pallid men in ragged green uniforms were moving about the camp doing various chores – cleaning weapons, sewing up torn clothes – while one directed the work of a party of natives who were repairing the roof of a hut. Quite close to me, a smart squad of native police were lined up on parade beneath the trees. A tall serious-faced man with a close-clipped moustache was quietly calling the roll, sucking hard on a chipped and blackened pipe between names. This, I knew, must be John Clarke, an old New Guinea hand who was in charge of the police and the native carriers at Bob's. When he had finished his roll-call I walked across to him and told him who I was.

He gave me a friendly smile and shook my hand warmly. 'I heard you were coming. I'm very pleased to see you. Now, I'll get you fixed up with a place to sleep, and you can have a clean-up, and we'll have a yarn after that.'

'Thanks, John. It'll be good to get these clothes off and into some clean ones. I think I'll have a swim in the Wampit to cool off. Is it safe to go in here?'

'Pretty safe. But don't go too far out into the current. There don't seem to be many crocodiles around.'

As we talked, John had been leading the way to a long hut containing only one or two beds.

'You'll be pretty private here,' he said. 'I'll get a couple of boys to put your bed-sail up at this end, where the roof doesn't leak.'

After his mosquito-net, the bed-sail is probably the New Guinea traveller's most useful item of furniture. It consists of a double sleeve of canvas about seven feet long and three feet wide. Two stout poles are inserted along either side to make a rough stretcher, and the poles are supported at the ends by a couple of stout sticks lashed together at the top like shear-legs. The result is a tightly stretched canvas bed, cool and springy, raised two or three feet off the ground. It can be erected in a few minutes, and the canvas is practically no weight to carry. Moreover, in the daytime, on the track, it forms a useful waterproof wrapper for blankets.

The boys summoned by John unwrapped the roll of bedding and ran to fetch suitable poles, while Achenmeri thrust himself importantly forward to supervise this weighty operation. John raised his eyebrows at the antics of this bumptious and comical constable, but he said nothing, while I groped in my haversack for some mail I had brought.

He glanced at the handwriting on the envelopes and smiled, before tucking the three or four letters into the breast pocket of his shirt, to be read and enjoyed later, alone. It was the first mail he had received for weeks. There was a paper for him, too, and he slit its wrapper at once.

'It's the *Bulletin*!' he exclaimed with a grin of pleasure as he unrolled it. 'I like to read that – it's my Bible, the *Bulletin*.'

'Isn't that a pretty old copy?'

'No, not very,' he said in a surprised voice, looking at the dateline. 'Only a couple of months. I've had it a lot older than that.'

I began to understand life at Bob's when I saw how excited John became over a two-month-old copy of a newspaper. Cut off by rivers and mountainous jungles, these men were isolated not only in a physical sense, but had their own time-scale as well.

I had found towel and soap in my patrol-box. 'How do I get to the Wampit, John?'

'Follow that gully straight on past the main track, where you came in, and keep going. It's about a hundred yards.'

'O.K... I'll be back soon.' By the time I had gone ten yards Bob's had vanished so completely from sight and hearing that I stopped and had to resist deliberately the desire to run back and reassure myself that the place was really there and that I had not been dreaming.

By the time I reached the Wampit bank the sun was already below the treetops, and the palms and wild bread-fruit-trees were outlined black against the brassy shine of the sky. The foliage rustled lightly in the breeze that blew upstream. I sat down on a log at the water's edge and slowly unlaced my boots, then pulled off my green shirt and shorts and let them fall in a sweat-soaked heap on the little beach of black sand.

The river here, in its lower reaches, was swift and muddy, but the water was cool. I waded gratefully in to thigh-depth and washed myself. New life seemed to return with cleanliness. At this somewhat open point the breeze was too strong for the mosquitoes to be a pest, so, having dried myself, I squatted naked on the log and looked downstream.

Not far away the Wampit almost lost itself in a vast flat area of swamp and sago-palms before emptying into the mighty Markham. Over the trees and across the Markham (which of course I could not see), I glimpsed again the Saruwageds. Filtered through an almost invisible haze of dust, the evening light cast a delicate softness upon them. They were blue, every conceivable shade from ice-blue to deepest purple. I knew that even the foothills were at least twenty miles away, but the mountains showed with startling clarity, mounting up and up, fold upon fold, until the tops disappeared into a level bank of cloud. I studied them intently, knowing that the next few weeks would find me somewhere in their remote blue fastnesses.

'Somewhere over there is Jock,' I thought. 'And somehow I have to find him.'

It was nearly dark. I pulled the towel about my waist and hobbled barefoot up the stony creek-bed, back to the camp. When I got there the others were putting on long trousers and gaiters, rolling down their sleeves, and rubbing their hands and faces with mosquito-repellent lotion; in short, making all the preparations for evening which characterize the mosquito-infested camp.

John Clarke appeared out of the gloom as I was getting dressed. He looked slightly embarrassed, I thought.

'You aren't an – er – officer, are you?' he asked.

My shirt carried no badges of rank, and his bore none either, though I knew he was a lieutenant. In fact, hardly anyone wore his rank in those days, partly because the store never had any badges and also because the Japanese made a feature of trying to pick officers and N.C.O.s off first, if they could identify them.

'No – I'm only a warrant-officer. Why?'

'Well, you see, we have an officers' mess here. I'd like you to eat with me, but of course – '

I cut him short. 'For God's sake don't worry about that! Just show me where the other mess is, and I'll be O.K.'

'It's not quite so simple. There's a headquarters mess, where the sigs and orderly-room staff and so on eat, and a sergeants' mess, and of course there's the men's mess. I suppose you'd better eat at the sergeants' mess.'

I stared at him. Here were forty or fifty men at the edge of the world, and pretty well on the edge of eternity too; bound together, one would have thought, by every important tie both of interest and sentiment. And yet, to take their meals, they split up into four groups. I could see that John's sense of personal hospitality was somewhat offended at having to send me to eat elsewhere, but that the system itself was crazy didn't seem to occur to him. And, to be quite honest, within a day or two I had so slipped into the way of things myself that I found nothing ludicrous in the spectacle of the same atrocious food from one central cookhouse being carried through the bush among the flies to four different mess-huts. Very few of the absurdities and injustices of army life worry you much at the time. You can't buck the system, so you put up with it, and pretty soon you don't notice. I don't think this means that most people are militaristic at heart. Real militarists are those who seek to justify the system, and find it good. The vast majority tolerate it because they have no choice.

As I finished buttoning up my sleeves John pointed out the sergeants' mess on the far side of the camp. The loud clatter of a beaten kerosene-tin announced that tea was ready.

'You'll be right, then, will you? I'll see you later,' John said, and made off into the darkness.

I strolled across to the sergeants' mess — a rough hut like all the others. A man was setting fire to little piles of green leaves all round it, making a smoke-screen to keep the mosquitoes away. A smoky hurricane-lamp spread a shadowy red glow over the interior. Four stout poles driven into the dirt floor supported the rough table-top provided by light sticks laid side by side. The five men round the table were perched in various attitudes of discomfort on old bully-beef cases. They were meditating quietly, saying nothing at all to each other.

As I introduced myself and asked whether I could share their meal, they hastily found another case for me, assuring me I was welcome. They wanted to hear the latest news from Wau, and would have welcomed the devil himself to supper, I believe, provided he had brought some diverting gossip with him.

I looked round the table at my companions as they told me their names. They were all young men – not one of them out of his twenties – but without exception they were heavily bearded. For all one could see of their faces they might have been middle-aged.

Among them was Bill Chaffey, a farmer and Member of Parliament from New South Wales, with an enormous red bushy beard that made him look like the prophet Isaiah. And there was Bob Sherman, an Englishman, whose glossy black whiskers reminded me of a melodrama villain. If he had suddenly exclaimed, 'Ha, my proud beauty! Out into the snow!' it would have seemed quite in keeping with his appearance.

The meal consisted of bully beef, sweet potatoes, and papaw, and no great plenty at that. When it was finished, tobacco was produced, pipes filled and cigarettes rolled. For weeks not one of them had smoked a shred of proper tobacco, and ancient pieces of newspaper had taken the place of cigarette-papers. Some smoked the trade twist that was issued to the natives – foul black stuff made, I should say, from the sweepings from cigar factories and bound together with molasses in plaited sticks. Others rolled their own cigars from brus, the native-grown leaf tobacco, purchased from the kanakas in nearby villages. This too, was terribly strong. After a couple of brus cigars a Capstan seemed tasteless.

The hurricane-lamp cast its smoky glow on the bearded faces of Bill and Bob as they played their evening game of chess. I saw that a number of chessmen were missing and had been replaced by buttons and bottle-tops. Faces grave, eyes deep-sunken, and foreheads lined, the two men made each move deliberately, shading their eyes from the lantern and occasionally brushing off with patient hand a more than usually vicious mosquito.

Another bearded patriarch of twenty-two, not so long-suffering, cursed and swore as he slapped at the mosquitoes swarming round his head. He was doing his best to write a letter home on a rather grubby piece of canteen paper.

A fourth man, who might also have stepped out of the Old Testament, was attending to his beard with all the care that a botanist would have lavished upon a rare specimen. With comb and mirror and folding nail-scissors he preened and pruned with loving care, until he achieved precisely that degree of elegance on which he had set his heart. Several reasons were given for this cult of the beard: one was that razor-blades were almost unobtainable; another, that beards were protection against mosquitoes, and useful camouflage in jungle fighting. While true to some extent, these were rationalizations. The real reason was that it helped to pass the time. It was a trifling diversion that helped bored men to endure a weary time of isolation, privation, and danger.

From time to time one of them would wind up the wheezy old gramophone and play a record. There were about twenty discs, which they told me had been taken, with the gramophone, from an abandoned house in Wau. When one group of men grew sick of the records the outfit was passed to another hut, with strict instructions to look after the only gramophone needle. It was carefully sharpened and resharpened till it was ground down to the merest stub.

The songs were a rubbishy lot – worn-out popular tunes and sentimental tangoes. The tinny sound of the banal words was flat and false as it disappeared into the surrounding darkness of the jungle. In that wilderness, a fruity tenor voice crying plaintively to men who had not seen a white woman for six months, 'The night was made for love', was about as appropriate as a juke-box on Judgment Day. But somehow the phoney sentiment struck home. We were all so starved for love and tenderness and all the deeply cherished private things that had made our individual lives worthwhile, that we seized upon even this fly-blown imitation to keep memory alive. And even today those tunes have a queerly evocative power. When I hear one of them memories crowd in upon me. I see bearded figures playing chess, surrounded by the brooding blackness of a fever-ridden camp; I hear the dull murmur of the Wampit rushing past, and see the wasted yet smiling faces of comrades who, side by side, faced jungle, hunger, and a savage enemy. Where they are today I do not know, but they were a good crowd, and it seems strange that a stupid, nearly forgotten tune should have the power to call up their images so vividly.

By eight o'clock we were all driven to bed by the mosquitoes. The only refuge was under a mosquito-net, but there was another reason for turning in early. Like all other supplies, kerosene for the lamps was short. If more did not come soon, they would have to fall back upon the very unsatisfactory flicker given by lighted strips of cloth floating in tins of grease. To avoid this further privation early lights-out was essential.

Bill Chaffey and I walked together to the sleeping-huts. The camp was already almost in darkness. On the other side of the dry creek-bed, where the native carriers and the police-boys had their huts, small fires were still burning. As the boys shifted in front of their fires, one could see their dark figures momentarily, and hear them talking in low tones. Occasionally the night was split with a gusty gale of laughter as someone scored with a good story. Otherwise the soft murmur of the Wampit was the only sound. Bill and I said goodnight and sprang hurriedly beneath our nets. Undressing was a matter to be performed in shelter. He would have been hardy who could have undressed calmly in the open, exposed to the attentions of the ravenous Markham mosquitoes.

I lay awake for some time in the clammy darkness. Gradually the talking of the natives ceased, and their fires burnt out. Then the rain started, hissing quietly through the trees and pattering almost inaudibly upon the sago-palm-leaf roof of the hut. To this monotonous whisper I fell asleep.

II

DAWN BROKE dull and humid. The rain had stopped, but drops of water were still falling from the trees and from the ragged edges of the roofs. Even at seven in the morning it was a steaming, sweltering day. I was sweating before I was fairly up.

As soon as breakfast was over – bananas and more bully beef – I settled down with John Clarke in his hut to find out all I could about the country I was going to. John spread a tattered map on the rough table before us.

'When you cross the Markham tomorrow, you'll be on the Huon Peninsula,' he said, indicating a huge bulge of land with his pipe-stem. 'I suppose it's about three thousand square miles, all told. The Saruwaged Range runs down the centre like a backbone, and it rises way up to fourteen thousand feet in places. The country falls away to the coast in the north; and, as you can see, the southern boundary of the peninsula is the Markham Valley.'

'How much of the peninsula is inhabited?'

'I think there are native villages pretty well everywhere – except very high in the mountains, of course.
Most of the area is fertile, but there are barren areas in the
Markham Valley, and they are pretty sparsely populated.
Actually you can't say too much about this country,
because a lot of it is unexplored. There are wild kanakas
too, higher up.'

'What about the Japs?'

'Generally speaking, we reckon they own the other
side of the Markham and we own this. We make an occasional visit over the other side, but Jock is the only one of
our blokes who's over there permanently. All the same, the
Nips stick pretty much to Lae and round the coast, though
they've been patrolling up the Markham Valley road a lot
more lately.'

I stared at this huge area on the map. Clearly, I might
wander there for the rest of my life without finding Jock
McLeod.

'How do you think I should start looking for Jock?'
I asked John.

He grinned, understanding what a hopeless job it
must have seemed to me.

'Jock's got a hide-out somewhere in this area,' he said,
circling a stretch of country behind Lae. 'It's known as the
Wain country. The Lutherans had a mission station at
Boana, a couple of days' walk from Lae, but of course that
was in peacetime. Jock has naturally kept very quiet about
his camp, but I think it's near the village of Gain. If you
start there you'll probably pick up his trail. You might have
to chase him a hell of a way, though. He hardly ever sleeps
twice in the same place, in case the Nips get wise to him.'

I found Gain on the map. 'How far would that be?'
I asked.

'Depends which way you go. The long way is the safe

way, and it'll take you about five days. You go up the Markham on this side for about a day,' he said, pointing to a spot on the map, 'and then cross over by canoe to this big village here called Chivasing. You can work north to the mountains pretty safely then – we've never heard of the Nips patrolling farther up from Lae than the Erap River.'

'The trouble is I've got so little food. How long would it take the other way?'

'Three days. You go straight down to the Markham to Kirkland's Dump, about two hours from here, cross the Markham, and dash straight up the Erap. It'll take you about five hours to get off the flat country, where the danger from the Nips is, and into the hills through the Erap Gorge. You can camp the night at Bivoro village, just inside the gorge. You should get to Gain easily in three days then.'

'I'm inclined to fancy the shorter route,' I said. 'What do you reckon the chances are of brushing the Japs?'

'If you're careful, and don't waste any time on the flat, I'd advise you to go up the Erap,' he replied. 'I'll tell you what I'll do: I'll lend you Kari, my police corporal, to go with you as far as Gain.'

He cut short my thanks. 'Forget it. I'm glad to help you out. Kari has been up there once, too, and knows the route. You'll find him a very reliable man.'

John called out to his native orderly, who was standing nearby, to tell Kari that he was wanted.

'You might as well meet him now,' he said. 'And I'll tell him he's to be ready to go with you in the morning.'

While we waited for Kari to come from the 'house-police' I told John how much his offer meant to me and how grateful I was. Now the party would have at least one experienced member.

A deep voice saying 'Yessir!' from the entrance of the hut made us look up. His arm raised in a smart salute,

Lance-Corporal Kari was standing at attention outside. He was as black as coal, six feet tall, and so broad that he filled the whole entrance. He wore only a pair of spotless khaki shorts, immaculately starched and pressed. On his bare right arm was buckled a cloth band, with the single stripe indicating his rank. His skin was smooth, glossy, and hairless, and you could see the magnificent muscles that rippled underneath it. His expression was rather stern, and his face was strikingly handsome, whether judged by European or by native standards. He was about twenty years old, and it was hard to imagine a more superb specimen of young manhood.

John told him to stand at ease, and, in a few terse words of pidgin, explained that I was crossing the Markham in the morning to join Jock, and that Kari was to accompany me up the Erap River, and as far as Gain.

Kari turned his handsome, serious face to me, and regarded me rather disapprovingly, I thought. Probably he felt the disgust of an old campaigner at having to put up with the inexperience of a tenderfoot. But he said not a word, and at the conclusion of John's orders he stepped back smartly, saluted, and was gone.

My hopes for a successful expedition rose a hundredfold as I watched Kari's erect, manly form striding back to the house-police. With such a companion anyone might have felt confident.

'What about trade goods?' John asked.

'What? Oh – sorry, John, I was thinking about Kari. I wasn't issued with any trade at all. I hoped you would be able to help me there as well.'

'I haven't got much. The only damned thing we have got plenty of here is malaria. Still, there must be a few things I can let you have. Let's have a look.' He led the way to the back of the hut and began hunting through boxes and drums.

'Here's a few dozen sticks of tobacco. What's this? Ah – a ten-pound bag of coarse salt! I can spare you that. And here's a pile of old newspapers – take as many of them as you want. Let's bring everything down to my table and see what we've got.'

I put this odd assortment on John's table, and he bent over it, shaking his head ruefully.

'There's not much, is there? I'll tell you what: just write me out a receipt for two quid, and I'll give you forty shilling-pieces from my official funds. That should help. If you're pretty stingy with all that stuff you can spin it out – for a few weeks, anyhow.'

Trade tobacco, sheets of newspaper, coarse salt, and New Guinea shilling-pieces! Strange currency, I thought, for paying the carriers who would move my gear from one village to the next, and also for food for myself and the police. But the purchasing power of these goods was high, for most Europeans had left the country when war broke out, and the natives were missing such amenities badly.

Newspaper, for instance, for rolling their foot-long cigarettes, was highly esteemed, and a couple of sheets was a considerable present. There is a story told of a village headman who, in peacetime, used to subscribe to the *Sydney Morning Herald,* not because he could read a word of it but because he required an assured supply of 'smoke-paper'.

Salt, too, was valuable, especially in the mountains, where it could not be obtained from sea-water. The people developed a craving for it, and a tablespoonful would buy anything up to thirty pounds of sweet potatoes or a large bunch of bananas.

New Guinea shillings, with a hole through the centre so that they could be threaded on a string, were also acceptable. Strangely, these shillings were called 'marks', a hangover from twenty-five years before, when the Germans ruled the Territory. The name of the German coin was still applied to the Australian government's minting.

The clatter through the trees of a beaten kerosene-tin made us realize with surprise that we had talked till midday. I thanked John again, and we went our separate ways to lunch – more bully beef, more hard biscuits, more soggy sweet potatoes.

In the hot afternoon I sat with Bill Chaffey in his thatched 'orderly-room' while he helped me draw a rough map of the nearer section of the country across the Markham. To keep the paper clean we had to stop every few minutes and wipe the sweat off our hands. Survey maps of the area were unknown, and even the best were little more than sketch maps. Bill, with careful accuracy, was gradually compiling a large-scale map from parts of earlier maps, sketches he had made himself on patrols across the river, and information obtained from the carefully sifted reports of others. He gave me a good idea of the main features of the flat Markham country and the nearer foothills, together with the names and positions of the more important native villages.

'Did John Clarke fix you up with trade goods?' Bill asked when we had finished the map.

'Yes. And he's lending me Kari, to go as far as Gain. I feel a lot happier about my chances now.'

'Is there anything I can scrounge for you? What weapons have you got?'

Bill was incredulous when he learnt I had nothing but a pistol.

'Good God, you should have a tommy-gun at least!' he exclaimed. 'I can't get you one, worse luck, because we're as short as hell ourselves. But I'll see if there's anything else I can do.'

The result of his scrounging was that I got half a dozen hand-grenades, a pair of powerful but old-fashioned field-glasses, and several boxes of ammunition for my .45 revolver.

At about half past five we walked down to the Wampit for a swim, and as soon as I had eaten my tea – the same old food – I turned in to sleep.

Next morning, as the trees were shedding their last drops of water from the night rains, and the steam was rising from the wet ground, Corporal Kari, Constable Achenmeri, and I set out from Bob's. John Clarke had helped again by securing six young men from nearby Mari village to carry my gear, for my other carriers had to return to Wau. As the line of eight natives swung into the jungle, heading north for the Markham, I waved goodbye to John, Bill, and my other new friends, and strode after the carriers. In a few seconds the camp was out of sight and the only hint of its presence was the put-put-put of the little motor that charged the radio batteries. Within a minute even this could not be heard. All round there was nothing but green, steaming stillness.

It was about eight o'clock when I set out, and my immediate destination was Kirkland's Dump, our farthest outpost on the bank of the Markham, nearly two hours' walk away. I had by now adopted the habit of reckoning distances in hours rather than miles, for distance as the crow flies is a meaningless term in New Guinea. In bad country a whole day's hard struggle might find one only three or four miles advanced, while twenty miles might be covered on the flat without great difficulty. For this reason one always thought in terms of how long it took to reach a place, and not how far away it was.

Most of my two hours' walk lay through swampy country, and the track wound its way hidden in the jungle which fringed the foot of a grassy ridge. In places the track was so boggy that poles had been laid along it to prevent its being turned entirely into a bottomless pool of mud. Covered with ooze and slime, and none too well anchored, the poles were a difficult obstacle unless one's boots were plentifully studded with sharp sprigs. The natives, with their bare feet, negotiated the poles with much less difficulty.

At about nine-thirty we reached a place where the track climbed up a kunai-covered hill. From the summit the view was not obscured by the jungle, and one could survey almost the entire Markham Valley. While the carriers had a spell I sat down on my patrol-box and studied the country.

The 'valley' was an immense plain, almost perfectly flat, and covered partly by large stretches of kunai and other grasses and partly by patches of scrub and jungle. Ten or fifteen miles away, across this level expanse, were the mountains in which Jock was living. They rose up sheer and blue from the valley floor, though the tops still could not be seen for the line of clouds that seemed to sit eternally upon them. In this line of mountains, like gates in a wall, were the dark gashes of the valleys of the three main tributary streams on the north side of the Markham – the Leron, the Irumu, and the Erap. Muddy and swollen from the rains in the enormous mountains they drained, these rivers hurled themselves out of the hills and rushed across the plain to join the Markham.

Almost beneath me, near the southern edge of the valley, was the Markham itself – a vast yellow-brown river consisting of three or four main streams which constantly joined and redivided and were interconnected by dozens of smaller channels. Between the main streams were grass-covered islands of considerable size, whose shape and position changed with every flood. Fifty miles to westward this incredible stream could still be discerned snaking its tortuous way through the malarious crocodile-infested valley. It was difficult to cross even at the best of times, but in the wet season, when it was full of floating trees and smaller rubbish, it was an impassable barrier.

The sun was now blazing from the metallic, cloudless sky. The oppressive blanket of stillness seemed more unearthly, intensified because we could see the vastness of the area it covered. The silence is bearable when you are walled in by the jungle, because you are conscious of only a small slice of it – the quietness of your immediate sur-roundings. But this vast landscape in which nothing moved or spoke was eerie and rather frightening. It was not the peaceful quiet of a friendly countryside, but brooding, malevolent, full of watchful eyes.

Kari pointed to a tiny smudge of smoke from the trees that fringed the river. It came from the camp at Kirk-land's, he said.

We followed the track down the grass-covered spur towards the Markham, and an easy twenty minutes brought us to the edge of the timber, where a big fair-haired young man was squatting in the shade. He stepped forward to meet me with a friendly grin, and we shook hands and introduced ourselves. As he pushed back his shabby and shapeless slouch hat I noticed that it was decorated with a magnificent flame-coloured plume from a bird of paradise, the unofficial emblem adopted by many members of the New Guinea Volunteer Rifles. His name was Tom Lega, he told me, and in peacetime he had worked on the Bulolo goldfields. At present he was the corporal in charge of the little detachment that manned Kirkland's.

'I was expecting you,' said Tom. 'They told us on the phone from Bob's that you'd left, so we put the billy on, and the brew is just ready.'

He led the way through the trees, and in a few moments we were in the centre of the camp – four wretched shelters of ragged sago-frond thatching.

'Come into the cage,' he said. 'We spend most of the day in here.'

He held aside for me the blanket which covered the entrance to a tiny room made entirely of fly-wire screening sent down from Wau. It was only the refuge of this room, I believe, which made it possible for anyone to live at Kirkland's, so bad were the mosquitoes. Even in the daytime they made life torture. As at Bob's, the men had developed a special technique for springing rapidly under the mosquito-net at night, otherwise a whole cloud of the pests would have swarmed under it too. Even so, it was impossible to get into bed unaccompanied by an odd mosquito or two. These were found in the light of a torch and dispatched by a momentary touch with a burning match. They disappeared with a fizz in a tiny puff of smoke.

It would be hard to imagine a more unhealthy site for a camp. Standing outside the cage, one could have tossed a stone to right or left and it would have fallen with a plop into stinking swamp. The sort of water they got from the well is better left undescribed. Yet these men had been here for months, and some of them would be here for months more, guarding the crossing of the river.

Four other men were leaning their elbows on the table that ran the length of the room. They wore only boots and shorts, and their greetings were terse, casually Australian.

'Hi-ya!'

'How y' goin'?'

'How y' makin' out?'

But on their pallid faces were grins which made the welcome warm enough. They passed the tea, for which there was the luxury of a little sugar to each cup, but no milk. Tom explained that the sixth member of the patrol was doing his turn of sentry duty on the landing-place a few hundred yards downstream.

While we drank the tea they explained to me the role of Kirkland's in the scheme of things, both at the present moment and as it had been in the past. It was now our most forward post in the 'Markham End', and was maintained from Bob's as a sort of watching-post. They were to warn Bob's by telephone if the enemy tried to cross the river, and to deal with them with their Vickers machine-gun if it was a small party. Against a force of any size, of course, they would have no hope. The telephone line was the constant burden of their lives, for the phone was faint at the best of times, and every few days a tree would fall and smash the wire.

Another of their jobs was to maintain the 'ferry service'. Earlier in the year, before the Japanese had begun effective patrolling of the Markham Valley, our most forward elements had been kept on the north side of the stream, principally in the vicinity of Nadzab. On the maps of the period appear names such as Mac's camp, Shep's camp, Zoffman's, and others. All these posts were cunningly hidden off the main tracks, and from them our scouts used to patrol to the very outskirts of Lae, and, on one or two occasions, right among the Japanese to the Lae aerodrome. The ferry service, consisting of a few canoes, with crews drawn from the native village of Chivasing, had been the link which maintained contact across the river and kept up supplies. An old New Guinea hand, Tommy Zoffman, had been in charge of this section of the operations, with the unofficial title of Admiral of the Markham Fleet.

Nowadays, however, in the face of much more intensive Jap patrolling, only quick reconnaissance visits were made to Nadzab. A few stores were left hidden in Mac's. As far as we knew, the Japs had never discovered the exact location of these camps, though they must have been aware of their existence. Our patrols seldom remained more than a night or two, and the ferry service was kept for these periodic visits, and was of course used by Jock McLeod.

As we sat round the table drinking tea and nibbling hard army biscuits, we talked about the possibility of my living over the other side of the river. The others did not seem to fancy my chances, and one of them summed up the general opinion:

'You're nuts! The Nips are a moral to get on to you sooner or later. Jock McLeod went over weeks ago, and we haven't heard from him since.'

'That doesn't say he isn't perfectly safe in the bush somewhere,' I argued.

'Ah, well, you're going to give it a try, so that's that!' Tom said as he swilled down the dregs of tea in his cup. 'The canoes and boats' crews should be ready now, so I'll walk down to the landing with you.'

I said goodbye to the others, and we left the wire room, hastily replacing the blanket over the door. Calling to Kari, Achenmeri, and the six carriers from Mari to follow, Tom and I strode along in silence through the bush and the kunai-grass at the edge of the Markham.

Five minutes brought us to the landing-place, a small shingly beach with overhanging trees that concealed the canoes perfectly, since only the very tips of their masts showed through. They were of a type well known in New Guinea, consisting of a single hollowed log for the main hull and an outrigger to give stability. A sail, made of old sugar-bags, was sometimes hoisted on the mast for sailing up the Markham before the strong breeze which blew upstream in the latter part of each afternoon.

For the present crossing we would require only two canoes, and the crews, powerful black-skinned natives from Chivasing, were bailing them out at the water's edge with half coconut-shells.

The northern bank was just discernible, low, muddy, and grass-covered. The six Mari carriers scanned it uneasily, and muttered among themselves. Achenmeri, too, looked nervous. He said nothing, but rolled his eyes round and round. It was plain that they did not relish the prospect of this trip up the Erap; but Kari, moving among them, and talking in quiet, confident tones, seemed to reassure them.

On a slightly rising piece of ground behind the landing was the sentry. He had been there since dawn, half hidden among the bushes, searching through his binoculars the opposite bank of the Markham and the mouth of the Erap.

Tom called to him. 'Anything doing over there?'

'Not a thing moved all morning,' he replied with a wave.

This, of course, was good news, but its significance was not very great, for the real danger lay higher up, where the main track which ran the whole length of the Markham Valley crossed the Erap. If the Japanese had decided on more extensive patrolling they would almost certainly begin by using this track, which I should have to cross in a few hours' time.

My patrol-box, blankets, and food had been loaded onto the two canoes, and with three carriers on each, Achenmeri and I squatted down on the deck of one, with Kari in charge of the other. We exchanged a quick hand-shake and goodbye with Tom, and then our near-naked crews pushed off into the swift, muddy water.

The current was so strong that it was impossible to cross directly from one bank to the other, so, sweeping rapidly downstream, we made diagonally for the first island. There was very little freeboard on the canoe, and from time to time water splashed into it. The crew did not seem very concerned at this, and it was one-third full before they began bailing with their coconut-shells. Meanwhile, with all three paddles on the right-hand side, with much panting and sweating, they were slowly urging our little craft nearer to the island. As soon as we reached the shallows they jumped overboard and began pushing, until we finally grounded at the lower end of the island. Then, by means of a rope made from vines, they hauled the canoe through slack water to the upstream end of the island, and we were off into the second main stream and over to the second island. Another repetition of the manoeuvre, and we had crossed the Markham and were on more or less dry land at the mouth of the Erap. The crossing had taken about half an hour.

It was a long way from this bank to the south one. Through the field-glasses I could see Tom and his sentry on the other side. They were waving, having seen my safe landing, and I waved back. Their figures, so small and distant, and the vastness of the stream between us, gave me a sudden feeling of inexpressible loneliness, which was cut short by the boss-boy in charge of the boats' crews.

As he squeezed the water out of his tattered loincloth he said, 'Suppose behind you like come back, all right, you shoot three-fella time long musket. All right, me-fella hearim musket 'e fire up, me-fella come quick.'

In other words, when I wanted to return, three rifle-shots would bring them over.

Without another word they scrambled onto their canoes and pushed off on the return journey.

I looked about me. It was a dreary stretch of country, all ooze and mud, and covered by a dense growth of cane-grass, or pit-pit, through which it was difficult to push a way. Even here, at its mouth, the Erap River was very swift, and carried such a burden of silt that its consistency was that of thin porridge rather than water. The Mari boys regarded it with misgivings, pointing upstream and chattering to each other in their own local language. It was so swift here, they said finally in pidgin, that it had certainly been raining in the mountains, and the higher we went the more difficult it would be to cross. However, after a little persuasion they picked up the loads and, with our eyes firmly fixed on the opening of the Erap Gorge in the distant line of blue hills, we set off across the flat.

We spent the first half-hour scrambling in and out of water and it seemed that at any moment the squelching mud would pluck the boots from my feet as we shoved our way through the pit-pit grass. We were heading almost due north straight through the tangled mass of distributary streams that formed the delta of the Erap.

Soon, however, the stream entered a more defined course, and the growth of pit-pit gave way to kunai. Although it was so swift, the river had virtually no banks, and one had the impression of a stream flowing over the plain rather than through it. The nature of the ground changed, too. In place of the mud there was an endless stretch of stones – water-rounded pebbles of varying size, but mostly about as big as a cricket-ball. They were extraordinarily difficult to walk on, rolling from underfoot and making one stumble every few paces.

In the course of a couple of hours we made about half a dozen crossings of the Erap, which snaked round and coiled itself across our path.

As we scrambled out of the water onto the right-hand bank after one of these crossings, Kari, who was at the head of the line, called out, 'Master, you come! Me lookim leg belong man.'

Tracks! I could scarcely see a sign of a footprint, but Kari and the other boys assured me that they were there, and led in the direction of a patch of jungle about half a mile from the stream.

'Who do you think it could be?' I asked Kari.

'It might be Japanese,' he replied. 'But I think it is more likely that they are kanakas from Bivoro, the village we are making for.'

'That's right,' the others chimed in. 'Whoever made those tracks was not wearing shoes.'

'The Erap kanakas often come down to these flats to hunt and fish,' added one.

A faint wisp of smoke curled up from the patch of jungle. Whoever they might be, they were now in the bush. We put the cargo in a pile and moved quietly in the direction of the smoke. A hundred yards or so from the edge of the timber we found a faint path, and in the soft earth were several clear footprints. These convinced Kari and Achenmeri that the people we were seeking were natives.

'Leg belong kanaka,' everyone agreed confidently.

We crept along the path and into the timber. Five minutes brought us to the edge of a small clearing, in which stood half a dozen tiny rough shelters of sago-fronds, the sort of huts which natives make for an expedition of a few days' duration. Eight or ten men were moving about, clad in the usual garb of tattered loincloth. There were a couple of women, wearing the typical grass skirt, short in front and knee-length at the back. There were also one or two small children. It was clear that they did not suspect the presence of any stranger.

While the rest of us remained quiet, Kari stepped forward. At the sound of his approach the women snatched up the children and fled into the bush. They had vanished almost before one realised that they had moved.

The men seized the long spears which lay handy, but they were reassured almost at once by the sight of Kari's police uniform. He told them of our presence and then motioned to us to come out. An elderly native with greying hair stepped up to me and saluted. He explained that he was the headman, or luluai, of Bivoro, and apologized for not having his official cap on.

'We have seen so few white men since the time of trouble with the Japanese came,' he explained in pidgin, 'that we expected nobody. Least of all did we expect anyone to come upon us here. In fact, when your police-boy stepped out of the trees we were afraid it was Japanese. They have sent native messengers up here to say that they are going to take over all this country and send some of their people up from Lae.'

With a loud yodelling call he summoned the women back, apparently telling them there was nothing to fear.

I asked him if there would be any Japanese in Bivoro, which was still some hours' walk away.

'No,' he replied, 'though it is nearly a week since I have been there myself. We have been down here hunting wild pig. But they would have sent for me at once from my village if anything of that sort had happened.'

This was good news. Bivoro was important, for it was the last village on our line of communications from the mountains back to Bob's. If the Japanese had not visited these people and spread the usual propaganda about all the Australians having run away, there was a good chance of our getting some help from the villagers.

The reluctance of the Mari carriers to make the journey up the Erap had increased visibly with every mile we put between ourselves and the Markham. I was afraid they might slip off into the bush and return home, so I asked the luluai of Bivoro if his men would take over the job and carry my six boy-loads of cargo to his village. He agreed at once, and shouted orders to the women to pack all their belongings – grass mats, blackened clay cooking-pots, and so forth. These went into the inevitable string bags. The men he instructed to collect the cargo, which still lay in the kunai outside the patch of jungle.

This arrangement pleased the Mari boys immensely. Now they would be able to sleep the night at home, and not in a foreign village. Kari lined them up to receive their pay, and I dropped a shilling and a stick of tobacco into each outstretched hand. By accepted New Guinea standards this was substantial overpayment for half a day's work, but it was important for them to be satisfied and in good temper. On their homeward journey down the Erap, it was quite possible that they would meet a party of Japanese and if they felt I had cheated them they might revenge themselves by setting the enemy on our trail. As soon as the last man had been paid, the six of them disappeared silently through the trees, stowing their shillings safely in their ears as they went.

'How are you off for tobacco?' I asked the luluai as I squatted on the ground beside him, waiting for the men to return with the cargo. (I spoke in pidgin, of course.)

'Not very well,' he replied. 'We do not grow very good brus at Bivoro. It is a long while since I had a piece of newspaper to roll my smoke in, too,' he added hopefully.

I gave him a stick of trade tobacco and several sheets of newspaper.

'Divide the paper up for the men, and I will give them a little tobacco when they bring the cargo up,' I told him.

He spread the paper on the ground before us and carefully tore it into strips.

'Look,' he said finally, 'there is one piece bigger than the others. I had better keep it myself, so as to avoid any dispute.' And the old rogue tucked into his string bag almost a whole sheet of paper.

In less than five minutes the women had packed all their belongings into the bilums, as the string bags were called, and the men had returned with my cargo. We were on our way once more.

The luluai walked beside me, carrying my haversack, and I asked him about the route we were to follow. He said that it would be necessary to cross and recross the Erap at least half a dozen times before we got to Bivoro.

'The river turns about and about so much,' he explained, 'that if we were to follow the one bank it would take us till tomorrow to get there. The water gets very swift as we go up, too, but we will help you to cross.'

We emerged from the patch of jungle and regained the kunai. It was terribly hot, and the sun was reflected straight back into our faces from the stony ground. I kept hoping that no enemy reconnaissance planes would fly over, because there was not a scrap of cover for several miles ahead. When we next came to the bank of the Erap I realized that even if there had been a Jap plane about we would not have heard it for the roar of the water and a dull rumbling sound which, Kari explained, was caused by rocks and boulders that were being swept along the bed of the stream.

'This stream is not deep,' he told me. 'The danger lies in those rocks, which could easily break a man's leg, and in the force of the water. I hope you are strong in the water, because if you fall over in crossing you will be lucky to get out much this side of the Markham, though the water is seldom deeper than your waist.'

The truth of this was demonstrated at our first crossing. The luluai had wished to hold my hand and assist me over, but foolishly I would not hear of it. 'If an old man like that can do it, so can I,' was my thought, and I plunged into the stream ahead of the carriers. The water caught me, and immediately I was struggling to keep my balance on the uneven stony bottom, though I was not even in the fastest part of the stream. The luluai, seeing I had learnt my lesson, thrust out his stick and hauled me to the bank.

He looked at me reproachfully, and explained that it was impossible to stand still and keep one's balance, because the stones rolled away from underfoot. It was necessary to keep running as fast as one could, never leaving the feet on the bottom more than an instant. In this way it was possible to cross the stream without falling. Having delivered his little lecture he grasped me firmly by the hand and led the way.

As soon as we entered the water we broke into a run, bobbing up and down in the current, with the water sweeping us downstream almost irresistibly. Without the assistance of the old man several times I would have fallen. By the time we had covered the twenty yards' width of the river we were at least fifty yards downstream from the point where we had entered the water on the opposite bank.

I took off my shirt to wring the water out, and watched the carriers, who were preparing for the crossing by rolling their loincloths up round their waists to leave their legs unhampered. Holding his load high in the air, each man plunged in and started running, jumping up and down as he went. My patrol-box, the only double load of the cargo, was carried by two men. Lashed to a pole, it swayed wildly to and fro between them as they held it clear of the water. I watched them anxiously, for the box contained all my essential possessions, including the precious map I had obtained from Bill Chaffey. In the course of several journeys up and down the Erap I never ceased to wonder how the carriers managed the distance without falling, with that awkward load jolting about between them. When I expressed my admiration for their agility they merely grinned, and twisted the water from their loincloths. 'Something – nothing, master,' they said. 'This river doesn't often become too flooded for us to cross.' And they went on to explain a phenomenon of the Erap – that as soon as it was seen to be raining in the mountains they knew they could safely cross the river, for the flood would not reach the flat for some time.

'When the flood does come, though, it is like a wave, and there is no hope if you are caught in midstream,' said the luluai as the men picked up the loads and set off again.

We walked fast, and without stopping to rest, across the stony ground, with the heat growing fiercer all the way. When we crossed the Markham 'road' – a faint dusty track that led down to Lae – Kari and the other boys could find no sign of its having been used recently. Certainly there were no footprints of Japanese to be seen.

Fast as we walked, however, the hills seemed to recede with every step. Even by two o'clock they seemed no nearer for our hours of marching across the plain. Then, about half past three, the Erap's banks suddenly became higher, and the stream took a more defined course. The hills all at once looked less blue, and quite close. Within half an hour we were well inside the Erap Gorge, its steep walls rising ever higher as we went. Kari said that another half-hour's walk and one more crossing of the river would bring us to Bivoro. A few stunted banana-plants were clustered here and there, and we passed one small garden of taro where people had recently been working.

Confined in this ever-narrowing bed, the Erap became even more swift and turbulent. The luluai called to us to hurry. There were signs, he said, that the flood was coming, and if we did not reach the crossing swiftly we would be forced to camp in the open for the night. He rushed to the water's edge and called to me to follow.

'We can cross here,' he said. 'You come with me now.'

And for what seemed the hundredth time that day we were struggling through the water. Actually, I think we had crossed the river fifteen times in all since leaving Kirkland's.

Once across, the luluai started to shout and wave his arms madly to the carriers, who had arrived at the water's edge; and they, in turn, gesticulated and pointed upstream. I could see that they too were shouting, but their voices were drowned by the roar of the river. Then, suddenly making up their minds, carriers, women with children, and the two police dashed into the water and struggled across to us.

They were just in time, for they had barely reached the bank when the level of the water started to rise. Within two minutes we were deafened by the roar of the stream and the rumble of the boulders. Nothing could have survived the boiling yellow swirl of water that rushed away to join the Markham.

We were close to Bivoro village now. It came into sight on a small area of flat ground near the junction of the Erap and one of its tributaries. I halted the carriers and squatted in the kunai, searching the houses with my binoculars. The village had all the appearances of a normal native settlement – a few men sitting smoking under the raised grass-thatched houses, women attending to cooking-fires and the preparation of food, and children running about playing among the banana-plants that encircled the houses.

I asked whether Bivoro boasted a house-kiap, or rest-house. (The pidgin name for the government patrol officer was kiap, and in peacetime it had been the custom for most villages under government control to build a rest-house of native materials, where the officer could spend the night.) The luluai indicated a large grass house a little apart from the village, and Kari drew my attention to a fire burning in front of it. I examined the house carefully through the binoculars. It consisted of two rooms with an open veranda between them. Hanging on the veranda, in full view, was a strange-looking sub-machine-gun of a type I had never seen before.

This seemed conclusive evidence that the Japanese were in the place, so I called to the carriers to remain hidden, and asked Kari and the luluai their opinion of the situation.

The luluai was positive that there were no Japanese there. 'We have heard of the Japanese, and are afraid of them. Long ago, we all agreed that if they came to our village we would run away, but you can see for yourself that even the women and small children are there. Would they be sitting round like that if the Japanese were in the village?'

While I admitted the force of his remarks, the machine-gun could not be explained. Kari examined it with the glasses and agreed that it was very different from any used by the Australians.

We moved back into the kunai a little, to consider the best thing to do. The luluai offered to go in and investigate the situation himself, and bring us word. Although he seemed a reliable old fellow, I decided against this. If he were, by some chance, playing a smooth double game with us and the Japs, it would be better for us to surprise them ourselves, rather than have them tipped off and prepared by the luluai.

Then again, there was no imperative reason for us to go in to Bivoro at all. We could sleep in the bush and push on next morning, having skirted the place altogether. I did not want to do this, however, because it would leave a grave uncertainty hanging over us the whole time we were in the Wain. We would constantly be wondering whether or not the Japanese were sitting near the end of our trail, waiting for us to come out.

The only thing to do was to investigate for ourselves at once, and we hastily planned our move.

Kari and I were to approach the house, while Achenmeri, concealed in the kunai, was to cover us with his rifle. The backward glances Kari kept throwing over his shoulder indicated that he felt the same misgivings as I did about Achenmeri's covering fire. I hoped it would not result in an accidental bullet in the back for either of us. We moved quietly down upon the rest-house, feeling confident that the owner of the gun was unaware of our presence, and anyhow would be dead before he reached it if he did realize we were coming. How we would deal with any other occupants of the rest-house was not so certain, but in the absence of a sub-machine-gun I relied on the hand-grenades, and both Kari and I had one ready.

We had almost reached the house when we heard a movement in one of the rooms. I raised my revolver, and out of the corner of my eye saw Kari's rifle fly to his shoulder. Then a fair curly head appeared in the doorway, and a voice shouted to a cook-boy to prepare some hot water for a wash. To our intense relief the voice was unmistakably Australian, and with a loud 'Hullo!' we hurried across the open space to meet the stranger.

He was so surprised that he almost fell off the veranda, and his relief when he recognized us as friends was almost as great as ours had been.

'Well, I'll be buggered!' was all either of us could say at first as we shook hands warmly and went inside the house to make introductions and explanations. Kari meanwhile shouted to Achenmeri that all was well, and told him to bring the others into the village.

The stranger sat down at once on the edge of his bed-sail, and I noticed that he looked pale and sick.

'Fever,' he explained briefly. 'I got here yesterday and

I've felt pretty crook since. It'll pass, though,' he added. He had the philosophical attitude towards his sickness that characterized most of the men who had had many attacks of malaria.

He told me his name was Les Williams, and that he was a member of a special party sent up from Australia on a secret mission into the Huon Peninsula.

'Do you know about Jock McLeod being in there?' I asked.

'Sure. I've met up with him already, and I'm just on my way to rejoin him. My chief is in there with Jock now.'

'Who's in charge of your show?'

'A bloke called Ian Downs. He's a lieutenant in the Navy now, but he was a New Guinea patrol officer in peacetime.'

Stacked at one end of the rickety bamboo floor was Les's patrol gear. A couple of the boxes looked as though they might contain a radio transmitter and receiver.

'Can you tell me some more about your set-up?' I asked. 'Or is there too much of the cloak-and-dagger hush-hush?'

'Seeing you're here, you might as well know. You'd pretty soon find out,' he added with a grin. 'Anyhow, I expect we'll all work in together, Jock and Ian have been co-operating.'

He shivered, and lay back on the bed, pulling a blanket over him.

'Before you go on,' I said, 'tell me about that sub-machine-gun. It had me tricked.'

'That's easy — it's only a Sten gun. They aren't on issue generally to Australian troops yet, but some special parties like ours are being equipped with them.'

Outside there was laughter and chattering as Kari and Achenmeri got acquainted with the natives of Les's party, and the luluai and his men told the rest of the inhabitants how astonished I'd been at finding another white man here. We stopped to listen for a moment, and then Les went on to give me more details of his plans.

It appeared that Ian Downs had established a base camp south of the Markham, at the native village of Tungu, on the Watut River. There he had a powerful radio set manned by signallers. The boxes on the floor with Les's patrol gear contained, as I suspected, a radio set, a small one intended for sending messages to Tungu, whence they could be relayed to Port Moresby or to Australia, but unfortunately it was out of action. Les had brought it to Tungu to see whether it could be repaired, but it needed some new parts, and he had arranged to have these sent after him. Our only means of communication, at present, therefore, was by runner, either to Bob's or to the Tungu base camp.

Ian Downs's party was collecting as much information about Japanese activities in this area as possible, as a prelude to a projected full-scale attack on Lae later in the year. Apparently Land Headquarters in Melbourne had had no idea of Jock McLeod's movements, and Ian had been astonished to find him on the peninsula.

Les was now on his way to rejoin Jock and Ian, after bringing the radio to Tungu. He had made his crossing of the Markham higher up than Kirkland's, moving across country to Bivoro.

Since he had been to Jock's camp near Gain, and expected to find him still there, we decided to make our way to Gain together.

Although next day Les felt better, he was still not well enough to travel, and we spent the day reading, yarning, and smoking, and drinking innumerable pots of tea. I took some pidgin English lessons from him, and though I was at last beginning to make some headway, I still found it hard to understand more than a fraction of what the natives were saying, because they spoke pidgin so rapidly.

At nightfall Les announced that he felt quite fit again, so we summoned the luluai and told him to have enough carriers ready in the morning to take our combined equipment – about a dozen boy-loads in all.

Before eight next morning we had packed our gear and were on the road. It was necessary to cross the Erap for the last time just opposite the village. The water was not running as swiftly as it had been two days before, and we got over easily enough. Once across, we found that the river swung away to the north-west, while our path lay in a north-easterly direction. We caught only one glimpse of the Erap after that.

The track was good, though it climbed steadily and the kunai slopes gave way more and more to areas of forest. The creeks were crystal clear and cold as they tumbled through their rocky courses.

A couple of hours' steady walking brought us to Munkip, a tiny village on the way to Gain. The 'doctor-boy' greeted us and we sat down for a few minutes in the shade of the house-kiap to catch our breath and glance at the remarks in the village book.

In peacetime, local government of the natives had been organized along the following lines: Three natives in each community were appointed by the government officer to be village officials. The luluai, or headman, was the senior, and would probably have been a leader of his people in their primitive state. Being an older man, he frequently had not learnt to speak pidgin English, the lingua franca of the Territory, and so a somewhat younger assistant and interpreter was appointed, called a tultul. The tultul had usually been away for a period of employment on a mine or plantation, and so had some slight acquaintance with the ways of the white man. The third village official was the doctor-boy, who had received elementary training in hygiene at one of the native hospitals and who also knew some of the principles of first aid. The official insignia of these three dignitaries was a peaked cap, sometimes of incredible dilapidation. It bore one broad red band, like a staff officer's cap, for the luluai; two narrow red bands for the tultul; and a white band with a red cross for the doctor-boy. Wearing their caps, and a loincloth round their middles, it was the custom for them to greet the kiap at the entrance to the village, each usually giving his own fantastic version of the military salute.

The village book contained the names of all people of the village, arranged in families. Births, deaths, marriages, and migrations were recorded by each officer who made the yearly census of the village, and at the back of the book were entered his comments and general remarks, and hints for the next visiting officer. It was to these remarks that we now turned, in search of any chance information about the country through which we were passing.

One interesting fact came to light: a company had sought the right to obtain kunai-grass in the area for the purpose of manufacturing paper. It was news to Les and me that the wretched stuff could be used for anything except thatching, but apparently it can yield paper of a very good quality. However, no active steps had been taken to put the project into operation.

We were thirsty after the long climb up from the bottom of the Erap Valley, and asked the doctor-boy for a drink of water. He shouted to one of the women, who presently hurried along with a length of green bamboo full of clean, cool water from a nearby creek.

The use of these bamboos was another instance of

the extraordinarily clever way in which these so-called primitive people had adapted themselves to their surroundings. The bamboos were cut in lengths up to five feet, and three or four inches in diameter. The interstices, or 'joints', were then knocked out with a long pointed stick, and the result was a clean, strong receptacle holding two or three gallons. It was a common thing every morning to see the women come up from the creek bearing two or three of them across their shoulders, the tops neatly stoppered with a wad of green banana-leaf. Smaller lengths were used for cooking purposes. Food was packed tightly into them, and they were placed on the fire for the contents to bake. When the food was cooked, the charred bamboo was broken away from the outside. An even more ingenious use of bamboo was in the irrigation conduits that were sometimes seen bringing water round parched hillsides from a spring to a flourishing patch of taro, often over distances of many hundreds of yards.

We drank and moved on, through the little rushing creek and out of the bush, to a steep kunai spur. Native fashion, the track followed the crest of the ridge – the shortest way, perhaps, but certainly the steepest – and led us to a forest-covered mountain. It was hard going, and the sweat soaked our clothes and dripped off our faces as we struggled uphill. But we did not mind, for the higher we went, the cooler the air would become, and the fewer the mosquitoes.

By midday we had reached a small hamlet called Badibo, where we halted to boil the billy. The local natives gave us a pineapple, which, with the tea, comprised our lunch. We bought some fine bananas, too, and the natives assured us that they had plenty of food.

'We are getting near the promised land now,' said Les. 'Just over this hill is Gain, the first village of the Wain country. The people there can grow almost any fruit or vegetable.'

It took an hour and a half to reach the top of the next 'hill'. The track, wide enough only for single file, climbed through thick forest all the way. The trees had been cleared slightly at the summit, and it was possible to look across the plain we had left behind, to the Markham. At the distant edge of the plain the great stream gleamed dully in the afternoon sun. On the south bank, where the hills came close to the water's edge, was the kunai spur of Kirkland's outlined against the dark background of the jungle. Through the binoculars we thought we could see a faint plume of smoke above the place where we knew the camp to be.

'Well,' I said, 'we're a long way from home now, if anything happens.'

We began the short descent of the other side of the hill to Gain, thinking enviously of Tom Lega and his five men at Kirkland's, mosquito-ridden and unhealthy as the place was.

Apparently the news of our coming had been sent ahead from Bivoro or Munkip, for the luluai, tultul, and doctor-boy of Gain stepped forward to salute us as we stopped in front of the house-kiap, and the village had a scrupulously neat look, which was usually lacking when a surprise call was paid.

The Wain country was to be my home for many months, and I grew to love it all. It contains many beautiful sights, but I have always had a specially soft spot in my heart for Gain village, possibly because of the contrast with the hot, flat, mosquito-ridden Markham. The house-kiap, a little apart from the village, was set in a grassy clearing on the hillside, whence one looked across the deep valley of the Upper Busu River towards tiers of blue mountains rising ever higher as they receded into the distance. The Busu, a considerable stream even here, flowed into the

Huon Gulf not many miles from Lae as a large muddy river. The hills, dotted here and there with gardens, were every conceivable shade of blue. Drifting smoke from some of the gardens indicated that the owners were clearing new ground. As Les had said, the natives grew abundant and varied crops in the rich red-brown soil – we were to see that this country was as productive as it was beautiful. The luluai shouted to the women that we wished to buy food for the police and some fruit and vegetables for ourselves. The food had obviously been gathered in anticipation of our visit, for within a few minutes half a dozen chattering grass-skirted women carrying large bilums, or string bags, walked across the clearing towards the house-kiap. They carried their bilums by putting them over their backs and suspending them by a string that passed across their foreheads. If the strain became too great the women would walk with hands clasped behind their heads to relieve the backward drag. In this fashion, loads that would almost have broken a mule's heart were carried. Often you could hardly see the woman who carried the load, which consisted of perhaps forty pounds of sweet potatoes, the next day's stack of firewood, a cooking-pot or two, and sometimes a child to top the pile. But no doubt they were used to it, and they seemed remarkably cheerful as they spread their wares on the grass, each standing by her pile waiting for me to buy.

The tultul translated my question into 'talk-place', or the local dialect, for the women did not speak pidgin. 'Do you want salt, money, newspaper, or tobacco?' I asked.

Without exception each chose a handful or so of coarse salt, and carefully parcelled it up in a leaf tied with vine. They were obviously delighted with their bargain, which astonished me when I looked at what I had received in exchange. There were piles of cabbages, sweet potatoes, English potatoes, tomatoes, papaws, bananas, sweet corn, and pineapples. The German Lutheran Mission, which had been established in the area for many years, was mainly responsible for the presence of these imported plants, and one could buy fine-quality English potatoes almost anywhere in the mountains of the Huon Peninsula, though they did not thrive in the low-lying coastal areas.

With a confidential wink, the luluai sidled up and handed me a small bundle tied up in a filthy rag. I opened it gingerly, to find six eggs. The old man's grin spread from one black ear to the other as I called out delightedly to Les, 'Hey, look at this! Eggs for breakfast!'

'Good-oh – they'll go well! Buy 'em and don't break 'em!' Les said enthusiastically.

I was about to give the old boy a shilling and a smoke when Kari stepped quickly between us. 'Master, you no can buyim! Me tryim first time suppose 'em 'e stink!'

Kari had been told to look after me, and he was taking it seriously. He called for a dish of water, but since none of the eggs floated we reckoned they were good, and handed over the payment. We also asked the luluai and tultul to come up to the house later in the evening, so that we could have a chat.

'Wash-wash' was the next item of camp routine. Two buckets of water were heated over the fire in the 'house-cook' – a small shelter attached to the house-kiap – and a couple of banana-leaves were spread on the ground for a bath-mat. With a mug we poured hot water from the bucket over ourselves, lathered up, and rinsed the soap off with more hot water from the mug. All this was watched by an interested throng of natives of both sexes and all sizes. It was the only way in which I took a bath in the next year or so, for to bathe in the icy streams of these mountains was to invite an attack of malaria.

Though Les had a couple of natives as servants and camp usefuls, we had no cook, so I prepared dinner myself. The menu comprised fried tinned sausages, cabbage, potato-chips, and fried tomatoes, and fruit salad, followed by several pints of very strong and excellent coffee made from coffee-beans grown in Wau – I had taken care to scrounge a big tin before setting out for the Markham.

Les sighed with delicious anticipation as I put his meal in front of him. 'By God, that looks good!' Settling the plate firmly on his knee, he ate ravenously.

Except for the sausages our meal was all of local produce. In this country the only rations we had to carry were the typically European foods – tea and sugar, tinned milk and meat, jam, biscuits, and flour. Fresh meat could sometimes be bought from the natives – they only had to kill a fowl or a pig. And if you had a shotgun you could sometimes bag a pigeon, which made succulent eating.

Dusk was approaching when we drained the coffee-pot and lit our pipes and sat on the edge of the house, which, like all native dwellings in this district, was built on piles a few feet above the ground. As we smoked, we watched the shadows darken in the valleys and the mountains change from blue to deep purple.

Through the glasses we picked out two iron-roofed houses on a distant hillside. These were the buildings of Boana Mission, the Lutheran headquarters for this area, and former residence of several German missionaries. Boana had long since been abandoned, for the missionaries had been either interned or removed to Australia. The buildings were also damaged, for Japanese strafing planes, under the impression that our forces were in occupation, had attacked the mission one morning and partially wrecked it. The question now was whether the Japanese would come and take charge. Boana was a sort of focal centre for the Wain, and was only a couple of days' journey from the enemy base at Lae. It seemed certain that soon the Japanese would venture into the mountains and establish a post there.

Though we had not received an unfriendly welcome, we were a little worried about the attitude of the natives towards us. Would they refuse to co-operate when we made the reasons for our presence known? More than twenty years before the Australian administration was established in New Guinea, German missionaries were exploring the Huon Peninsula and making contact with its people. Some of these missionaries were unfriendly to the administration, and they had not encouraged the natives to co-operate with any white men except themselves. Because of their greater numbers and more or less permanent residence in one district, they naturally had a greater hold on the natives than the transient government officer had. Although all these European missionaries had gone we feared that their influence would persist, for we knew that some of the native mission helpers (or 'black missions') also bore the government no great love. We felt a greater sense of confidence, however, when we were told that most of the 'black missions' had left their posts and returned to their home villages. Now, perhaps, we would have a chance to influence the natives to our way of thinking.

It had become quite dark. The evening was very cool, and we pulled on sweaters and long trousers. I felt contented as I sat and watched the little disc of Les's pipe glow and fade. A good dinner, clean clothes, a pipe, and a cool, pleasant climate – what more could one ask at the end of a hard day's walk, I thought, as I compared this with evenings at Bob's, where one sweated all night and slapped continually at mosquitoes. Below us in the valley the Busu River thundered as it rushed down towards Lae. Across the little clearing came the murmur of conversation and an occasional roar of laughter from the police-boys. We saw the flicker of their fire and the red points of their cigarettes. Les and I sighed as we knocked out our pipes to refill them. In the midst of war, it seemed, one could find peace.

A quiet 'Me fella come up now' announced the presence of the luluai and tultul. They had approached so silently on their bare feet out of the darkness that we had not heard them. They squatted down close by, and we passed them a couple of sticks of tobacco and some newspaper. While they rolled their long cigarettes we talked, the tultul translating our remarks from pidgin English to 'talk-place' for the luluai, and rendering the old man's comments into pidgin for us.

We chatted generally about the war. They knew the Japs had driven us out of Lae, and they wanted to know what the situation was in other parts of New Guinea. We told them of our growing strength – of the planes which would bomb Lae and Salamaua in ever-increasing numbers, and of the great base being built at Port Moresby. Yes, they knew Lae was already being bombed more heavily – the explosions could be heard clearly in Gain as the sound travelled up the valley of the Busu.

'But what about men?' they said. 'The talk comes up to us from Lae that there are more Japanese there than there used to be white men in the whole of New Guinea in peacetime. There are now only four white men that we know of for certain: you two here and the two over there' – they waved their hands vaguely over the hills where they supposed Jock and Ian to be.

We told them of our successes at Milne Bay and Kokoda, and that before very long we would be in a position to regain Lae. We also impressed on them the necessity for avoiding any contact with the Japanese, and for hiding in the bush if any Japs came into the area. They agreed to do this readily enough, for stories had come up from the coast about the harsh treatment of the Lae natives by the Japanese.

The conversation drifted to other topics – food and gardens, and the scarcity of pigs. As they left to return to the village, we told them that we wished to leave early next day, and asked them to make sure that sufficient carriers were available by daybreak.

We lit the hurricane-lamp and undressed, filling a last pipe to be smoked in bed before going to sleep. It was three-blanket country here, and the world seemed a pleasant place as we stretched out on our bed-sails. The risky journey up the Erap had been accomplished safely, the local natives seemed well disposed, and we were happy.

We took a last look across at the house-police, which was now silent. Squatting by the dying embers of the fire was the sentry posted by Corporal Kari. His black skin shone in the faint light; when he drew on his cigarette the whites of his eyes gleamed, and the shape of a fixed bayonet could just be discerned.

'Well, shut-eye now,' said Les. 'We must be on the track before sparrow-fart tomorrow.'

I was too nearly asleep to reply.

III

I N THE morning we drank a cup of tea by the first grey
light and were on the road again. A dozen men would
have been enough to carry our gear, but we were surrounded by a throng of people, all anxious to help. Chattering loudly in their own tongue, tiny brown-skinned
lads seized lamps and buckets and other light articles and
fell into line with the men carrying the heavier loads. Of
course, this was not done purely out of a desire to work:
they knew very well that they would share in the distribution of salt and tobacco at the end of the carry. But
there was a good-humoured spirit about the whole line of
carriers which made us confident that even if the enemy's
propaganda had penetrated as far as this, it had failed to stir
up feeling against us.

We descended the track, which wound steep and
snake-like, through grass and forest, to the Busu River. We
crossed the river by a rickety bridge of bamboos and
began the climb up the other side. These steep climbs up
and down the valleys were the most difficult feature of

travel in these mountains, where all the streams were so deeply entrenched. Indeed, in some settlements one could shout to another village and be heard, though the walk to it involved the best part of half a day's solid climbing.

On the top of the ridge forming the east side of the Busu Valley was another small settlement, whose people were already assembled, waiting to take over the carrying. We sat on our patrol-boxes to rest for a few minutes, and paid the men from Gain with a stick of tobacco and a piece of newspaper each. The lads who had joined in the line, carrying the lamps and other odds and ends, asked for salt, so we gave them a tablespoonful each. One by one they stepped gravely forward and presented a leaf for the salt to be placed on. Then they squatted down and made neat little bundles, folding the leaves and binding them tightly with pieces of vine. I often noticed the serious expressions on the faces of some of these ten-year-old brats. When they had a job to do they tackled it much more purposefully than the majority of European children of the same age, displaying a sense of responsibility far beyond their years.

We walked for a further hour and a half along the main track, a well-defined and more or less graded bridle-path, with Les at the head of the line and myself at the rear. The police-boys were interspersed among the carriers. The carriers from Gain had gone home, after handing over to these new carriers, but the luluai and tultul of Gain were honouring us with their company as far as the camp. The tultul walked with me at the rear, pointing out features of interest and telling me the names of all the mountains. The men in front, he told me, were watching carefully for a certain mark on a tree – indicating the turn-off to the camp. Before long the line stopped. They had come to the marked tree. Loads were put down and everyone took a breather before continuing on the last lap of the journey. Moving off again, we plunged straight into thick bush, grasping saplings and vines to haul ourselves up a steep, slippery slope. It took only about twenty-five minutes to reach the camp on the summit of the hill, but we were exhausted. Only a couple of days off the Markham plain, we were not yet in training for mountain walking.

The camp consisted of two small grass huts concealed in a patch of thick bamboos. It was an excellent spot for a hide-out, for there was a back way out for escape into another valley; anyhow, a Japanese who had just climbed that hill would be in no condition to put up a fight. He would doubtless feel just as we did now – about ready to drop.

We looked inside the huts, but they were empty; then round the encircling green walls of bamboo. All was silent. The place seemed deserted. Then a native holding a rifle stepped out of the foliage, and approached Les, whom he obviously knew, with a broad grin.

'Goo' mornin', master,' he said.

' 'Morning, Buka. Master Jock 'e stop?'

'No-got. 'Im 'e no stop,' the boy replied.

' 'Im 'e go where?'

'Master, me no savvy 'im 'e go where.'

That was that. Jock had left. The boy added that he had moved on two days earlier, and had taken the tultul of the nearby native village of Wampangan with him. When this man returned we would be able to find out where Jock had gone.

I had been studying Buka during this conversation. He was the blackest man I have ever seen, as black as polished ebony, and his glossy skin shone in the sun. His real name was Ure, but he was called Buka after his home island in the Solomon Islands group. These people probably have the blackest skins of any New Guinea natives. Buka was a police-boy, though at this moment he was not wearing his uniform. Instead, he sported a long silk loin-cloth of brightest canary yellow.

As Les and I moved into one of the huts we told Buka to get a fire going.

'I suppose we might as well wait here until we hear something from Jock or Ian,' I said.

'Might as well. It's no good chasing round the country until we find out where they've gone or what's happening.'

We paid off our carriers and gave the luluai and tultul of Gain a small present each. Not far from the spot where we had turned off the track at the foot of the hill, there was another little hamlet of six or seven houses, and we told the departing carriers to call in there and ask the people to bring us up some food. Then we sat down and started on our lunch, polishing off the six eggs we had bought the day before from the luluai of Gain.

'The camp looks a bit damp,' I remarked as we lay reading on our bed-sails after our meal. 'Why did Jock have it built directly on the ground?'

'Mainly a question of time,' Les replied. 'The whole joint was run up in about half a day, and you can't have hot and cold water in that time – or a raised floor, either.'

'Fair enough, I suppose. Anyhow, they tell me Jock's pretty tough, so I don't suppose he'd notice the difference!'

'Tough? Boy! Wait till you've been round the bush with him for a while – you'll find out just what toughness is! Jock's one of the toughest things on this island.'

There was some tinned meat and some biscuits in the house, and we set about making an inventory of our combined stock of food. My own rations were few, but Les had quite a lot, all specially prepared for his expedition. Oatmeal, dried meat, sugar, tea, chocolate, were made up in separate cellophane packets, each containing sufficient for one man for one meal. With the local vegetables and fruit we reckoned we would have enough food to last four people for about ten days. But our supply of trade goods was running low, and when the salt and tobacco were exhausted we wouldn't be able to buy any more native foods. The greatest drain on our trade goods was the food that we had to buy for the police and our other boys, who lived almost entirely on local produce. However, we calculated that we could make the trade goods last at least three weeks. Also, it was possible that Jock had some with him.

Next day a small group of men and women from the hamlet below came up to sell us some of their produce. While we purchased bananas and sweet potatoes they chattered freely among themselves in their own language. We couldn't understand what they were saying, of course, but two words of pidgin kept recurring – sheep-sheep and bulmacow, meaning sheep and cattle. We pricked up our ears.

'Wonem this-fella sheep-sheep now bulmacow?' asked Les.

'Master, some-fella sheep-sheep now bulmacow 'e stop long place belong mission,' replied one of the men.

'Fresh meat!' Les and I exclaimed at once.

Taking Kari with me, I set off almost at once for Boana Mission, which lay on the far side of the valley of the Bunzok River, a couple of hours' walk away. If we could find a beast to kill for meat we would not only have the rare pleasure of eating some fresh grilled chops or steak but would be able to spin out our rather meagre tinned rations.

Through the hot sunshine we followed the winding track down into the valley of the Bunzok to Dzendzen village. As we passed between the grass houses and halted in the clear space in the centre of the village, I felt that the people received us with anything but enthusiasm. They stood glowering sullenly on the outskirts, making no effort to approach us. However, we managed to persuade three or four of them to come to Boana and help us bring back the meat we hoped to get.

A few minutes' walk from Dzendzen we had to cross the Bunzok, which, like all rivers in these mountains, was a foaming torrent that thundered through a course strewn with enormous boulders. The bridge consisted of a huge tree felled across the stream, the top roughly flattened with an adze. The natives told us that the missionary used to ride his horse over this log without dismounting.

The climb up the far side of the valley was steep, and we paused half-way, in a small garden, while the boys cut lengths of sugar-cane for us all. It was wonderfully refreshing stuff, and we eagerly sucked the cool, sugary juice, spitting out the coarse, tough pith.

Before the war Boana Mission had been a little community on its own. There were about a score of small kunai native dwellings, several very large and lofty thatched buildings made of native materials – these were the school and church buildings – and the European dwellings, the two iron-roofed houses that Les and I had glimpsed from Gain. One consisted of only a couple of rooms, while the other was a typical mission building – rectangular and very spacious, surrounded entirely by a wide veranda. The country immediately about the settlement was open and undulating, and all around dark-forested mountains rose up. There were some citrus-trees, an orchard, a little coffee, and the overgrown remains of several large gardens. The most level piece of ground had been made into a small airstrip for the planes which brought stores up from Lae on the coast.

Kari and I sat on the veranda of the larger house. We were hot, and I spread my shirt on the ground to dry out the sweat. We looked about curiously at this abandoned, half-ruined settlement which lay so silent in the baking sunlight. Suddenly a serious-looking middle-aged native stood before us. Neither Kari nor I had seen his approach; a ghost could not have materialized more silently. But he smiled gently, and the cool, ripe papaw he handed us was real enough. Kari halved it with one stroke of his bayonet, and we ate greedily, talking between mouthfuls to the man who had brought it.

He explained that he had been a mission employee and had run away to his distant home village when the war started. After a few months he had returned, and had been dismayed at the ruinous state of everything. He had decided to settle down alone and do his best to look after the place.

As the native pointed out the damage we could see he was near tears. Japanese planes had bombed the house, believing it to be occupied by Australian troops, and water had leaked into almost every room. The scene was one of utter chaos. A large ornately carved organ seemed to be the only thing that had escaped. A loose shutter squeaking and banging in the wind was unnerving me, and everywhere was the smell of decay. I shivered. From the encircling mountains a thousand pairs of Japanese eyes might be watching us. Even the mission boy, friendly and helpful though he was, seemed a little unreal and sinister.

Kari did not like the atmosphere either. 'Place no good, master. Me no like!' he rumbled in his deep voice.

I could see several sheep grazing near the edge of the clearing. 'Come on,' I said. 'Let's get one of these animals and get out of here.'

The four men from Dzendzen were resting in the shade a short distance away, and we called to them to follow us. Kari shot the nearest sheep neatly through the head, and after we had skinned it we gave the entrails to the carriers. They wrapped the carcass in leaves to keep the flies off, and fastened it to a stout pole for carrying.

The mission boy had been wringing his hands and muttering as he watched all this, but we did our best to soothe his feelings with a handful of salt. Then, having instructed him to tell nobody of our presence and to warn us immediately upon the first sign of Japanese patrolling, we made our way back across the Bunzok and up the hill to the camp.

In high hopes of fresh meat, Les had delayed lunch, but had the kettle boiling and the pan ready for the sheep's liver. We cut off some chops for ourselves and handed the rest of the carcass over to the police, who divided it. They dispatched most of it that night at one sitting.

Shortly after dawn next morning, just as Les and I were getting dressed, Kari stepped into the house.

'Master,' he said, 'me like go back long Markham.'

I looked over at Les, who pulled a wry face.

'Pity, isn't it?' I said. 'I promised John Clarke I'd send Kari back as soon as I got the hang of things here.'

'Nothing for it, I suppose. We could do with an experienced policeman, though.'

I nodded to Kari and told him it was all right to leave. He went out to the house-police, thrust his few belongings into his pack, rolled up some scraps of meat left from the night before, and was ready for the road. I gave him a couple of sticks of tobacco, and a hastily scribbled note for John, telling of our safe arrival. Kari stowed them carefully in his haversack, and took a backward pace.

'All right, master – me go now.'

He smacked the butt of his rifle smartly in salute, turned about, and his big black figure was almost instantly swallowed up by the bamboos. Travelling alone and unencumbered, he would be back at Bob's soon after nightfall.

'He's a real man,' I thought, as I looked at the bamboos into which he had vanished. 'I hope I see him again.'

Midday next day brought a visitor in the person of Singin, tultul of nearby Wampangan village. A smooth-tongued, plausible, and intelligent man, Singin had a thin, keen face with yellow-brown skin – he looked as though he had Malay or Chinese blood in his veins. He had been away with Jock, and from his little string bag he fished out a crumpled scrap of paper bearing a message. In it Jock ordered Buka to follow Singin and bring the trade goods and the box of food. Clearly Jock had no idea that Les and I were at the camp, for the message was written in pidgin – to be read to Buka by Singin, one of the few natives in the area who could read and write.

Singin told us that he had left Jock in the village of Samandzing, about four days' walk away. Singin was not sure where Ian Downs was, but said that he was some-where 'farther on'.

I pulled out the map I had drawn with Bill Chaffey. There was no sign of a village called Samandzing.

'What about your map, Les?' I asked.

'Soon see. It's in my pocket,' he replied, pulling out something that looked like a handkerchief. It was a map Ian had drawn on a piece of silk. It could be screwed up in the pocket, put under water, rolled in the mud and washed out, emerging from all this as good as the day it was made.

It covered a much greater area than my map, and we found Samandzing high in the mountains, a considerable distance to the east. It seemed to be on a river called the Sankwep, the most easterly tributary of the Busu. So as to plot the track, we asked Singin to name one by one the villages passed through on the way to Samandzing, and as he did so we sketched in the route from village to village. It was a roundabout way, and seemed to lead across several very high mountains.

'What are you going to do?' Les asked.

'My orders were to join Jock, so I suppose I'd better shift on. What about you?'

'I'm expecting the missing parts for this radio set to

be sent on by runner. If I go too far away he might never find me. It'd be better for me to wait, and follow in a few days when I've got the set working.'

Although it was now half past twelve I decided to set out at once, hoping to reach Gumbum village, on the far side of Boana, by nightfall. I told Achenmeri to pack my gear, and Buka to make ready the stores that Jock needed. Les sent Singin to the hamlet at the foot of the hill to tell the natives to come up and carry my cargo.

It was well after one o'clock when Singin returned with nine puffing men, each armed with either a coil of vines or a pole. I had spent the interval roughly tracing part of the silk map on a piece of paper. The result was a crude piece of cartography with which to guide a person across some of the roughest country in the world, but I was only thankful that my chance meeting with Les had enabled me to have a map at all, however rough. I had already walked to the edge of the map Bill Chaffey had given me, and by the next day would have had only the cloudiest notion of where I was, or where I was heading. It seemed strange that such a vital thing should have come to me only by chance. If I had crossed the Markham higher up, if I had wasted another day at Bob's, if Les had not gone down with fever… No doubt coincidence enters into everyone's life: during my time in New Guinea it certainly played an important part in mine, both for good and ill.

With Singin and Buka at their head the carriers passed through the thick bamboos and started, slipping and swearing, down the hill. Les and I shook hands. 'See you in a few days,' we both said. But in fact our next meeting, an accident just like our first, took place several years later, in a luxury hotel in Melbourne.

I followed the same course to Boana as on the previous day. The mission boy materialized just as mysteriously as before, this time to sell me a few eggs from his hens. I paid for them with salt, and repeated my instructions – to keep silent about our movements and to warn Les instantly if there should be any sign of Japanese patrols.

Singin left me here, to return to his home village of Wampangan, whose grass roofs could just be discerned through the trees on a mountainside, about half an hour's walk away. We struck off east, across the little airstrip and into the bush. An hour's walk found us at Karau, a village of some twelve or fourteen neat and well-made grass houses grouped round an open space. We sat down here while the men came in from their gardens to take over the carrying. Wild yodelling from the surrounding bush told us that they were passing the word along. In the meantime I paid the others with salt and let them go. They set off homeward at a trot, hoping to beat the afternoon rain.

As soon as sufficient Karau men had come in, Buku lined them up and assigned them their loads, and we moved off down the wide, well-graded track to Gumbum.

This village was a singularly pleasant spot. The house-kiap and the house-police were set in a greensward surrounded by breadfruit-trees, and the paths were lined with gay red, green, and yellow croton plants. There we spent the night, first telling the old luluai to have sufficient carriers on the spot in the morning. The police put up my bed, but I was still doing my own cooking, not yet having secured a satisfactory cook-boy. The natives preferred to stay at home because of the unknown dangers and the difficulty of the work we required them to do. I wanted a boy who would accompany me readily, rather than one who required persuading and who would probably desert and go home as soon as we struck hard going.

Next morning we were on the road shortly after dawn. Our route for the day lay through Monakasat and Banzain to a village called Karangandoang. We were climbing high into the mountains now, and the scenery was wildly magnificent in the early part of the day, but by three in the afternoon the hills were often blanketed in cloud, which rose slowly from the depths of the valleys until it covered the whole countryside. The walk between villages meant a precipitous descent into a valley and a backbreaking climb up the other side. In the mornings the grandeur of the country was some compensation for the effort. Later in the day, with the mist shrouding everything, it was unnerving to walk into the valley as the unseen stream roared below, or to make what seemed to be an endless ascent into space, for the tops of the mountains were invisible and one could not see where the track was leading. By the time we reached Karangandoang a misty rain was falling and the red earth of the track was very greasy and slippery. It was cold, and the boys spread a layer of earth over part of the bamboo floor of the house-kiap, so that, native fashion, I could have a fire in the house to cook on, and to dry my clothes. There was no house-police, but the boys arranged accommodation for themselves in the village, a couple of hundred yards away. The natives greeted us with no great affection – for which, I suppose, they could hardly be blamed, because our presence meant only the nuisance of a carry next day. However, they brought us food, asking for salt in return.

A strong wind was blowing through the house, and I had put on dry clothes and an extra sweater and was about to eat my meal when Buka, his eyes and teeth flashing white against the blackness of his face, burst into the hut.

'One of Master Jock's police-boys is coming! He says there has been trouble!' he exclaimed.

A few seconds later a weary, muddy, but grinning policeman, his cap and loincloth dripping wet and his bare torso steaming, appeared out of the night in the weak yellow shaft of lantern-light. He said that his name was Buso, and that he had a message for Les.

'Give it to me,' I said. 'I'll read it before it goes on to him.'

Buso fished in the depths of his haversack and produced a large sealed envelope. I was glad to see that it had not yet been penetrated by the water, though it was damp. I told Buso to go down to the village to eat and get dry, and to come back in an hour.

The letter was from Ian Downs, describing how he had gone down from the mountains to the coast near Hopoi to reconnoitre a beach on which our assault troops would land to begin an attack on Lae. Unfriendly natives had betrayed him, and he had been chased by a party of Japanese and nearly caught. 'Managed to climb a ficus-tree and watched the Nips walking round underneath. Fortunately they didn't look up,' ran one passage. At another stage the enemy caught sight of him and opened fire, but he managed to shake them off in the bush. He had trouble in fording the swift Bulu River, and apparently injured himself as he crossed from side to side in an effort to cover his tracks from the enemy. Studded through the letter, like a new kind of punctuation mark, was the sentence, 'Had another swig at the whisky-flask – felt a bit better.' The whisky kept him going until, on the second day, he reached a remote mountain village, where he was now resting.

I didn't think the Japs would let Ian get away with this. Although up to this time they had never gone far inland, they must now realize the danger of allowing people like Jock and Ian to continue to live freely in the mountains. A concerted drive by the enemy to hunt such people out of hiding seemed quite a possibility.

I decided that in case there was trouble ahead it would be better to have with us reliable police, and so, when Buso returned, his belly swollen from an enormous meal of sweet potatoes, I told him that the letter would be taken back to Les by Achenmeri, the recruit, and that he, Buso, would guide me to the village where Jock was staying.

The following morning, as Achenmeri turned back towards Boana, the rest of us set out for Kasenobe. It seemed to lie well off the direct line to Samandzing, and I asked the natives whether there was a shorter route. No, they told me, this track was the only one. An hour later we came to a small village, where the Karangandoang carriers handed over to a new line.

Although the sun was fairly high, we were now at such an altitude that the air was quite cool. The country became increasingly rugged and beautiful with every mile. On distant slopes plumes of blue smoke curled slowly up from native gardens – gardens which in this fertile soil produced an abundance of almost all temperate-climate crops. Here and there, like a white ribbon draped over the hillside, a mountain stream plunged hundreds of feet into the valley, and at intervals the brilliant green of the valley sides was broken by the red scars of landslides.

About midday we obtained our first clear view of the enormous central spine of the Saruwaged mountain range, which runs down the middle of the Huon Peninsula. Though about ten miles away, it was almost frightening, it seemed so high and remote. I knew it had been crossed in one or two places, but as I looked at the jagged line its peaks cut across the sky, it was hard to imagine anything as tiny as a human being attempting to overcome such an obstacle. Between the soft blue of the peaks and the sparkling blue of the sky we saw gleaming patches of white. One had the impression that some of the mountains were snow-covered; indeed, the German explorer Detzner, who spent four years of the First World War hiding in the interior from the Australians, described them as snow-bearing. This curious misapprehension is explained by the fact that on these mountains there are large areas of bare, windswept limestone which glistens in the sun and could easily look like snow to a distant observer.

At about two o'clock, when the surrounding country had already vanished into the fog, Kasenobe, perched on top of a cliff, appeared suddenly out of the swirling greyness. As we clambered over the slab stockade which surrounded the settlement, we saw that it was quite a large village for this area, consisting of over thirty houses. There was a big church, its thick, well-thatched roof in sharp contrast to the wretched, poky dwellings.

The feeling of remoteness became complete here. In the other villages, though I had been conscious that many things were new or strange, somehow they seemed different only in degree from life as I had known it in Australia. But even another planet could have been no more unfamiliar and eerie than this savage village. If I had to convey my main impression of it – and of the many others like it – in one word, that word would be greyness. The fog, the stinking village pigs, the weatherbeaten roofs, the dirty, scaly-skinned, near-naked kanakas – all these were dismal, grey, and dispiriting, beneath a sombre, leaden sky.

Only one man spoke pidgin, and none of them had ever been away from the village to work. There was not a shred of calico to be seen. All the men wore the traditional dress known as mal, which is a strip of rough 'cloth' made by beating a section of bark from the wild mulberry until it becomes pliable. It is wound tightly round the waist several times, and then passed between the legs to enclose the genitals. The women wore only a flimsy petticoat, less than a foot long, made of reeds. They were decrepit hags, in keeping with their village; their pendulous breasts reminded me of razor-strops hanging on a barber's chair. The missionaries, in their efforts to preserve their charges unspotted from the world, had seen to it that no minor amenity of civilization – such as a piece of soap – penetrated to this fastness. Their church, with its rough wooden cross, seemed a pious incongruity among stone-age savagery. I thought of the Indian villages of early North American history, where mission churches had been no barrier to acts of fiendish barbarity.

The men stood glowering as we piled the cargo in the middle of the village. Occasionally, with angry gestures, one would jabber unintelligibly in the local dialect. I noticed that several of the kanakas were armed with bows and arrows.

'They are wild men here,' Buso remarked – a trifle superfluously, I felt – as he and Buka unslung their rifles. 'Master Jock taught them a lesson, though, when we passed through, so I don't think they will attack us.'

Buka grinned in agreement. 'Master Jock 'e strong-fella man too much! Kanaka all 'e no can humbug long Master Jock,' he said happily.

They pointed out the man who spoke pidgin, and I called him over. He came slowly, sulkily, and stood in front of us with his head bowed. I told him quietly that I wanted sufficient food for the police and myself, but he continued to stare at the ground, and would not answer. I suppressed my anger with some effort, and explained to him patiently that we were hungry and must eat. They had plenty of food, and if they brought it to me they would be paid for it. If we had to help ourselves we would take it for nothing. They could please themselves.

He translated this into 'talk-place', and the other men discussed the ultimatum. In the end they shouted to their women, and a few minutes later we were supplied with potatoes, sweet potatoes, cabbages, and beans. The women were as timid as the men were aggressive, advancing just near enough to seize the proffered salt at arm's length, and then dashing back hastily, as though afraid I would bite them. A crowd of ten-year-old brats had gathered behind me, but they rushed away to hide whenever I turned, however quietly, in their direction.

As there was no house-kiap I decided to sleep in the church. It was at the edge of the clearing, so we would have some hope of escaping into the bush if we were attacked. Buso and Buka put up my bed-sail on the dais at one end of the building, and, feeling rather like a sacrificial lamb on the altar, I lay down there to write up my patrol diary. It was still very early, so I spent the rest of the afternoon writing letters home to Australia. It seemed an odd thing to do in this place: I felt that I might as well have been writing to people on the moon. How any letter would be sent I did not know, but I wanted it to be ready in case a runner should be sent back to Bob's.

Late in the afternoon the whole church building suddenly began to creak and rock, and I could see the beams of the roof heaving and straining against the ridge-pole. I sprang off the bed in fear, not realizing for a moment that it was only an earth-tremor – almost a daily occurrence, though this was an unusually violent one. When it had stopped, after about two minutes, and I had calmed down, I wished it had been the volcanoes at Rabaul erupting – we'd have been saved the trouble of clearing out the Japanese.

As darkness drew on I ate my solitary meal. The cold and damp crept into the church, and the whole world seemed to shrink to the dim sphere illumined by my small hurricane-lamp. There was no sound from the kanakas, no sign of cooking-fires. I shivered, checked over my pistol, and crawled miserably into bed.

Kasenobe looked more cheerful in the morning. Bright sunlight warmed the sparkling air, and not a cloud spoilt the clear sky. But the houses were the same grey ramshackles, and the kanakas as sullen as ever. Naturally, in such a place, latrines were unheard of, so I retired to the edge of the bush. While still squatting, I was knocked flying by half a dozen ravenous village pigs, squealing and fighting for the excrement that forms a large part of their diet.

Nine surly Kasenobe boys shouldered our cargo, but they were so unwilling to come that I decided Buso, Buka, and I should watch three of them each, in case they tried the favourite trick of throwing down the cargo in some difficult spot and vanishing into the thick forest. We hoped to be in Samandzing – the village where Buso had left Jock a couple of days before – by nightfall, but I began to doubt our chances when I saw the track. It was both rough and steep, and so badly eroded by rushing water that on the hillside immediately above Kasenobe we found ourselves walking in a ditch three or four feet deep. The map showed that we had to cross two high mountains, and Buso confirmed this. Though they were very steep and difficult, he said, we ought to make Samandzing before dark.

Eleven o'clock found us regaining our breath on top of the first mountain. The carriers seemed to have settled down, and happily accepted tobacco and newspaper to roll smokes. Many aeroplanes passed overhead as we rested, but we could not identify them because of the thick trees that stretched above us. However, within a few minutes the boom of anti-aircraft fire and the heavy rolling thunder of exploding bombs told us that our planes were making a strike on Lae. The noise of the explosions was a healthy reminder that, however isolated it might seem, this country could easily be reached by the Japs from their base at Lae in about three days' walk.

An hour or so from the top of the mountain brought us to a stream which the natives called Dimini. On the far side of the valley was a ruined village of the same name, whose inhabitants had moved to Kasenobe. We sat down for another rest on a cliff above the stream, where a cleared space enabled me to get a good view of the surrounding country. Looking downstream through the field-glasses I could see in the distance a thatched building which seemed somehow familiar. The more I looked, the more it puzzled me, but I could not identify it. I passed the glasses to Buso, who instantly recognized it as the house-kiap at Karangandoang in which I had slept the night before last. The Karangandoang people had indeed been fooling us when they said that to reach Samandzing it was necessary to pass through Kasenobe. Down this valley Karangandoang was not more than five miles away, and I felt sure that there would be a track, even if only a rough one. I made a mental black mark against the people who had caused us to lose a whole day through unnecessary travelling. We started off again to climb the second mountain. It was not as high as the first one which I had estimated as being about nine thousand feet, but the track was much rougher. In one place a landslide had carried away a section of it, and we had to scramble round the bare rocky hillside holding on to roots and trees as we went. Every now and then we had to stop to scrape leeches off our legs.

By two o'clock we were trotting down a steep slope into Bungalamba village, where we boiled the billy. Native fashion, I laid a couple of ears of corn in their leaves on the fire for lunch. As I ate I studied the map, finding out where Bungalamba fitted into the general picture. This village was of considerable strategic importance to us, I felt, for it was on a river along whose valley a path led direct to Lae. From where I sat I could see down the river to Mililuga village, which was only two days' walk from Lae. If the Japanese decided to come looking for people like Jock McLeod, this seemed a likely route for them to take.

Bungalamba was important for another reason: it was the last inhabited point on the southern end of one of the few known crossings over the Saruwaged mountains to the north coast. Jock was well aware of its dual importance, and in a tiny dependent hamlet of the main Bungalamba village, perched high on the far side of the valley, a police-boy was stationed. His job was to watch for any signs of a Japanese move up from Mililuga which would cut us off, and to listen to the gossip of the local natives, reporting to Jock any news he picked up.

As we passed the hamlet, which consisted of three or four miserable grass houses, this police-boy was waiting by the track. He saluted gravely. I saw that he was a small middle-aged man, with the hair receding from his wrinkled brown forehead and turning grey on his temples. His name was Watute, he said, and he came from Pema, at the mouth of the Waria River. He had been in the police force nearly twenty years, and it was not long before I saw why Jock had picked him for this job: he heard everything that was said, shrewdly separated wheat from chaff, the idle chatter from real news, and built-up a complete and accurate picture of the situation, often from the flimsiest of clues, in a manner which would have done credit to Sherlock Holmes.

Leaving this elderly native detective at his post, we hurried along the track through the thickening fog. Luxuriant green vegetation crowded upon us from either side, cold and dripping with moisture. The tops of the trees faded to invisibility behind swirling grey wisps of cloud. Sometimes, on downhill stretches, we broke into a jogtrot, and I think something of my own excitement at the prospect of meeting Jock spread to Buka and Buso, for I heard them urging the carriers to go faster and faster.

When we reached Samandzing the fog was so thick that twilight seemed to be approaching, though it was only about half past four. I could not see the more distant houses, but the village seemed a large one, with well-built grass houses laid out in neat rows. There were a few men strolling about, and I called the nearest one over and asked him which house Jock was using. He stared at me for a few seconds, blank and dumb, then shook his head and slunk away. The other people, too, seemed to be avoiding us, and I was glad when Buso, who had been walking at the tail of the line, came up. He would know where Jock had set up house.

'Master Jock 'e sleep long house-lotu,' he answered promptly to my question, and together we made our way quickly to the big church house which dominated the village. Inside it was gloomy, but there was enough light to see that the building was deserted. There was no sign of Jock's patrol gear. I sent Buso to find the luluai, while Buka and I kept a sharp watch about us, rather disturbed by Jock's unexpected absence.

Buso returned in a few minutes with a reluctant luluai in tow. As soon as the luluai appeared outside the church I knew from his surly face that he would be small help to us.

'Master 'e go where?' I asked.

' 'Em 'e go long Bilimang, lik-lik place close to.'

He was telling me that Jock had moved to the small nearby village of Bilimang. Further inquiries established that it was in the next valley, a couple of hours' walk away. The luluai obviously wanted us to go, for he kept assuring us that we could reach Bilimang shortly after nightfall if we hurried. Come what may, he was determined that we should not sleep in his village of Samandzing.

But I felt too tired to go any farther that night, though I wanted badly to see Jock. I knew he never spent many days in the one place, so it seemed reasonable to suppose that the luluai was telling the truth. To make sure Jock did not leave Bilimang before I arrived, I scribbled a note to say I was following, and asked the luluai to send a lad at once to Jock with the message.

I was a bit dejected, for I had come from Kasenobe at great speed, buoyed up by the prospect of Jock's company that night; now I felt rather let down at the thought of spending another night alone, not knowing what had happened to Ian Downs and wondering whether the Japanese were even then hunting us.

I could see that Samandzing was under strong mission influence, for the churches and schoolhouses were almost as numerous as the dwellings. The people' were unfriendly, and when I asked the luluai to sell us sufficient food for a meal he replied with a smirk that it was Sunday and that his people could not possibly break the Sabbath by digging food. His response had me floored for a moment – until, through the mist, I caught sight of a number of women toiling up the hill from the gardens, laden with bilums of food and bundles of firewood. Apparently the Sabbath Day's rest from labour did not apply to women! I hinted gently that if he could not supply me with a few vegetables in return for payment it might become necessary, however undesirable, for the police to shoot and eat one of his pigs – without payment. The threat was sufficient: after taking one uneasy glance at the gusto with which Buso and Buka unslung their rifles and looked about for a pig, the old scoundrel shouted to the people in 'talk-place'. Within minutes plenty of food was laid out at our feet. There was no house-kiap, so I had a cooking-fire lit on the earth floor of the church, and slept as I had at Kasenobe, perched up on the dais.

By ten o'clock next morning I had put most of the zig-zag track from Samandzing behind me and was clambering down the last hill to Bilimang village – a hill so steep that we should have had parachutes and jumped.

Jock was lounging against the side of a hut waiting for me. He was a big tough-looking man. Above his ruddy face his dark hair was close-cropped, almost shaven.

His deep chest and broad shoulders were scarcely covered by his too-small shirt, and his massive legs, bare below the shorts, were disfigured by ugly running sores. These were tropical ulcers, which start from the smallest scratch and need months of persistent treatment if they are ever to be cured. On his feet was a pair of dirty old sandshoes.

He sauntered forward to meet me, hand extended.

'I got your note,' he said with a grin. 'I don't know how the hell you made it. They must have gone completely nuts to send you out here alone! Anyhow, I'm glad to see you. Come inside and have a cup of tea.'

We bent double and squeezed through the doorway of the tiny native hut. It was almost dark inside, and we could barely stand upright without banging our heads against the smoke-blackened roof. Still, it was the only spare house, and much warmer than camping out.

Over the tea Jock continued to grumble about the stupidity of headquarters.

'I don't think the silly bastards have woken up about the war!' he fumed. 'It was bloody well criminal to send you through that country by yourself! In this letter you brought, I'm ordered to instruct you in routine patrol work. Christ Almighty! Do they think I'm just sitting happily here on my arse, seeing the kanakas keep their villages tidy? Hasn't anybody told them about the Japanese yet?'

He gulped the scalding tea, and tossed the dregs out the door.

'Did they give you a radio set?' he asked at length.

I shook my head. 'I mentioned it, but they just laughed. I thought you must have one.'

'Hell! Here we are, just behind the Nips' main base, and they won't give us a radio! If we find out some red-hot news we have to send it by runner, five days to the nearest radio at Bob's. The intelligence is stale when it arrives! And what about the risk the poor bloody police-boy runs, going up and down the Erap! But a radio? Hell, no! Those bludgers in Wau and Port Moresby might find it too hard to get the Randwick starting-prices if they gave away too many radios!'

'There's certainly not much point in staying here without one. Let's hope Les Williams can get his set going.'

Jock grunted. 'It'll help, but we should all have one. We might get scattered from one end of the Huon Peninsula to the other. One set wouldn't be much use then.'

He sat looking moodily out the door. Rain was falling now, and cold gusts of wind rushed into the dark little hut.

'How about food?' he asked more hopefully. 'Surely to God they realized I was just about out of kai-kai?'

I shook my head. 'No. I've only got about a week's food for one man.'

Jock's anger flared high again. 'The bastards! No comforts. That's all right – you can't expect comforts on a job like this. No food. That's not too bad either – you can always get hold of a bit of sweet potato or pumpkin or something, even if you have to pinch it out of a native garden. But no radio! We'd do more good drinking ourselves happily to death in a nice pub in Australia!'

He made one last effort. 'How about trade goods? Did you manage to get a decent supply?'

'Not much. I've got a few pounds of salt and a few dozen sticks of tobacco. There's an odd newspaper or two, and that's the lot.'

Jock laughed, instead of raging as I had expected.

'Well, we know the worst now,' he said. 'No use worrying at this stage. It's only when you've felt hopeful that you get wild like that. Let's talk about something else.'

'Tell me about Ian Downs,' I said. 'Where is he now?'

'I don't know exactly. He's somewhere in the mountains of the Momalili country, having a rest. I reckon we can expect him back in a day or two. At least, I hope so. There's one thing that's got me a bit worried, though.'

'What's that?'

'Well, there's a track that leads up from the coast between here and the Momalili country. If the Nips get wise to it they might cut him off before he gets here.'

'Do you reckon they will?'

'I'm not really frightened about it. Up till now the bastards have stayed pretty close to the coast and the main tracks. They aren't keen on the bush and the mountains.'

'I don't know that I blame them,' I cut in. We both laughed.

'No. They show more sense there than we do,' Jock said.

Until we saw Ian we could make no definite plans for the future, but Jock mentioned several possible patrols that might yield valuable information. Jock himself was keen to cross the Saruwaged Range over to the north coast, to see what was happening there. As far as we knew, no white men had been there since the war started. Another suggestion he made very much intrigued me: he said that the Japanese were holding prisoner in a compound near Lae the whole peacetime Chinese population of the town. They had been captured when Lae fell, and put behind barbed wire. From time to time some of these Chinese – the tradesmen – were taken into Lae to do work for the Japanese. It was certain therefore that they would have vital information about enemy installations, the strength of the garrison, and the effects of our increasing air raids. However, Jock thought that the sensation caused by Ian's appearance on the beach at Hopoi would make the Japs very careful for a while, and it would be much too dangerous to attempt to visit the Chinese compound just now – for a few weeks, he thought.

At lunch, it did not surprise me when Jock's cook-boy produced porridge made from crushed army biscuits. It was a common dish in those days when rations were short. But at tea-time, when he brought more porridge and said that Master Jock always had a dish of it, I was puzzled and asked Jock the reason. Surely no-one could like the gluey stuff that much!

Jock laughed. 'It's the only way I can eat those bloody slabs of concrete. I haven't got any teeth of my own, and I lost my false ones over the side of a ship in Townsville. You'd better tell the cook you don't want a side dish of porridge every meal yourself. He probably thinks I have it so often because I like it.'

Jock had a few books with him, among them a cheap and battered edition of Winwood Reade's *Martyrdom of Man*, which we dissected and discussed late into the night. When we came to the passage which described religion as a force that commonly softens the head and hardens the heart, Jock told me of some of his own peacetime experiences with some of the missionaries. On one occasion he remonstrated with a missionary who was making some sick natives work in a garden.

'Mr McLeod, you do not understand!' retorted the indignant missionary. 'We are not interested in the miserable bodies of these people, but in saving their immortal souls.'

All next day it rained. We sat on the floor, wrapped in blankets, our backs to the little doorway so that the faint light would fall on our books. From another hut a few yards away came the monotonous drone of a mouth-organ as one of Jock's police-boys played 'Auld Lang Syne' over and over again.

Late in the afternoon a native lad ran into the village through the gathering gloom and rain and handed a wet, crumpled scrap of paper through the doorway to Jock. It was a note from Ian, saying simply that he had arrived at another hamlet about half an hour's walk away, higher up the mountain, and was camping the night there in an empty house. Jock at once rolled up his blanket and bed-sail and went to join him, leaving me to arrange for the packing and carrying of all our gear next day.

Ian was squatting on the veranda of a little native house when I arrived. He seemed fairly fit, though his legs were badly cut about. He was a stocky, fair-haired young man. The old sea-boots into which his feet were thrust were one obvious relic of his past years in the Navy.

We all crowded into the house to escape the cold wind. There was hardly room to move, but we sat shoulder to shoulder, and plunged at once into a discussion of what we should do. The many things to be considered, such as our lack of food, tenuous communications, danger from Japanese patrols following Ian's betrayal at Hopoi, and so on, took some time to discuss, and evening was approaching before we had worked out definite plans. What we decided was this: Jock was to cross the Saruwaged Range and find out what was happening on the north coast; Ian was to return to the Wain country, somewhere near Boana Mission, and rest for a while; I was to return to Bob's with all speed, obtain as much food and trade goods as possible, and rejoin Ian and Les Williams in the Wain. For his journey over the range, Jock would take all the stores we now possessed, and Ian would arrange by radio message to Australia for further supplies and a wireless set to be dropped by plane on the north side for Jock. This meant that he would be able to travel light on the difficult cross-ing, and take very few native carriers.

Accompanied by Buka I set out at first light next morning on the return journey to the Markham. As Jock had taken over my stores I needed only a couple of men from the hamlet to carry my bed-roll and patrol-box. I intended to sleep at Bungalamba that night, or, if we made particularly good time, to camp under one of the abandoned houses at Dimini. Jock and Ian were still in camp. Because Ian could still travel only slowly, they were going to make a leisurely day's walk of it to Samandzing. Next day Jock would go to Bungalamba, there to start his journey across the mountains. When I said goodbye they merely grunted, half asleep under the blankets, and turned over to snore again.

As we wound our way up the tortuous track nearing Samandzing, Buka suddenly stopped and pointed to a tiny figure far above, coming down the track towards us. Even with the naked eye we could see that he wore the police-boy's peaked cap and was carrying a rifle, and I whipped my binoculars from their case and focused them on the track above.

'Well, I think I know who it is,' I said. 'See what you think.' I passed the glasses to Buka.

At once a grin covered his broad black face. 'Master, me savvy this-fella man! Achenmeri!'

We sat down at the side of the track to wait, wondering what news Achenmeri would bring from Les.

When he came round the bend in the track about twenty minutes later, puffing and blowing, Achenmeri told us that he had seen us from a distance, and that he had put on a spurt to reach us quickly. He handed me a letter and flopped on the ground nearby to recover his breath.

Les's letter said that the runner with the spare radio-parts had not arrived, and that he himself was making a flying visit to the Tungu camp across the Markham, to try to get the set working.

We had counted on Les's radio to send the message requesting the supply-dropping for Jock, so I decided to wait for Jock and Ian to see how Les's going to Tungu would change our plans. We walked steadily on to Samandzing, where I set up house again in the church, obtained food from the kanakas for the whole party, and had the billy boiling for a mug of tea when Jock and Ian arrived about midday.

I stayed the night with them at Samandzing, and we slept side by side in the church. The natives treated this larger party with more respect than they had shown me, but they were still far from friendly. We posted a sentry to watch the village, and Jock advised me always to do so in future.

'You never can be too sure of these kanakas,' he said. 'If they reckon the Japs have won the war, they'll all be on their side, just as they abandoned the Germans to come over to us thirty years ago.'

'Would they change as quickly as all that?'

'Why not? What chance would they have of resisting the Japs with bows and arrows? Anyhow, all these years, some of the Lutheran missionaries haven't done anything to make them loyal to the Australian government. The Germans used to boast openly that the Australians would be chucked out of New Guinea. One of them actually told me that Hitler would soon sweep through here like a fire. He didn't seem to care a bit that I was a government officer.'

'Why weren't the missionaries interned, or deported?'

'God knows! Everyone here knew what was going on! Look, you'll hardly believe this: right at the end, when the government just had to evacuate them, and the steamer was pulling out of Lae, some fat-arsed fraus lined up at the ship's rail and heiled Hitler!'

While Jock grumbled, Ian said nothing. He leant back in the shadows on his bed, eyes nearly closed, with cigarette-smoke dribbling slowly from lips that turned slightly in a half-sceptical smile. I looked at Jock's indignant face and back to Ian's expression of doubt. Was this story about some of the missionaries true? I was to learn the answer to this later.

The fact that Les had gone back across the Markham to Tungu caused only one slight change in our plans. I was now to send Watute after Les to Tungu, carrying the radio message arranging the dropping of supplies for Jock.

'It'd be kinder not to take Watute across the range,' said Jock. 'He's probably old enough to be our father. He remembers when the Germans ran this joint. He can attach himself to you when he's delivered the message, and then you'll have three police: Buka, Watute, and Achenmeri – if you can call Achenmeri a policeman.'

We set out at dawn next day, stopping for a few moments while Watute rolled his blanket and got ready. He grinned with pleasure at the idea of being on the move – life in this miserable hamlet, perched up in the fog and cold winds, was uncongenial to his old bones. The thought of warmer sun and lower altitudes brought a happy smile to his wrinkled face as he trotted beside me down the steep track.

From the ruined village of Dimini we took the short cut down the river to Karangandoang. We would be saved a day's walk, and would also avoid another meeting with the Kasenobe kanakas, with their ostentatiously unfriendly bows and arrows. But the walk down the Dimini stream was harder than we had expected, and for a long way we struggled round steep cliffs or splashed knee-deep through the rushing, icy water.

For the rest of the journey I merely retraced my steps of a couple of weeks before through Boana and Gain to Bivoro and across the Markham plain. From Bivoro, Watute struck off across country to the south-west, to cross the Markham higher up and make his way along the

Watut River to Ian and Les's base camp. He would then return to the Wain country and join me, wherever I might be camping.

I slept the night in the house-kiap at Bivoro, and before dawn next day hid all my gear except bed-roll and mosquito-net in the roof of the luluai's house. A bright, mischievous-looking young man called Dinkila offered to carry the bed-roll to Bob's, and I took him on, so the party which set out on the final stage numbered four, including Buka and Achenmeri.

The most dangerous section of the journey lay in this final day from Bivoro to the Markham. Gossip travels from one New Guinea village to the next as fast as it moves across any suburban back fence, and native informers had probably told the Japanese commander in Lae of our earlier trip up the Erap. This, coupled with Ian's sudden appearance on the beach at Hopoi, might persuade him of the necessity to patrol all the country surrounding his base; we might find a Japanese patrol sitting astride the Erap, waiting to intercept any Australian party entering or leaving the mountains by that route. The country was so flat and open that a vigilant enemy sentry would certainly have no trouble spotting a large party. However, we hoped that our small group would be able to slip through.

Buka led the way. He had left his uniform at Bivoro, and instead of a rifle was carrying a hand-grenade in a little string dilly-bag at his side. We walked very fast, breaking into a trot occasionally, just keeping Buka in view ahead of us. If he spotted danger he was to put his hand on his head: we would then find what cover we could in the grass.

The river was less swollen and did not hinder us as it had on the journey up, but a tense moment came when we reached the Markham road. While we others hid, breathless and watchful, in the grass, Buka made a quick search up and down the track, looking for enemy footprints. The grin that flashed across his shiny face told us that he saw none. He beckoned us to follow, and we hurried on, hopeful now of reaching Bob's safely. About two-thirty, tired, sweat-soaked, hungry, and thirsty, we pushed our way out of the ooze and pit-pit grass of the Erap delta to the edge of the Markham. I searched the low bank opposite through the glasses. Across the rushing, muddy water we saw no smoke from the camp, nor any movement at the canoe landing. I fired the prearranged three shots to summon the canoes, and looked again. There was still no movement. I was going to fire once more, when the tiny figure of the sentry stepped to the water's edge and waved. He had been studying us carefully before emerging from the bushes. After some minutes the black specks of the crew could be seen launching a canoe. They disappeared from time to time behind the islands, coming towards us so slowly that I kept glancing over my shoulder, kicking at the ground in nervous impatience, afraid that the Japs too might have heard the shots and would hurry to attack us from behind, here at the end of our journey.

We did not wait for the canoe to touch, but splashed out through the shallows to meet it. As we sprang on board with an enthusiasm that almost sank the little craft, I ordered the boss-boy to push off at once for the south bank, and we manoeuvred from island to island in the same zig-zag fashion as we had crossed in the other direction a fortnight earlier.

Tom Lega was waiting as the canoe scraped ashore. He grinned in casual greeting as I dashed the sweat from my eyes and shook his hand. 'Come up to the hut,' he said. 'The others'll want to hear all the good guts from the other side.'

We crowded into the little wire cage, and I told them first of Ian's betrayal and escape at Hopoi. They had never seen Ian, but Jock was an old friend, and they bent closer, silent, to hear of his decision to cross the range to the north coast.

They whistled quietly, looking sideways from one to another.

'Over those mountains! Jesus!' one exclaimed.

'Hell, I didn't think they could be crossed!' another muttered.

Tom laughed. 'In peacetime they used to say Jock was a tough guy, even among all the tough guys on this island. If he wants to get there he will, even if he has to crawl every bloody inch of the way on his hands and knees.'

The others shook their heads doubtfully. Once or twice, for a few fleeting minutes at dawn or dusk, these men had seen the clouds roll clear from the Saruwageds. A couple of bets were made, and the odds all favoured the mountains.

While a billy of tea was prepared, Tom rang through to the orderly-room at Bob's. I heard him shouting with all his lung-power to Bill Chaffey through the faint and feeble field telephone. 'That's right – he's here now! What? What? Yes, he's O.K., What? What the hell was that? Jock? He's gone over the range! Range! R-A-N-G-E! Listen, Bill, ask him yourself when he gets up there. So long!'

Tom came back from the phone groaning in mock despair. 'What a phone! I'd rather use smoke-signals or native drums, I reckon. Bill wants all the news, but you can tell him yourself. You'll be up there in a couple of hours.'

I laughed, downed the remaining black tea in my pannikin, and called to my boys to follow as I struck off up the grassy hill towards Bob's.

IV

I N MARI village, half-way to Bob's, I paused to drink the cool effervescent milk of a green coconut and swap a little gossip with the people. Mari was almost a model village: it was well laid out, and the houses were large and solidly built, many of them with carefully carved wooden ornaments in the shapes of lizards, fish, and turtles. The bare ground between the houses was swept clean, and a rough fence of bamboos kept the pigs away. However, there was a curious tension in the atmosphere, as if many strange things were happening beneath the surface, unsuspected by the casual observer.

The village was under the domination of a native of strong personality and character called Kwila. Some of the men at Bob's suspected him of giving the Japs in Lae information about our movements in the Markham Valley. This was never proved, and in fact he was eventually awarded the Loyal Service Medal. But even if he had been playing ball with the Japanese, who could blame him? The war was not of his making. If, for some reason unknown to him, white men and yellow men wanted to fight like animals in his country, what was more natural than for him to work for the safety of his own people? Until it became clear who was going to win the war, a sensible politician would speak softly to both sides. At that time, however, with our lives at stake, it was hard for us to take this detached and reasonable view, and we treated as traitors all natives who associated with the enemy, no matter what the circumstances.

I talked to Kwila as I squatted to drink the coconut milk. He was tall, broad-shouldered, and impassive of face. His dark eyes flickered – now narrowed to slits, now wide open. The answers to my questions came volubly, and seemed phrased to please rather than simply to tell the truth. He could speak English well, but was careful to use only pidgin, for painful experience among the whites in Lae had taught him that a 'coon' who spoke English was 'cheeky', and liable to be put 'in his place'. I finished the coconut milk, and he walked with me to the edge of the village, where we parted with mutual assurances of esteem; but I had learnt nothing, absolutely nothing, from our twenty minutes' conversation.

The fading light was already shutting us in in an ever-narrowing circle when we reached Bob's. With its haze of blue smoke hanging in the trees, the camp appeared before us out of the jungle just as mysteriously as it had a couple of weeks earlier. Clammy sweat glued the green shirt to my back, and the mosquitoes hummed and bit. I thought rather wistfully of the Wain country, cool and high, across the river. And yet it was pleasant to be back, to taste the illusion of security produced by the presence of numbers of other white men. Here, too, was a sense of contact with a world outside the swamps, mountains, and jungles of New Guinea, for the wireless picked up the Australian news bulletins, and sometimes letters were delivered. Compared with grey Kasenobe on its fog-smothered mountain-side, the rough camp at Bob's was civilization.

In the sergeants' mess they were waiting for tea. The same bearded men sat rolling their own cigars while they cursed the mosquitoes. The gramophone was still playing, in spite of the fact that the only needle had been lost. In its place they were using thorns from a lemon-tree which grew in a native village a few miles away.

The first person to see me as I approached was Bill Chaffey, who was in the act of pruning his red beard. He sprang to his feet. 'Ha! How was my map? It couldn't have been too bad, seeing you got back here O.K.'

'It was all right as far as it stretched,' I told him, 'but that wasn't far enough. I walked right off the edge of it. I've just come back for a day or two, to get more stores. What's the set-up now? Is there plenty of food?'

Bill fixed me with that firm, half-humorous look which must have been such an asset to him in Parliament. Before he could speak, the shattering racket of the beaten kerosene-tin announced tea.

'That saves me the trouble of answering your question,' he said. 'You just come and see for yourself.'

We sat down at the rickety table. Bully beef, pumpkin, papaw, black tea without sugar.

'There you are, my boy!' Bill said. 'More eloquently than words could express, you have before you the whole stores position of Bob's!'

'When are you expecting more?'

'They're overdue already, but I hear there's a big carrier-line from Wau likely to reach here today or tomorrow. I hope they do. We're out of tobacco, and we've bought so much brus from the local kanakas that even that's getting scarce.'

Two days later the new rations arrived on the sweating shoulders of a long line of carriers. I persuaded Major John Taylor, the officer commanding Bob's, to give me a month's stores for one man. It was a generous gift, for his own men had long been on short rations, and it was not his responsibility to provide for those across the river. The people who should have supplied us apparently thought we could live on grass or air, for they never once sent us so much as a single tin of bully beef. Even the special Christmas parcels provided for each soldier were not sent on to Jock or me, or kept for our return. Somehow they just vanished mysteriously.

Bill Chaffey and John Clarke helped me again with trade goods and other valuable stores. There were two large drums of salt and a good supply of stick tobacco and newspapers, all of which would buy more local produce and thus help to spin out the rations. Bill supplied me with a couple of gallons of kerosene, a case of hand-grenades, and some gelignite with fuse and detonators. The gelignite would be useful for setting booby-traps, to protect us against enemy patrols which might try to surprise us in camp.

As soon as all this gear was put together and made up into fifty-pound boy-loads I sent Achenmeri to Mari village to ask Kwila to send up twenty men to carry it as far as Kirkland's. From Kirkland's, Buka crossed the Markham alone, to bring boys from Bivoro to continue the carry for me, because the Mari natives were too afraid and suspicious to go farther, and I, in turn, was suspicious of them.

Tom Lega gave me a spot for the night in one of the crowded little sleeping-huts. I expected Buka back next morning with the carriers, but it was not until after midday two days later that the sentry on the canoe landing reported a group of natives across the river, and we heard the three shots from Buka's rifle. They had been two anxious days, for we were afraid Buka had been captured, and perhaps forced to reveal the movements of Jock and Ian. However, the delay had been caused by difficulty in locating the natives' houses, which were scattered among the gardens on the hillsides.

Only two canoes were serviceable, one having been dismantled for repairs. Two trips were needed to ferry over our gear, and it was nearly four o'clock before it was all piled among the cane grass on the north bank.

Making so late a start, we could not reach Bivoro that night, so we camped in the hunting shelters halfway up the Erap, where I had met the luluai on my first trip. They were dirty, ramshackle affairs, but we were glad to be out of the light rain which fell during the night. So far there had been no sign of enemy activity, and we left before dawn next morning, to get away from the flat country. In the mountains one felt reasonably safe, but here the line of heavily laden carriers would be visible for miles as it snaked slowly across the grassy plain.

We stayed in Bivoro only long enough to pick up the gear I had hidden on the way down. Dinkila, the boy who had carried the bed-roll, said goodbye here, because he wished to remain in his village.

By nightfall we were in Gain, where we slept, and the following day moved to Boana, where I took up my quarters in the smaller of the two iron-roofed houses. I did not know where Ian was camping, for when we parted he had not decided on a place. It was arranged merely that I should meet him 'somewhere in the Wain'. I had thought Boana, in the heart of the Wain country, would be the best place to pick up news of him.

My night at the mission was restless. Full of wreckage and smelling of decay, the house creaked and groaned rheumatically. The unaccustomed softness of a proper bed drove sleep away from me rather than induced it. There was a cuckoo clock in the room, which I had wound up for fun and then forgotten. When its sudden sharp note struck in the darkness I jumped to the floor and grabbed my revolver, ready to blaze away at the first thing that moved.

Next day was cold and dreary, and when the chill wind blew aside the veil of mist I saw the silent, watchful mountains staring balefully at us all around. I went into the big house and gathered up a bundle of papers from the piles which littered the floor. There was also a copy of the German-language edition of Hitler's *Mein Kampf* which I took with the papers over to my 'bedroom' in the other house. I intended to pass the time reading as much of them as I could with my scanty knowledge of German. My room had two windows: one was shattered and the other one was jammed open, and I was soon shivering. As I already had my warmest clothes on, I could only pull my blankets round me as I settled down to read.

Almost all the magazines were filled, from cover to cover, with Nazi propaganda articles, and elaborate gravure pictures of Nazi rallies featuring Hitler, Goering and Goebbels. None of the publications seemed to deal with missionary activities. I mumbled aloud as I read, skipping the most difficult passages, but I got the gist of things. Some of the papers and circulars were easier to read than others, for they had been typed on a machine with ordinary roman letters, unlike the difficult German black-letter of the printed books.

There were several letters referring to the establishment of a branch of the Nazi Party in New Guinea, and in one of them the writer warned that the activities of the party should be carried on with discretion, 'lest we should lose the great freedom of action which the Australian government has so far permitted us'. In case I had misunderstood these letters, I took some of them back to Bob's on my next visit, where Jim Hamilton, who worked in the cipher office, and who spoke German well, confirmed and amplified my rough and incomplete translation. I was glad that I had shown them to him, for I then sent them, with a report, to the district office in Wau, but a year or so later, when I tried to follow the matter up, nobody seemed to have seen either the documents or the report, and I could never find out what had happened to them.

The wind dropped, and the mist, which had been rushing past in little clouds, turned to a slow, steady rain. I huddled gloomily in the blankets, looking across over my drawn-up knees at the larger house. On its veranda, Buka and Achenmeri were staring just as despondently back. It was plain that the queer atmosphere of the mission was getting on their nerves too, so I decided that we would move to Wampangan or Karau, or some handy village, to spend the night. Why one should have felt more comfortable in a smelly native village than in a proper European-style house I did not stop to think. One thing was certain – we would not sleep again at Boana.

Just as the boys started to get their gear ready a Wampangan kanaka came panting up the hill carrying a crumpled piece of paper. It was from Ian, who had heard of my arrival at Boana. He said that he had established himself at Bawan, about four hours' walk away, and would we join him in the morning.

'Morning nothing!' I grunted aloud. 'We're going right now!'

I sent the Wampangan boy hurrying back to his village, with instructions to send twenty men for carriers as fast as they could run. Then Buka, Achenmeri, and I got all the cargo lined out and ready for the road. It would almost certainly be dark before we reached Bawan, but anything was better than another night here.

The walk to Bawan was steep, largely through thick rainforest country, but once we reached the top of the first mountain the rain stopped and the sky became clear. The track was thickly overgrown, and though this meant extra effort for us it would make patrolling much more difficult for the Japanese, who did not know the area. From a clear spot in the track the boys pointed out the 'ficus belong Lae' – a huge ficus-tree on the hill behind Lae township, and a famous landmark. It stood out clear against the sky like a big mushroom. When I looked through the field-glasses I was startled at the clarity of the detail – I could practically distinguish the branches. Once again I was reminded of the nearness of the Japanese base, a fact easily forgotten in the sensation of isolation produced by the rugged mountain country.

Bawan, the village which was to be my headquarters for some time, is worth describing in detail. Being about four thousand feet above sea-level it was cool and pretty well free from mosquitoes. I first saw it just before dusk, from the far side of the valley, in that brief half-hour – there is no long twilight in New Guinea – when the valleys darken and the hills soften from green to palest blue, and when the chill that comes into the air causes a little shiver, for one's clothes are still wet through either from sweat or from rain. I could see the main village far below me, on a level space near the foot of a deep gorge. Smoke was rising from the many little cooking-fires in front of the houses, and men were standing round a larger fire which blazed on the red earth of the open space in the centre of the village. Above the roar of the water we heard laughter – tiny, feeble sounds almost lost in the distance. A crazy bamboo bridge spanned the river, and opposite us, on the other side of the gorge, several hundred feet up, was a group of about fifteen houses. Their occupants stood in a little cluster at the edge of the cliff, pointing across the valley in our direction. We waved to them and they waved back, and when I studied them at close range I saw that they were all kanakas. There was no sign of Ian or his police.

About half a mile farther round the side of the valley a faint wisp of smoke curled up, barely discernible against the blue of the hillside. A careful search through the binoculars showed the roofs of three more houses. This was where the doctor-boy of Bawan lived with his relatives. Since I had not been able to see Ian in either of the other two hamlets, I concluded he must be living chez doctor-boy.

We hurried down the steep track, anxious to reach at least the outskirts of Bawan before dark. The carriers shouted encouragingly to each other, and their loads of cargo swung and bounced about as they scrambled eagerly downward.

Darkness had fallen when we reached the houses, and as we strode into the circle of firelight there were surprised shouts from the natives. Unlike their fellow villagers on the cliff above, they had not seen us coming. They were most friendly, running to help the carriers with their loads, and offering us sugarcane to suck.

Ian was not to be seen.

'Master 'e stop where?' I inquired of one of the men.

'Master 'e stop on top. 'Im 'e workim two-fella house.'

Apparently Ian had built two houses for himself and was not living in either of the hamlets, or with the doctor-boy. I hoped he would not be far away. We had made the journey from Boana at such a cracking pace that I was very tired, and so were the carriers.

'House belong master, 'e long way, nau close to?' I asked.

' 'Em 'e long way lik-lik,' was the reply. 'Long way lik-lik' literally interpreted means 'A little long way!'

Further inquiries about the exact distance would have been profitless, so I asked whether someone would guide us to Ian. Willingly, three men picked up blazing sticks from the fire for torches and, shouting to their womenfolk – presumably that they would be late for their meal – led the way across the river.

The dark water that roared beneath the rickety bridge reflected the flames of the torches, and I looked down, fascinated, till I almost lost my balance. I would have fallen in but for the grip on my hand of one of the Bawan guides, who pulled me firmly off the bridge, saying in a kind but determined voice, 'Master come now', as though remonstrating with a wayward child. In a few moments we were clambering up the black wet rocks on the side of the valley.

Twenty minutes' climb brought us to the second hamlet, where the people, outlined in the doorways of their houses, called out greetings, both to us and to the Wampangan carriers. I heard Buka's voice in querulous inquiry above the din, 'House belong master close to?'

' 'Em 'e close to finish,' I heard the reply.

'Ha! Suppose 'em 'e long way, me buggerup finish,' sighed poor Buka, who was not at his best in the mountains.

Five minutes later we came to a clear level space, where the torchlight dimly showed two large houses. More torches appeared, and there was excited chattering and laughter as Buka and Achenmeri were greeted by Ian's boys. Ian, lantern in hand, advanced to meet me from the farther house, and as we shook hands I saw that he was dressed warmly in sweater and long trousers. His tousled fair hair shone in the flickering light.

'Hi! Didn't expect you till tomorrow. But there's hot water all ready for a wash-wash – we put it on the fire as soon as we spotted you across the valley. By the time you've cleaned up, the cook-boy will have some kai-kai ready.'

'Thanks, Ian, but I think I'll just have a mug of beef tea and then turn in. I reckon we made record time for the Boana to Bawan Stakes. I've just about had it.'

'You must have gone like blazes to get here tonight – I didn't send that messenger till nearly midday. Why didn't you wait till tomorrow?'

'To be quite honest, I wasn't game to spend another night in that mission. It was giving me the horrors, and the boys too. They all reckon it's 'place no good'. If your messenger hadn't come I was going to move into one of the native villages. They may be dirty, but at least they don't give you the creeps.'

Ian nodded sympathetically. 'I know what you mean. You feel you're being watched all the time – and not just by the Holy Ghost, either. Well, you go and wash up, and I'll see all the stores are put away. I made the ground floor of the house a storeroom in expectation of plenty, but it doesn't look as if you got too much.' He strained his eyes, peering at the cargo the carriers were lining out at the edge of the clearing.

'There's a full month's ration for one European – that's a fortnight for the two of us – and a fair amount of trade goods. There's a few odds and ends, like gelignite, hand-grenades, and some kerosene.'

'I suppose we ought to count ourselves lucky to have that much, really,' said Ian, though the disappointment in his voice was obvious. 'Were they hard up at Bob's?'

'They certainly were! They were even running out of brus to smoke.' I went into the house as soon as I had washed. Ian handed me a steaming mug of beef tea; one of his boys was still putting up my bed, so I sat down on the end of Ian's, taking in the details of the hut as I drank.

For the camp, Ian had selected a grassy clearing, the only flat piece of ground for miles around. The ground floor of our house was a storeroom, while the upper storey comprised a kitchen at one end, a large living- and sleeping-room in the centre, and at the other end a spacious veranda. The building had been done with great care. The eaves hung low over the walls, which were double thicknesses of bark sheets lined with parts of an old tarpaulin of Jock's. The doorway could be covered with a strip of canvas also. All this was necessary to keep out the cold and the heavy nightly fog.

As soon as I had drained the cup I rolled into the blankets and was asleep. My last recollection was of Ian arranging the hurricane-lamp above his head as he lay on the bed to read an old newspaper I had brought from Bob's.

Breakfast-time was cold. We ate dressed in long trousers and sweaters. Outside, fog limited visibility to about fifty yards, and everything looked grey and dismal. Drops of moisture off the ends of the grass thatching dripped softly onto the ground. However, even while we ate, the fog was becoming thinner and the sun could be seen trying to break through. By the time we had eaten breakfast and shaved, the fog was completely dissipated, and we had a beautiful day of warm sunshine. Almost always it was the same – cold night with fog or rain, and warm, sunny day till about three or four in the afternoon, when the mists rose up from the valley floor. Sometimes there were several clear hours in the evening, when, if the moon was shining, it was bright enough to read and write outside.

Stripped of all our clothes, we lay on our ground-sheets and basked in the sun while we formulated our plan of campaign.

Bawan was an extremely good choice for a camp. It was near the border between two native districts, the Wain and the Naba country. It was centrally situated, close to several main tracks, and was not too remote from Lae, while being within easy reach of the wild mountains to the north if it became necessary to hide from enemy visitors. Moreover, in this spot it would be very difficult for the Japs to surprise us. Anyone coming from Boana would have to wind his way down the steep track on the far side of the gorge and then climb an equally steep path on this side. He would be in full view at least half an hour before he reached us. There were only two other approaches – one from Gewak village and the other from Monakasat – and a sentry posted on a rise five minutes' walk behind the house could command both these paths, which were mere goat tracks, exposed and narrow. A machine-gun could dispose of a party of Japs here without a hope of their escaping. Another most important point in Bawan's favour was that the surrounding country was exceedingly fertile and carried a fairly dense population. This meant that native foods would be in good supply – as an enormous pile of sweet potatoes, taro, pumpkins, and other vegetables under the house-police testified.

I congratulated Ian on his choice, and we went on to discuss the work we could do. He contemplated moving to Bawan all his stores from the base camp south of the Markham, together with his radio set, remaining quiet till the Japanese had more or less forgotten the encounter near Hopoi, then making quick patrols down to the back of Lae to find out what was happening there. The interim period of lying low we could devote to securing our position with the natives, so as to be assured of their support, and perhaps training a number of them to shoot, forming a small local guerrilla band. This seemed to me a good scheme. Having the radio on the spot would enable us to cut out the long and dangerous walk back to Bob's every time we wished to send a message. As soon as Constable Watute returned with news from Ian's base camp, we would know whether Ian's cloak-and-dagger organization would allow him to go ahead.

Two days passed, and one afternoon we heard the sentry call out that someone was coming down the track from Boana. With the binoculars we saw that it was Watute, and in about half an hour he stepped up to us, puffing and panting. He saluted, and handed Ian a letter.

The message dashed our hopes completely. Ian was instructed by his headquarters in Australia to leave the area immediately. That night he packed his gear by lantern-light, and early next morning, leaving me most of the food, he set out on the long road back – to Australia, ultimately. I watched him through the glasses as he climbed slowly up the far side of the valley. He turned momentarily, waved, and then plunged into the forest and out of sight. Again I had that feeling of loneliness which had first come over me when I crossed the Markham on my original journey into the Wain – and a terrible certainty that now there was no one to turn to for help, no matter what happened. I had just spent my nineteenth birthday alone in the bush, I remembered, and now it seemed that Christmas, a couple of weeks off, would be celebrated alone too.

Before he left, Ian had suggested that I should send a message to Jock telling him what had happened and pointing out that now he would probably be employed better here than on the north coast. As I had left Achenmeri at Bob's to receive further training, Watute and Buka were my only police. Though both were experienced men, I did not want to send either of them on the difficult journey across the Saruwageds. Watute had just come back from his long walk to Tungu, and Buka was not at his best in the mountains. The last we had heard of Jock was a message he had sent to Ian with his returning Bungalamba carriers, saying that he had made the crossing but that it had been very difficult and bitterly cold. I did not know exactly where he was, but I decided to send Buka to Bungalamba with a letter for him. Buka was to find a native willing to take it to the first village on the north side and ask the kanakas there to pass it on to the next village, and so on until it caught up with Jock. I gave Buka a big parcel of salt and some coloured calico: the man who made the trip across the range was to get this as payment, and Buka was to tell him that I would reward him further when Jock either came back or sent me a message. Buka went off, and four days later he returned to say that he had found a young man to do the job and had actually seen him set out on his arduous trip.

The terrible loneliness I had felt when I waved goodbye to Ian, a vanishing speck of khaki against the green mountainside, was not to assail me again; for one thing, life became too busy for loneliness to have a chance. And again, Lethe River itself has no greater power to bring forgetfulness of all past things than New Guinea's mountains. This green, strange, wild country had become home. My everyday companions were half-naked black people; pidgin came more readily to my lips than English; the seething movement of a big city had faded to the faintest memory, and even a piece of ordinary bread would have seemed unfamiliar. The crude thatching that sheltered me at night had become as homely and comfortable as the roof I was born under.

To make friends with the natives from the surrounding villages was my first aim. If these natives were hostile, the Japanese could capture me as soon as they chose, but if they supported me wholeheartedly it should be possible to escape even from intensive enemy patrolling. Therefore I set about learning the local dialect, and before long was able to talk reasonably well about everyday things.

Each morning, as I ate breakfast in the sun, a couple of bright-faced youngsters would squat at the edge of the veranda, to teach me new words. When I made a slip they would rock with shrill peals of laughter, and then they would put their faces close to mine, repeating the words patiently over and over until I mastered them. They were good teachers, and I used to reward them with some trifle like a packet of biscuits or a box of matches. Strange sounds not used in the English language were much easier to distinguish when made by the children's clear voices than in the adults' deeper tones. Conversation practice was at night, when some of the older men would sit in the house yarning and smoking in the dark. When I stumbled badly they would chuckle and nudge each other, and help me out of difficulties with a word of pidgin. They seemed pleased that someone was taking the trouble to learn their tongue, and for my part I felt flattered every time I used a new phrase successfully and they complimented me on my progress.

Each morning that I remained in camp we sat on the rising ground above the house and waited for our bombers to make their daily raids on Lae and Salamaua. The buildings of Lae itself were hidden by the low hills just behind the town, but the famous ficus-tree stood out clear against the skyline. Salamaua, across the waters of the Huòn Gulf, was in full view, though of course much farther away. Often, through the binoculars, we saw fierce fires raging, and pillars of black smoke creeping higher and higher into the sky.

Our planes used to make their runs quite low over the house, and we could count them and see all their markings clearly. It was strange, after they had passed, to see the first puffs of smoke from Lae's anti-aircraft guns bursting silently round the planes like little balls of cotton wool. Forgetting the slow speed at which sound travels, one wondered at the silence. Then, when the air was full of puff-balls, the first sound of the explosions would thud echoing up the valley.

I found the bombers were great company and encouragement, and used to wish that I had some way of telling their crews that every strike they made was excitedly cheered by a little band of natives and a white man standing on the hills behind their target. 'Olaman! Make 'im savvy you!' the police used to cry every time there was a particularly heavy explosion. 'Hey! Japan 'e sorry too much now!' the Bawan kanakas would shout as the smoke climbed skyward.

Sometimes the raids were less successful. The American planes had particularly bad luck, and several times all their bombs fell into the sea. Such a detail had small effect on the exuberance of the communiques from General MacArthur's headquarters, for I checked back on them every time I visited Bob's. If one believed these announcements, never a bomb was dropped in New Guinea that failed to find its own special little target. A native from a coastal village near Lae told us with a grin that more often than not the raids made from a high altitude were ineffective – except that they saved the Japanese the trouble of fishing, for the explosions stunned or killed thousands of fish, and small boats were always held ready to pick them up when the raid was over.

Any raid, however, was good propaganda material for me. The Japanese were spreading stories among the natives that there was scarcely a white man left in New Guinea. These tales were beginning to filter in to the Wain country, and might easily have been believed – for, after all, there was only one white man they could actually see. The raids, in ever-increasing strength, were a more effective answer to this Japanese propaganda than I could have hoped to provide.

My days at Bawan were a constant round of calls, some social, some business, and some which could not quite be fitted into either category, though one had a shrewd suspicion that business of some sort was at the bottom of them. About ten o'clock the grassy clearing in front of the house would become filled with chattering women from the surrounding villages bearing food. Each woman made a pile of her own food and stood by it while I went down the line asking each one what she wanted. Almost always salt was the answer, and Watute would follow me and deal out an appropriate quantity to each. Sometimes they asked for newspaper, of which I had plenty, or razor-blades, of which there were still a few among the trade stores. All their loincloths were wearing out, so occasionally, for a very large pile of sweet potatoes, I gave a strip of calico. In this way I bought, in addition to sweet potatoes, taro, bananas, and lavish supplies of introduced European vegetables. I was never once short of tomatoes, ordinary potatoes, sweet corn, cabbages, or beans, while several dozen eggs a week was nothing unusual. Every now and then someone would come along with a fowl, for which I gave two or three shillings, or perhaps a couple of razor-blades.

We bought far more food than we really needed, but it helped the people to get some of the trade goods which they had lacked for so long. Besides, I did not want the women to have to carry bundles of food home again.

Their visits kept me in touch with the villages, too, and helped me to preserve friendly relations and to hear the local gossip. The police and other native boys were also able to have plenty of food: the more contented and comfortable they were in camp the better, for they had to face such great danger and discomforts on the track.

Buka often went out in the afternoon, with a shotgun Ian had left me, in search of pigeons, which made very fine eating. As we had only a couple of dozen shotgun cartridges, he was rationed to one shot each day, but he often managed to bring back two birds, having walked round for hours until he found two sitting close enough to knock both with one shot. To complete the diet Ian had somehow, somewhere, found a few goats, which gave a pint or two of milk a day. Food therefore presented no problem, so long as one had salt or other trade goods to exchange for it. As I look back on this part of my life in New Guinea, I don't wonder that the boys at Bob's jokingly accused me of taking the risk of living in the Wain for my stomach's sake!

Another market I conducted daily was for brus, the native-grown leaf tobacco that was planted round almost every house. The leaves were picked and hung to dry underneath the house. When partly dried they were attached to a long length of thin vine at intervals of an inch or so. This was wound up tightly, and the whole bundle was bound with other pieces of vine. The result was a tight sausage-shaped bundle of tobacco-leaves, very aromatic, from which one could get really good smoking tobacco. The quality varied from leaf to leaf, and after a while one developed the knack of selecting a good leaf. For more than six months I smoked nothing else but brus in my pipe, and I grew to like it as well as any store tobacco. In a few weeks I had bought over two hundredweight of the stuff, which we hung on the veranda of the house. I intended to take it all back to Bob's, where the tobacco famine for both whites and natives was acute. This trade pleased the natives very much, for before the war the mission had bought quantities of it. Now the villages were able to dispose of part of the surplus that had accumulated.

Many people came for medical treatment, frequently offering food in payment for quinine or for a dressing on a sore. But we took no payment, for we had enough food, and Ian had left plenty of ordinary drugs and medical supplies. Unfortunately there was no hypodermic, so I could not treat the many cases of framboesia, or yaws. This is one of the commonest and worst diseases in New Guinea, and produces huge revolting ulcers, rather like some syphilitic sores. It clears up almost magically after two or three injections with an arsenical drug, and the hope of getting treatment made people drag themselves to Bawan from places three or four days' walk away. Mothers who had carried infected children from distant villages would ask hopefully if their piccaninnies could have a 'shoot', as they called the injection. When told no, they would turn away sad-eyed and patient. Life was always hard for them, and they met calamities like disease and hunger with a philosophical resignation that civilized races have forgotten.

Jock told me that the pidgin word 'shoot', for injection, was once amusingly misinterpreted in peacetime. A group of kanakas were waiting at a hospital to receive treatment for yaws. Lunch-time came and the three white men attending to the patients went to eat. Two of them were old hands, and the third was a young man, a new arrival from Australia. 'We'll shoot those boys after lunch,' one old hand remarked. 'Yes, might as well finish them all off in one go,' the other agreed. Neither noticed the look of horror on the younger man's face, and while they ate heartily he sat there and left his plate untouched. After hearing a couple more casual references to 'shooting the kanakas' he pushed his plate away and stamped from the table. 'You people get hardened to anything up here!' he stormed. 'As far as I'm concerned, they may be black but it's still plain bloody murder to shoot them!'

More ceremonious calls were made by the village officials from all the surrounding communities. It was common for ten or a dozen luluais, tultuls, and doctor-boys to arrive to have a talk and smoke some of my tobacco. They often gave me useful information or passed on village gossip, all of which helped to build up a complete picture of what was happening in the country. Watute used to talk to them for hours in the house-police, and often they would stay overnight with him, helping to eat the enormous pile of food which was always on hand. Watute was a shrewd fellow, and his long service as a detective in the police force had made him something of a psychologist. A tultul who called upon Watute with a secret in his mind usually went away having said more than he intended, and perhaps without realizing how much he had said, so skilful was the questioning.

We gathered that the Japanese, though still inclined to confine their activities to the coast, were now warily extending patrols up the valleys, and all the villages near Lae were now completely under their control. The villages of the Wain and Naba, which had never been visited by the enemy, and had had no contact with them, would almost certainly assist me if there were any trouble.

However, there were villages whose allegiance wavered and which I classed half-way between the ones completely enemy controlled and those which supported me, for some of them had been trading with the enemy as well as visiting me. It was chiefly villages of this sort I had to fear. A native of, say, Wagun village close to Lae, could safely be treated as an enemy. The luluai of one village who came to see me had obviously had dealings with the enemy, and yet I did not wish to antagonize him and prejudice my chance of winning him over to our side. So I was obliged to let him wander about our camp, though I took the risk that tomorrow would find him in Lae telling the Japanese where we were. Circumstances had made shrewd politicians of these natives, for they were caught between two opposing forces and were determined to side with the ultimate winners. They sometimes argued with me that the Japanese were so numerous that they must win. 'Look,' they would say, 'you know for yourself there are now more Japanese in Lae alone than there were white men in the whole of New Guinea before. The Japanese must be stronger.'

I would point to our air raids. 'If the Japanese are so strong, why don't they stop those aeroplanes from bombing them?' I asked. 'Every day more and more of our planes come over; we are getting stronger and stronger, and will soon finish the Japanese off.'

They would rub their woolly heads and look worried. 'Yes, perhaps,' they would say with a shrug, and go off puzzled, trying to decide whether to back the side that had many men or the side that had many aeroplanes – a small-scale edition of the problem that arm-chair strategists were arguing about all over the world.

Some days I would spend walking from village to village, learning all the streams and paths and short cuts, and stopping to talk to the people as they worked in their gardens. By arriving unannounced, and doing away with all the ceremony that usually attends the visit of a patrol officer, I managed to get the people to accept me as someone who really lived among them – not one of themselves, perhaps, but at any rate a sympathetic fellow human, instead of an irritating visitor who made them waste time by lining up to be counted, and who told them that their village was not clean enough. As time passed I felt more and more confident that these people trusted me and would help me if they could.

One morning, as I was handing out the usual remedies for malaria and for constipation, there was a howl from Buka, who was filling my lamp in the storeroom beneath the house. 'Hey, master, come quick! Some-fella man 'e stealim kerosene!'

I hurried to the store and found him excitedly waving an empty tin in the air.

'Kerosene 'e go finish! Kerosene 'e go finish!' he chanted.

I grabbed the tin – our only one. It was empty right enough, but theft was not the reason. The kerosene had all leaked away through a small hole in the bottom. The tin must have got knocked in the carry up from the Markham.

The gloomy prospect of spending every night in darkness set me hard at work to make an emergency lamp, and Watute helped me to rig a strip of cloth for a wick in a shallow tin of dripping. The light it gave was dim and flickering, and the smoke and smell were unpleasant. It was useful for an emergency, and nothing more, but it would have to do until I could get more kerosene from Bob's.

Darkness came suddenly at six o'clock each night. Almost always there was a violent thunderstorm and heavy rain, then the wind rushed up the valley, shaking the house, blowing down huge trees with rending crashes, and whistling through chinks in the bark walls. I used to sit at the door of the house and watch the brilliant lightning flashing over the stormswept mountainsides and flickering on the roofs of Bawan village, just down the hillside. After half an hour the weather would become calm and the drifting mist would shut the little clearing tightly away from the rest of the world, and I would shiver in the cold. Unless men from the village came up to gossip I would go straight to bed.

A fire seemed the best way of cheering up the dark and silent house, so I sent Watute to Boana Mission to collect three old sheets of roofing-iron we had seen lying about. When he returned, with two Bawan men carrying the iron fastened to a pole, we tried our hands at making a fireplace. A pile of rocks and earth protected the bamboo floor, and we fastened one sheet of iron as a protection for the wall and made a hood over the fireplace with another. A chimney was out of the question, but we cut a slot in the wall behind the fireplace, rather like a letterbox, and lit an experimental fire to see what happened. The draughts went the right way, and most of the smoke went through the slot and out the side of the house. Always afterwards the police lit a fire there just before nightfall, and from a gloomy cavern of darkness the house became a friendly, cheerful dwelling.

So that Buka and Watute could celebrate Christmas suitably, I bought them a pig, which cost £3. Its owner wanted to put it on the fire alive, and apparently regarded me as rather eccentric when I insisted on its throat being cut first. 'Why bother?' was his attitude. 'The fire would pretty soon have killed it, anyhow.' But he happily counted his sixty shining perforated New Guinea shillings, and strung them on a thong for safe keeping, content with his bargain even if the pig was dispatched in a somewhat messy way.

The two policemen invited friends from the village to eat with them, and they all gorged themselves. The following morning there was still a quarter of the pig left, so they made a basket of bamboo slivers and hung the remnant in the smoke to cure. The ham surprised me by its tender juiciness, though the smell was rather uninviting.

So Christmas passed, and then New Year. There was still no word of Jock. Every day some new speculation filled my mind. Had he perished crossing the mountains? Had the natives on the north side failed to send my message after him? Had the Japanese caught him? Had he been attacked by wild natives? My mind fastened on these questions one by one, and spun round and round upon them till they became obsessions. I used to say angrily to myself, aloud, 'For God's sake stop wondering about it! Thinking won't help him, and it'll only drive you nuts!' But, just the same, when the storms came at night I would still find myself wondering whether, at that moment, Jock was exposed somewhere on the bare peaks to the cutting rain and freezing wind.

Medical stores were now running out, and I had only a bare personal supply of quinine and sulpha drugs and other vital necessities. I decided to make another quick visit to Bob's to get more, if they could spare them, and also to send in a report about our activities in the Wain. Buka was left in charge of the camp, with a supply of food and trade goods for Jock in case he returned, and a note saying that I would be back from Bob's within a week. Watute and I set out for Bob's, taking our bed-rolls and arms and also the hundredweight or so of brus we had collected to give the boys back at Bob's a smoke. When we reached Bivoro, Dinkila, the lively young man who had carried my bed to Bob's on the previous trip, squatted down to talk to us. Life in the village was too quiet, he said discontentedly. The old men kept nagging at you, and work in the gardens was drudgery. Could he join the police force, and have a uniform, and come with us?

'What did you do in peacetime?' Watute asked quickly.

Dinkila looked at him. 'I was a cook-boy in Lae, first of all for some white women and then for Master Jacobsen.'

Watute grinned. 'There you are, master – he'll be a good cook if he worked for Master Carl Jacobsen! Master Carl knew all about food. Why don't you take this man on as a cook?'

I put the idea to Dinkila. The wages were ten shillings a month and all found, and he would have to accompany us wherever we went. If he wanted a change from village life, what about it?

He had set his heart on a uniform, but after a few moments' consideration he took the job of cook, and from that moment on became the tyrant who ruled the details of my personal life: what I should wear, what I should eat, how my bed should be made, how strong my tea should be. It was no use arguing with Dinkila. What he thought I should have, I got, but he was a devoted servant and worked tirelessly to secure my personal comfort. How often he nursed me through attacks of fever and sickness I have forgotten, but whenever I awoke he seemed to be there with a cool drink, a mug of soup, or a cup of coffee with aspirins and quinine.

We hurried down the Erap again, stopped for the usual welcome cup of tea and gossip with Tom Lega at Kirkland's, and rushed straight through to Bob's. The men fell upon the parcel of brus, tearing leaves out to roll themselves cigars, upon which they drew fiercely, exhaling with luxurious contentment. We had arrived in the middle of their worst tobacco famine, and none of them had had a smoke for days.

Next morning I was surprised when Bill Chaffey called me to the orderly-room. There was a phonecall for me from Kirkland's. Tom Lega's voice, faint and blurred, came out of the earpiece. 'One of Jock's police-boys has just swum across the river!' he said excitedly. 'He's got a letter for you, and he's coming on at once to Bob's. He says Jock got back across the range O.K.'

I was so excited that I hardly thanked Tom for calling, but slammed the field-telephone down and strode off along the track to meet the policeman. About half-way to Kirkland's I saw him come round the bend and I recognized him as Nabura, an intelligent man who could read and write a little. He was weary, and though he grinned when he saw me he was too tired to quicken his pace. When we drew near to one another he fumbled in his haversack and handed me a thick bundle of papers tied together with a piece of vine. This was Jock's official report to the district officer, with a short note to me asking me to type out a copy of the report for him, and to forward the original to headquarters. The note said Jock would wait in Bawan for my return.

The official report told of the crossing of the range; of the cold that had almost killed Jock and his native companions; of the dreadful storms; of the rocky cave in which they had sheltered one night; of the wild bush kanakas who had attacked them. He had reached the north coast and come upon a lonely Australian there watching the activities of the Japanese as they moved supplies in barges round the coast from Madang to Lae. At a coastal village he secured a canoe and travelled with his boys to the island of Sio. It was not occupied by the Japs, but they visited it periodically. A Japanese reconnaissance plane flew low over Jock's canoe on his return journey to the mainland. He dropped into the water and remained hidden under the decking while the plane circled above. His boys kept paddling doggedly, expecting at any moment to be sunk by a burst of machine-gun fire, and eventually the Jap pilot decided it was only a harmless native fishing-party, and flew away. Jock scrambled back onto the canoe, thankful that the sharks had left him alone, only to find a few days later that his immersion had result-ed in a case of 'coral ear', an intensely painful infection that lies in wait for anyone unlucky enough to get tropical sea-water in his ears. In his note to me Jock said he was in such pain that he was practically living on aspirins at the camp in Bawan, and he asked me to get something from the doctor to fix the ear up.

I hurried back to Bob's, where Bill helped me type the report. Then we got medical supplies from the doctor, and the few items of food that could be spared. I was going to return to the Wain next morning.

At dawn we woke to the deafening roar of aero-planes. The thunder from the bombing raids on Lae was terrific, and went on ceaselessly. Through the trees we saw flight after flight of our heavy bombers droning over, and soon a phonecall from Kirkland's told us that enormous columns of smoke could be seen downriver, and that all Lae seemed to be ablaze. I decided to defer my return until we knew what was happening. There was another ring from Kirkland's, a personal one for me, and I almost fell out through the grass wall of the orderly-room when I heard the voice. It was Jock!

'Ear's too bloody crook!' he bawled into the phone. 'Can't sleep at all, so I've come in to see the doc. Be seeing you in an hour or two.'

I hurried down the track to meet him. He was much

thinner than when we had parted, and it was plain that the journey had affected him. 'Bastard of a trip,' was all he would mutter, however, concerning the crossing of the range itself.

Bill Chaffey was waiting for us back at Bob's. He took us aside to talk quietly, and though his tone was humorous his expression was troubled.

'I'll tell you what all that racket down at Lae's about,' he began. 'We've had a signal to say that the Japs have a big convoy of ships there, and they're unloading reinforcements and a hell of a lot of stores. Our planes have been belting hell out of them since dawn, but naturally there's a lot of gear and troops got ashore in spite of it.'

Jock and I were silent.

'You know what it means, don't you?' pursued Bill.

'Yeah,' said Jock, rubbing his bristly head thoughtfully. 'It means the Nips are going to hang on in Lae and Salamaua and drive all us poor bastards out of the bush and out of Wau and right off this side of the island.'

'What about you blokes staying here?' Bill asked. 'We can get away through the bush all right from here, if they come up in force. If you're across the Markham you'll be trapped.'

Jock squatted on his heels. I noticed that his sandshoes were worn out and that the tropical ulcers on his legs were eating bigger and bigger patches out of the flesh. 'Point is this, Bill,' he said after a pause. 'If the Nips are going to take over in Wau, there'll be more need than ever for us to keep in touch with the natives and see what's going on. I think we could manage to live in the bush there.' He turned to me. 'What do you reckon?'

'I'll give it a go if you think so,' I said. 'I wouldn't care to try it on my own.'

From then on, things moved so quickly that the rest

of the day was a confused jumble of events. By evening I found myself, with Watute and Dinkila, asking Tom Lega at Kirkland's for a bed for the night. Jock had to remain for a few days to have his ear treated, but would join me at Bawan as soon as he could. And all the time, in the background, there was the roar of our planes and the rumble of the bombs on Lae.

Next day, just after dawn, Tom had the canoe ready for me to cross the river. He had become used to saying goodbye on the banks of the Markham, but he made it pretty plain on this occasion that he didn't expect to see me again. His handshake was firmer and longer as he followed the canoe out into the shallows.

In midstream we looked suddenly upriver. Almost at water-level three Beaufighters were bearing down on us. We reckoned it was the finish, for our planes had had orders to regard all movement along the Markham as hostile. They saw us, banked off, and came at us in another run. The boat's crew sprang overboard and struck out for the shore, leaving Watute, Dinkila, and me rushing downstream wildly. I snatched my slouch hat off and waved it frantically above my head, almost overbalancing the canoe. Watute did the same with his khaki cap. In spite of the panic we were in I felt a momentary pang of annoyance as my pipe slipped and fell into the water with a dull little plop. Then, with a screaming whistle, the three planes passed over us. They had recognized us in time, and with wings dipping in salute they hurtled off towards Lae. At the rate the current was racing us seaward we would soon be in Lae ourselves if we didn't do something about it, so we paddled madly with our hands and managed to land the canoe on one of the islands. Through the field-glasses I saw the boat's crew get new paddles from the landing and start swimming over to us, to finish the journey so ignominiously interrupted. While we waited for them I became conscious of something like a pebble in my mouth. It was the end of my pipestem. Apparently I had bitten it clean through in the excitement.

When we reached Bawan two days later the tultul was waiting for us at the outskirts of the village. With an apprehensive glance up the track that led to my house he drew me nervously aside.

'Master, this-fella police-boy, name belong 'im Buka, 'em 'e long-long finish. Me-fella fright too much long 'en.'

He was telling me that Buka had gone mad, and went on to explain that he was rampaging round the countryside, stark naked, brandishing rifle and bayonet, threatening to rape all the women and shoot all the men. The tultul said that Buka had not actually molested anyone yet, but the people were all too scared to leave their houses, and no gardening had been done for days.

Watute stepped forward as the tultul finished speaking.

'It's the full moon, master,' he said. 'It's happened before, but he's never harmed anyone yet.'

The tultul was watching me anxiously, and I was vaguely conscious of other scared faces peering round the corners of the houses, so I said in a firm and confident voice that Buka would be kept under control, and we moved on to the house. I had not the faintest idea of how we would deal with the situation, and when I caught sight of Buka I was really frightened. He was squatting naked by the fire at the end of the house-police, crooning a senseless, monotonous tune. His usually fat and jovial face seemed wasted and sullen, and his eyes were dull and empty. He took no notice whatever when we spoke, so Watute climbed up beside him and quietly grabbed his rifle and bayonet and handed them down to me. Then we went into my house to consider what to do.

Watute reckoned that Buka would soon be himself

again, for in the past the attacks had seldom lasted longer than a couple of days. Disarmed, Buka was now much less dangerous, so I accepted Watute's suggestion that he and Dinkila should take it in turns to watch him, and I told them to call me instantly if he attempted to leave the house or wander down to the village. We hid the rifle in the thatching of the roof, and Watute returned to the house-police while Dinkila prepared my tea.

I was filling an after-dinner pipe by the fire when soft footsteps padded across the veranda. A quiet voice at the doorway said, 'Master!' The tultul had pushed aside the canvas cover of the door and stepped inside.

'What is it, tultul?' I asked.

'Master, one-fella piccaninny, 'em 'e sick too much. Papa belong 'en like you come lookim.'

This was the first time they had asked me to see a sick person outside the usual morning 'visiting-hours'. I picked up the medical kit and followed the tultul out into the cold night and down the track to the village. He led me to a small house near the edge of the cliff, and helped me through the tiny doorway. The hut, its timbers and grass roof smoke-blackened and glazed, was so hot that I could hardly breathe. The smouldering fire in the middle of the floor gave off a little light and a lot of smoke, and I could see the sick child's mother and father squatting in the shadows by the back wall. When the fire blazed up a little I saw the hopeless look on their faces.

The child, a boy about eight years old, lay stretched out naked on the rough floor near the fire. His head was resting on the lap of a hideous old woman – probably the grandmother, I thought, shuddering at the sight of her. She too was almost naked, and her whole body was covered with a grey, scaly skin disease. One breast had shrivelled almost to nothing, while the other hung, skinny and straplike, to her navel. Her head was shaved. From time to time, through shrunken toothless lips, she mumbled, dribbling and idiotic. As I stooped to look at the child I glanced up and saw her glinting old eyes flash hatred. Then she stared straight ahead and ignored me.

The child's pathetic, skinny body was rigid, the stick-like limbs immovable. The eyes were turned up so that only the whites showed – and they were not really white, but a muddy bluish colour. When I touched the eyeballs there was no more reaction than if I had pressed my finger on a marble. His pulse was so feeble that for a while I could not detect it, and thought he was dead already. The tultul leant forward and picked up a piece of wood from the fire. He blew gently on it till it flamed, and then held it close to the child's head so that I could see better. Death was already in the little black face, I thought, and put the glowing stick back on the fire.

I could not treat a disease I was unable to diagnose, and anyhow I felt certain that the child was beyond help. No one spoke. As I squeezed out the doorway the mother and father looked bewildered, and the old woman followed me with her eyes, detesting my interference. I felt angry at my own helplessness.

The cool air outside was like a cleansing bath after the murky stink of the little hut where death was waiting just a few minutes longer. In his quiet, calm voice the tultul thanked me for coming. The child's father would be grateful too, he said, though unwilling to say so in front of that terrible old woman.

I walked slowly back to my house and raked the fire together. Life is bloody tough for these people, I thought, as I stared into the coals. They were naked both bodily and morally, victims of every cruel and senseless whim of fate and nature. But not quite naked, perhaps, when one recalled their gentle, stoic patience. The cloak of their philosophy was probably no more threadbare than the scientific cloak in which civilized people have tried to shroud themselves for the last half-century.

A piercing, terrible wail shivered through the air from the village. It was like a dog howling, but infinitely tragic. The child was dead. I went to the door and looked out. Little points of light moved in the blackness where the village was, as people came out of their houses holding torches. The wailing became general, taken up, swelling and fading, by every voice in the community. Sometimes low and moaning, sometimes shrill and harsh, it went on all night.

Tossing wakeful on my bed-sail, I remembered Jock's idea of trying to visit the Chinese prisoners in the compound behind Lae. These people would have on-the-spot news of the Japs' recent landing of reinforcements, and perhaps some knowledge of how they intended to employ them.

The more I thought about it, the more exciting the idea became. I decided not to wait for Jock's return, but to go alone next morning. To the sound of the weird wailing down the hill, and with one ear cocked for any sound of trouble from Buka, I sat all night over my maps and notes of the country between Bawan and Lae, trying to work out the safest approach and to devise escape-routes in case we were discovered.

I was still making notes and sketches when dawn showed the grey outline of the doorway. As I went outside to call Dinkila, a loud, hollow banging echoed from the village. The men were knocking together a coffin from rough hand-hewn planks, to bury the little boy.

Buka seemed sane again – but exhausted, like a man who has just been on a hectic drinking-jag. He had no recollection of what he had done or said, and seemed mildly surprised to see us all. I decided to leave him in camp and to take only Watute and Dinkila down to the Chinese camp.

The three of us set out about eight o'clock, carrying blankets, a little food, trade goods, and a tiny hurricane-lamp. We had our usual arms, and our pockets were stuffed with hand-grenades. I told the tultul of Bawan that we were merely doing a routine tour of the villages and would be away two or three days. To make sure that gossip could not precede us, I did not tell even Watute and Dinkila our real destination until we were well clear of Bawan. Dinkila's eyes lit up at the prospect of excitement, but Watute merely gave his queer tight little half-grin and said nothing.

'Did you know where we were going?' I asked.

'I guessed,' he said. 'After all, we've got all these hand-grenades, and you've got those maps and papers. I realized it wasn't going to be just routine stuff.'

We walked fast all day, over ridges and valleys, drenched alternately by sweat and icy river water. We did not stop to eat, for safety depended on speed – to get in and out again before unfriendly natives could warn the Japs. Evening found us in a little village called Lambaip, near the edge of the foothills behind Lae. The few people in the village greeted us quietly, showing neither hostility nor enthusiasm. They gave us some vegetables to eat, and pointed out an empty house where we could sleep.

We were to be on the track by four o'clock next day, so I divided the night into three-hour watches – mine from seven o'clock to ten, Watute's till one o'clock, and Dinkila's till four.

Among the Lambaip kanakas Dinkila found an old friend with whom he had worked in Lae. The two of them talked and laughed so loudly at bawdy peacetime recollections that in the end I yelled at them to shut up, so that I could go to sleep. Dinkila came sheepishly to the door, leading his friend.

'Master, this friend of mine will come with us tomorrow, if you like,' he said. 'He knows the language of all the villages on our way.'

I held the little hurricane-lamp up. The boy was young and merry-faced like Dinkila, and was nodding his head in energetic agreement with the proposal.

'All right – it's a good idea,' I said. 'Now, for God's sake let me get some sleep, and go to sleep yourselves!'

Next morning before starting we gathered every scrap of wrapping paper from the army biscuits and burnt it, and carefully buried the bully-beef tins. If any of the natives told the Japs we had been here, we were determined that there would be no scrap of evidence. I even packed my boots into the bed-roll and walked barefoot, for the print of an Australian army boot, with its distinctive horseshoe heel-plate, would have been certain proof that we had passed along the track.

The ground was rough, and my feet were soon covered in cuts. As I watched Watute's leathery feet padding along in front of me I wondered how long it would take for my soles to become as tough as his.

We walked rapidly, continually downhill, roughly following the course of the Busu River towards Lae. It became very hot after the sun rose, for we had left the high country behind and were approaching the coast. About midday we passed a huge bomb-crater in the jungle on a nearby hillside. Probably the bomb had been jettisoned by a lost or damaged aircraft.

A few moments later we reached the large village of Musom, about fourteen miles from Lae. Natives who had been lounging about sprang to their feet in angry astonishment as we strode into the centre of the village. An uproar broke out as men rushed from the houses waving pig-spears and bows and arrows, and shouting. I slipped the safety catch off my rifle, and saw Watute do the same, and we backed up against a large house so that nobody could sneak in behind us, while we waited for the row to subside. Dinkila's friend from Lambaip stood close by, translating freely as the kanakas yelled and gesticulated. We gathered that some of the people were for killing us off at once, while others were trying to restrain them. The noise died down to a threatening rumble, and an elderly man stepped sullenly forward.

'Me luluai,' he announced in a defiant tone, making no attempt to salute.

'Where's your cap, luluai? And the village book?' I demanded sharply.

'Hat now book 'e something belong gov'ment belong Australia,' he said bluntly, and went on to explain that cap and book had both been destroyed, and any Australian who wanted to go on living had better keep clear of his village.

His speech received an ugly growl of approval from the crowd. They had the numbers to shoot us down quite easily, even if it cost them a few casualties. Probably, however, we would be picked off by bowmen hidden in the bush that fringed the village.

Bluff seemed our only hope.

'You've seen that hole the bomb made on the hill-side up there, haven't you, luluai?' I asked.

He grunted a surly assent.

'That was caused by just a single bomb,' I went on evenly, trying to infuse a note of menace into my voice, to cover up very genuine fear. 'Just one bomb cut down all those trees and made that enormous hole.'

The crowd was quiet now, listening intently.

Jumping suddenly forward I stuck my face up close to the luluai's face, shouting at the top of my voice, 'You'd better look out, luluai! My friends with all those aeroplanes know where we are now! If anything happens to us they'll come over and drop hundreds of bombs, all over the place!'

As the luluai fell back a step, I took a step forward, still shouting at him. 'Bombs everywhere! No gardens, no houses, no women, no children, no luluai either!' I went on, piling horror on horror.

The luluai melted back into the crowd, but I called him out by himself again, and painted in the full ghastly details of the imaginary air raid. As the crowd began looking upwards apprehensively, as though fearing vengeance from the skies at any moment, I thought of the parson who used sometimes to add a marginal note to the draft of his sermon: Shout like hell here – argument very weak. That parson apparently understood an audience.

Before long most of the kanakas had put their weapons down and moved to the other end of the village, where they stood murmuring uneasily. The luluai was reduced to a state of unwilling civility.

We asked him about the movements of the Japs.

'I suppose an ignorant old man like you thinks the Japanese are the government now?' I said.

'Master, me no lookim Japan. Me-fella no savvy long Japan.'

' 'Em 'e gammon, master,' Watute said quickly at my elbow. 'Look at these things I found in the houses.'

He held out several Japanese newspapers, and a bottle with a Japanese label, half full of kerosene.

'Where did you get those, luluai, if you haven't been dealing with the Japanese?'

The old rascal squirmed and wriggled, but stuck to his story that he and his people had had nothing to do with the Japs. It was obviously untrue, but he was unshakable, so I fell back on more idle threats, to prevent him rushing straight to Lae to tell the Japs what had happened.

'We'll be round here for a day or two, luluai, so don't tell the Japanese. Remember – no matter whose fault it is, if any harm comes to us in your country the aeroplanes will come and bomb you.'

He gave me an ugly glare – he was quite shrewd enough to guess that the whole business might be a bluff, but was too terrified of the bombs to gamble on his luck.

Watute drove the point home: 'You see, luluai? If you want to save your own skin, you'd better look after us, and do everything you can to make sure we leave here safe and sound.'

We munched a few bits of biscuit and had a drink of water. Then, with a final warning to the luluai not to try any funny business, we hurried along the track towards Gawan, a large village one stage nearer the Chinese camp.

We reached Gawan by mid-afternoon, and though the people were anything but pleased to see us they concealed their feelings and showed at least formal politeness. The local luluai and tultul wore their hats and made some gestures of cordiality, giving us a house and a supply of food.

'Have you been dealing with the Japanese?' I asked the tultul.

'Certainly not – we wouldn't dream of such a thing.'

'What about the people of Musom?'

'Yes, they have been down to Lae. But not the Gawan people.'

Watute and I grinned at each other. They didn't mind telling tales on other villages, while protesting their own innocence.

'Tultul, do you know the camp down the river where the Chinese are living?' I asked.

He was silent, licking his lips and swallowing, and curling his toes in the dust.

'Do you hear the master asking you a question? Speak up!' snapped Watute.

'Yes, me savvy,' he whispered.

'We want to go there tomorrow, and we would like you to guide us.'

He looked piteously from Watute to me, and back again, hoping that we might be joking. Oh no! his expression seemed to say. No – anything but that!

'Come on – you heard,' Watute prodded him.

'No – it's not safe!' he blurted out. 'What if the Japanese shoot you? Then I'll be in trouble with the Australians.'

'You'll be in trouble with the Japanese if they find out we got even this far, and you'll be in trouble with me if you don't do what you're told. You're in plenty of trouble, tultul.'

'Please don't go!' he implored, groaning and almost weeping. 'It's not that I won't take you, but it's too dangerous.'

After pleading unsuccessfully for half an hour, he finally gave in, and with a terrified expression muttered 'Yessir' to Watute's order to be ready at three o'clock in the morning. Then he went off, shaking his head and trembling, to his own house across the village.

The sun set brassily behind the timbered line of black hills as Dinkila prepared my tea. It was dark when I finished eating, and I lit the little lamp while Watute and Dinkila squatted on the floor to eat their meal of boiled sweet potatoes. We sat there, talking and smoking for some time, and then, leaving the lamp burning low where it stood, we took our rifles and dropped quietly out the back of the house and into the edge of the bush. If the tultul should fetch a Japanese patrol to surround the house, we could now easily escape to the river and make our way upstream to safety in the Wain country.

All night we sat huddled together in the bushes. Time stretched out unmercifully, and I remember trying not to look at my watch, and being disappointed, whenever I did steal a glance, to find how slowly the night was passing.

The village was fairly quiet. Sometimes a glowing cigar-end betrayed a figure moving, and in a nearby house an old man coughed and spat. Shortly before midnight, as the moon rose, we were surprised to see the women and children, with large bundles on their backs, slip out of the houses and glide like shadows along the track that led north to the hills.

'What does it mean?' I whispered to Watute. 'Do you think they're expecting a Japanese raid?'

The moonlight showed his old face creased with thought. 'It could mean that,' he said at last. 'But probably they're just playing safe. If they were sure a raid was coming, the men would have gone too.'

We sat on in silence, letting the mosquitoes bite us as they would. The minutes ticked painfully by, gradually adding themselves together to make slow, reluctant hours.

'I'm hungry,' I complained. 'And all the food's up in the house.'

Watute chuckled softly, and fumbled in his haversack, bringing out a strange black object with little bits of dust and tobacco adhering to it.

'What's this?'

'Pig. Master kai–kai,' he replied, offering it to me.

It was a knuckle of camp-cured ham from the boys' Christmas pig. I hacked off a piece with my sheath-knife and nibbled it gingerly, more with the idea of not offending Watute than of enjoying it. It tasted surprisingly good, and I soon asked for another bit.

Three o'clock came at last, and while I covered him with my rifle Watute went across the village to wake the tultul. He emerged yawning and stretching from his house, accompanied by a friend, and as soon as he saw me he began to make excuses and fresh protestations against going with us.

'It's no good, tultul,' I said. 'We're going, so that's the end of it.'

He looked as if he might burst into tears, so we gave him and his friend a packet of biscuits and tried to cheer them up. The tultul wasn't a bad sort really, but circumstances had put him into the damnable position of having to placate the implacable and somehow help each side in turn without being caught by the other.

Watute took off his uniform and borrowed an old black loincloth from Dinkila. Then he ruffled up his hair and rubbed his face and body with ashes from the fire, till he looked like any grubby kanaka from the bush. I told him to leave his rifle behind, and gave him two hand-grenades, which he put in a little string dilly-bag with his tobacco and matches.

We followed the tultul and his friend down the winding track. For the first couple of hours the bright moonlight enabled us to walk swiftly, but by five o'clock we were so deep into the valley, and in such thick jungle, that we had to sit down and wait for dawn. The soles of my feet were stinging, for though I had patched the cuts up with sticking-plaster it had been washed off by the wet grass and the many small streams we had crossed. Leeches worried us too, swarming up our legs and fastening onto the skin till they dropped off, gorged to bursting.

At first grey light we hurried on, and sunrise found us halted on a cliff above the river outside a village called Gwabandik. Watute went ahead to reconnoitre alone in his guise of kanaka, while the rest of us waited in the jungle just off the track. He was back in five minutes with the news that there were no Japanese about, and that the Gwabandik people, while surprised at our visit, were quite friendly.

The tultul and his friend and Watute and I perched on the edge of a house and ate a couple of tins of bully beef, while the Gwabandik people gathered round curiously to hear what was going on in other parts of the island. They were so near to Lae that they had a good idea of the devastation our bombing had caused.

I asked them about the Chinese camp. Yes, they knew it well. It was quite close – in fact some of them were going there that morning with a supply of vegetables. Yes, they would take me down with them, provided I was careful and first let them make sure there were no Japanese about. I told them I was in a hurry, and they obligingly rushed about, getting their loads ready.

In the middle of these preparations Watute suddenly leapt to the ground and raced to the end of the village, where he intercepted an aged native he had caught slipping into the bush. In true police-boy style Watute grabbed his arm and propelled him up to me.

'Master, this-fella man, 'em 'e tultul belong Tali!' he said excitedly.

Tali was a village near Lae known to be under Jap control.

'Is that true? Are you the tultul of Tali?' I asked.

He was a tall, thin grey-haired man, and he drew himself erect and said in a dignified voice that Watute had made a mistake.

Watute was scornful. 'I don't make mistakes like that,' he said. 'This man gave the kiap trouble in peacetime, and I've seen him both in Tali and in Lae.'

The old man denied it, saying that he belonged to another village nearby. Though he remained calm, I could see that Watute's certainty worried him.

I asked the Gwabandik natives about him, but they were evasive. 'Just an old man,' was the gist of their replies.

I felt that Watute was probably right. Even if he had made a mistake, there was something suspicious about the old man – the evasions of the Gwabandik boys seemed to point to that. At all events, it would be dangerous to let the old native go, so I told him he would be kept under guard until we left the area, and motioned him to get in the line in front of me. He began to protest, but thought better of it, shrugged, and moved into line. We started off downstream, led by about a dozen Gwabandik natives carrying bundles of vegetables and fruit.

Most of the time Watute walked at the head of the line. He appeared indistinguishable from the kanakas, and no one would have guessed that he was usually a trim, clean, uniformed police-boy. Neither would anyone have suspected that his innocent-looking little dilly-bag held two deadly 'hand-bombs', as he called the grenades, with which his aim was unerring.

Once he dropped back beside me to mutter about a theory he had worked out regarding the tultul of Tali, if such were really the identity of our prisoner. For some weeks we had been hearing stories which suggested that white missionaries were still living near the coast and carrying on under Japanese auspices. The reports, which came from natives in widely separated villages, agreed in substance, and seemed authentic. Watute had a theory that one of these missionaries had sent the tultul, a strong mission supporter, to see whether it was safe to resume missionary activity in this area.

I put this to the old native, but he only mumbled unintelligibly in reply. However, I noticed that he no longer denied that he was the tultul of Tali, nor that some Europeans were working near Lae with Japanese approval.

On its far side the river was joined by a large tributary and became a huge torrent, its tawny surface broken and foam-flecked.

'Which side of the river is the Chinese camp on?' I asked the tultul of Gawan.

'Place belong Kong-Kong 'e stop long other fella half.'

'Well, how do we get there? Look at that river!'

'Bridge 'e buggerup finish, me-fella savvy brokim water.'

'Yes, you can get across, I dare say. But what about me?'

'Master, more better you stop. Now me-fella bringim number one belong Kong-Kong, name belong 'en Peter, now you-fella talk-talk along this-fella half.'

In other words, I should stop on this side of the stream, and they would fetch the unofficial leader and spokesman for the Chinese – a man named Peter Ah Tun, whose name I had heard from Jock.

Watute and I weighed this suggestion and decided in favour of it. It had the advantage of keeping the river between us and the Japanese and also of cutting out the dangerous crossing.

We were soon led on to a flat, open stony beach, and the Gwabandik natives announced that they would make the crossing here. They would ask Peter Ah Tun to come back with them at once. Three of them were needed to get over safely, they said. If I watched them I would see what method was used to pass these flooded streams. They grabbed a dry log of driftwood from the beach – a sizeable tree about fifteen feet long – and tucked it under their left arms, with one man at each end and one in the middle. Then they plunged straight in. The current caught them, and they would have been swept rapidly downstream, but, as they bobbed about, they struck out strongly with their right arms, and each time their feet touched bottom they kicked powerfully forward. In this way the three natives reached the other side in a few minutes. They pulled their log up clear of the water, took off their loincloths and wrung them dry, and set off at a run down the far bank.

I followed their movements through the glasses, and as soon as they had disappeared round a small bluff Watute and I withdrew the rest of the natives about a hundred yards upstream, where we crouched in the cane-grass out of sight.

Watute and I kept looking at each other, he with his funny little half-grin flickering about his face. Unspoken, the same question was buzzing in both our heads: Would the Gwabandik natives return with Peter alone, or would they bring a Japanese patrol? We had our answer in less than five minutes, for the three natives, still running hard, reappeared round the bluff, followed by a single flying figure in white athletic singlet and white shorts.

While I kept the binoculars fastened on the bluff, straining my eyes to detect any sign of Japanese coming round the corner, Watute gave me a ball-to-ball description of the movements of Peter and the three natives: 'Four-fella 'e go down long water. All 'e brokim water now. Altogether man 'e come up long this-fella half. All 'e look-look nabout, now all 'e no lookim you-me,' ran his commentary.

Transferring my gaze from the farther bank to the flat below us, I saw that they were indeed searching for us, in a puzzled way, in the spot where we had been squatting when they crossed the river. I handed the binoculars to Watute with orders to shout a warning if there were any suspicious movements. Then I advanced to meet Peter.

We introduced ourselves, shaking hands warmly. He was of medium height, with gold-brown skin, and a face that looked as much European as Chinese. Through the wet singlet that stuck to his skin his ribs showed up like a washboard, and he was panting and heaving as I led him to a patch of long grass where we could hide while we talked.

'Are you all right?' I asked. 'They won't be looking for you?'

'I've been down in Lae, in jail,' he said bitterly. 'They only let me go a few days ago. Look!'

He held out his wrists and indicated his ankles for my inspection. All were encircled with black bruises, and on the inner surfaces the skin had been worn away, leaving raw, open sores which were starting to fester.

'Handcuffs?'

'Yes. And leg-irons! They keep you chained hand and foot. You can't move. You can't eat. You just lie there. You shit yourself, you piss yourself, for days! And they beat you!'

His voice became shrill and loud – almost a scream, for a moment – as he recalled his ordeal. Then he calmed down.

'Some natives told the Japs I was spying for the Australians,' he said. 'So they had me in there for questioning.'

'Do they leave you alone in your camp? Isn't it always guarded?'

'They don't bother to watch us all the time – they know we haven't much chance of escaping. Every few days a patrol comes to look at us, but that's all... But we'd better not waste time – today's a likely day for them to come, and there'll be trouble if I'm missing.'

A rapid-fire burst of question and answer began concerning the number of ships, the strength of the force landed from the convoy a few days ago, the amount and type of equipment brought ashore. To all my questions, and many others, Peter gave answers either from his own observation or from the reports of his fellow Chinese.

'What effects are our bombing raids having on the enemy?' I asked.

'They aren't killing many – the Japs have got tremendous deep shelters everywhere. But the raids do a lot of damage, and they've affected the troops' rations. Only yesterday one of your planes burnt up a huge dump of bagged rice. And the enemy lose a lot of petrol the same way.'

'Do you think the supply position is really acute yet?'

'It must be fairly bad because they bring stores in by submarine now. The subs don't surface till night-time, and the stores are unloaded offshore, in the dark.'

'Do you think the Japs know there are any white men in the mountains?' I asked. I was scribbling furiously with a stub of pencil on a grubby sheaf of papers.

'Yes, they know several white men are there, and that one recently crossed over the Saruwaged mountains. Only last Wednesday a party came up to look for you. They got as far as the old broken vine bridge over the Busu – they tried to swim the river but after a couple of them were nearly drowned they gave up.'

This intelligence was important, for it meant that our movements were certainly being reported to the enemy by natives, and that the Japanese believed them. On the other hand, the fact that the enemy had abandoned their expedition at the first serious obstacle seemed to indicate that they still had no stomach for inland patrolling into the wild and, to them, unknown mountain country. On the whole, in view of our tremendous initial advantage, I felt we could still consider ourselves fairly safe in the high country.

'How do they treat the rest of your people?'

Peter Ah Tun answered that the Japanese gave them only enough food for their subsistence, made them work in Lae, but generally treated them with reasonable humanity. They had not molested their women, and had provided food for their old people. 'Our rations have got worse, though,' he added. 'Once we used to get oil and dripping and tinned fish, but now it's only rice and a little salt. We get a bit of stuff from the natives, as you see today.'

'Things are going to get worse still,' I said. 'Before we actually make an assault on Lae the bombing will be terrific. Would you like to come out with me? I think we can still get out O.K.'

His eyes lit up for a moment, but he shook his head slowly. 'No, I couldn't do that. I must stick to my people. The Japanese would ill-treat them all if I disappeared. I must stay. We'll manage somehow. We'll go bush with the natives when the time comes.'

'You're sure you won't come?'

Peter shook his head again, without speaking. I gave him the cake of American ration chocolate I carried for an emergency, and having arranged that any further meetings should be at this spot we shook hands again. He and the Gwabandik boys went down to the water with the food, while Watute and I, with the tultul of Gawan and his friend, set off rapidly into the bush, to return to Dinkila at Gawan. We still had with us the supposed tultul of Tali, now under Watute's watchful eye.

This man, and many other people like him, was one of my worst headaches. If I made him a prisoner he would be a constant millstone round my neck, for I had no proper jail at Bawan, nor did I have enough police to guard it if I built one. On the other hand, if we let him go he might make straight for the Japanese. We decided he was to come part of the way back with us, and that we'd let him go along the road. At least we'd have time to get clear before he could raise the alarm.

The tultul of Gawan was like a man who has just been reprieved. He grinned and laughed now that his distasteful job was over. He was looking forward to our departure from his country with unconcealed pleasure, and he made the pace of our journey back to Gawan a cracker, breaking into an enthusiastic jog-trot from time to time. I found it hard to keep up with him, for there was almost no skin left on my feet and I was suffering a good deal from recurrent malaria that somehow could not be shaken off. My legs were weak, and I was short of breath.

All the way I was swearing, in a manner which would scarcely have disgraced Jock himself, at the idiocy of the headquarters crowd in insisting still that we needed no radio set. All the precious information from Peter Ah Tun instead of being in the hands of New Guinea Force Headquarters within a few hours, would have to be written out and sent to Bob's by runner – a delay of at least three days. Not only was the delay infuriating, but the messenger would be risking his life and jeopardizing the safety of our whole set-up – if he were captured the Japs might easily torture him into telling where our camp was. As Jock had said the day I met him in the mountains, without a radio we would be better employed drinking ourselves quietly to death in a nice pub in Australia.

Dinkila met us at the entrance to Gawan village. The billy was boiling, he assured me, and a mug of tea would be prepared in an instant.

As I ate some biscuits and drank a couple of pints of the hot black tea I was busy with paper and pencil roughly drafting the report. I told Dinkila to pack the few bits of gear we had, and to be ready to leave in ten minutes. Watute, his mouth crammed with sweet potato, grinned at me and pointed to the overjoyed expression on the face of the tultul of Gawan as he heard me give Dinkila the order to prepare to move. He was probably the happiest man in New Guinea at that moment.

Evening was near when we left. There was no hope of reaching Lambaip to spend the night, so when it became dark we slept in the bush a few miles up the side of the mountain above Musom.

I must have been more tired than I realized, for it was dawn before I woke, drenched from the heavy rain that had fallen in the night, and burning with fever. Watute, too, had slept through the rain. Dinkila and his friend from Lambaip had taken it in turns to guard our prisoner.

We stretched our stiff and creaking limbs, and I struggled painfully into my boots again. When we reached Lambaip we released the captive and said goodbye to Dinkila's friend. I had nothing to reward him with for his services, but I wrote a note explaining what he had done for us, telling him to give it to the first government officer to visit the village, unless of course I returned there myself. Then we struck into the hills towards Bawan, arriving about four o'clock.

As I stepped over the low fence which kept the village pigs away from the house, a strange police-boy in full uniform stepped forward and saluted smartly, handing me a folded paper, and murmuring that he had arrived at Bawan just a few moments earlier. I dismissed him and the others and went into the house to read the note. It was from Bob's, and contained a radio message from the district officer who had just taken charge in Wau. The message said, 'Return south of Markham at once. Bring all gear from Wain country.'

I sat down to consider what might lie behind this unexpected order. The instruction to bring all gear was clearly an indication that the Wain country was to be abandoned. It almost seemed that in Wau they expected the Japanese attack to be successful, and were withdrawing me while it was still possible to make contact. Again I cursed the lack of a wireless. If we should lose Wau, it was enormously important that someone should remain to watch Lae. If the new D.O. were taking this action for my safety (as he was in fact doing, I found later), a radio message would have told him that we could safely remain for a year or more in the mountains. As long as we kept contact with the kanakas they would protect us from the Japanese. Once lose touch, however, and one would hardly be able to blame them if they concluded that the Japanese had won the war.

Without a wireless I realized I could not argue. That slip of paper in my hand told me clearly what must be done. So I called all the boys into the house and translated the message into pidgin for them.

'The district officer thinks our work is ended,' I continued, 'and we must do what he says. Now go and call the luluai, the tultul, the doctor-boy, and some of the old men. I want to talk to them.'

They filed silently outside, except Watute, who lingered a moment near the door.

'Well?' I asked. 'What are you thinking about?'

'Master, we are not afraid, you and I?' he questioned, as though to clear up a doubt.

'No, of course not,' I assured him.

'That is all that matters, then,' he said. 'Now, if the Number One says we must go, we must do as he says. But it is a pity. This is a good country, the Wain.' And as he went down the steps he looked wistfully round at the blue hills and at the lengthening shadows in the valleys.

By the time the luluai and other natives of Bawan arrived it was dark, and Dinkila had lit the fire. My blankets, still damp from the drenching the night before, were steaming beside it. Dinkila, his glossy black skin gleaming in the firelight, moved quietly about the room, packing things for our journey next day, and occasionally turning his attention to the pots on the fire, in which he was preparing tea.

I told the Bawan men that I was leaving, but hoped

to return one day. In the meantime they must bear in mind all the things I had told them. They must avoid the Japanese, and help any white man who came to them, just as they had helped me. Then, when the government returned, they would have a good name, they would be well rewarded. But if they did not heed my words it would be no use their appealing to me to intercede for them against the wrath of the government.

'Oh, sorry, master,' they replied. 'Me-fella hearim finish talk belong you. Me-fella no can loosim talk belong you.'

Warning them that all the men must be ready to carry my cargo in the morning, I gave each one a calico loin-cloth and a couple of pounds of salt, and they lifted the canvas curtain across the doorway and vanished into the misty blackness of the night. I heard them ask Watute, at the door of the house-police, for a lighted brand from the fire to show them the path home, and I could hear their voices receding as they went down the track to the village.

'Do you think they will remember what I have told them?' I asked Dinkila.

That cynic shrugged his shoulders. 'How do I know? Men forget everything sooner or later. I suppose they will remember for a while.' And he busied himself again at the pots on the fire.

There was a case or two of meat left, which I did not feel disposed to carry back to Bob's, so I opened one and distributed it and a good deal of other extra food to the police. I saw by the pile of native food they were cooking that their last night in the Wain was to be a memorable one, and upon returning to my house for tea I found that Dinkila seemed to have the same idea for me. The first course came on three plates, one piled high with potato-chips and rissoles, and the other two with cabbage, sweet corn, taro, sweet potatoes, spinach, and fried bananas. I could see him completing the preparation of an enormous dish of fruit salad to follow.

'Good heavens!' I exclaimed. 'How many men do you think I am?'

'You can eat it,' he said. 'You haven't had a proper meal for days.'

He was right. I was terribly hungry, and finished the meal without any trouble.

Dinkila watched with approval.

'Master 'e like sleep now,' he said mischievously as he cleared away the last dish and replaced it with some black coffee. Then he ran quietly down the steps and up to the house-police, to get his own meal.

More than anything in the world I wanted to go to sleep but the report had to be written. Dinkila had left a whole kettleful of black coffee, and this helped me stay awake until eleven o'clock, by which time the report was complete in draft form, and it remained only to make a decent legible copy. I called out to the sentry to see that everyone was out of bed by four o'clock next morning, and fell asleep without waiting to undress.

V

IT WAS morning. By lantern-light Dinkila prepared a cup of tea, while Watute supervised the lining out of the cargo by the other police, ready for the carriers. The air was cold, and a light breeze was drifting the mist up the valley. The fuzzy hair of the boys was silvered by countless tiny droplets of moisture. The police were reasonably warm in their sweaters, but the carriers, wearing for the most part only a loincloth, shivered as they adjusted ropes and carrying-poles. Those who were not working stood silently by, shoulders hunched and arms clasped across chests to conserve as much bodily warmth as possible. Jock, expecting to return to the Wain shortly, had left all his patrol gear in the camp, and that, together with my own equipment, made a total of twenty-five carrier-loads. The news of our departure would spread quickly, and I hoped the Japanese would not send a patrol to sit astride the Erap, or perhaps wait for us at the canoe landing. To forestall any such move, we would travel rapidly, sleeping the first night at Gain, and the following day pass straight through Bivoro to Kirkland's. This would require a tremendous spurt, and we took ten extra carriers to relieve the men with the heavier loads from time to time.

We reached Boana Mission not long after sunrise. The buildings had the same ill-omened atmosphere about them as ever: even the usually irrepressible Dinkila was subdued. We stayed only long enough to receive the respects of Singin, tultul of Wampangan, and to give him charge of a case of meat to be handed to the next European who entered the area. Then we moved on through Dzendzen, Kasin, and Wasinim to Gain, and at all these villages relays of people were waiting to take over the carrying, while the village officials, complete with hats, were there to salute me at the roadside as I arrived, and then to bid me farewell.

There was an hour or two of daylight left when we reached Gain, and I was uncertain whether to camp or to push on to Badibo. I decided to camp, but sent Watute ahead to warn the people to be ready to carry next day. The old chap was pretty tired, and said his 'skin was paining'. However, he rubbed nettles all over his arms, back, and chest, and announced that he felt much better. It was not uncommon to see a native doing this. Once or twice I had inadvertently brushed against a clump of nettles, and the pain was considerable, so I do not know how the boys could have borne to rub them all over themselves, bringing up great weals. No doubt it had some beneficial effect, or else they supposed it did.

The track from Gain was a good one, and before daylight next day we had passed through Badibo, and shortly after dawn arrived at Munkip. Watute had done his job well, as usual, and the people were standing by in readiness. He had also sent a lad ahead to Bivoro to warn them of our coming. We reached that village, the last one of our journey, about eight o'clock.

I was feeling sick and weak when the carriers put down the cargo outside the house-kiap, but news travels so quickly that we dared not remain. I told Dinkila to make some beef tea, which I tried to get down, but it was difficult. Then the line moved ahead, out of the last few miles of the Erap Valley and into the bare, stony plain.

Walking in my usual place at the rear of the line to keep the stragglers from falling too far behind, I suddenly felt a wave of great nausea and weakness, and the next thing I remembered was Dinkila and Buka bending anxiously over me as I vomited violently. While Dinkila lifted me into a little patch of shade behind some bushes, Buka rushed ahead to stop the line of carriers.

'Get my bed,' I called after him.

'All right, master. Me-fella savvy,' Dinkila said, in a tone which implied that all could safely be left in his hands.

Buka was a long time returning. Apparently I had been lying on the ground unable to move for about half an hour before I had been missed, so the carriers were a good way ahead. Buka brought four Bivoro natives with him, the biggest and strongest in the line. They were carrying my bed-sail, blankets, stout poles, and lengths of vine. They set to work at once to make a rough stretcher.

Despite the intense heat of the sun I was shivering, and Dinkila wrapped me in blankets and lifted me onto the stretcher. At a word from Buka the Bivoro natives, one at each corner of the stretcher, picked up their additional burden and hurried down the track after the rest of the line. Every time they stumbled, which was often, I felt as if my frame would jolt apart.

We reached the Erap River and to judge by Dinkila's shouted instructions they found the crossing hard going, but I was too sick to worry. To have been dropped beneath the cool water would have been a blessing, for the shivering stage had passed and I was now burning with fierce dry heat.

About midday we overtook the main line of carriers. Watute had halted them, out of sight, at the edge of a patch of scrub.

'The kanakas wanted to stop in some hunting shelters for the night, and continue the journey in the morning,' he said. 'But I kept them on the move. The sooner we get out of this the better. We can still reach the Markham by sundown, if we hurry. I'm going ahead to scout,' Watute added, as he handed cap, rifle, and bayonet to Buka. 'We are getting near the Markham road now.' And he vanished silently into the cane-grass.

I called Dinkila and told him to take my maps and papers, which lay beside me wrapped in oilskin.

'If the Japs attack us,' I told him, 'your job is to escape across the Markham with these papers. Never mind about anyone else. You get this packet to the Number One at Bob's.'

With a muttered 'Yessir' he tucked the parcel under his arm and dropped back, while at Buka's command the line picked up the cargo, which now included me, and resumed the long southward march.

Two hours later, so the watch said, I was conscious of Watute's voice beside me.

'We have passed the Markham road, master,' he said. 'The Japanese could not have known we were coming, or they would have lain in wait. Unless they see us from behind now, and give chase, we should be safe.' And he moved away, to exhort the carriers to an even greater turn of speed.

I must have fallen asleep then, for the next thing I remembered was throwing aside the leafy branches with which Dinkila had covered me from the sun, and raising myself on my elbow to look around. The sun was nearly down, and I could see by the slack water surrounding us, and the density of the cane-grass, that our journey was almost ended. The dark forest-covered hills of the south side of the Markham and the kunai spur of Kirkland's could be seen close at hand. I sank back on the stretcher with a sigh of relief. Almost safe at last! Three shots rang out from Watute's rifle. He had hurried ahead to give the signal summoning the canoes, and a few moments later the carriers laid the stretcher down at the edge of the muddy, swirling Markham.

Buka was studying the opposite bank with my binoculars. There was smoke from the camp, he said, but no sign of the canoes.

'Fire again,' I ordered Watute, and he let fly another volley of three shots into the air. This time there was an answering shot, and the canoes, Buka told me, could be seen pushing off from the distant shore.

It seemed ages before they grounded, and I heard the excited questions of the boats' crews asking why I was being carried. While the canoes were coming across, Watute had paid off the Bivoro carriers. They had been wonderful, sharing between them the four extra loads caused by my having to be carried, in spite of which they had made the journey in record time. I told Watute to give them each two shillings and some tobacco, and enough meat and biscuits for a meal, since it was nearly dark and they would not be able to return home until next day.

As I lay on the canoe I felt I did not care how long it took to cross. The Japanese had no hope of catching us now. Dinkila gave me back my papers, and I managed to sit upright to respond to the greeting of the white man on the shore. He splashed into the shallows to help me to the bank.

'Where are you wounded?' he asked.

'Not wounded – just a bad go of gastric fever.'

'But the blood?' he questioned.

'What blood?'

'On the rag you had round your head.'

For a moment I was puzzled. Then, simultaneously, we caught sight of a red and white towel Dinkila had put under my head for a pillow. Through the low-powered binoculars it had seemed that my head was covered with a blood-soaked bandage.

'Thank God for that, anyhow!' he said, laughing. 'You look as if just about everything else had happened to you, though.' He pulled my arm round his neck, to help me as we made our way up the track to the camp.

Tom Lega was away at Bob's for the day, but I said a feeble hullo to the others, and within ten minutes had swallowed a cup of tea and half a papaw and was asleep beneath a mosquito-net.

I woke at midday next day, and we pushed straight on to Bob's. I could walk only very slowly, and often sat down to rest. We arrived just before dark, and the doctor sent me straight to bed. He told me I must go to Wau as soon as I could travel, for a large weeping sore had broken out on my face, caused by exposure to the sun while I had been lying on the stretcher, and he insisted on my seeing a skin specialist.

During the couple of days I was in bed Jim Hamilton and his brother Rob typed out a copy of my report on the visit to the Chinese compound and sat and talked to me. Bill Chaffey thrust his huge red beard under the mosquito-net from time to time to tell me the latest news. Jock had been sent up to Wau, he said, for the ear was getting worse and causing him severe pain.

The typed copy of the report was sent on to Wau by police-boy runner, and on the third day, accompanied by Buka, Watute, and Dinkila, I set out after him.

While I was sick at Bob's, and during the three-day walk to Wau, one of the closest battles of the New Guinea campaign was being fought. Japanese troops who had just landed at Lae were brought across the bay to Salamaua, and advanced through the bush to attack Wau.

Our reinforcements had only just begun to trickle in there from Port Moresby, and the attacking Japanese took them utterly by surprise, outnumbering the defenders many times over. The enemy came unnoticed along an old mining track, and were in Wau before their arrival was even suspected. The curious thing is that the existence of this trail was known to many of us who had been around the bush, but was nevertheless left unguarded.

The Japanese entered the streets of Wau and reached the foot of the steeply sloping aerodrome. Overcast weather had delayed the landing of planes from Moresby carrying reinforcements, and it seemed that the Japanese would capture Wau. Then, through slightly cleared skies, Douglas transport planes roared in to land right among enemy machine-gun fire. 'Right! Where are the bastards? Let's at 'em!' shouted one massive infantryman as he jumped down from the plane waving his sub-machine-gun. Crack! went a Jap sniper's rifle from the end of the drome. They picked up the soldier and took him back to Port Moresby in the same plane, a casualty in thirty seconds.

The new troops were the 17th Infantry Brigade, among the most famous fighters in the whole A.I.F. They had fought in the desert, in Greece, Crete, and Syria, and now they were about to add New Guinea to their honours. They were the wildest and the finest group of men I have ever known, a unit one is proud to have been associated with.

Wau showed me a new aspect of war. Instead of the quiet of the jungle, and outnumbered men spying on the

Japs but not daring to attack them, all was hurry, noise, and determination. Gone was the placid quiet of the lovely Wau Valley. Now white men outnumbered black, and the streets were crowded with men and vehicles, field telephone-lines were everywhere, improvised signs and direction posts had been put up at every corner. Mechanics had repaired some of the cars and trucks partly destroyed the year before when, following an unconfirmed and (as it turned out) untrue report of a Japanese attack, orders were given to burn Wau township down to prevent it from falling into the enemy's hands. I was in Wau at the time and remember the panic that accompanied its abandonment when it was fired.

The most picturesque of the mechanics' repair jobs was the Stonkered Taxi Service − consisting of a nearly wrecked sedan car which had somehow been put back on the road and which now served as an ambulance.

By the time I arrived the Japs had been driven off from Wau itself, but twenty-five-pounder guns right in the heart of the town were pouring shells onto nearby Wandumi Ridge, along which the enemy was retreating. The enemy suffered frightful privations on the march back to Salamaua, and in some cases ate their own dead. I saw one corpse with pieces hacked off the thighs to feed the survivors.

At the casualty clearing station set up in one of the few houses which the torch had spared, the doctors took one look at the sore on my face.

'Over to Moresby, and then to Australia for you,' they said.

I went back to my headquarters, the district office, to wait for a plane back to Moresby. Jock, whose patrol gear and maps I had brought from the Wain, was out with the troops near Skindiwai, on the road to Salamaua. He was in charge of their native carriers and was also acting as guide. These troops had been cut off from Wau by the Japanese, but the latest information was that they were fighting on, and it was hoped that they would soon be relieved.

I tied up Jock's boxes, marked them, and put them in the store for him.

'I hope he needs them again,' I said to Watute, who was helping me.

He grinned happily. 'Japan 'e no can killim Master Jock 'e die,' he said confidently. ' 'Em 'e strong-fella man too much.'

Next morning, in bright sunshine, Dinkila and I boarded an empty transport plane returning to Port Moresby.

Watute and Buka were waiting to see us off.

'Oh, sorry, master!' they said. 'Behind you come back lookim me-fella.'

As they saluted I promised to return as soon as I could. Then the plane's doors slammed shut, and we lost sight of them.

It was Dinkila's first ride in an aeroplane. He was not at all afraid, but rather excited, and he watched Wau disappear and the mountains slip beneath us, his nose flattened against the Perspex window. I watched with interest too, for this was the very country over which I had walked from Port Moresby in the early days of the war, before we had any aeroplanes. As I saw the incredible succession of precipitous ridges and valleys pass beneath us I marvelled that every round of ammunition, every tin of biscuits, every case of meat, had been carried on human shoulders across those heart-breaking obstacles to the weary, outnumbered troops who had held the Bulolo Valley all these lonely months. Now we were making the return trip in a comfortable couple of hours. I remarked on the contrast to Dinkila, but he was not interested. He had turned that queer green colour peculiar to a sick native, and I could see that he was retaining his breakfast with difficulty. He stumbled down the steps of the plane into the dusty, blinding glare of the aerodrome at Port Moresby, but his spirits were at their usual high level ten minutes later.

A jeep took Dinkila and me from the aerodrome to the headquarters of Angau (the Australian New Guinea Administrative Unit), a vast collection of buildings that stretched right round the beach from Hanuabada native village to the old civil government house.

From here I spent some days visiting various intelligence agencies, answering their questions as best I could about affairs across the Markham. There was now nobody in the country behind Lae, and the intelligence officers felt it was important for someone to be there so that we should not remain ignorant of enemy activity in this important area. For instance, it was rumoured that the Japanese were opening overland communications between Madang and Lae, following a track up the Ramu River, over into the Markham headwaters, and down that river to Lae.

I was keen to return to the Wain country. With adequate supplies and a radio set it would be possible to hole up there for the rest of the war, provided I got back quickly, before friendships with the natives had cooled or been forgotten. Various officers in these intelligence groups said they would support me if I applied to go back, and offered assistance in supplies, equipment, and information.

The sore on my face was gradually healing, and on one pretext or another I put off visiting the hospital for a fortnight – until I was nearly better – hoping to avoid being sent to Australia. When I finally reported at the hospital I found that it was all under canvas. There were about forty beds to each ward, and they were stretched out in a great double row on bare dirt floors. Most of the time the sides of the tents were kept brailed up to let the breeze in. Many of the patients had been wounded in the Wau battle and in the subsequent pursuit of the Japanese across the ridges to Salamaua.

While I was sitting in the registrar's office waiting to be admitted a sister walked into the tent. A white woman! And a girl fresh from Australia at that, a girl whose cheeks had not yet been stained yellow by constant doses of atebrin tablets. She must have noticed the astonished look on my face, for she asked what was the matter, and laughed when I explained that she was the first white woman I had seen for more than a year.

'There are plenty of us here,' she said. 'You'll probably want to go back to the bush before you've been a patient very long.'

After a week under observation, which I spent resting in bed, I was told by the skin specialist that I could remain in New Guinea, and was discharged from hospital with a warning to keep my face always well shaded with a hat.

I went back to Angau headquarters to seek permission to return to the Wain. There was a delay of a couple of weeks while my plan was debated by my senior officers, and eventually approval was given.

In the period of waiting I learnt about another phase of warfare – base areas and headquarters. I was learning that war had no redeeming features; that in its every aspect it was futility compounded with varying degrees of degradation. I had already seen something of the physical suffering it entailed. But the dangers and hardship of active service seemed tolerable when I compared them with the shabby atmosphere of service base areas.

In a fighting unit in action there was the comradeship of proved friends, the tradition of things endured together, which evoked a very definite generosity and loyalty. In such a unit, however dreadful material conditions might have become, the moral climate at least was fairly healthy. By contrast, base areas, where living conditions were usually reasonably good, seemed to smoulder with stupid and petty personal jealousies. There were all sorts of rackets. For instance, in some places, sick natives, or even ones who should have been at work, were employed by the officer in charge of them to make crude and shoddy 'curios', which the officer then sold at fabulous prices to souvenir-crazy Americans. The black market in liquor, smuggled to New Guinea by service aircraft, made the civilian black market appear a gentlemanly affair. More often than not soldiers who were actually doing the fighting and taking the risks seemed to be regarded with aversion, or at best tolerated as inescapable burdens who disordered the even routine of life. The worst of the food seemed to come our way, and we were not welcomed in the mess. To prevent contamination by rude interlopers such as myself a notice was erected at one of the top tables saying: NO OUTSIDERS AT THIS TABLE. At this base camp there were several other 'outsiders', whom I had known in Wau early in the war and who were, like me, waiting to return to active service. We retired together to a lower table, which we protected – a little childishly, it must be confessed – with a notice of our own: NO BASE BLUDGERS ALLOWED.

At the quartermaster's store anybody seeking equipment or supplies was greeted with a mixture of rudeness and obstructionism. The quartermaster, who was enormously fat, glared when I asked for a tin of baking-powder, screwing up his lard-ball face and squinting through his glasses.

'What do you want that for?' he squealed.

'To make scones and damper with.'

'Humph! I don't know what's the matter with you people in the bush. Why can't you be satisfied with biscuits?'

The question came from a man who ate bread every day of his life to one who had not tasted it over a period of eight months. I stood still and waited without replying. Slowly, grudgingly, as though parting with the elixir of life, the pudgy fingers moved across the counter, pushing a tin of baking-powder. Item by item I squeezed six months' rations out of him, and every time he handed something over he did so as though it meant he would have to take his enormous belt in another notch. But when Dinkila and I went back to Wau two days later we had nearly half a plane-load of food, arms, trade goods, and medical stores. Dinkila had enjoyed his stay in Port Moresby, but I felt that it would be preferable to live at Bob's, or even Kirkland's, than to get caught up permanently in Port Moresby.

VI

I WAS TO wait in Wau for final orders for the expedition, and as I walked into the district office the first person in sight was Jock McLeod. I had last heard of him cut off by the Japanese near Salamaua, and it was good to see him safe. He was noncommittal about his adventures.

'We got out of it O.K.' was all he would say.

About the proposed return north of the Markham he was more vocal. He thought things would be more difficult now.

'If I were the Nip commander I'd have occupied Boana,' he said. 'I bet you find Japs all through the Wain.'

'Well, then, why didn't they occupy it before? They had just as much reason to do it a year ago,' I argued.

Jock shrugged. 'It will have sunk through their commander's skull now, I reckon. Anyhow, you'll find out,' he added with a grin, and he introduced me to Major Donald Vertigan, who had just taken over as district officer.

Vertigan, a government officer in peacetime, was not one of the most popular men in Angau, and at my first interview with him I certainly didn't like him. He was a thin man with a thin face and a close-clipped moustache. He had a strange way of peering at you unblinkingly as he sat, for quite long periods, silent and unmoving. He told me that I was to have a companion on this trip – a Captain Les Howlett, an old New Guinea patrol officer, who was coming up from Australia for the purpose. He was working for the Far Eastern Liaison Office, and his interest would be largely propaganda among the natives.

Vertigan sat cold and staring as I explained that I would rather go alone. Divided responsibility was bad, I urged, and the larger the party the harder it was for the natives to conceal it, the more supplies were needed, and so on. Finally, I pointed out that two Europeans together in the bush nearly always quarrelled, no matter how tolerant and sensible they might be under ordinary circumstances.

He was unmoved. 'Howlett will be going, anyhow,' he said in a flat voice. 'He's bringing the radio set for your party, by the way.'

That was all. I got up and went out, feeling that the new district officer was unfathomable. I had not the faintest idea whether he liked or disliked me; whether he approved of my scheme for a patrol into the Huon Peninsula or thought it a hare-brained venture; whether he would support me if I got into trouble, or would let me stew in the mess I had made for myself.

As the weeks went by, however, and I saw more of him, I realized what an immensely valuable job Vertigan was doing and how helpful he was. Every instruction he gave me, or suggestion he made, was sound or constructive; he saw that I was given every reasonable thing that I asked for, going out of his way to get me the proper stores for the expedition. Vertigan worked prodigiously hard at his own job, and seemed to have small interest in or energy for the Army's personal jealousies and feuds. When he was finally awarded his M.B.E. I felt that no man had merited recognition more, for an important job well done in the face of great difficulty and discouragement. It is the greatest thing in the world for the morale of men engaged in lonely bush work to know that their superior officer at headquarters is someone who understands their problems, and will help them if he can. Later in the war, working for a man who did not bother even to acknowledge urgent radio messages, I realized just how lucky I had been to have Vertigan for a boss.

I had to thank him for my superb detachment of police. Corporal Kari, who had taken me up the Erap on my first patrol the previous year, was to command them. Old Watute, and two of Jock McLeod's former police, Nabura and Witolo, were the others. These were all men of experience and proved integrity. Because of his slowness in the mountains, Buka had to be left behind, to my sorrow. Dinkila, gay as ever, was still my cook, and for my other servant I had Pato, an elderly man from Gumbum village, in the Wain. He was a steady, intelligent man, speaking both Wain and Naba dialects. Moreover, he enjoyed considerable prestige in the country we were going to – there was scarcely a village where he did not have at least one relative. Before the war, he told us, he had had a responsible job as a boss-boy for Ray Parer, the famous aviator.

Being older men than the others, Watute and Pato became very friendly, and with their combined experience and local knowledge were a particularly valuable team.

I had to wait several weeks for Les Howlett, and I filled in the time doing odd jobs: helping to build a native hospital, guiding parties of troops through the bush, sometimes taking native carrier-lines with supplies to our troops in the forward areas. It was during this period that the Japanese made their last big air raid in that part of the island. About thirty planes came over, shining silver specks, very high and in perfect formation. We took cover in slit trenches nearby, and could hear the bombs whistling overhead as half the raiding force made their run. As the second group of bombers approached, there was a scuttering of earth outside the trench in which I was crouching with another man, and a panting figure tumbled in on top of us. It was Dinkila, and he stank horribly.

'My God, man, what have you done! Shit yourself?' I demanded holding my nose.

He gave a quick, nervous grin. 'Master, me hearim bomb 'e come, now me fall down long house pek-pek.'

He had jumped into the pit of the primitive latrine in his hurry to escape the first of the bombs! We hardly waited for the second lot, which fell harmlessly on a nearby hillside, before we sent him packing to the river to wash. Dinkila never lived the incident down, and was the butt of the natives in our party for months afterwards.

In the second week of April I moved the police and all stores to Wampit, there to await the arrival of Les Howlett. I thought it better to move down in advance of him, since the two of us together would have placed too much strain at the one time on the limited carrier-lines serving the Markham end. After I had been there for a few days a message came through from Major Vertigan saying that Les had left Wau. On the afternoon of 20th April, when I thought he ought to arrive, I went a short way along the track to Timne to meet him. It was a steaming Markham day, and I walked for only half an hour or so, then sat down on a log to wait.

The first hint of Les's approach was the passing of a line of about forty laden carriers, in charge of four young police-boys wearing their brand-new navy serge uniforms with red sashes. At the end of the line marched a medium-built man of about thirty. When I approached he pushed his battered felt hat off his perspiring brow and ordered the police to halt the carriers for a spell.

'Are you Les Howlett?' I asked.

He regarded me with dark humorous eyes. 'Yes. I suppose you're Peter Ryan?'

'That's right.'

We shook hands, and I said, 'Wampit Camp is just about half an hour away. What about pushing on?'

'Let's,' he replied briefly. 'I'm a bit keen on a wash-wash and a feed. All right, walkabout!' he called to the boys, who lifted the cargo and moved off again down the track.

It was dark by the time Les had had a wash and we had eaten our tea. Heavy rain poured onto the low-pitched grass roof of the hut, and for the first of many nights to come we faced each other across the lantern and planned.

'What are those police of yours like, Les?' I asked.

'Not bad. They're smart lads, but they haven't had very much experience yet.'

'I'll turn them over to Kari and old Watute, two of mine. They'll make policemen of them.'

'Good idea. Now about those stores...'

And so on, planning, scheming, making a hundred suggestions and discarding most of them, and laughing often. Les chain-smoked cigarettes; my pipe was never cold. By midnight we felt we had straightened out a lot of problems, and had got to know each other. I had discovered Les's quick, quiet sense of humour, and had come already to look for the gleam in his smiling dark eyes across the hurricane-lamp. It was something that buoyed me up often in the months ahead.

Next morning, in front of the hut, Corporal Kari paraded our little squad of police – eight in all. There was a striking contrast between my boys and those Les had brought fresh from the depot at Port Moresby. Mine, wearing patched and faded khaki loincloths and battered peaked caps, lacked the parade-ground smartness of the recruits. But they were tough, steady, and reliable, old soldiers tempered in the fire of many campaigns. The difference in the faces was interesting, too. My boys looked like a bunch of thugs compared with the fresh-faced youthful recruits. However, the newcomers seemed keen and eager, and I felt that with experience, and after a spell under the stern hand of Kari, they would be as good as any. I watched them drill for a quarter of an hour or so, till Kari dismissed them.

Les had brought six other boys over with him – they all came from various parts of the Huon Peninsula. With them to help us there was a good chance that wherever we might go we would be able to make ourselves understood. And they would be most useful for propaganda purposes, for they had seen the tremendous progress made since the early days of the war, and the huge aerodromes and enormous troop concentrations at Port Moresby, and would be much better able than we were to convince the people of their own villages that the Allies were now possessed of real military strength. It was easy to understand the scepticism of the natives in the villages when I, a single white man, talked about our enormous resources. They used to retort that they had only my word for it that we had large numbers of troops, while they could actually see, not far away, thousands upon thousands of Japanese. Now, they would listen with much more attention to our story, for it would come from the lips of one of their own people.

Although we firmly rejected all equipment that was not absolutely essential, our combined stores amounted to nearly seventy carrier-loads. Most of it was either food or trade goods. We were gambling on being able to sneak this very substantial quantity of material into the Wain, for we wanted to be independent of cargo-dropping from aircraft – as well as being unreliable, it was likely to betray our position to the enemy.

The large supply of trade goods comprised knives, axes, beads, mirrors, calico, matches, tobacco, newspaper, salt, and a thousand razor-blades. This last item was a rare prize, for razor-blades were highly valued by the natives, and were very easy for us to carry round in our pockets. A couple of packets represented payment for food for our whole party for days. At that time they were very hard to get, even for the troops, and the Army was reluctant to part with such a large number 'just to issue to natives'. It had taken a good deal of persuasion on Major Vertigan's part to get them.

I looked at the pile of trade goods with satisfaction. For the first time I could go into the Wain without being a beggar and depending for charity on the good nature of the natives. Now, I thought, I would be able to give things away with a lavish hand, mindful of the anthropologists' warnings that natives despise nothing so much as meanness.

Our wireless set, an Air Force job, was a masterpiece. It was light and compact and could be unpacked and set up quickly. Moreover, it operated on dry batteries, which was an advantage; an accumulator set would have needed a charging unit for the batteries and petrol to run the unit on, both of which would have added to our problems. The noise of a recharger's engine would have echoed for miles round those hills, too. When packed into the special padded box Les had made for it, and complete with spare valves, batteries, headphones, tools, aerial, and other spare parts, our wireless set could easily be carried by two men, and though it was often severely battered during carries through rough country it never once let us down. Les and I thought of it with the affection one bestows on a faithful friend.

Because of rumours circulating among the natives that the Japanese were making regular patrols from Lae to the Erap River, we decided not to go by my usual route up the Erap Valley, but to cross the Markham higher up, opposite Chivasing, on the north bank. Chivasing was one of the bigger villages, and we hoped to get enough carriers there to take us across the uninhabited stretch of the Markham plain to the villages of the more densely populated Middle and Upper Erap, through which we would pass to the Wain. This route would take several extra days, but it was safer, and would enable us to visit many villages that had seen no European since the last peacetime patrol, in 1941.

We sent a message to Mari village telling all the able-bodied men to present themselves for carrying next day, but only twenty-five of them turned up, and it was clear that we would have to make two trips to get all our stores to the Markham.

We decided to make two short carries the first day, moving all the gear as far as Kirkland's. By three o'clock the carriers, under the leadership of a native called Sela, had returned from the first trip. Picking up the remaining cargo, they set off at once on the second trip. I walked at the tail of the line, intending to spend the night at Kirkland's. Les was to follow in the morning.

Half-way between Wampit and Kirkland's I called in at Bob's. Although I knew the camp had been more or less abandoned, it was a shock to see it manned by only four men. The long huts were empty, the door of the store lay open and broken, and the sergeants' mess where I had eaten so many happy, if frugal, meals was falling down. Without any laughing, chattering natives, the silence was more unearthly than ever; and the smoke from the single cooking-fire still hung motionless among the trees. I asked the four men, all of whom I knew from those earlier days, whether they felt the same sense of awful desolation as I did at this moment.

'Feel it!' they exclaimed. 'You notice it just by walking in here. You can imagine how it's affecting us after all these weeks.'

I felt sorry for them as I looked at their strained and pallid faces.

'Remember how we used to play the old gramophone at night, and gather round the signal hut to listen to the news?' they asked, and we talked a while of the old days, when Bob's was, in a sense, 'home' to us all, and its fires and bustling activity made it a place of comfort and refuge in the hostile jungles that surrounded us.

Kirkland's was unchanged, except that Tom Lega had obtained leave to go to Australia, and the place was in charge of another corporal, Curly Lee. I had met Curly the previous year, on a brief visit to the Salamaua front. He had been camped at Skindiwai, a wet, cold little group of bark shanties almost buried in the dark, mountainous rainforest.

'Fair dinkum, it's enough to give you the horrors!' exclaimed Curly. 'We used to huddle round the fires at Skindiwai and say we'd give anything to get warm. Down here in the flamin' Markham we'd give anything to get bloody well cold again!'

'And the mossies!'

'I don't mind mosquitoes biting at night,' chipped in one of the other men. 'I've been on this ruddy island now for so long that the mossies are just part of life – we'd miss them if there weren't any. But when the bastards go all day and all night, like they do down here, it's a bit over the odds.'

We sat and yarned in the mosquito-proof room for the rest of the afternoon, but the conversation continually came round to guesses at how much longer the war would last, and how much longer it would be necessary to go on living in this dreadful spot.

'When I stop to think about it,' said Curly, 'it beats me why this rotten, lousy hole hasn't sent us all off our heads!'

About five o'clock, when the last of the Mari boys had gone and I had checked over all the cargo, Curly and I walked up to the kunai-covered hill at the back of the camp to watch the cook-boy and his mate catch flying-foxes, or black bokis as they were called in pidgin. These passed over in a cloud every night, and the method of snaring the creatures showed once again how intelligent these 'savages' were. They took the long, light, spear-like midribs of coconut-fronds and covered one end of them with an entanglement of thorny vines. These missiles would be hurled among the flying-foxes as they made their way overhead, the thorns would catch in their wings, and the weight of the midribs would bring the creatures tumbling to earth. Their smell was repulsive, and they were infested with vermin, but when skinned and cooked they were tasty enough.

Kari put my bed-sail up alongside Curly's, and we talked till quite late that night. Curly told me there were no canoes or boats' crews at Kirkland's now, because no patrols went over to the north bank of the Markham. The Chivasing natives had dismantled all their canoes because they were frightened to be on the river in case they were shot at by aircraft.

Early next morning the Mari carriers returned to bring our gear up to Naraguma, an hour or so farther up the Markham. Naraguma was really a dependent hamlet of Mari itself, but had been abandoned by order of the district officer. He did not want natives moving about near the Markham, for they might be spying for the Japanese. For this reason, it was felt that the whole south bank of the Markham between the Watut and the Wampit rivers should be kept uninhabited.

The Mari boys would leave us at Naraguma, and carriers would be brought down from Chivasing for the remainder of the trip. Curly walked up to Naraguma to keep me company, and we made our way together through the thick jungle that fringed the river. When we reached the little village the carriers dumped their loads and at once set off back to Kirkland's for their second lot. Curly helped me stow the loads beneath the houses. We noticed that though the buildings were in good repair the jungle was already starting to creep in upon the settlement. A few months more, I thought, and it will be a hard job to find Naraguma.

Curly waited while I sat on my patrol-box to scrawl a brief note home – the last I would have an opportunity to send for several months. He wrapped it in the oilskin folder we all carried to prevent our papers becoming soaked with sweat, and buttoned it into his shirt pocket.

We shook hands.

'So long – see you in Sydney or Melbourne,' was all he said. With a quick glance at his tommy-gun to make sure it could be brought instantly into action, he disappeared into the surrounding jungle.

By three in the afternoon the boys were coming in by ones and twos with their second loads. As each man stacked his cargo beneath the houses I paid him off – a shilling and a stick of tobacco for his day's work.

Les arrived at four, behind the last load of cargo. He had made sure that nothing was left behind. As soon as he came into sight I called out to Dinkila:

'Cookim hot water long wash-wash belong master!'

'All right, master, me lookim,' he replied as he ran down to the river to fill a bucket.

As soon as Les had bathed and changed his clothes we set Dinkila and Les's cook to prepare a meal while we sat down to learn our list of code words.

'This is the list,' Les said, pulling a paper from his pocket. 'These are the keys to the code we will use, and we must memorize them in that order. We don't want to carry any papers of that sort on us, in case we are captured.'

The words – there were about a dozen – were ordinary enough. 'Attractive' and 'evidently' were two I can recall, but it took us a little time to learn them in the right order. Then we dropped the paper in the cooking-fire and watched it blacken, curl up, and slowly burn. Somehow it seemed symbolic. I felt a link had been severed, and Les must have thought the same.

'It's almost like burning our bridges, isn't it?' he asked with a smile.

As we lay beneath our mosquito-nets that night we speculated on how we should fare when we had really crossed our Rubicon, and how the natives of the north side would receive us.

Early next morning we sent Kari to Chivasing, several miles upstream on the other side of the river. He had often been there when he was in charge of the police at Bob's, under John Clarke, and he knew some of the villagers. We expected him back the next day, but he did not turn up. The morning of the following day advanced and there was still no sign of him. We became more and more anxious.

We discussed possible reasons for Kari's non-appearance. Like all the Manus people he was a powerful swimmer, so there seemed little likelihood of his having been drowned when crossing the river.

'There's only two things could have gone wrong, Les,' I said as we squatted at the water's edge. 'He may have been taken by a crocodile, or the Nips may have grabbed him.'

'Pretty crook alternatives for Kari,' Les replied grimly. 'We'd better watch out, in case he has been captured – the bastards might have forced him to give us away. You know their form with prisoners.'

I called for Watute, who was second in command of the police.

'Tell the boys not to move away from the camp without their arms, and post two sentries on the track and on the riverbank instead of one,' I told him.

'Yes, sir – me talkim all boy look-out good long Japan,' he replied with impassive face, and a few moments later his voice came across the clearing as he called his orders to the others.

About midday there was a loud shout from the river-bank, and we hurried down to the spot where Watute had posted a man in a tree so as to command a better view of the surrounding country.

'What is it? What's happening?' we asked.

'You hearim master 'e talk!' Watute snapped to the boy above. 'You lookim wonem something?'

'Master, plenty man 'e come. All 'e come long water.' Les scrambled up the tree beside him and pulled out his binoculars.

'There's a hell of a lot of people drifting down the river hanging onto logs,' he announced after a few moments. 'As far as I can see they are all natives.'

We ordered the boys to stand to. Not only the police, but the cooks and every other native member of the party were armed, so we had in all quite a respectable little force. Nevertheless, five minutes later we breathed a sigh of relief when Kari stepped ashore, wringing the water from his loincloth, to tell us that seventy natives from Chivasing and the nearby village of Teraran were accom-panying him, and that the luluai of Chivasing had come to 'boss' the men. Though the danger from crocodiles was great, they had made the journey downstream in the usual

Markham way – gripping a log or plank and floating with the current.

Kari tossed his rifle to one of the police to clean the muddy Markham water out of it. He then explained the reason for the delay. It had taken him some time to assemble the men, he told us, for in these troubled times most of them were living in houses widely scattered among the gardens. He had found that there were not enough natives to cope with all our gear, and there were further delays while he sent a message to Teraran asking for extra assistance.

We interrupted the luluai to give him a couple of dozen sticks of tobacco and some newspaper to distribute, so that each man received a smoke for the road. Then he told us how he proposed to transfer our party and gear across the river. We were to move that afternoon to a little group of rough shelters a few miles upstream, and spend the night there. In the morning he would arrange for the construction of rafts to take us over the river. We felt that to have to spend another night on the south bank of the river was not only irritating but dangerous: we were most anxious to get out of the flat country, where we might at any time encounter a Japanese patrol from Madang or Lae. But there was nothing we could do but accept the luluai's suggestion.

We asked Kari what he thought of the general attitude of the people. Could they be trusted? He replied that they had probably been telling the truth when they said there were no enemy patrols in the vicinity, but he thought we should take no risks.

The walk to the shelters took till almost sunset. There was no track, and we had to crash through kunai and jungle, from time to time splashing through the shallow water at the edge of the stream. We passed many gardens and many clumps of bananas. Several rough houses belonged to the Chivasing people, we were told. They spent a good deal of their time on the south bank of the river, we were surprised to hear. This would be unwelcome news for the district officer, who had planned to keep the area between the Watut and Wampit rivers an uninhabited no-man's land.

The huts where we were to spend the night were just rough thatch-covered platforms, dirty and rather smelly, standing a couple of hundred yards from one arm of the Markham on a low-lying piece of ground which looked as though it would be inundated during the wet season.

Upon our arrival the luluai announced that he and his people would go back across the river to Chivasing for the night and return in the morning. Les and I discussed this with Kari and Watute, and finally agreed to let them go provided a couple of his men remained with us. The word 'hostage' was not actually mentioned, but the old man knew well enough what we were getting at, and selected two men to stay. They were so ready to remain in our camp that we felt sure the natives were not contemplating any treachery. They seemed pleased at their luck – looking forward, no doubt, to a good feed of tinned meat and plenty of smokes at our expense. When the luluai started off home with the rest of his people Kari and Constable Witolo were sent with them, to sleep in the village and keep an eye on things generally, and to make sure that they really did return.

The only water came from the Markham, and when dipped from the river in a billy it was so charged with silt that it resembled porridge. The natives drank it unconcernedly, though they admitted that it sometimes made their throats sore. In spite of our raging thirst Les and I waited for about an hour while half an inch of mud settled on the bottom of the billy, and then we carefully transferred the somewhat clearer water to another billy, to be boiled for tea.

There was a steady breeze, and the night was cool and almost free from mosquitoes. We sat for a couple of hours round the fire, smoking our pipes and yarning to the police, who kept us in gales of laughter with Rabelaisian tales of their experiences. These were mostly lies, no doubt, but it was all good fun, and each strained his imagination to outdo the others. By eleven o'clock a faint silvery light reflected from the few scattered clouds indicated that the moon would soon rise, and Les and I turned in. But the story-telling went on, in a lower tone – and probably continued most of the night, but we were not awake to hear it.

It was midday before the luluai returned, accompanied by about thirty men carrying great lengths of vine which they had cut in the bush earlier that day. Under the luluai's supervision, they started making four rafts, which he said would carry all our gear. They cut down banana-plants for the job. No doubt the cellular inside of the banana-palm makes it very buoyant, but to us it seemed a waste, for the hard cooking banana is one of the staple foods of these people.

Eight or ten banana-plants, laid side by side and lashed with vine, formed the main body of the raft. Several short, very thick logs were then laid crosswise over it, and a rough platform of smaller poles was built on top of them. The solid lower part, made of banana-palms, would be under water, while the platform of poles would keep our gear high and dry. Such at least was the theory of it, but when the cargo was piled aboard, all the lowest things were awash. It was just as well they were all more or less impervious to water – our iron patrol-boxes and cases of meat – not the radio set or our blankets.

Four of our boys could not swim at all, so we ordered one to board each raft. This extra load settled the rafts even deeper into the water, and we asked the luluai anxiously whether they were safe. He dismissed our foolish fears with an airy wave of the hand. Hadn't he been arranging this sort of thing for years and years? That was true, but we felt far from happy about those four extraordinary craft moored to the bank by vines and stakes. This was only a minor channel of the mighty Markham, yet even here the current was plucking at them as though eager to hurl them away to destruction.

By the time loading was complete the sun was getting low and the luluai wished to start. However, there had recently been great activity by a slow, old-fashioned Japanese observation-plane known to the troops as Photo Joe, and so we waited till almost dusk, when there would be less chance of being spotted if Photo Joe happened to be on the prowl.

Finally, about five o'clock, we pushed off. The four boys on the rafts had Owen sub-machine-guns across their knees, for they would be the only ones able to shoot if there were trouble. The strong swimmers of the party plunged gaily in, each pushing a log in front of him for support. Those of us whose swimming was nothing to boast of – this included Les and myself – clung to the sides of the rafts, to be carried along as the Chivasing boys pushed and hauled and strained. All the hazards of a sea voyage were to be had in a trip across this incredible stream – reefs, islands, currents, waves, and sand-banks – any one of which might have wrecked us. Our method of progress was much the same as that used by the canoe-boys at Kirkland's – across to the first island, haul the raft upstream to the top of the island, then off into the current of the second channel. After three such operations we were into the last and largest stream, and the real north bank of the Markham came into view.

'Master, me lookim Kari now Witolo!' called one of the boys from his raft.

'True! Two-fella 'e wait long you me!' another cried from his vantage-point on top of the cargo. They waved and called to Kari and Witolo, who were waiting at the water's edge about three hundred yards downstream.

The bank seemed to be flying past at a terrific rate, and the boys grunted and panted as, pushing with one arm and swimming with the other, they strove to force their reluctant craft across into slacker water. Les and I, no longer merely passengers, threw our weight into the struggle. Inch by inch we drew nearer to the shore, until the men who were standing with Kari and Witolo were able to throw out long vine ropes and haul us to dry land.

Stepping ashore, we found our pockets, socks, and boots full of silt and gravel drifted in by the river, and our tempers were not improved by the sight of several tall canoe masts showing above the kunai. It seemed that these people had canoes after all! We called upon the luluai to explain.

'Ah, they are very old canoes!' he said glibly. 'They could not possibly be used to make a crossing of the river.'

But Watute, sent to investigate, reported that the canoes were in perfect condition, some of them new. They were partly concealed in a small backwater, and this had caused the illusion that their masts were rising out of the kunai.

Confronted with this, the luluai was silent, and with downcast gaze curled his toes up in the dust with embarrassment.

We were furious that all our gear should have been entrusted to those crazy rafts, and we had had such an uncomfortable crossing, when it all might have been accomplished with speed, safety, and comfort. However, we restrained our anger, for we dared not antagonize the people, or they would refuse to carry for us next day. With a few general remarks expressing our low opinion of liars, we moved off up the path to the village, followed by the people carrying our cargo. The motive in concealing the canoes was plain enough of course: they had grown tired of maintaining the 'ferry service' at Kirkland's, and now that it had been discontinued they sought to prevent its re-establishment by hiding the canoes.

Chivasing, with a population of about five hundred, was built on a strip of slightly rising ground about a mile from the river. Round about the village the people had planted thriving coconut-groves, which supplied them with much of their food, fuel, and building material. The houses stood in lines, radiating, like the spokes of a wheel, from a large open space worn bare and smooth by the passage of many feet. They were well built, designed for this hot region with the rooms well above ground and largely open at the sides. These neat dwellings were another example of the mastery over their environment achieved by these 'backward' people. I remembered the reflection of Joseph Conrad, looking for the first time upon the Bangkok of his day, that in all the habitations he saw in that city 'there was probably not half a dozen pounds of nails'.

As soon as we had found a house to sleep in, and seen the gear safely stacked beneath it, I had a look round the village, though it was now nearly dark. I always studied the surroundings of a new camp – a precaution that saved my life, a couple of months later, in this very village. A broad, clear creek, from which the villagers drew their water, flowed across the north end of the clearing. The farther bank was covered with dense jungle and vines.

As there would be a moon shining in the early hours of the morning we decided not to wait for sunrise but to leave at about four-thirty. The luluai was told, and we arranged for the sentry to call him in the morning.

'Do you reckon it's worth unpacking the cooking gear for a meal?' Les asked.

'I don't think so. What about just having a tin of bully beef and some biscuits?'

'Suits me all right. We'll have the milk of a green coconut to drink, too. I don't fancy that water unless it's boiled.'

We squatted in the dark on the edge of the veranda and ate the rough meal in our fingers. Then, stripping off our wet clothes, we rolled beneath mosquito-nets and slept.

VII

I SEEMED HARDLY to have fallen asleep when I felt a hand on my shoulder and heard the soft, husky voice of Constable Nabura:

'Master! Four o'clock! You-me go now.'

A grey light filled the village, and I thought for a moment that we had overslept and that it was already morning. The watch, however, showed exactly four o'clock, and we saw that the overcast sky and a slight misty rain had diffused the moonlight, giving it the appearance of the dim light of early dawn.

We tossed the mosquito-nets aside, shivering slightly as we pulled on our damp boots and clothes. The stillness was being broken by the grunts and yawns of sleepy men as the police went from house to house rousing the carriers. Here and there flickering lights appeared as almost-cold embers were blown into a blaze, and one by one the men wandered over, yawning, rubbing their eyes, and hitching their loincloths about their waists.

By the light of torches of flaming coconut-fronds the cargo was lined along the track and a man told off for each load. Half a dozen women were coming with the party, not only to carry food for their men but to help them with the carrying. Accompanied by Kari and the luluai Les went along the line, checking each load and making sure that it was securely fastened. Then, at the command 'All right, walkabout!' the long line of natives picked up their loads and headed north along the narrow track through the kunai, towards the mountains.

We passed the last house of Chivasing and made our way between the tall rows of coconuts. Two towering palms at the end of the row looked like gateposts against the grey-silver sky. They were, in another sense, like a gate, for each time I crossed the Markham on my way to the mountains I felt I had passed through a door into another life. The door closed behind me, and the life on the far side of it was forgotten. The whole universe seemed to be contracted to a few score native villages and their black inhabitants.

We hoped to reach Sintagora village, in the Middle Erap, that night. There we would be well into the hills, off the flat country, among a dense population where carriers would be readily available, and whose foods were plentiful and easily purchased. This first day's journey was the most hazardous, for in a few hours' time we would cross the important foot-track which ran the whole length of the Markham Valley, and which the Japanese were now using for increasingly frequent trips from Madang to Lae. We would have to pass right through a place where they usually camped – namely, the old Wawin rest-house, in peacetime a sort of half-way house for the patrol officer making his way from Lae to the Upper Markham. The surrounding country was so flat and devoid of cover that an enemy reconnaissance plane, or a sentry on one of the low foothills, could scarcely fail to see us. Nabura and a couple of the local men hurried ahead to the Wawin rest-house – if there were any signs of the enemy they would return and warn us, otherwise they would wait at the junction till we arrived.

An hour or so out from Chivasing, in a hamlet comprising about a dozen houses, we paused for a few moments to allow the stragglers to catch up. It would soon be daylight. Already the darkness seemed to be less intense, and the drizzle of rain had ceased.

We had made a further mile or two on our north-ward journey when the sun rose, an indistinct yellow blot in the grey sky, and the oppressive, steamy heat of the Markham day began in earnest. At a quarter to seven Constable Nabura suddenly materialized out of the bushes beside me.

'Master, road belong Markham close to now!'

'Japan 'e stop? You lookim leg belong 'en?' I asked.

There were quite a number of enemy footprints, he said, made by the well-known rubber shoe with the heavy tread on the sole. None of the prints seemed to be very recent.

The two local men who had gone ahead with Nabura were immediately posted as sentries on the road, one on either side of the junction.

By the time Nabura had finished his report Les had moved up, and I repeated swiftly to him what the native had told me.

'That's good. But I don't think we ought to stop here, do you?'

'No. We ought to push on and cross the road, and keep going for at least an hour before we have a spell.'

We called all the police together and told them they were to keep the line tight and compact and allow no straggling. We wanted to cross the danger spot as quickly and inconspicuously as possible.

In close order, the line moved forward. From this point onwards there was no track to Sintagora, and we either had to break our way across country through the kunai, or follow the bed of the Wawin River. Deciding to go by the river, we plunged in and began plodding upstream against the current. In the lower reaches we often sank to our waists in the soft ooze, and had to be extricated by the boys. Higher up, where the bed was more solid, fine gravel worked its way into our boots and socks, chafing every inch of skin from our feet, which were softened – almost as if they had been parboiled – by long immersion. In spite of these disadvantages it was an excellent route for us under the circumstances, for we were walking in the bed of the river some ten feet below the level of the plain, and were thus hidden from observers on the ground, while the trees which lined the banks and overhung the water gave perfect concealment from patrolling aircraft. Moreover, we left no tracks behind.

Shortly after midday Les came splashing up to me. 'Do you notice how the banks are increasing in height?'

'Yes – it's almost a gorge we're getting into.'

'You might say we're into the foothills, in fact. There are small tributary streams coming in from the sides now.'

With every mile we advanced, the stream became more and more a mountain river, and the valley walls grew higher and steeper, while the water became cooler on our legs.

About four o'clock the luluai and a couple of the older men held a brief conference, and it was decided to leave the Wawin and follow one of the small tributaries which joined it from the east. This stream rose up steeply, its bed rough and boulder-strewn. Half an hour's climbing

brought us out on an open kunai spur, which we ascended to the top of the ridge, and Sintagora came into view,
a further half-hour's walk round the ridge.

We had seen no Erap natives: unless they had spotted
us earlier in the day our coming would be a complete
surprise to them. When we entered the village at sunset
surprise was hardly the word to express the looks on the
faces of the people as they saw white men and a long line
of carriers approaching from that unexpected direction.

When they had recovered their composure, however,
they proved to be friendly, and showed us the way to the
house-kiap and then helped the exhausted Chivasings
with their burdens.

Sintagora was a lovely place. It was, we estimated, a
couple of thousand feet above sea-level, and commanded
a splendid view of the Markham Valley. We could just see
Salamaua across the blue waters of the Huon Gulf.

Scarcely had we asked for food when the open grassy
space in front of the house-kiap was filled with women
carrying bilums of excellent sweet potatoes, bananas, and
papaws. Several natives ran up with English potatoes from
the gardens.

It was too late for the Chivasings to return home –
they were too tired to make the journey, anyhow – so we
bought a lot of food for them and asked the tultul of Sintagora to see that they all found a place to sleep. We were
tired too, after thirteen hours on the track, and after a quick
meal we turned in, rolling ourselves in three blankets, so
cool was the night, and not bothering about mosquito-nets,
for there was no sign of the pests.

Early next morning the Chivasing people assembled
in front of the house-kiap and were paid for their day's
work. Each man received a shilling and a razor-blade, and
the women who had accompanied the line were each given

a strip of calico for a loincloth. These were substantial presents in those days of scarcity, and the natives were delighted. The luluai, too, came in for a little extra present, and with a smart salute he led his people quickly away, to get as far as possible along the track before the sun became hot.

We decided not to move farther that day, but to remain among the people, making friends with them and learning all we could of enemy movements and propaganda. As far as we could discover there had been no visits by the Japanese to the area, and the people seemed to know very little about them. Of course, they knew that Lae and Salamaua were in enemy hands, but that was the extent of their knowledge. We were uneasy when they told us that a native mission teacher who was living in the vicinity had run away into the bush and would not come to see us.

A lot more food was brought in during the morning, and we paid for it in salt, which the people craved for. It was well that we had brought three big drums of it. The slightest amount spilt on the ground was at once carefully scraped onto a leaf by some thrifty mother and carried away as though it were a rare gem.

Les looked at the pile of native food with satisfaction.

'It's good to see the food situation's O.K. I think we only brought one bag of rice for our boys, didn't we?' he asked, drawing reflectively on his after-breakfast cigarette.

'That's right – only one,' I replied. 'It'll do for a while if we have to hole up and remain hidden. We can all feed from it without having to approach the villages for food.'

'Not only that, of course – we may easily be forced into an uninhabited area where we can't buy food anyhow.'

I spent the morning giving medical treatment to the natives of Sintagora and surrounding villages. There were many bad cases of yaws. I treated the huge, sickening ulcers by injecting an arsenical preparation. In a few days this would dry up the open, running sores as if by magic. The natives, no doubt, imagined that it was magic, and elderly men who hadn't a sign of a sore presented themselves for a 'shoot' – not with the idea of having any disease cured, but to keep themselves strong and virile. I suppose I gave a hundred injections that day, besides doing dozens of dressings for tropical ulcers and minor wounds.

Towards evening Les set up the radio to test it for the first time. We were quite tense with excitement as he called Port Moresby and then switched over to see if we had been heard. The usefulness of the patrol depended entirely on effective radio communications. If they failed we had taken the risk of coming to live in the mountains for nothing.

The voice of the operator in Moresby was clear and loud: 'You're coming through well, old chap. Go ahead and pass your message.'

Les shot a quick, smiling glance of triumph at me, and then bent intently over his Morse key. Although we could receive the powerful Port Moresby station clearly, the transmitting power of our little set was so small that we had to send our messages in Morse. Les tapped out a brief message, merely telling Moresby where we were, and that all was quiet.

'All O.K., AVL, all O.K. See you again,' replied the Moresby operator – thereby breaking all formal rules of radio procedure.

The air was fresh and very cool when, with a sigh of contentment, we rolled into bed. We were into the mountains; the natives seemed friendly; food was abundant; our communications were in good order. What more could one ask? With a shout to Corporal Kari to make sure a sentry was posted, we pulled the blankets about us and were asleep.

The next stage of our journey was to Fi, a village eight or ten miles north. We started at dawn, with Sintagora people and men from all the surrounding settlements bearing the cargo. The Erap, swinging round to the west, lay across our path, as formidable a stream in the mountains as it was on the flat country. Assisted by the local men, who knew almost every stone in its bed, we made the crossing without accident, clutching a stout vine that was stretched from bank to bank. There could have been no more dangerous enterprise than trying to cross this stream without the assistance of the people who lived on its banks.

We were established in the house-kiap at Fi by two o'clock, before the afternoon rain began. Our meal was prepared by Tauhu, the substitute cook, for we had sent Dinkila on a visit to his home village of Bivoro, to pick up any gossip about the Japanese. The alacrity with which he seized the opportunity to call at his home town suggested to the other boys that he had a girlfriend there, and they made countless ribald jests about it. Dinkila only gave a rather smug smile, which seemed to say: You're jealous — you wish you were coming with me.

About four o'clock we set up the radio to hear the weekly talk in pidgin English. This was designed as a propaganda service to natives, who could not, of course, speak English. This day the talk was given by John Murphy, a leading expert in pidgin and the author of the first pidgin dictionary with any claim to completeness.

Murphy's talk was listened to intently by our police and other boys, but the natives of Fi gave it only a perfunctory hearing, and sat there without the slightest glimmer of enthusiasm, or even understanding. No doubt these broadcasts had a certain value in some areas, but as far as we were concerned they were a failure.

When the talk was over I wondered whether the natives were having a sly joke at our expense when they asked us to see their tame cockatoos. The birds seemed to have a large vocabulary of their own, but when I tried some pidgin on them I caused much amusement. 'Cocky savvy talk-place, master! No savvy talk pidgin!' the kanakas said, laughing heartily.

Another pet in this village was a tame hornbill. He sat calmly in the branches of a breadfruit-tree, catching with unfailing accuracy in his enormous beak the bits of banana we threw up to him. He seemed to understand the local tongue, and would fly down to be petted whenever they called him.

Fi showed no sign of enemy influence, and in the morning we walked eastward to Sugu, across the steep valley of the Nambuk River. The Sugu people showed us to the rest-house, and we stopped, astonished, when we saw it.

'Hey, look at that!' exclaimed Les.

'Brand new! Look – the grass thatching hasn't even dried out yet!'

'I'd say it's only been finished a few days,' said Les, who had moved over closer. 'Yes. Look here – there's still sap oozing from the ends of some of the logs.'

'Now, why would they bother building a rest-house when there's nobody to use it?'

'You'd think they'd be only too glad to get out of it. Let's talk to the tultul and see what he's got to say.'

We summoned the tultul and asked him why the house had been built. He replied that when he had heard of our arrival at Sintagora he expected us to pass through Sugu, and had at once made arrangements for us to be properly accommodated.

'Look,' he said to support his point, 'the house is quite new.'

'Why did you build it so big?' asked Les. 'There's room enough for twenty men to sleep in it!'

For just a second the tultul was stumped, but his recovery was magnificent. His eyes fell upon our huge pile of stores and equipment.

'I heard from the talk that you had a lot of cargo,' he said calmly, 'and so I thought I ought to see there was plenty of room for it.'

We looked at each other, and Les shrugged his shoulders in response to my raised eyebrows.

'All right, tultul, you can go. Tell some people to bring us food.'

He vanished at once, and we heard him shouting to the women to bring food.

'What do you think?' I asked as soon as we were alone.

'I think it stinks!' Les exclaimed. 'But why has he built it? There isn't a single sign of Japanese patrolling. I feel certain that if the Nips have been through here we'd have heard at least a whisper of it. It's got me beat.'

Till late at night we puzzled over the building that sheltered us, and got nowhere. We dropped off to sleep at last, still wondering.

Next morning we set out for Gain, which I had last visited on the way out of the Wain country early in the year. If the large new rest-house at Sugu had been a mystery, the condition of the track to Gain was an even greater enigma. Grass had been cut, fallen trees removed, landslips cleared, and a serviceable bridge constructed over each stream. Such diligence on the part of the kanakas and zeal on the part of the village officials had been uncommon even in peacetime, when there had been regular routine patrols to inspect such things. At a time when patrolling had ceased, it was nothing short of extraordinary to see a bridle-path so well tended, and we asked the village officials to explain their new-found conscientiousness. But they would say nothing. Apart from an occasional mumbled 'Work belong me' from the tultul, they maintained a stubborn, though embarrassed, silence.

This was only our first taste of an attitude which prevailed over almost the whole of the Huon Peninsula. We were to encounter many such strange activities, and nowhere would the people explain the motive for their unwonted energy. Model villages, well-tended cemeteries, a high standard of cleanliness, especially in regard to latrines – in fact, all the things that a hardworking administration had been trying for so long to introduce to village life – seemed to have become a fait accompli overnight. All our inquiries failed to breach the blank wall of silence that the natives had erected. But it could not conceal the profound uneasiness which lay behind it. In the end, our nerves began to be affected, for the continuous sense of being alone in the midst of some vast but intangible force imposes a strain even on the most unimaginative temperament. Not till the following year, and then only by piecing together many shreds of evidence, was it possible to construct even a partial picture of the sinister and, to a white man, almost incomprehensible forces then at work in the area.

At Gain everything seemed to be the same as when I had passed the previous January. Dinkila, who was waiting for us at the entrance to the village, said there had been no news of the enemy at his home village of Bivoro, and apparently no Japanese had been near Gain either. Nevertheless, he said, something seemed to be happening here at Gain which he could not quite fathom. The natives would tell him nothing.

The buildings of Boana Mission could be seen from Gain, and we studied them carefully through binoculars.

There was no sign of smoke from cooking-fires, and it was too far away to see whether there were any people about. The luluai and the tultul of Gain declared that to their knowledge the enemy had never been in Boana. We felt that if the Japs had visited there, the news would certainly have reached Gain. And so we decided that we could safely go on to Boana the next day, by my usual route through Kasin, Wasinim, and Dzendzen.

I ate tea in a cheerful mood that night.

'I'm thinking of Jock McLeod,' I said to Les, who had looked up inquiringly at my chuckle. 'Wait till I tell him his pessimistic prophecies were all wrong! I felt all along that the Nips wouldn't have found their way in here yet.'

Next morning we had our gear lined along the track and were about to order the carriers to move off along the road to Boana when I noticed the tultul of Kasin, which was the next village on the road, hovering at the edge of the clearing. He caught my eye, blinked, and looked away. Then he cast another quick glance at me. He seemed in two minds whether to approach me or run away. This was very strange behaviour, for he had always been most friendly and helpful. I called him over.

'Why didn't you come and talk to me?' I asked in an injured tone. 'I thought we were friends.'

'Master, me like talk lik-lik long you,' he mumbled. 'Me got talk.'

'Well, what is the news?' I asked, as he stood there silent for some moments.

He stared at the ground and shifted his shoulders uncomfortably. Then, trembling and swallowing, he told us in barely audible monosyllables that a Japanese patrol had visited Boana. By painfully minute cross-examination we placed the date of the visit as 17th April. It was now 1st May. He either could not or would not tell where they had come from, nor where they had gone. He knew only that they had been there on the 17th and were now gone.

I retracted mentally the things I was going to say to Jock. An enemy patrol – almost certainly much stronger than ours, if the Nips were following their usual practice – had appeared out of the blue and then vanished just as mysteriously. Not the least disquieting feature was that the natives were concealing what they knew: either lying to us or keeping silent. For all we knew, the enemy might be making a systematic tour of all the villages – might swoop down on Gain itself at any moment. As the realization burst upon us we almost unconsciously cast a glance over our shoulders at the high mountains behind. I called Kari, told him briefly what had happened, and ordered him to post a policeman a few hundred yards along each track leading into the village, so that we could not be surprised.

Using the map, and information supplied by kanakas, we found another route to my old camp at Bawan, skirting Boana itself. It involved penetrating deeper into the mountains, to a village called Sedau, and a long walk over what appeared to be rough and difficult country. It would have been most foolish, however, to have risked contact with the enemy at that stage.

'If we get into a scrap now,' said Les, 'the only thing that'll happen is that we'll lose a good part of our supplies. I'm all in favour of keeping well clear of trouble until we've got all this junk planted somewhere.'

'Me, too. The longer we can keep out of strife the better.'

It was no part of our duty to seek combat. Our role was to see and not be seen: once we clashed with the enemy they would become so wary that our chances of obtaining worthwhile information would be much reduced.

We set out at once for Sedau, some four hours' climb into the mountains behind Gain, where we felt it would be safe to spend the night. By the time we had been going a couple of hours we were enveloped in dense fog which, though it had the advantage of concealing us, prevented us from observing the surrounding country.

Through occasional breaches in the fog we watched Sedau from a hillside a few hundred yards above it. Natives were moving about, and there seemed to be no sign of anything unusual happening, so we marched into the village. The people received us without enthusiasm or any other emotion, showed us to a house to sleep in, brought us a reasonable quantity of food, and left us alone. They said they had never seen, and practically never heard of, the Japanese.

Towards evening Kari and Watute, who had been poking about the village, asked us to look at a large house in course of construction a little distance from the village, and an enormous latrine nearby.

'What do you suppose they are for?' Watute asked, after he and Kari had drawn our attention to the unusual design of the house.

Les and I could not guess their purpose, and asked Kari and Watute what they thought.

'I think these people have heard the Japanese are coming, and want to have houses ready for them,' Kari said. 'The natives here are much more frightened of the Japanese than they are of us, you know. They have heard all these stories of the Japanese cutting people's heads off.'

'It is only a guess, master, but it is the only thing I can think of,' Watute put in. 'As if the Japanese would know what a latrine was for!' he added with a chuckle, for he was familiar with the filthy habits of many of the enemy soldiers.

Les sent for some of the villagers again, and we questioned them closely, trying to detect any inconsistency in their stories. They were unshakable: they knew nothing whatever of the Japanese, and were building the house and the latrine for their own use.

'Do you use that latrine yourselves?' Watute shot in suddenly.

'Yes,' said the tultul.

'How long has it been finished?'

'About two weeks.'

'See, master!' Watute said triumphantly. 'They are lying about something, for that latrine has not been used at all.'

But even this could not shake the tultul's composure. He had his story, and he was sticking to it.

In the morning we called for men to carry our gear to Sokulen, a small village in the hills directly behind Boana. There was no dearth of men: willing carriers appeared from all the houses, each man eager to be on the road. This anxiety to be rid of us confirmed our suspicions that something was amiss.

Watute watched their hurried preparations with a sardonic grin.

'Master lookim?' he asked. 'Altogether man 'e hurry up too much long rausim you-me.' And indeed their indecent haste to see us beyond their borders could not have escaped even the most unpractised eye.

The track to Sokulen led up a tributary creek of the Kusip River, over a low divide, and into a tributary of the Bunzok. Most of the way we walked knee-deep in icy water, slithering and stumbling on the stony beds of the streams. The wear and tear on our boots was very great, for at least half of each day's walking was along a watercourse, and the boots were never dry from one day's end to another. They were soon reduced to a sodden pulp, which fell to pieces. Already, only a week out from

PETER RYAN

the Markham, our first pair were showing signs of disin-
tegration, and it seemed that our five spare pairs each
would be none too many.

Where the track to Sokulen lay across the divide it
seemed as though it had been subjected to recent heavy
traffic. The ground was muddy and churned up, and the
track was much wider than the usual native pad. Bamboos,
which grew in thick clumps on either side, had been
slashed and cut – a thing no native, appreciating their value,
would ever do. It looked as though a Japanese patrol had
passed that way, but heavy rain had obscured all definite
footprints, and we could not tell whether the travellers had
worn boots, or in what direction they had gone. The
police, however, were of the opinion that those who had
passed before us were not natives, and that they had travelled in the opposite direction to ours. They indicated the
angle at which the slashes had been made in the bamboos,
and pointed out that if we, for instance, wished to make
such a cut we would have to stop and turn round, whereas
a man travelling the other way could do it as he walked.

'I wonder if we would have thought that one out?'
said Les.

He called the tultul of Sedau over and questioned
him on the state of the track. The tultul still insisted that
he had never seen a Jap, but he was so ill at ease that we
did not believe him.

While we were talking to the tultul one of the police
noticed two natives running down the track from the
direction of Sokulen. They made straight for Les and me
and, without waiting to get their breaths, told us excitedly
that a large party of Japanese had arrived at Bungalamba on
their way to Lae, and that all the village officials of the
surrounding settlements had gone to meet them. The two
boys did not know what had happened then, because they
had hurried to tell us about the arrival of the Japs. We

pointed to the track, and asked what had caused it to get into such a condition.

The boys looked at us in astonishment, saying, 'Japanese, of course! Didn't the tultul of Sedau tell you about them? They slept one night in his village, and told him to build a house for them, because lots of Japanese parties would be coming through here.'

Les and I noticed the venomous look the tultul shot at them, and we could not help laughing, in spite of the grave news.

'Where did they go after they left Sedau?' I asked.

'Through the Kisengan, in the Erap River. They slept at Sugu on the way.'

My scalp prickled, and I heard Les's sharply drawn breath. So that was it: the new rest-house at Sugu, where we had slept, had, only a few nights before, housed Japanese, and the track, which we had remarked as being uncommonly well tended, had been cleared in honour of the enemy! Twice already we had crossed the trail of that party, and now there was news of another one ahead of us.

The game played by the natives was understandable and, from their own point of view, justified. They wanted neither Japanese nor Australians wandering round their country. Both were merely nuisances to them – useless people who ate their food, had to be carried for and shown their way round the bush. The natives were frightened, too, that there would be a battle between us in which they would inevitably suffer, and they were bending all their energies to keeping us apart, each in ignorance of the other's presence.

From our point of view things were as bad as could be, and we could not continue wandering round the mountains blindly crossing and recrossing the paths of enemy patrols. It was a shock to find that the Japanese had departed from their habit of the previous year and were now patrolling extensively in the wild mountain country into which they had been once so reluctant to venture. But it was a worse shock to find that the natives were giving them as much assistance as they gave us: this attitude I blamed largely on the fact that for two and a half months the area had been abandoned by us. If I had never left the country, but had stayed on in the villages, I felt sure that things would never have come to this pass.

There was only one thing to do now: we must get all our cargo safely into some remote spot and then find the enemy patrols for ourselves. We told the tultul and the two messengers from Sokulen of our intention, and the three of them joined in tearful entreaties to us to leave immediately.

'Go back to the Markham at once,' they pleaded. 'If you go now you will be able to reach your own people safely. If you stay here you will certainly be killed. There are so many Japanese, and if they find we are hiding you from them they will cut our heads off. Some of them are coming to sit down at Boana Mission,' they added.

Jock's words came back to me: 'If I were the Jap commander I'd have a standing patrol at Boana.' It seemed as if his gloomy forecast was being fulfilled in earnest.

In spite of the pleas of the local natives we resumed the journey to Sokulen quickly, after having told the police what the situation was and sending Watute and Pato ahead to scout. At a point on the track which offered a particularly good view of Boana we paused for ten minutes to let the carriers catch their breath, while we watched the mission. Through binoculars we could see right into the houses, and since there was still no movement we concluded that the mission was, at any rate up to this moment, unoccupied.

At Sokulen we set up the radio and informed headquarters in Port Moresby that the Japanese seemed to have taken up inland patrolling in a big way. Then, still keeping the unwilling Sedau people as carriers, as punishment for having lied to us, we pushed up the Bunzok Valley to an out-of-the-way village called Bandong. It was dark when we arrived, and raining hard. The Bandong people received us with indifference and showed us to the only spare house in the village. Wet through, and too tired to eat, Les and I and all the boys lay on the floor and went to sleep.

In the morning I awoke to a depressing sight: a packed mass of black, brown, and white humanity lying steaming in their wet, dirty clothes, and a house looking even filthier than it had appeared by torchlight the night before. I sat up and shivered. Bandong, one of the highest villages in the Wain, was about six thousand feet above sea-level. No wonder it was cold. I roused Dinkila and Tauhu and told them to light a fire and prepare some tea. Les woke, and we went outside with maps and compass to plan our next move.

'This is a pretty remote spot, all right,' said Les. 'But if the Nips are visiting all the villages it won't do to stick round the houses. We must get out among the gardens, disperse our stores, and lie low till that mob at Bungal-amba has gone on.'

'These people grow yams,' I remarked. 'They proba-bly have little storehouses scattered about the gardens.'

'They're sure to,' Les agreed. 'Let's go and sink this tea, and then we'll have a look round.'

The sweet black tea, scalding hot, gave us new life. As we drank it, we called some of the Bandong people to us, to explain what we intended to do and to seek their help. They were shy, for they had had very little contact with white men. Only one of them spoke pidgin, and he had to translate for the benefit of the others. They soon caught the idea, and brought us to a spot about an hour's walk farther upstream, leading into a tributary valley.

There was a garden here – it had been abandoned the year before, the Bandong men said. Dotted here and there about it, but hardly visible till they were pointed out, were five tiny shacks used for storing yams and firewood. The valley was so steep that it was possible to approach the houses only by the narrow path we were following. Even if we were discovered there, it would be no easy matter for the enemy to take us while our ammunition lasted. This was an ideal hiding-place.

Les and I decided to sleep in one of the shelters with Kari and Watute, and the other boys, with part of the stores, were to use the other four shacks. They were minute houses: one could not stand upright, even in the middle of the floor, while at the edges it was necessary to crawl. The one we were in, the largest, was not quite seven feet long. Les said that if you even wanted to change your mind you had to go outside the house to do it!

As soon as we had posted a sentry we ordered Dinkila to cook a large meal for us, and told the boys to prepare one for themselves. Then we changed into dry, warm clothes and squatted by the fire to read.

'We're safe for the present,' Les said. 'And, anyhow, it's no use trying to think about these things on an empty stomach.'

Dinkila excelled himself, and even made a batch of pancakes. When we had demolished his good work we lay on our blankets, maps spread before us, to make an appreciation of the local situation, and work out what we should do to meet it.

At present we considered ourselves pretty safe from attack, and probably would be safe as long as we remained here. On the other hand, it was too remote a spot for us to hear what was happening. It would be necessary, we decided, to move nearer to some of the more important tracks which traversed the Wain and Naba, but we could leave most of our food here as a reserve.

We were worried about the attitude of the native inhabitants of these parts. It was decidedly disturbing. In 1942 the kanakas would have informed me instantly if even a whisper of enemy patrols had reached them. Now they were at pains to conceal every enemy movement from us. The reason was that they feared the Japanese patrols – which moved in greater numbers than ours – more than they feared us. Stories of beheadings carried out by the Japanese seemed to have had a great effect upon the natives. We would have to try very hard to regain some of our influence with them, partly by propaganda through the local men Les had brought over from Moresby, and partly by judicious distribution of presents to influential natives.

We decided to remain two more days in our present hide-out, then venture out cautiously, ascertain the whereabouts of the Japanese, and if possible reach my old camp at Bawan, where I was better known and had more close friends among the local natives. It was no use, at the moment, formulating a detailed plan, since there were too many unknown factors.

We folded up the maps, opened a cake of ration chocolate, and addressed ourselves to reading again.

'Ha, what do you know! A crossword puzzle!' Les exclaimed as he turned over the last page of his magazine.

'Let's help do it,' I begged.

'No fear – I'll do it on my own first! But I'll only write very faintly in pencil, so that I can rub the letters out before I hand it over and give you a turn.'

'O.K., do that. I'll have my go tomorrow.'

Trade goods and other supplies had made so many carrier-loads that we had been forced to leave nearly all our books behind at Wampit. We had squeezed in a few paperbacks and a magazine or two, but it would not be long before we had read everything.

Next day brought a surprise visitor – Singin, tultul of Wampangan village. He had been among those village officials who had gone to meet the Japanese party at Bungalamba, and when we heard this we hoped to get some detailed first-hand information, for he was a shrewd, observant man. But we were disappointed, for Singin said that when he and his companions reached Bungalamba the Japanese had left, proceeding down the river through Mililuga and Gawan to Lae. There were about thirty of them, and they had come from Sio, on the north coast. Apparently the trip had been hard, for two of them were sick and were being carried.

We heard all this with mixed feelings. On the one hand, it was good to know the Japs were out of the way for the moment. On the other hand, if they had really come from Sio, and had crossed over the Saruwaged Range to do it, the mountains had clearly lost all terrors for them, and they would probably be prepared to chase us wherever we went. There was no certainty that the Japs had made the crossing, of course, and we could not understand why they should bother to do so when they could easily have walked round the beach or come by barge. Still, they had gone, and this was our chance to get to Bawan. We gave Singin a very handsome present – a tomahawk – and told him to return to his village and remain there until he heard from us, meanwhile having nothing to do with Japanese patrols. He agreed to do this, saying that he would send all his people into the bush if the enemy approached Wampangan.

We watched his long, lean figure disappear up the hillside.

'Too smooth by half,' Les said, shaking his head.

'Yes. He saw the Japs all right, I bet. All the same, I don't think we have anything to fear from him. He's shrewd enough to realize that we might win the war. He knows that if he tipped us off to the Nips and we were the victors he'd be in bad. I think he'll play a politician's game, but will see nobody gets hurt — as far as he can.'

That night Les went down with a sharp attack of fever, and we had to wait two days, until he was well enough to travel. The little houses were so cold that it is remarkable we were not all laid low with fever or pneumonia.

On 7th May we set out for Wampangan, travelling round the head of the Bunzok River and passing through the villages of Kawalan, Ganzegan, and Kwamboleng. Although the country was wild and steep, we moved much more quickly than before, because we had left more than half our cargo hidden in the garden at Bandong.

The road showed signs of recent maintenance work. But it was the villages that astonished me. In each case, including Wampangan, the old site had been abandoned and a new village of model houses had been built. There was also a great increase in the area of cultivation.

Singin greeted us effusively and announced his intention of co-operating whole-heartedly. His was not a very convincing performance, and one could quite easily have imagined him saying the same thing to the Japanese. However, we thanked him and gave him a small present, telling him to have carriers ready in the morning.

As we sat down to eat our tea by lantern-light Dinkila asked whether we would consider going to the mission, seeing we were so close, to shoot a bullock. He hinted that, though he was equal to the task if need be, it placed a strain on even the best cook's ingenuity if the meat always came out of a tin. A piece of nice grilled steak, now, he said...

He had struck the right note. Les and I looked at one another, our mouths watering.

'I'll go down there in the morning if you like,' I said. 'You can go straight to Bawan with the cargo. If all is well I should be there almost as soon as you are.'

'Do you think it's worth the risk?'

'I'm pinning my faith on Singin. I don't think he would let me go if the coast weren't clear. It's pretty safe, I reckon.'

In the morning Kari, Watute, and I set off for Boana, having received Singin's assurance that the mission was deserted. On a hill overlooking the mission station we hid for half an hour or so in a clump of bamboos, watching. One or two natives moved about the grass houses, but the usual brooding quietness lay over the iron-roofed ones. Of the enemy there was no sign, but we approached warily, Owen guns cocked. The mission schoolhouse seemed still to be in use, though we got the impression that it had been hurriedly vacated as we approached. As before, the feeling that hostile eyes were watching our every movement assailed us. Kari, who had been with me the first time I visited the mission, said he still thought it was 'place no good'. I agreed with him.

In the mission house various signs of the enemy visit remained. The organ had been broken open, and there was a pile of cigarette-butts on the veranda, as though a sentry had been posted there. All small pieces of cloth had been removed – presumably to patch clothes with, for native reports all agreed that the clothing worn by the Japanese was in an extremely tattered state. In their usual filthy way they had covered the veranda with excreta not six feet from where they had slept.

There was nothing of real interest to be seen, so we hurried across the now much overgrown and boggy aerodrome in search of the cattle, which we found grazing at the edge of the bush. It seemed as though the Japanese had tried to round them up: they had been very tame and quiet before, but now they fled as soon as they heard us approaching. Kari dropped to his knee and shot a big black bullock clean through the head as it ran. I looked at him approvingly. 'A good man to have around when the Nips turn up' was my unspoken comment on his marksmanship.

We skinned and quartered the bullock and hung the meat up under the trees. It would be brought on to us at Bawan by some of Singin's men. Then with a quick backward glance at the mission we hurried off to catch up with Les.

As we strode along the track I saw that it too had been cleared and levelled and that my last orders to the people – to let the roads revert to bush – had been ignored.

When I reached Bawan village Les had already arrived and told the people that I was following. They were standing about waiting for me, and though some of the older men greeted me with some show of affection, the tultul and the younger men made no attempt to conceal the fact that our presence would be a serious embarrassment to them. The camp itself was unchanged. Les had quickly installed himself, and out in the kitchen I could see a fire blazing, and Dinkila and Tauhu at work with billies and frying-pans.

'Rather cosy set-up,' Les said approvingly as he looked at the double roof and the canvas–lined walls. 'It'll keep pretty snug even on the coldest nights.'

'Yes, it's warm and comfortable, all right. When we get a fire going it'll look fine.'

Les examined the unorthodox architecture of the fireplace.

'Does it really work?' he asked.

'Most of the smoke goes out. After all, you aren't staying at the Ritz!'

Les grinned. 'No. I suppose I shouldn't complain. Ought to be glad to have a camp like this all ready made.'

For a few days it seemed that our routine at Bawan would be very much the same as it had been in December. Food was good and plentiful, and the people came every day to sell it. By ten each morning the grassy space in front of the house was filled as usual with chattering women bearing string bags of potatoes, bananas, beans, tomatoes, and every conceivable kind of vegetable. On one occasion, while buying food, I made one faux pas which might have spoilt our relations with the people. One woman stood a little apart, holding her string bag on her back, while the others had spread their bags open on the ground to display their wares. I bought all the food on the ground and then approached this woman.

'What have you got there?' I asked, peering at the indistinct shape in the bottom of the bag. 'Potatoes?'

'Potatoes!' she exclaimed indignantly. 'Piccaninny belong me!' And she produced from the bag her first child, a fine little boy about three months old. She was as proud as could be of him, and I hastily gave her a little present of salt to soothe her outraged feelings.

'Potatoes!' I heard her snort as she walked off down the hill with the others.

While I did medical work Les talked to the natives of the surrounding villages about the war, telling them of the ever-increasing air raids on Lae. As he spoke, planes were passing over the camp making their runs on the township, and the sound of bombing and anti-aircraft shelling could be heard clearly.

There was a series of earth-tremors while we were at Bawan, and a lot of heavy rain, resulting in numerous landslides. Often as we lay in bed at night we heard a loud crash followed by a thunderous roar, lasting sometimes for a couple of minutes, while the whole house trembled and creaked. And then in the morning there would be a huge piece of the mountainside lying in the valley below, often with trees still growing on it much the same as when it had been a few hundred feet higher up and part of the mountain.

At night, after Dinkila had placed the little kettle of black coffee on the table and fastened the canvas cover across the door, Les and I drew closer to the fire and, to pass the time away, played the old children's guessing game of Animal, Vegetable, or Mineral. We attained a high degree of proficiency in detecting such improbable objects as 'the left boot of the Japanese commander in Lae'.

Another little game after lights-out was to make up limericks about young girls from Bawan, Wampangan, and other villages in the district. Many of them were rather ingenious and amusing, but I cannot recall any which could properly be printed here.

Unfortunately this pleasant existence was not to last. On 12th May, just at dusk, two exhausted natives staggered into the camp, having run almost all the way from Samandzing. We helped them up into the house while, between great sobbing breaths, they told us that a Japanese party had arrived in Samandzing from Lae and had announced their intention of proceeding to Boana via Bawan. In 1942 this would not have been very serious news. The camp was some little distance from the main track, and I would merely have kept a very good watch and let the Japanese go past, secure in the knowledge that the local natives would not betray me. Now the situation was different. The attitude of the natives, though becoming friendly again, was far from certain. Worse still, they had been so busy with their road-building that a newly made track from Samandzing, twelve feet wide and as smooth as Collins Street, lay right in front of our door.

As Les set up the radio to tell Port Moresby of this latest development we wondered what to do next.

'We have to get out of here, that's certain,' Les said. 'You've been all round here before — where do you reckon is the best spot?'

'I think we ought to keep as close to the centre of things as we possibly can. There's plenty of villages where they would never find us in ten years, but which would be no good to us because we wouldn't hear a word of what's happening. I think if we go to Orin, a couple of hours away, we'll be safe enough for the present.'

'I'll take your word for it,' Les said as he plugged in the ear-phones. 'Get us a lamp, will you? I can't see what I'm doing.'

I told Dinkila to get Les a light, and ordered the rest of the men to prepare everything for the road so that we could get out of Bawan first thing in the morning. Kari doubled the sentries and sent one man to watch the track from Samandzing about half a mile out of Bawan. I was not seriously worried about an immediate attack, for if the Japanese had only just arrived in Samandzing it would be a good two days before they reached Bawan. But we would take no chances.

At first light next day all the men of Bawan came to carry our gear to Orin. I looked sadly at the vegetable garden I had planted in January. It was showing great promise, and we had already eaten in imagination the succulent peas and beans it would soon produce. I cast several regretful glances backwards as we moved up the hill to Gewak village, an hour away, and then round the hillside to Orin, a further hour.

The tultul of Orin, an old friend, greeted us warmly, and the people of the village seemed much better disposed than those of Bawan. There was no house-kiap, but they offered to clear out a couple of their own dwellings for us.

'I'm against sleeping in the villages now,' I said to Les. 'It's too risky. Even if the kanakas don't give us away deliberately, the Nips might wander in any time.'

'Yes – it's better in every way to keep out in the bush. We won't compromise the kanakas with the Nips then and to keep themselves in the clear they won't say anything about us hiding in the bush.'

'It's just a question of where to go. Look up there.' I pointed to the towering mountain which overshadowed Orin.

Les gave a low whistle. 'Do you reckon we can climb it?'

'I don't know, but let's ask the tultul. I'd like to have a go.'

The tultul was dubious. There was a way up, of course, he said, but it was not easy, and with all our cargo...

'Come on, tultul,' we said encouragingly. 'You show the way, and let us try.'

I have seldom seen a wilder place. We climbed almost eight hundred feet, straight up from the village, mostly over well-nigh vertical sheer rockfaces. In two places we had to pass beneath a torrent of water which drenched us and almost sent us flying into space. When we reached a small level clearing which looked as if it would do for a camp, we flopped to the ground.

'Fair enough! This will do me for the rest of the war!' I panted.

'Me too,' Les agreed. 'If the Nips get us here, they've earned the scalps.'

The Orin people helped us build two rough shelters out of the large shiny leaves of the wild breadfruit-tree, and we sat down to take careful stock of our situation.

Though safe, it was a miserable spot, for even when the sun came out, which was seldom, it did not penetrate the thick foliage. All next day it poured with rain, and our crude huts leaked badly. Only with difficulty could Dinkila and Tauhu keep a fire alight long enough to make a billy of tea. The rest of our food we ate cold from the tins.

I spent the day wrapped up in blankets, pretending I wasn't cold, while I read Noel Coward's autobiography, *Present Indicative*. Dusk was approaching when I put the book aside. I looked round in the green twilight and marvelled that for a short time I had forgotten my surroundings and been so lost in the picture Coward had painted of the bright footlights and the brilliant uniforms of *Cavalcade*. Uniforms! What grubby rags Les and I were wearing! What sodden felt hats, without chin-strap, badge, or pugaree! There had been a time when we had both appeared smart and shining on parade, but it was so long ago, and so much had happened in the meantime, that we could hardly remember it. In fact, everything seemed far away and long ago – dry clothes, cleanliness, safety, music, love – everything except green foliage, endless rain that hissed down through the trees, and natives squelching the mud between their bare toes and swearing continually at one another.

The momentary spell of Coward's stage had gone. I was aware of Watute and Pato standing beside me, legs caked in mud and wet sweaters steaming.

'Well, what is it?' I snapped.

They understood that I had not meant to be rude, for they just grinned and said they wanted to talk to me about an idea which had occurred to them. I passed them tobacco, and while they rolled themselves cigarettes Pato spoke for the two of them.

He was a local man, and knew both the Wain and Naba dialects. From remarks overheard in Gewak and Orin villages, he had learnt that the Japanese had put in a supply of food at Samandzing. He had discussed the matter with Watute, and between them they had evolved the theory that the food must be intended for Japanese troops being evacuated from Lae. Pato and Watute thought the party which was supposed to have crossed the range might have been looking for an escape-route.

'Evacuated? Escape-route? What do you mean?' I asked. 'Do you think the Japanese are going to give up Lae?'

They shrugged their shoulders. The air raids were getting heavier. No ships could get in with supplies. The submarines could not feed them. It was not for them to say whether the Japs were going to abandon Lae, but it was possible.

(As we discovered later, it was indeed the purpose of some of these Japanese patrols to discover tracks by which troops might be evacuated from Lae, and when the attack by the two Australian divisions came in September, the commanders were surprised at the enemy's extensive knowledge of the mountain trails, over which a great many of the Jap Lae garrison had made their way to safety. Our generals need not have been so surprised however, for having thought over what Watute and Pato had said it seemed to us more and more likely that they were right, and we therefore passed on the idea, for what it was worth, to headquarters. Apparently they did not think it was worth much, for they did nothing about it. And so the brilliant deductive work of two 'simple' natives was wasted.)

The present purpose of Pato and Watute was to visit Samandzing and see whether the information about the dump of food was correct. They would also do what they could to prove the other part of their hypothesis, and generally listen to the gossip around the villages. Pato said that his kinsmen would conceal their presence from the enemy if any Japanese were encountered, and he was sure they would be quite safe.

'It sounds a good idea to me,' said Les, who had been listening to the whole discussion intently. 'What do you think?'

'I agree. I think they ought to take plenty of trade goods, to buy food and information. I don't see how it could possibly do any harm, especially since Pato has all the local contacts.'

'All right, master. Tomorrow long too-light, me-fella go.' And having announced their intention of leaving at dawn next day, the two elderly warriors moved out through the rain to their own shelter among the trees a few yards away.

During the night I heard several of the boys coughing.

'Les, are you awake?' I asked softly, not wishing to arouse him if he should be asleep.

'Yes. I suppose you're thinking what I'm thinking? Those coughs...'

'Yes – they aren't too good. Several of the men come from warm coastal villages, and aren't used to this sort of climate at all.'

'It's serious for them too. Colds turn to pleurisy or pneumonia so damned quickly.'

'It's no wonder, of course – this spot is so dark and damp. We'll be sick ourselves if we stay too long.'

'Tell you what. The tultuls of Orin and two other villages are coming up tomorrow. Suppose we go for a walk round this mountain with them and look for a better camp? They ought to know of a decent spot.'

I agreed that we should do this, and to the sound of constant coughing we fell asleep, rain still falling about us and plopping in big drops from time to time upon our beds.

Next morning the tultuls came as expected. We set off at once with them on our quest for a drier and warmer camp. While we were winding our way round a steep, grassy section of the hill overlooking Orin, two of the tultuls gave sudden startled cries and vanished into the bush. We looked at our one remaining tultul, the one from Orin, in astonishment, but he was just as amazed as we were. The mystery was soon solved. From the road below came a rapid succession of rifle-shots, and buzzing bullets seemed to fill the air round us, clipping through the grass and ricocheting. The three of us hurled ourselves into a narrow watercourse out of sight, and the firing ceased. We sorted ourselves out, and helped the tultul out of the mud. He had been first in, and Les and I had landed on top of him.

'That was a surprise!'

'To us, but not to those other two black swine!' Les snarled. 'They've been as nervous as a couple of cats all morning. They were waiting for it to happen.'

We crept to the edge of the gully and carefully parted the fringe of long kunai-grass which grew on its lip. Down on the track we counted seventeen Japanese, most of them with rifles held ready to let us have it again if we showed ourselves.

'Oh for a Bren gun!' Les wailed. 'We'd get the lot — we couldn't miss them!'

'That one with the white topee on must be the officer,' I said. 'You couldn't miss him.'

But our only weapons were Owen guns, and for them the range was so great as to make a hit the merest fluke.

We remained there for some minutes, noting with satisfaction that none of the Japanese made any attempt to come up the hill after us. The tultul drew our attention to a great crowd of native carriers, and a pile of boxes which had been left farther down the road. Apparently this was no shoe-string expedition, but was travelling well equipped. It was clear, too, that the Japanese were having no trouble in getting native carriers.

After perhaps ten minutes the leader put his pistol back in its holster, and we heard him shouting to the natives to pick up their loads. A few moments later the whole procession moved off towards Gewak.

'Well, they seem to have given us away.'

'Let's hope they aren't going to try and sneak up again tonight. We'd better get back to the camp and see what's going on there.'

We set off as fast as we could, through the bush and round the steep hillsides, still accompanied by the loyal tultul of Orin.

At the camp we found that Watute and Pato had heard of the enemy's arrival and had hurried back to warn us. By the time they reached the camp, however, we had gone.

Kari had taken charge of the situation in our absence. The radio had been dismantled and packed into its box, and all our stores hidden in scattered spots in the bush. Each boy was standing to with a rifle or sub-machine-gun, and hand-grenades had been issued all round. We complimented Kari on his efficiency, and then called a council of war with him, Watute, and Pato.

'Do you think we ought to shift?' I asked Les.

'It depends what the Nips are likely to do. We don't want to credit them with over-confidence. They're new to these mountains and they won't feel sure that there are only two of us. The natives will tell them, but they'll still be pretty suspicious.'

'They seemed to lose interest in us as soon as we ran

away. Do you think you could find out anything about them, Pato, if you went down to the villages? Do you think it would be safe?'

Pato grinned. It would be safe enough for him, he said. He thought if he went down about evening he might even be able to find the Japs himself.

We decided to let Pato go, and that for the present we would stay where we were.

Towards evening we said goodbye to him and wished him luck. After we had radioed our headquarters to tell them what had happened we sat down, with what patience we could, to wait for his return. We dared not light a fire, so we boiled up some coffee on a little tin of solid fuel, and huddled round in blankets, trying to keep warm. We could hear the roar of the waterfall below us, and soon the rain started again. Every hour we changed the sentries, one near the camp at the edge of the cliff, and another about ten minutes' climb down the hill. As time went on we became more and more nervous. Perhaps Pato had been captured and the Japanese would try to surprise us?

I saw Les peering at the luminous dial of his watch.

'Two o'clock,' he muttered. 'Time drags, doesn't it?'

'I can't stand much more of this,' I murmured. 'I almost wish the Nips would show up, to put an end to the waiting.'

I had hardly finished speaking when a grunted challenge from the sentry nearby caught our ear:

'Who's 'at 'e walkabout?'

'Me Pato! You no can shoot!' came the hurried response. Pato, realizing that the suspense would make us all a bit trigger-happy, was taking no risk of getting bullet by mistake.

We hurried him into the house, wet through, covered with mud, and panting from his rapid climb up the hill, and Dinkila at once prepared a mug of steaming beef-tea for him.

Meanwhile, the whole party of natives crowded into the little hut to hear Pato's story, muttering excitedly beneath their breaths. It was so dark that as we looked around we could not distinguish any of the boys: only their whispers or movements told us of their presence. We made notes by the faint light of a lantern while Pato talked, and all we could see of him was the flashing whites of his eyes behind a cloud of vapour rising from his mug.

Pato had gone right up to the Japanese patrol, he told us. They were camped in my old house at Bawan, and had a wireless set, a lot of rice, tinned meat, and fish. They also had about ten wooden cases whose contents he could not ascertain or guess at; but when he showed interest in them he thought the officer in charge of the patrol looked at him suspiciously, so he wandered off.

Les and I glanced at each other as Pato calmly related all this. If only that Jap officer had known!

'Did you find out where they were going?' I asked.

'Yes. My cousin in Bawan says they are going to Boana tomorrow, and the next day they will go on the way to Lae.'

'Do they know anything else about us?'

'They know it's your house they are camping in, but they keep asking whether there are only two of you. They don't seem to believe it.'

'Thank God for that! I hope they think there's a hundred of us!' Les said fervently.

We thanked Pato warmly for his good work, and lay down to sleep for the remaining two or three hours of darkness.

Early next morning we radioed Moresby, asking whether planes could be sent to strafe Boana next day, and suggesting dawn as the best time, in order to catch the enemy party before they set out on the next stage of their journey to Lae. We were told that this would be considered. The following day we would have to move on, in case a special party of Japs should be sent out to hunt us down.

About ten o'clock Watute and I walked back to Bawan, approaching cautiously through the bush for fear the enemy were still about. They had gone, but so had our camp. The house had been burnt, the vegetables dug up, and the whole area fouled.

'Look at it!' Watute said disgustedly. 'The dirtiest kanaka out of the bush isn't as filthy as that!'

We retraced our steps to Orin and found that Les had already decided upon a place to move to – a village called Kiakum, higher in the mountains of the Naba country.

We went there next day, not following the tolerable track that wound round the edge of the valley, but moving along obscure hunting-trails which ran across the mountains, used by the natives when they hunted possums in the forest. The path was rough and steep, and not a little dangerous in some places.

Nearing Kiakum we passed several independent homesteads standing alone in little clearings among the tall cane-grass. It was a sign that the people had not acquired the village habit encouraged by the government, but still preferred their own way of life. Obviously these families had never been seen by the patrol officer in peacetime. It was a reflection on the superficial patrolling of the peacetime administration, but not really to be blamed on the officers themselves, who had to work so hard, and cover such enormous distances, that they could not possibly do more than pay fleeting visits to each village. Quite often one would see entered in the village book a remark by a patrol officer to the effect that the people lived in their village only at census-time, and spent the rest of the year in their real homes among the gardens. There was something to be said in favour of the more scattered dwellings: during epidemics infection was not likely to spread so rapidly as when the people lived all crowded together.

The inhabitants of the homesteads that we passed near Kiakum must have thought we would be angry with them for living in this way, for upon our approach they fled into the bush with startled cries. This, again, seemed to be a sign that the administration had not really enjoyed the confidence of the population. How could the natives have much affection for people who came to see them only to inspect things, and probably to complain, or to make investigations when there had been trouble? To them the patrol officer was at best a nuisance who, once or twice a year, stirred up a lot of trouble, had to be carried for, and then disappeared. The system made it humanly impossible for most of the officers to establish any solidly based relationships of real understanding and affection with the remoter settlements. Perhaps the blame, in the final analysis, should be placed on the Australian governments, of whatever political colour, which, before the war, had consistently starved the Territory of funds and forced district administrators to manage on shoe-string budgets. It was the legacy of that sort of patrolling which was now making it difficult for us to have any influence, in any real sense, on the people, though my stay at Bawan had convinced me how ready they were to be friends once an interest was taken in them as individuals and not just as entries in the village book, to be censused and, probably, censured.

At Kiakum we found that the natives knew very little about the war. They had never even seen a Japanese, and had met so few white men that Les and I were regarded as curiosities. It was a relief to find that the mission had no hold up here – we would certainly find the people much easier to get on with. Only one man spoke pidgin, and though he offered to clear out his house for us to sleep in, we declined the offer and slept beneath the house. On the following day we asked the natives to build two thatched houses in a secluded spot about half a mile up the hill from the village proper.

For the next ten days we remained at Kiakum, receiving many visitors from the remote mountain villages, all eager for definite news of the war, of which, up to that time, they had heard only the wildest rumours. We would go down from our house each morning at about ten o'clock and remain in the village till the afternoon, receiving all our visitors there: only Kiakum people were allowed to approach the house. We got on famously with the natives, relations being as cordial as they had been with the Bawan people in 1942. Each day I took the medical kit with me to the village and gave injections, dressed wounds and ulcers, and dosed colds and malaria. Once we had to cut the tips off two toes of a boy who had kicked a stone and developed such a bad infection that the toes were just rotting away. The job was done neatly and successfully with a pair of sterilized wire clippers and a local anaesthetic, and the patient was walking round again the following week.

While I did medical work Les talked to the people, losing no chance for pushing our cause, and noting every scrap of information they brought. Pato unearthed one story which, whether true or not, amused us. He was told that when the Japanese heard of my visit to the Chinese camp they were so enraged that they put a price on my head – two cases of meat and £5 (in Australian money) to any native who brought me in, dead or alive.

Les laughed. 'Two cases of meat and a fiver! I didn't realize anyone valued you as highly as all that!'

One constant visitor to the camp was the village idiot, a powerful man clad only in a strip of bark. Unlike most natives – whose skins are usually very clean – he had a heavy beard, and a moderate growth of curly hair all over his body. He was extremely dirty, and one could smell him from a distance. Our introduction to this man was startling. We were bending over the wireless one night deciphering a message, when there was a loud thump behind us, and there he was. He had leapt from the doorway right to the centre of the floor. In his hand we could see an enormous savage-looking bush-knife glittering in the lamplight. Les and I looked at each other nervously, uncertain whether to dive out the side of the house or to tackle him and risk having a limb severed by the knife. Our dilemma was solved when we saw the agitated countenance of the pidgin speaker from the village appear round the doorway.

'Long-long man, master,' he said. 'Master sit down, now 'e all right.'

We sat down rather reluctantly. 'Long-long' is the pidgin word for 'mad', and it was well applied to our visitor. With a weird gleam in his eye he stuck his knife quivering into a beam of the house and came to inspect us more closely. He felt our boots, hands, and faces, rubbing his paws all over our clothes and making queer chuckling noises in his throat. Scared as I was, I could not help laughing at Les's expression of girlish coyness when our grimy friend put a hand down the back of his shirt. Then, apparently satisfied that we were human, he moved about the house inspecting all our belongings.

The Kiakum pidgin speaker crept inside and explained to us that all the people were frightened of the long-long man, though he was never violent unless violence was offered him. We gathered that the poor man enjoyed a kind of prestige among the people, though they also feared him. We thought they would probably resent it if we did not treat him well, and for that reason we allowed him to come and go at will, giving him little presents of meat and biscuits from time to time, and even establishing a kind of friendship with him. We could not help wishing, however, that he would confine his social activities to the daytime. Several times at night we woke with a start to hear an extraordinary chattering in the hut, and the torch revealed this naked, gibbering madman dancing round the bed, bush-knife in hand. When, later on, we finally left Kiakum, he broke down and cried like a child.

Our radio could not pick up ordinary broadcast programmes, but we found that at two o'clock in the morning we could receive a news broadcast and some music from an American station – I think it was in San Francisco. We had not realized how much we missed music, nor how ignorant we had become of what was happening in the world outside. We had developed a state of mind which suggested that the Markham River was the boundary of creation. As soon as we discovered that we could tune in to this programme we ordered the sentry to call us at two every morning, and spent half an hour or so listening first to music and then to the news bulletin, 'just in case the war has ended, and they haven't told us', as Les put it.

On 29th May we made an inventory of our stores. We were running low in certain items, especially sugar, biscuits, and salt. The last-named of these shortages was the most serious, for it represented our currency and was our means of buying vegetables, fowls, pigs and labour.

I decided to visit the dump we had left in the little huts near Bandong, and replenish our supplies. I would also try to go to Boana and find out whether the Japs had moved in yet. If they had not, there was a good chance of shooting another beast and so being able to issue another couple of meals of fresh meat all round. I would take Pato, Watute, and Dinkila with me, and a couple of the Kiakum men as guides. As it was unsafe to use the main tracks, because of the number of Japanese who seemed to be moving about, we would go over a little-known and little-used pad straight across the mountains, which came out near Kawalan, in the Wain country.

We set out on 30th May over what was assuredly one of the worst tracks in New Guinea. It was incredibly steep and rough, through moss forest all the way. We all, even the Kiakum men, suffered violent headaches which seemed to split our skulls in half. Probably they were caused by the very great altitude. To cap our miseries, leeches were swarming everywhere. The whole surface of the ground seemed to be covered with their tiny waving shapes, smelling blood and stretching out for it. We dared not sit down, but we halted every twenty minutes or so while I scraped them from under my gaiters and the boys picked them from between their toes. Despite our exertions in climbing we shivered all the way. When almost in sight of Kawalan, the first Wain village, we met with an obstacle that was almost enough to make us turn back. A landslide had carried away a large section of the hillside, where the track had once been, leaving a rock-face without a foothold of any description, a sheer drop of fifty feet or more. After half an hour's search in the bush the boys found enough vines to fashion a rough rope ladder. We tied it to a tree and hoped for the best as we lowered ourselves into space bumping hard against the rock from time to time as the rope swung round, and scraping the skin off our knees and elbows. We left it hanging there, hoping that no one would come along and move it. If they did, the only way of getting back to Kiakum would be to make a two- or three-day journey through Wampangan and Bawan.

There were only two men in Kawalan village when we arrived, and not a sign of the women and children. I questioned the two men about this, but they declined to say where the others were, and both affirmed that there were no Japanese in Boana. I was not at all happy about this 'ghost town' of several dozen empty, silent houses. After a while one becomes very sensitive to the 'atmosphere' of native villages — there is an air about them which tells you whether everything is as it should be. In this case I had the strongest possible premonition of something being wrong, and so as soon as it became dark we crept quietly out of the house we were occupying, and spent the night at the edge of the surrounding bush.

In the morning the tultul of Kawalan appeared mysteriously out of the blue, and he too assured us that there were no Japanese at Boana, nor would he give us any hint of where the rest of the Kawalan people were.

I still did not believe what these people had said about Boana, and decided to investigate. Telling Watute and Pato to approach it down the left side of the Bunzok Valley, I went off with Dinkila down the other side. We were to call at Bandong en route to prepare the cargo I wished to take back to Kiakum. If one of us were blocked the chances were that the others might get through and see what was happening.

Bandong I found almost as empty as Kawalan. In spite of the assurances of the few old natives who were there, the people were not merely away at work in their gardens, for every cultivated patch we passed was deserted. Something mysterious was happening. But what? In the hope of solving the mystery Dinkila and I set off for Sokulen after only a short pause to regain our wind.

We had covered about half the distance when a native lad about twelve years old came panting up behind us. He brought a message from Watute, saying that he and Pato had discovered that Boana was inhabited by a strong force of Japanese, and that almost every native in the Wain had gathered there at the summons of the enemy commander, who intended to announce the new Japanese government of the area. Watute and Pato were still investigating, and they suggested that I should wait for them in Kawalan, and not take the risk of proceeding to Sokulen.

Dinkila and I turned back towards Kawalan, but did not go into the village. Instead, we camped in the bush on the side of a small hill nearby, commanding a good view of the track along which Watute would come.

Late the following afternoon we saw him limping up the hill, and it was Dinkila who first spotted the fact that he seemed to have lost all his belongings except his rifle, bayonet, and ammunition. When he reached us, mud-caked, scratched, and weary, he had a grim story to tell.

Pato and he had decided to spend the previous night in a house at Wampangan, intending to go to Boana the next day disguised as bush kanakas, he told us in a bitter voice. Two natives who had come up from Lae with the Japs, heard of their presence and betrayed them to the enemy. A party of twenty Nips attempted to trap them in the house, but they heard them coming just in time, and managed to escape by tearing up part of the light bamboo floor and dropping down beneath the house. In the darkness, and with all the shooting and confusion, Watute became separated from Pato. He did not know where Pato was now – but feared he might have been killed or captured. The Japanese got onto Watute's track and chased him up the valley. They had heard about my presence there, and were out for my scalp too. He thought they were still a few hours behind him, but whatever happened we should get out of the way quickly.

As there was not a kanaka to be seen anywhere we had to abandon all thought of taking extra stores back to Kiakum. Before darkness fell we had made a few miles along the road back, and when we could see to walk no farther lay down to sleep in the bush at the side of the track. It poured with rain all night, soaking us as we huddled together for warmth.

At dawn next day we moved on. We had no means of knowing whether the Japs would continue the pursuit past Kawalan when they found us gone, but after we had struggled up our vine-made Jacob's ladder we cut it away behind us and felt reasonably safe. It was about three o'clock when the house at Kiakum came into view, and we hurried down the hill for the last few hundred yards, with only bad news for Les, and a bitter blow to give the rest of the boys, who had been very fond of Pato.

We drafted a radio message to headquarters, to give them our latest information on Japanese movements. According to Watute, the patrol now at Boana was surveying the overland route the enemy proposed to set up between Madang and Lae. They would shortly leave for Kaiapit, in the Upper Markham, travelling through Sedau, Sugu, and the Erap, by the same route as that taken by the party we had so narrowly missed last month. Their destination, Kaiapit Mission, was being watched by an old New Guinea resident, a gold-miner called Harry Lumb. He moved about the district in much the same way as Jock and I had patrolled the Wain, and knew the area and its natives intimately. I had last met him in Wau some weeks earlier, when he had just discovered a case of canned beer in somebody's abandoned cache. We drank a few tins, and then buried the remainder at the foot of a tall dead pine-tree. 'There it is now – a nice little drop for our next meeting,' Harry had said with a grin of satisfaction as we piled earth on top of it. Then we parted, he bound for his post at Kaiapit, I on my way across the Markham .

I had thought of Harry as soon as Watute said the Japanese were bound for Kaiapit, and now mentioned it to Les.

'Do you think Port Moresby will warn Harry Lumb?' I asked. 'He's quite likely to be poking round that Kaiapit country now.'

'Sure to, I should think, when they get our news that the Nips are bound that way. Why? Do you think we ought to suggest it?'

'No. I suppose they would do it as a matter of course, and we have to keep our radio messages as short as possible.'

And so the message went without any suggested warning to Lumb. I wished later we had put it in.

While I removed my wet and stinking clothes, Tauhu cooked a meal and Les sat down at the radio and tapped out the message. I was so tired that I ate more or less mechanically, half asleep. I thought in an idle sort of way how pleasant it would be to return to the old humdrum life of the Wain of last December. It had seemed so dull then, but what a welcome change it would be now.

We spent most of the night trying to decide what to do. The position, as we saw it, was briefly this: The native situation was very bad. The kanakas had thrown in their lot with the Japanese, having apparently decided to regard them as the new rulers of the island. We could remain alive only by hiding in some quiet spot like Kiakum. But that would achieve nothing. The alternatives were to attempt to escape back across the Markham and admit failure, or to try to cross the Saruwaged Range and see what was happening on the north side. We had heard that two men, Lincoln Bell and Fairfax-Ross, were somewhere on the Rai coast, and we hoped we might be able to find them, and perhaps help them.

'Anyhow, if you ask me,' said Les, 'getting back across the Markham just now is not only inglorious — it's impossible!'

'All right. That leaves the Saruwageds. What about it?'

'Yes — let's have a go at it.'

So it was decided that next day we should try to cross the range, and if we failed we would consider trying to get back to Wau. Following our usual plan of keeping the native members of the party well in the picture, we sent for Kari and asked what he thought of the idea. He said he was quite prepared for the crossing, and he was certain all the others would feel the same way.

'All right,' I said. 'Tell all the men to pack their gear at dawn tomorrow.'

We talked of our chances of making the crossing. I remembered how Jock had described the mountains, though the track he had used was a different one and lay ten miles or so to the east. If anything, the range was a trifle higher where we were going to try. All day long the mountains were covered with clouds, but at dawn and sunset the summits were frequently clear. Often we had risen early at Kiakum to study the bare windswept rock-faces, the sheer precipices, and the yawning cavern-like valleys that scarred the sides of the range. Here and there, like white threads, streams coursed down. We knew our task would not be easy, but the valley of the Sanem River seemed to offer the best approach, and the Kiakum people said the range could be crossed from there, though none of them would admit to having made the crossing. Probably they feared we would ask them to come as guides.

In the morning, to the great grief of our friend the village idiot, the Kiakum people lifted our gear to take it to the village of Mogom, the most northerly habitation in the Sanem Valley shown on our map. North of that was unexplored, and we had no idea whether people lived there, or whether it was just a barren waste. Even if it were inhabited, it was likely that the people would be so wild and shy that we would be unable to establish contact with them, much less induce them to undertake the long and arduous carry across the range.

We left Kiakum with some regret. Our quarters had been comfortable and the people friendly, and it had been a place of wild, magnificent beauty. We would probably never see it again in our lives, and we felt sad to think it as we looked ruefully at the plot of ground we had already turned up to make ourselves a garden. The plot seemed a symbol of man's incurable optimism, even in the face of every possible reason for being pessimistic.

We could find no track to Mogom. We struggled round grass-covered hillsides, through patches of bush and old long-abandoned gardens. Once we descended into a gully, were unable to climb the other side, and had to retrace our steps several miles and try a new approach. At four o'clock we reached the spot where the Kiakum boys said they had found Mogom three years before. None of them had been into this part of the country since then. Now there was only one house. It showed every sign of being in use, but its owner had apparently fled at our approach. We checked the place on the map and found that we were certainly standing on the spot where some years earlier a patrol officer had put a dot for Mogom village. The kanakas had moved, that was all: in this wild tangle of country it would be useless to search for them, who knew every inch of it and could elude us without effort.

We studied the country farther north for signs of habitation, and for a long while we could see none. Blue mountains, fold upon fold of them, cold and distant, were all that met our gaze. Then we found a clear patch of country with just the faintest wisp of smoke going straight up to the sky, and, almost simultaneously, we picked out two large gardens. We knew then that there were people living higher up the valley, and our hopes of reaching the north side rose.

With some difficulty we persuaded our Kiakum people to stay the night with us, so that they might carry our gear as far as those gardens. Even the prospect of substantial rewards did not arouse their enthusiasm, so we warned Kari to keep a careful, though unobtrusive, guard upon them in case they attempted to leave us silently as we slept.

Although we walked all the next day we advanced only another four or five miles. The country, already rugged and difficult, became increasingly so as we moved up, but once the higher part of one of these valleys was entered, there was no alternative but to follow it to its head. To cross the ridges which composed the sides was not feasible. Notwithstanding the steepness of the ridges there were many gardens, showing how fertile the soil was and how extensive and uniformly good the native agriculture. The neatly fenced plots of corn, sugar-cane, and sweet potatoes, terrace-like round the valley sides, were a remarkable sight. The natives, it seemed, understood the problem of soil erosion in this country of steep slopes and heavy rainfall, for all large trees that had been felled were carefully laid across the line of drainage, to reduce the amount of soil carried off by surface water.

About midday we were astonished to hear someone calling out to us in pidgin from the valley below. To our joy and amazement we were overtaken about ten minutes later by Pato, whom we had imagined dead or captured at Wampangan. With a grin all over his lined old face he told us that after he lost contact with Watute he had tried to creep away, but had been detected and chased, with shots whistling all round him. It had taken him a long while to shake off his pursuers, but he had finally made his way to his home village of Gumbum, arriving there pretty well exhausted. He had had to rest there for a couple of days.

Pato's return had a wonderful effect on the morale of the party. Dinkila the irrepressible jumped wildly up and down on the track, giving piercing whoops like a Red Indian. Pato would be invaluable in negotiations with the natives we hoped to find, for they would speak the Naba dialect, we supposed, and he would be able to interpret for us.

In the late afternoon we came upon Amyen village – so far unmarked on any map – at the end of a track we had been hopefully following for the last couple of hours. It was built in much the same way as the more 'civilized' villages – with the houses grouped about a small clearing. This was better luck than we had dared to hope for: people who lived in a compact group like this would be easier to find and deal with than those who lived miles apart in scattered homesteads.

About a dozen men were waiting in the village to receive us. There was no doubt that they had observed our approach afar off, for all the women and children had been sent away and the houses had been cleared of all goods and chattels. Since the place had never been visited before by government officers, there had naturally been no village officials appointed, but it was not hard to distinguish the leading man. He was old, and of fine, upstanding carriage, and he advanced to meet us with dignity and grace. His was the type of personality that commands respect from anyone, black or white.

He said something that was unintelligible to us.

'He wants to know why we are here,' Pato said.

'Tell him we wish to stay in his village for a while, but that we will not harm his people or touch his pigs or gardens,' I said.

The old man inclined his head gravely to me, and then turned to Les, who had walked forward with a large handful of salt. He took it, tasted it, smiled his approval, and then, not to be outdone in generosity, called to his companions, who hurried forward with great bundles of sugar-cane cut in two-foot lengths. It was thick, and dripping with juice, and we tore the skin off it with our teeth and sucked the sweet sap to quench our thirst.

Formalities were over. Police and natives joined in the eating of cane, exchanged tobacco, and, though not understanding a word of each other's remarks, chattered amiably. The old headman took Les and me by the hand and showed us a house for ourselves. When we pointed to the police and other boys, he indicated a large house for them nearby.

The buildings had been made with great care and cunning. This village we estimated to be nearly eight thousand feet above sea-level, and a freezing wind blew down at night from the Saruwaged mountains. To cope with this the natives had built their houses some four feet off the ground and roofed them with pit-pit grass from eight inches to a foot thick. The walls were made with strongly laced strips of bark, in which was a small doorway. Then, round the whole house, another bark wall with a small doorway in it was built, stretching from the edge of the roof to the ground. The two openings were carefully placed so that they were not opposite one another, and one had to crawl on one's stomach to get in. Not only the cold wind but almost all air of any sort was excluded, and the huts were quite dark inside. What the atmosphere was like in there after a fire had been burning is better left to the imagination.

The women and children started to drift back into the village in twos and threes, and we were pleased to see them, for it showed they trusted us. Despite the cold, they looked healthy — fat and well fed, and with clean, glossy skins. Very few sores were to be seen, and I did not notice a single case of yaws. These natives had a physical peculiarity we had noticed before among people in the highest mountains — namely, extreme muscular development of the buttocks and thighs, which gave them a slightly deformed appearance. There was not a single piece of cloth to be seen, but the men wore a strip of beaten bark cloth round their waists and enclosing the genitals, while the women wore a very short petticoat of rushes. Both sexes had capes of beaten bark. I tried one on, and found it as soft as a blanket, and very warm. The only disadvantage I could see about it was the vermin that infested it.

The old man was very reluctant to help us in our trip across the range. It was the wrong season, he protested, and if a big storm came up while we were on top we would all assuredly perish. However, after more than an hour's session with him, Pato translating, we persuaded him to let us have a try, and lined up his men to pick out the fittest for use as carriers. We selected fifteen fully developed men who seemed to be in perfect condition. Anyone with signs of a physical defect we rejected, lest he should prove a liability on the mountain.

Since we would have only fifteen carriers, it was clear that we would have to abandon a large part of our gear, so we rewarded our Kiakum carriers with tinned meat, cloth, knives, and other things useful to them, with such liberality that they were staggered. They were really sorry to see the last of us when we sent them off home. All the next day was spent preparing for the journey. The natives cooked large quantities of sweet potatoes for themselves, and parcelled them up in leaves, explaining that it was often impossible to light fires up above, so they always took the precaution of cooking their meals in advance. I felt sorry for them having to depend on food like sweet potatoes for a journey such as the one that lay before us, for the water content was so high that one had to eat a prodigious quantity to get an adequate meal, and after an hour or two on the track one felt empty. One might be distended at twelve o'clock, and starving again at one.

We took stock of our own rations and found that the only things we had plenty of were tinned meat and powdered milk. There were practically no biscuits, jam, or flour left, and the tea and sugar were almost exhausted too. Dinkila made a couple of dozen pancake-like objects out of the remaining flour and some powdered milk, and these, with the tinned meat, were to be our rations for the crossing, with a few tins of Marmite from the medical kit.

We sent a radio message to Moresby saying that we were going to make our big effort in the morning, and then packed the wireless very carefully into its box. If anything happened to it we were finished. We knew, of course, that it would get a certain amount of rough treatment on the mountains.

At about four o'clock, the clearest hour of the day, Les and I walked up to a gentle rise behind the village, to search the Saruwageds for any secret we could wring from them. Remote, cold, incredibly high and distant-seeming, they frightened us. Their icy stillness possessed a secret no human heart could share. No wonder the natives held superstitious beliefs about these mountains. It would have been better if they had remained always mist-shrouded –

245

never showed themselves morning and evening in this fashion, naked in all their inaccessibility. We realized with fearful hearts that our lives, and the lives of our natives depended on whether we could master the range.

As we stared into the distance the faintest vapour of cloud appeared in front of the highest peak, became thicker, and was joined by others. Before we realized it the whole range was covered in a swirling mist, thickening every second into black clouds. We turned to walk back to the village, and saw the lightning flash, while thunder rolled and echoed down the valley. Outside the house the police were watching the storm too, their black faces expressionless. But I could not bring myself to ask what they were thinking.

VIII

WE LEFT Amyen early next morning. The first couple of hours led through gardens, some planted with sweet potatoes and sugar-cane, others abandoned. The system of shifting agriculture employed by these people necessitated clearing a new patch of ground every few years and letting the old gardens revert to forest to recover their fertility. We also passed many tiny lakes, like fishponds in a landscape garden. They had been formed when water collected in depressions dissolved in the limestone.

Then began our approach to the range itself. We were off the foothills and advancing upon the Saruwageds, using as our route a long steep razor-backed ridge which climbed ever up and up. In less than an hour we had left the open country behind and entered the moss forest. It was like going out of the sunlight into a dark cavern. The trees were encased in green spongy moss that oozed moisture. The moss festooned the branches and encrusted the trunks — in some places it was up to eight or ten inches thick. There was no soil at all in the accepted sense of the word – just a spongy moss-covered mass of rotting vegetable material into which we often sank to the thighs. Even at its firmest the ground felt like sponge-rubber under our feet. How deep this mass went we could not tell, but we pushed a sharpened eight-foot pole full length into the ground without encountering any resistance. The silence was unearthly. There were no birds or insects – the only living things we saw were possums and little kangaroo-rats. The footfalls of the party made no sound; and even a shout sounded flat and dull. A curious effect of this atmosphere on both the natives and ourselves was a tendency to speak only in whispers.

In places the ridge, maintaining its north-north-easterly course, became so narrow that we were forced to straddle it and work ourselves forward on our hands. How the carriers managed remains something of a mystery to me to this day. In some parts we took half an hour to move forward a hundred yards. And it seemed that worse was to follow – for each Amyen man had a length of vine rope over his shoulder, for use 'when the road became hard'.

As we advanced, the timber, still moss-festooned, became more stunted and twisted. All the time we were crawling either over or under it, or squeezing between branches. This was exhausting enough for Les and me who were carrying only our packs and Owen guns, but it must have been almost unendurable for the carriers, with their awkward loads slung on poles between them. We saw with apprehension that the wireless, in spite of the greatest care, was knocking against tree-trunks and branches.

About half past two light rain began to fall, and our carriers at once put down their loads.

'What's going on?' Les asked. 'I hope we're not going to have an argument about wet and dry pay at a time like this!'

We called to Pato to catch up with us: an argument, if there was to be one, would have to be conducted through him. We pointed out what had happened, and he crossly asked the old man to explain the delay.

The headman answered in about three words, and Pato turned to us with a smile.

'It's all right,' he said. 'They are just going to put their raincoats on!'

The Amyen men were rapidly undoing bundles which had been slung across their shoulders. We were amused to see them donning curious tent-like coverings of laced pandanus-leaves, which went over their heads and the upper parts of their bodies. As they moved off again, they looked like a row of houses on legs, with high-pitched thatched roofs.

Half an hour later, about mid-afternoon, we reached a spot on the side of the ridge where the carriers said we were to camp for the night. We guessed the altitude at something like nine and a half thousand feet. There was a small cave here, which was partly natural and had been partly hollowed out by the natives on their periodic trading trips across the range. Apart from possum-hunts, these were the only occasions when they went on the mountain. There was of course no permanent habitation higher than Amyen, and we knew we would not find any villages until we got down to about seven or eight thousand feet on the north side.

The carriers were to sleep in the cave, and since there was not enough flat ground outside for even one man to stretch out, the police built one rough platform of boughs for themselves on the slope above, and another for Les and me.

We badly wanted a drink, but though we could hear water rushing far underground, beneath the rocks and moss, all our attempts to discover a spring were in vain. The carriers said there was no water, but several of them were subsequently seen drinking from a bamboo receptacle, and after a good deal of persuasion they led us to a small trickle which they had carefully covered with stones.

Enough firewood was found for the police and the carriers to have some sort of fire all night, and to make a hot drink. We issued a pint of hot Marmite to all our own boys, but when we offered it to the carriers only one or two accepted. Les and I, wet through, crouched in our ground-sheets while we ate cold bully beef out of tins, and spread with Marmite the 'pancakes' Dinkila had made in Amyen. Then came a drink of tea which Tauhu had contrived to brew. We cupped our hands round the mugs, holding them close to our bodies to keep the rain out of the tea, and warming our frozen fingers at the same time.

Darkness would soon be approaching, and Les and I erected our only shelter – half a one-man tent – over the platform of boughs, and prepared our beds.

Before turning in we paid a visit to the cave where the carriers were housed. It was almost underneath us, and Les referred to it as the basement.

The sight that met our eyes as we peered into the cavern mouth might have been a scene from the Inferno. In the smoke-laden, stifling interior grotesque black figures squatted round a fire, gobbling food. Occasionally, when the flames leapt up, unearthly shadows danced on the walls, and eyes and teeth flashed through the dimness. The carriers were all quite naked, having taken off their bark coverings to dry them. When they noticed us looking in upon them the talking ceased, and with an air of acute embarrassment they cupped their hands over their private parts to hide them from us.

'Shall we go in?' I asked.

'We can try,' said Les. 'It'll be a squeeze.'

They made way for us, and rather diffidently offered us pieces of charred sweet potato to eat. As we had issued them with a packet of biscuits each, we did not feel it would be putting them on short rations to accept, so we took the potato and nibbled away as we squatted round the fire with them. The shyness soon wore off, and we carried on a lively and friendly, though unintelligible, conversation which lasted some twenty minutes. Then, feeling in danger of asphyxiation, we left them with expressions of mutual esteem – also unintelligible – and stepped into the freezing air outside.

It was almost dark. We saw the police huddled together round their little fire – this they somehow always managed to keep going throughout the night. There were no complaints from them, and I could see by their determined faces that they had made up their minds to stick it out until morning. As Kari squatted there with the others I bent over his shoulder and murmured that he ought to place a guard over the carriers, for if they should run away in the night we would have no hope of getting over the range. He replied that he had thought of this, and that Constable Yaru had already taken up his position in the bush near the mouth of the cave.

Les and I crawled into our own bed. We were wet, cold, not particularly well fed, and yet it would be wrong to suppose we were miserable. Long ago we had developed the stoicism in regard to little things that acted as a sort of filter for unpleasant experiences. Putting wet and dirty clothes on again when one has become warm and dry, for instance, is probably one of the most disagreeable of sensations, trivial though it may seem. But we had developed a state of mind where the physical sensation of such things did not register upon the consciousness, and so we were spared much misery.

We put on all our spare clothes and wrapped our blankets round the two of us, but we were so cold that we hardly slept at all, except in fitful dozes. Whenever one of us moved, the freezing air rushed in under our coverings. Steady rain fell all night, pattering onto the rough shelter and gradually finding its way in upon us. About midnight there were two terrific hailstorms, and we hardly dared think how the police and other boys must be suffering. Occasionally we heard them swear or mutter as a hailstone registered a direct hit.

At the very first sign of light we were happy enough to get out of our cramped, uncomfortable bed and prepared to resume the climb. I noticed ice on a billy of water, and hurried over to see how the police had fared. Apart from being cold, and passing a few uncomplimentary remarks about mountains, which really had no business to be as high as this, they seemed well enough. Strangely, it was the carriers who reported casualties, comparatively well protected though they had been. Five of them, through Pato, protested that they were too ill to continue. To make sure they were not shamming illness I decided to take their temperatures. It was only after much persuasion and explanation from Pato that they would consent to this indignity, and, even then, one of them showed a distinct desire to bite the end off the thermometer. To prevent this I kept a finger between his teeth while the mercury registered, which caused Pato great anxiety. He stood nervously by, afraid that the kanaka would bite my finger too. The temperatures of all five men were high, and there was no doubt that they were ill. We would just have to leave them behind in the cave and hope that they would recover sufficiently to be able to make their way back to Amyen.

With five carriers ill we were forced to abandon nearly one-third of our gear. We were already carrying heavy packs ourselves, a thing which white men find difficult in New Guinea even under the best conditions. Up on these mountains they were almost the end of us. They chafed and cut, made our backs ache, and several times nearly caused us to overbalance down a precipice. We put on our best boots and threw the others away, and abandoned most of our food. The wireless and the trade goods were the most important things to keep – the trade goods to buy native foods (and native co-operation) and the wireless to send messages to Port Moresby.

We were on the track again shortly after six o'clock. No more depressing sight can be imagined than this moss forest in the half-light. Damp, green, dim, unreal, it made the journey like a combination of a bad nightmare and a scene from one of Grimm's fairy-tales.

I shall never understand why the natives, with their unprotected feet, did not suffer more. It is true that Watute stumbled on a broken branch hidden in the moss, and a sharp sliver of wood passed right through his foot, but though the injury proved troublesome later, the foot was so cold at the time that he felt hardly any pain, and there was very little bleeding.

As we pushed onwards the track became increasingly vague and faint, but there was no fear of losing the way, for travel in any direction except along the top of the ridge was impossible.

At ten o'clock, at an estimated height of ten and a half thousand feet, the moss forest ceased abruptly, giving place to a growth of short prickly grass, and small shrubs about two feet high. We felt freer and less oppressed. There was a little pale, weak sunlight, which seemed to warm us and lift our spirits. Far below, spread out like a map, was the Wain and the Naba country and, beyond, the flat country of the Markham. Lae and Salamaua were both visible, and a huge stretch of coastline which we imagined must extend as far as Buna. Smoke was rising from the gardens of the Naba, where men were clearing the bush. Down below us, infinitely remote, natives were working, white men and yellow men were fighting, people were being born and people were dying. But these mountains seemed to put the momentous battles and affairs of mortals into another perspective: it seemed as if they did not matter at all, and as the clouds blocked out our view we felt that other people and other lives were little more than an unsubstantial memory.

We still had several thousand feet to climb, and we set ourselves to do so before midday. We soon saw why the natives had brought their vine ropes. Bare rock-faces, smooth and polished by the water that had trickled over them for countless ages, blocked our way every half-mile or so. To walk round them was like walking round the side of a brick wall. To enable us to negotiate them, not once but many times a native crawled round to the other side, and the others tossed lengths of vine over to him, to be made fast to rocks, or, when convenient rocks could not be found, to himself. Then, hardly daring to breathe, we crept over, feet on one rope and hands gripping the other. When we got there we always found ourselves sweating profusely, with a pain in the chest from tensed muscles and constricted breathing.

The top of the range was a semi-plateau some six or eight miles wide, a scene of utter desolation. A howling wind, with nothing to break its force, lashed us pitilessly as we struggled forward. The great limestone outcrops seemed like bones poking through the crust of the earth. When not struggling across the treacherous face of the range we were plodding painfully through a black, sodden bog of spongy earth that sucked at our feet as though it would pull us down for ever. Walking, instead of being a natural rhythmic movement, became a matter of individual footsteps. Every time we lifted our feet we wondered if we had the strength, or the desire, to put them forward once more. Once – but only once – we made the near-fatal error of sitting down for a rest. Intense lassitude caused by lack of oxygen in the atmosphere overcame us, and we wanted to sleep. As soon as we realized what was happening we forced our protesting legs to resume our weight, and stood up for the remainder of our brief spell.

Headaches, faintness, giddiness, and attacks of nose-bleeding plagued us all. Then the carriers started to give trouble, and we caught some of them trying to throw their loads down and run away. The vigilant eye of Kari spotted the move, and he at once halted the line, made them walk closer together, and ordered the police to keep them hemmed in so that escape was impossible. But he was no slave-driver, and understood that the carriers were really distressed with their heavy loads in this frightful country. In spite of his own heavy pack, rifle, and ammunition, he moved in among the cargo and, one by one, gave each carrier a spell for half a mile or so, shouldering their loads himself.

I pointed this out to Les. He had no words to express his feelings, but we both looked at Kari and marvelled as he ran from one end of the line to the other, bullying here, coaxing there, and sparing no one less than himself.

'If we ever arrive wherever it is we're going,' I said, 'the credit will be due to Kari more than to us.'

Les nodded. 'Whenever I look at that man, I feel that though we give the orders, in his strange stolid way Kari is the real guts of this outfit.'

Another thought was constantly in my mind as the afternoon advanced: it struck me how little we knew of what lay on the other side of the range. We knew neither where we would come out nor the name of the first village we would find. For all we knew, the Japanese might be waiting in force for us, and all we would earn, at the price of the endeavour of this nightmare journey, would be a miserable and lonely death, which we might have found more easily by staying in the Wain. To me the irony of making such an effort only to meet the fate one was trying to escape from was overwhelming. I tried to tell Les what was in my mind.

'It's been gnawing at me a bit too,' he confessed. 'I know it's no use fooling ourselves about what we may find here; but, all the same, I think we ought to try and put those ideas aside until the worst does happen.'

'You're right, of course, Les. We might take a leaf from Kari's book again. He's so intelligent that he must have thought of that horrible possibility, but he's coping with the minute-to-minute problems and not worrying about what can't be altered.'

Watute, limping from his pierced foot, his old face screwed up with pain, moved towards us.

'Master, look!' he said grimly, pointing beneath a large overhanging limestone boulder.

We followed the direction he indicated. Huddled together were the bones of several people.

'What happened? Who are they?' I demanded.

'Pato 'e talk kanaka – all 'e buggerup long cold (Pato says they were kanakas – they all perished from the cold),' Watute replied briefly.

It was a salutary, if grisly, warning. It was no use worrying about what might happen after we got down off the range. The thing to do first was to get down. With an apprehensive backward look at the pathetic pile beneath the rock, we hurried on.

About half past four we began the descent of the
north side. At first it consisted of a perfectly vertical cliff,
down which we had to lower ourselves on the inevitable
vine. This continued for the first three-quarters of an hour
or so, and thereafter it was still almost vertical until we left
the grass behind and came to the forest level. About six
o'clock darkness and heavy rain descended on us almost
simultaneously. The old Amyen man who was leading the
carriers kept saying 'Meka! Meka!' and pointing ahead.
'Meka' meant 'house', but when this had been going on for
over an hour of darkness and no house had materialized,
we lost patience. We felt sick from the combined effects of
cold, hunger, altitude, and weariness, and had decided to
roll up in our groundsheets and sleep where we were in
the bush when Watute hurried up to us.

'Master, place close to! Master, smell!'

We sniffed, sniffed again. Very faintly, in spite of the
rain, and the sweaty reek of ourselves and the boys, there
came the tang of wood-smoke, a smell which hungry men
can detect miles away. Though our shoulders seemed
likely to crack with the effort, we lifted our packs up once
more and staggered down the track in the wake of the
carriers, to whom the thought of houses, warmth, and
food had given a new lease of life.

After twenty minutes' hurrying through the rain and
darkness we heard excited cries from the boys ahead and
caught sight of flickering lights through the bush. In a few
moments we had pushed our way, stumbling and breathless, through a clump of thick cane-grass and were in the
middle of what appeared to be a fairly large village.

An old man wearing the red-banded cap of a luluai
stepped forward into a circle of torchlight and saluted.

We had no idea that patrols from the north side had
penetrated so far in peacetime, but there was our luluai, as

large as life, giving orders for houses to be cleaned out to accommodate us. We threw ourselves exhausted on the ground beneath one of them, too worn out to speak or move for nearly half an hour. Then we hauled ourselves inside the tiny dwelling, where two of the police, who had recovered sooner than we had, were already engaged in putting up our bed-sails.

Our first action was to take off our boots, which were sodden, heavy, agony to wear, and nearly ruined. Then we went over to the other house to see how the boys fared, whether they all had a dry place to sleep, and if food had been brought to them. While we crouched round the little fire in the centre of the floor, talking about the day's walk, some of the village people brought in two huge blackened cooking-pots full of steaming boiled sweet potatoes, English potatoes, pumpkin, and other vegetables. The boys squatted round the pots and thrust their hands into the boiling mass. The smell of food was too much for us: we joined the circle and dived in with the others two white hands among a dozen or more black ones, and gorged till we felt we would burst. Then we staggered off to bed. We slept right round the clock, not waking till ten next morning.

All day it poured with rain, and the cold seemed to creep in on us through every chink of the house. The ground, the houses, the men – everything looked grey, sodden, and dispirited. We crouched by the little fire that was burning on a pile of earth in the middle of the floor, but our aching limbs gave us no rest. When we got up to stretch our legs we found them almost too weak to support us.

' "Damp rusts men as it rusts rifles; more slowly, but deeper" ' quoted Les. 'I can't remember who said that – can you?'

'No. But he must have been a soldier.'

'Too right he must have been!' Les said fervently as he drew his knees up to his chin and then creakingly straightened his legs again.

The village we had come to was called Gombawato, and it was at the head of the Yalumet River. It had taken us a walk of nearly fourteen hours to reach it, and we had crossed the range at an altitude of somewhere between twelve and thirteen thousand feet. We put this information in a brief radio message to Port Moresby, and settled down to rest again.

We hardly moved from the house all day, for neither of us could stand steadily, but I was able to dress the bruises, scratches, and cuts of the rest of the party during the morning. Hardly anyone seemed to have escaped without an injury of some kind, and Watute's foot was now very painful.

About midday I walked over to the house-police. Through the smoke I could see the younger ones lying on their blankets on the floor, talking of their adventures of the day before in the awe-inspiring mountains we had left behind. Dinkila was telling a story of an argument he had had with an Amyen man. The point of it escaped me, but it set the others laughing.

Watute and Pato sat together, blankets draped over their heads and shoulders, and looking like a couple of amiable old chimpanzees as they conversed gravely in low tones about our best course of action for the future.

Kari sat by himself near the door, sewing up a rip in his loincloth, looking seriously out into the rain from time to time. I tried, somewhat clumsily, to tell him how grateful I was for his magnificent work the day before.

He flashed me one of his rare, quick smiles. 'Something-nothing, master. Me police-boy – work belong me.' I realized that Kari, in his way, was a truly great person. The dangers, the difficulties, and the petty annoyances of

PETER RYAN

our precarious existence never troubled him: he thought
only of his duty and the responsibility which command
had put on his broad black shoulders. I had come to
understand why the other boys never resented the stern
discipline he imposed on them. It was not merely his
enormous physical power that maintained his authority: it
was an authority which sprang from a realization by the
others that in Kari they had a man who, merely by being
what he was, deserved respect.

No one in Gombawato spoke pidgin, so our only
way of talking to the people that day was to get Pato to
put our questions into the Naba dialect, and have the
Amyen carriers put them into the language of Gombawato. The answers, of course, came back through the same
channels. However, the problem was solved by the arrival
during the evening of a young man from another village
some hours' walk farther down the valley. He spoke
pidgin English and had been summoned by the Gombawato people as an interpreter.

Our Amyen carriers also spent the day in the village,
resting instead of hurrying back, as we had expected them
to. During the afternoon we paid them, in salt, razor-blades,
and lengths of cloth, for their two days' hard work, and
told them that they should have, of course, all the stuff we
had been forced to abandon on the range. All in all, they
had no cause to complain of their bargain, but I wondered
what they really thought of these two curious white men
who insisted on crossing the Saruwageds in the wrong
season and who had only the vaguest idea of where they
were heading. I suppose that is a question which will
never be answered.

I remember these Amyen carriers with affection.
They were manly, dignified, and utterly unaffected. They
treated us from the first as equals, unaware of the white
man's traditional arrogance with native peoples. The great-

est boon I could wish for them is that they be left alone for ever in their wild, fantastically beautiful mountains.

Towards evening we set up the radio to see if there was any reply to our message of that morning. There was, and we decoded it breathlessly, for it would tell us what our future was to be. To our disappointment it instructed us to withdraw altogether from the Huon Peninsula, since headquarters considered the risks of remaining there not commensurate with the value of any information we might be able to secure. It seemed that things had become just as grim for parties like ours on the north side of the range as we had found them in the Wain, for of the two men we had hoped to meet they could tell us only that one had disappeared and the other was at that very moment withdrawing. The message ended by telling us to use our discretion about the route we chose to escape by, and suggesting that we should either try to get back across the Markham where we had crossed it, or make our way to Bena Bena in the Central Highlands. There was a landing-strip there, and an aircraft would be sent to fly us out.

To go to Bena Bena we would have had to pass through the country of the Markham headwaters – country neither of us knew – so we resolved to try to cross the Middle Markham and return to Wampit, whence we had set out. If we failed in this, we would try to walk up the Watut Valley to Harry Lumb's camp, and thence to Wau.

The following morning there was another wireless message, which disturbed us a good deal. It read: REPEAT INSTRUCTIONS TO WITHDRAW OF MY PREVIOUS MESSAGE STOP HARRY LUMB KILLED BY ENEMY NEAR KAIAPIT STOP MOVE QUICKLY STOP GOOD LUCK.

As we decoded it, letter by letter, our hearts sank. We looked at each other grimly.

'Well,' Les said at last, 'they don't put "good luck" in radio messages unless they think you're pretty much in need of it!'

We sent for Watute and Kari and told them the bad news. They clicked their tongues with vexation, and looked glum.

'If Master Lumb was killed in the Upper Markham we had better keep clear of that country,' Watute said. 'For Master Lumb knew that country better than anyone else.'

Kari started to speak, and then hesitated.

'Go on. What were you going to say?' I prompted him.

'I know,' Watute said abruptly. 'He was wondering if it was the same party of Japanese who surprised Pato and me at Wampangan. They said they were going to Kaiapit.'

Les and I looked at each other.

'It could have been,' Les said.

'I wish we had put a warning to him in our message.'

'Well, we have no way of knowing that he wasn't warned, if it comes to that. You know what Harry was like. He never seemed to be afraid of anything. He was quite capable of staying over there regardless of warnings.'

I thought of the last time I had seen Harry, when we parted cheerfully on leaving Wau a month or so earlier. It was a pathetic memory now. We would never keep our assignment to drink the remainder of the case of beer.

We made it clear to Kari and Watute that our work was now ended, and that our orders were to save ourselves if we could. They, as the senior men, would have to see that there was no deterioration in the morale or discipline of the others. They replied gravely that they understood their responsibilities, then saluted and withdrew.

Despite the injunction to move quickly, we made no attempt to travel that day. We still could not stand steadily, and would only have collapsed on the track.

The following day we made our first move, to Imom village. It was only five hours' walk away, but the country was rough and we seemed permanently short of breath. Walking downhill was more difficult than climbing, our knees frequently giving way and bringing us to the ground. Watute was still suffering a good deal from his injured foot, which had been made worse by the roughness of the track.

We found that Imom was under strong mission influence – which is tantamount to saying that we found a non-co-operative attitude among the people, if not open hostility. When the war with Germany broke out, a number of German Lutheran missionaries had been interned; apparently the idea had been conveyed to their congregations that this was a blow at the missions as such, rather than a legitimate rounding up of enemy aliens. Then, at the outbreak of war with Japan, when all missionaries were evacuated, the native mission teachers – or 'black missions', as they were called – fled from their stations to their home villages. During this period the native situation from our point of view was satisfactory, and the black people were friendly and helpful. After a time the black missions began returning to their work, and the attitude of the natives changed. When we found them aloof and disagreeable, it was a pound to a penny that a black mission teacher was resident in the village. The contrast, for instance, between the helpful courtesy of remote, heathen Gombawato and the churlish behaviour of Christian Imom is only one illustration which could be multiplied many times.

Mission interests in Australia have vehemently denied that the German Lutheran mission played an unhelpful role in New Guinea. The evidence, I feel, does not support them. After all, the Germans, with their mission, were established long before Australia took charge of the Territory. Again, as rivals with the civil authorities for ascendancy over the natives, they had no particular reason for supporting an alien government which, at best, merely tolerated them. Something of this attitude communicated itself to the natives, and some of them talked openly, though not very intelligently, about a return to German rule.

At Imom we made a tolerable meal from locally bought food, but Dinkila brought our tea to us with a long face.

'Master, no got some-fella tea more. Sugar 'e got lik–lik.'

'It had to come,' Les said philosophically. 'But, all the same, I'm not looking forward to the next few weeks – or months, as the case may be – without any tea.'

'It's not only tea we'll be without,' I replied. 'All we have is a few tins of bully beef and a huge tin of powdered milk. That's going to get pretty monotonous.'

'Never mind. The trade goods are holding out, so we'll be able to buy plenty of native food.'

'That's where the razor-blades are going to be handy. We've got enough trade goods in them alone to survive a six months' siege.'

When we had eaten, we spread our maps before us for what seemed to be the thousandth time since we had set out from the Markham. Our object was to find a place where the mountains could be re-crossed, and so get back to the Markham. We had a vague notion that there was a dip in the country between the end of the Saruwageds and the beginning of the equally formidable Finisterres. We intended to move westward looking for this, and traced out a tentative course from village to village, as they were shown on the map.

'One thing I'm bloody sure of,' Les said as he folded the maps and pushed them back into his haversack. 'Even if we go kanaka and spend the rest of the war with a bit of bark round our middles, eating sweet potatoes in Gombawato, we aren't going over the top again at thirteen thousand feet.'

The next night we spent in Kosuan, a pleasantly situated village. Three tame hornbills fluttered round the houses, swooping to catch any morsel of food that might be thrown to them. The people sold us enough to eat, but were not disposed to enter into closer relations.

In the morning we lined the few remaining loads of cargo in front of the house, and I called for men to come forward and carry it. As I spoke, silence fell, and one by one the men started to drift away into the bush that fringed the village.

'Quick!' I called to Les. 'Grab some of them, or we'll be stuck in this joint for the rest of our lives!'

Les sprang down from the house, pistol in hand, and we were about to rush after the vanishing natives. We need not have bothered. Suddenly, from behind trees and bushes, the police appeared, together with old Pato, rifles held ready. They closed in on the village in a circle, forcing the kanakas into a group in the centre. The villagers saw the trick had failed, and made no further attempt to escape, though they carried with surly faces and unconcealed ill-temper.

There was now no doubting the un-co-operative attitude of the natives of this part of the country, and as we walked along the track to Hamdingan, our destination for the night, Les and I discussed how best to handle them. We felt that at any moment the people might refuse to carry for us, and go bush at our approach. We decided to make a surprise entry into Hamdingan. Leaving the carriers under the guard of a couple of the police outside the village, the rest of us swooped down on the houses and had the populace locked inside their large new church before they realized what had happened. We selected enough young men for carriers and kept them under guard all night. Once the women saw that we had their men in custody they brought us plenty of food, for which we paid in razor-blades.

The road over which we had walked from Kosuan to Hamdingan was, for New Guinea, a great highway. It was at least twelve feet wide most of the way, and in some places up to twenty feet. Drains and culverts were neatly dug, and bridges had been built across all the streams. It was but another example of the way in which the 'black missions' had exercised their new-found supremacy. As natives told us afterwards, they had made the people of each village devote a certain amount of time each week to work on churches, schoolhouses, and roads. The work on churches and other mission buildings was harmless enough, but the road construction was in direct defiance of the orders of the government and of the few white men who had been through the area. It also showed that the pamphlets in pidgin English dropped from our aircraft, instructing the natives to allow any tracks to revert to bush, had been ignored. The purpose of these instructions was of course to make it as hard as possible for the enemy to find his way into the back country. It was plain that if he had chosen to come this way he could have marched twelve abreast with the greatest of ease.

In Hamdingan there was one man who spoke pidgin, but unfortunately he seemed half stupid, and it was with great difficulty that we secured any information at all from him. He gave us a very garbled account of another white man having left the Huon Peninsula by the same route, and from his vivid description of the red hair of this man we recognized 'Blue' Pursehouse, who had been doing work similar to ours behind Finschhafen. The fact that he had pulled out indicated that things had got tough in his area too, and we tried to find out how long ago he had left, and whether we had any hope of overtaking him. Our half-witted informant was no help. One minute he would raise our hopes by saying the man had gone two days ago, and then infuriate us by saying two years ago.

We were able to pick up a certain amount of useful information, however. He told us Hamdingan was only about a day's walk to the coast, and that news of Japanese activities often came up to them. Sometimes, he said, the Japs walked round the beach, and sometimes parties in charge of barges pulled in to hide from our planes during the daytime, to resume their journey to or from Lae at night. This news was disturbing, for we had not realized how close to the sea we had come. At nightfall, however, when all was quiet in the village, we heard the surf breaking on the beach, and we posted double sentries on the track in case the Japanese should hear of us and hurry inland to cut us off.

We told our pidgin-speaking native that next day we intended to go to Boksawin village, the place which seemed to lie nearest to the route we had in mind. He replied that it was at least two days' walk and that we would have to spend a night in some bark shelters on the way.

We had become so irritated by his silly and self-contradictory statements in other things that we told him flatly we did not believe him, and that we intended to walk without resting until we came to Boksawin, however far away it might be. Then Kari locked him in the church to keep him safely out of the way till morning.

Next day, at 4 a.m., we started our walk to Boksawin. There was no moon, and daylight was about two hours off, but the first part of the track was well defined and even. Shortly after sunrise the limit of the good road was reached, and we began to climb a steep mountain. Half an hour later our pidgin-speaking native paused beside a small stream, which, he said, was the last water we would see for another day. It seemed that he spoke the truth, for the carriers – about half a dozen of them – filled small bamboo receptacles with water and, having stoppered the tops with wads of green leaves, tied them to their loads. Les and I had no waterbottles with us – they were among the gear we had abandoned in crossing the range. In New Guinea mountain country one usually crosses a stream of some sort every mile or so, and we had not expected to need them. We took a good long swig, and then resumed the climb, hoping to make the distance to the next drink.

Before long the track, climbing steeply, became more difficult. Hundreds of huge trees had been felled across it and were lying in all directions. We progressed by walking along the trunks and springing from the end of one onto another, but they were very wet and slippery, and we often fell off. It was only through good luck that none of us was badly hurt.

Our boots had worn to paper thinness, and the nails, sticking through, were gouging holes in our feet. As the boots were more hindrance than help I threw mine away and walked mostly in bare feet, putting on an old pair of sandshoes occasionally, when the track was specially rough. In spite of my assurance that one soon became used to bare feet Les stuck to his boots until they dropped apart.

At midday we were still climbing steadily, and before entering a dense moss forest caught a glimpse of the sea across to Rooke Island, off the coast. We thought we could also distinguish the outline of New Britain on the horizon, but were not certain. Shortly afterwards we found the hunting shelters, where our guide urged us to spend the night. However, the cryptic 'Move quickly!' of the radio message rang in our ears, and we decided to push on.

The track became very bad as it led us along the crest of a narrow, level ridge which seemed to stretch on into eternity. It was clothed in dense forest, which prevented us seeing more than a few yards ahead or catching any glimpse of the surrounding country. The carriers were making very heavy weather of it, so we sent Kari and Constable Witolo, both strong walkers, to move ahead as scouts.

About half past four Les had a sudden violent spasm of vomiting, which left him so weak that it seemed he would have to be carried. However, with a great effort he managed to continue, from time to time holding on to me or one of the police. By nightfall he had recovered completely.

Shortly before dark we found a small stagnant pool of green, slimy water. The smell was revolting, but we plunged our hands and wrists into it and swilled it about our mouths and throats. Foul as it was it revived us and gave us heart to continue.

We plodded painfully on, wet through from a short, sharp downpour that had come about seven o'clock. It began to seem as though we would spend the rest of our lives struggling along this ridge as it stretched on and on endlessly into the blackness. We were worried about our hearts, which were pounding in a most alarming fashion – even worse than they had behaved crossing the Saruwaged Range.

Then, at ten o'clock, the track took a slight downward turn, and by half past ten the moon had risen and we came out of the forest into more open country with alternate patches of jungle and grassland. The condition of the track also improved, and it was now a well-graded zig-zag carved out of the steep mountainside.

Just before midnight, with the moon shining brightly, we came out upon the flat, open country near the Uruwa River. We were all barefooted now, and on the stony ground our footfalls made no sound. It was as if we were already dead, shades without weight or substance drifting through space. We had not the energy to look about, but plodded drearily, half consciously, forward. Suddenly two ghostly figures rose from a patch of shadow, saluted, and one said in a clear voice, 'Master, place belong me-fella close to now!'

Les and I were too tired to be startled by their sudden appearance. When one of the two men told us he was the tultul of Worin, and that Worin was the village we were approaching, we were too weary even to protest that we had been heading for Boksawin. Kari and Witolo had arrived a couple of hours earlier, the tultul told us, and were waiting in the village. We seemed hardly to have heard his encouraging news, and staggered silently, drunkenly, along the track behind him.

Worin looked unearthly in the moonlight. The mists from the valleys which surrounded it had blotted out from sight all the rest of the country, and the village seemed built on an island floating in space. Bananas grew among the houses, and the leaves of the plants, like tattered elephant's-ears, threw weird shadows on the ground. As we entered the village we eased our Owen guns forward and called to Kari and Witolo. There was no answer. We slipped off the safety catches and looked about uneasily.

'I left them here,' the tultul said anxiously, running to a dwelling and peering inside. 'Master, come lookim!' he said after a moment.

We went forward and Les flashed his torch inside the dark hut. Kari and Witolo, exhausted by their dash through the forest, lay asleep on the floor. Witolo had slumped forward, his forearm and head leaning in a mess of boiled bananas. Kari, sleeping no less soundly, lay near the door, rifle beneath his hand. We did not attempt to waken them, but moved across to another house. They had ordered the tultul to cook bananas and sweet potatoes for the boys, and two fowls for us. This had been done, and Les and I raised the dirty blackened clay cooking-pots to our lips and drank the soup first. Then we seized a fowl each and, ripping them apart in our hands, wolfed every scrap. We had not had a meal for thirty hours, and had been walking for about twenty hours without a pause. In the morning we woke to find ourselves lying amid the picked bones of our supper, pistols and sheath-knives still on belts round our waists, Owen guns still slung round our shoulders.

We watched the boys as they lay in front of the houses warming their aching limbs in the morning sun. Our bodies had been chilled for days and now seemed to soak up the cheering rays as blotting-paper absorbs water. We did not feel well ourselves, but the condition of our natives caused us more concern. They seemed utterly exhausted both in body and spirit, and by some queer illusion seemed to have shrunk in their misery. Later, Les and I observed the same change in each other. When Les shaved off the beard that had grown in the last three or four days I was shocked to see how thin and bony his face was. I realized later, of course, that I looked just as bad. Fever had been troubling us a lot, and we were very tired from the combination of great physical strain and the worry of the expedition. The safety of the native members of the party disturbed us, for they had all volunteered to come, had served us faithfully, and had stuck to us when they might easily have run away. Now we felt that we had to do something to get them out of the mess into which they had trustingly accompanied us.

We decided it was no use trying to move farther, when nobody could do better than drag himself painfully round the village. The best thing was to stay a while and recruit both our strength and our morale. There was plenty of food about, so we bought a very large pig and

PETER RYAN

decided to have a barbecue that night. This helped a lot, and there was a perceptible lift in spirits as soon as the pig's expiring squeals were heard.

The tultul of Worin — whose name, to my sorrow, I have forgotten — was a most remarkable man, and we spent the day sitting under one of the houses talking to him. He had for some years been a cook for Leigh Vial, the first patrol officer to penetrate this area, and upon his return home he had been made tultul. He was a person of great strength of character. He told us that mission teachers had been pestering him to get rid of the village book and his official hat, but he had steadfastly refused to do so. Indeed, his was the only village on the north side of the Saruwageds where the book and hat could be produced at our request. In spite of all discouragements he had endeavoured to acquaint his people with the ways of the government, and had taught several of his relatives to speak pidgin, though none of them had ever left the village. He would have liked to come with us to meet Leigh Vial again, whom he obviously admired almost to the point of hero-worship, but the tultul was now a married man with a family, and could not leave. However, he asked if we would take his younger brother with us, for the boy was very anxious to see something of the world beyond his own valley. Les and I discussed this but decided against taking the young fellow, for there was a good chance that before we reached Wampit again we should come in contact with enemy patrols, and we did not think it fair to take him into danger.

Vial was our 'contact man' in Port Moresby, and we could scarcely have had anyone more co-operative. Having worked in the bush himself in circumstances of fantastic danger, as the famous 'Golden Voice' behind Jap-occupied Salamaua, he knew how much it meant to us to have our signals answered promptly, and to feel that there was someone who would give us help and support wherever possible. It was he, for instance, who had arranged the strafing of Boana Mission. (When finally, some months later, I reached the comparative civilization of Port Moresby, I learnt of a curiously ironic and tragic coincidence: almost at the very moment when we were talking to the tultul of Worin, Vial himself was out on a leaflet dropping flight not far away. His plane crashed into a nearby valley and everyone aboard was killed. We wondered why we no longer heard from him by radio. Quiet, capable, unobtrusive, he was one of the greatest heroes of New Guinea.)

Late in the afternoon, while the pig was being prepared for the fire, we tried to send a message to Port Moresby informing them of our position and asking for any information that might be available about enemy movements in the surrounding country. At first we had some difficulty in passing the message and receiving the signals from Moresby but the trouble was only a flat battery, which was easily changed. Afterwards we heard some of the police discussing this failure to hear the 'talk', and were very amused at their theories:

'I suppose it's because we are too deep in the valley for the talk to get down to us,' one said.

'That isn't the reason,' another replied. 'It's because those high trees up on the mountain won't let the talk past.'

A third boy staggered them all with his superior knowledge. 'If you knew anything about wireless, you would have noticed that the wind was blowing the wrong way. How can the talk get all this way from Port Moresby if the wind is against it?'

Afterwards, whenever I built a new post, I put the house-police close to the house-kiap, for it was lots of fun at night-time to listen to the conversation, which was usually dominated by the 'old soldiers' telling extravagant lies about their deeds in the peacetime police force before the war spoilt things.

Feeling much refreshed by our day's rest, we left Worin about seven o'clock next morning, and at about eleven reached the village of Moren. There was a fine church here, but all the natives had run away, so after a short spell we followed the track down into the deep gorge of the Uruwa River, where our tultul said there was a bridge. He confirmed our belief that there was a place where the range could be crossed easily into the head of the Leron River, which flowed into the Markham, and agreed to come with us as our guide as far as Ewok, the first Leron village. He had made the same journey some years before with Leigh Vial.

The bridge over the raging torrent of the Uruwa was nearly broken, and we had to wait over an hour while the boys cut vines in the bush to repair it. While we sat in the shade waiting, we took note of the unusual rock formations exposed by the river. They were all manner of brilliant colours, varying from a rich ochre, through red to pale pink. They were very soft and chalky, which no doubt accounted for the fantastic shapes into which the water had carved them.

The country we were now in (and through which we were to pass for several days) was rather different from any I had seen hitherto. It was undulating, and the greater part of the ground was covered by kunai-grass, forest being confined to the hilltops and watercourses with the exception of a few patches here and there. For the first time since leaving the Markham it was possible to command a fairly extensive view of the surrounding country as a whole. Even in the most open parts of the Wain and Naba one was restricted to a view of one valley at a time. This Uruwa region was rather hot and dusty, but we welcomed the free feeling of open spaces, a contrast from the shut-in sensation we had had in the jungle.

We climbed up the steep western bank of the Uruwa, passed through a small hamlet set in a banana-grove, which the tultul said was called Sugan, and reached the village of Sindamon late in the afternoon.

This village, we were told, had never been visited before by either missionary or patrol officer, and of course it was not shown on our map. There was a legend that the people had fired such a number of arrows at the only missionary who had dared to approach that they were left in peace thereafter. Whether any of the arrows found their mark I was never able to find out.

Although they spoke no word of each other's language, our tultul and the Sindamon men soon established friendly relations. They were big, upstanding, dignified men, their bodies painted red with clay and their hair tied up tightly in dome-shaped hats of bark. Keeping a tight hold on their bows and arrows, they willingly exchanged food for razor-blades, which they had never seen before but for which they developed an instant liking. All our bargaining was done by signs, and we soon became very friendly.

When we indicated (again by signs) that we wished to sleep in one of the houses they nodded politely, removed a rotting corpse from the veranda, and motioned us to enter. It was apparently the custom here for a dead man to be left in his house until he had decomposed, when his bones were interred in a shallow grave beneath the veranda. Naturally the stink still clung to the place, but heavy rain fell and we were glad enough to be dry, though a large number of fleas did nothing to improve our night's rest.

We left Sindamon early next morning, really sorry to part from these friendly savages, and struck straight across the grassy hills to Kundam. There was a track we could have used, but it would have taken us through Goriok: with our binoculars we had seen a wide road leading into that village from the south, so we decided to avoid it. Though it was more difficult walking, the line we were taking across country was at least more direct. The Som River, swollen from the heavy rain the night before, was difficult to cross, but we joined hands and plunged through, a human chain.

At Kundam village, one of the most primitive I had ever seen, there were extensive gardens. We were unable to establish any contact with the people, who stood silhouetted against the brassy evening sky, black forms lining the crests of the nearby ridges, hurling their choicest terms of abuse at us. Now and again one more impetuous than the rest fired an arrow at random, though the range was much too great. Since nothing would persuade them to come down and talk to us, we had no choice but to help ourselves to the produce of their gardens. When they saw their bananas and taro being plundered their fury knew no bounds. 'Hopping mad' is the only expression that describes it. They screamed and danced with rage, and with loud yodelling cries discharged a whole cloud of arrows in our direction, though they must have known that their chances of hitting anyone were remote. In case they made a night attack, we doubled the sentries before rolling in our blankets on the ground at the edge of the village. Here again the fleas were too plentiful for a really restful night.

Before leaving Kundam in the morning we tied several pieces of cloth and a dozen razor-blades to a tree in the middle of the village, by way of payment for the food we had taken. There was now no sign of the inhabitants, and we hoped this did not mean they were lying in ambush for us somewhere along the track.

We could see the village of Ganma, the next on our route, about four miles away across the valley, but though we spent two hours searching for a path, there was none to be found, and we had to march on a compass-bearing, cutting our way through the bush and secondary growth. When we arrived at the village shortly after midday we found that it consisted of two or three very poor houses. At first none of the natives was to be seen, but about three o'clock a party appeared on a hill nearby and made a hostile demonstration. We could not understand a word of what they said, but their gestures, obscene and defiant in turn, left nothing to the imagination. We called to Nabura, the best shot in the party, to climb quickly onto the roof of the tallest house, from where he would be able to detect anyone crawling through the grass. He was told to keep the people just out of arrowshot, and not to fire to kill or wound unless the situation seemed dangerous. We asked the tultul what our chances were of making friends with them, but he did not seem to think it worth while trying, saying that they were notoriously bad hats and that it would take us at least several days even to open a conversation.

The next day we were to cross the mountains once again, onto the Markham fall of the Huon Peninsula. We expected to reach Ewok village in the afternoon, for according to the tultul the crossing was nowhere near so high as the one we had made over the Saruwaged Range proper.

The tultul asked to be allowed to return home from here, though the other Worin boys would stay with us until we reached Ewok. We let him go. He had done us good service: none of the other natives would have directed us to this easier crossing, and we would merely have blundered along, hoping to find it by good luck. The only other person who might have been able to advise us was Vial, and he, though we did not know it then, was dead.

We abandoned most of our gear at Ganma – keeping just the wireless, our personal packs, and a small parcel of trade goods. We gave our shotgun to the tultul, together

with a packet of cartridges. He was doing a fine job, pre-
serving government authority all on his own, and the fillip
to his prestige from the possession of a shotgun would
greatly ease his unenviable burden. He asked whether he
could also have two empty cartridge-boxes in which we
had kept tobacco. We gave them to him and asked why he
wanted them.

'It's like this,' he explained in pidgin. 'If I go back
home with a carton of a dozen cartridges they will spy on
me when I am hunting, and every time they hear a bang
they will say "Another one gone", until they know I have
used them all up and the gun is useless. However, when
they see these three boxes they will think I still have
plenty left.' With a sly grin he filled the empty cartons
with pebbles, and then closed them securely.

We also gave him a bottle of oil and told Kari to
show him how to care for the gun. I never saw a man so
proud of a present. He would allow nobody to take it
from him, and as he lay down to sleep that night the gun
lay beside him.

This place was the worst for fleas that I had ever
been in. The whole surface of the dusty ground seemed
to be crawling with them. During the afternoon Les and
I amused ourselves by seeing how many of the pests could
be caught in one blanket, killing upward of seventy before
tiring of the game. The sort of night we spent, lying on
the ground, is better left to the imagination. In the
morning it would have been literally impossible to put a
pinhead between the bites anywhere on our bodies; we
had the appearance of suffering from some skin disease.
Even the police, not unduly fussy over a flea or two, said
they had spent a sleepless night.

Shortly after sunrise we shook hands with our tultul
and turned our faces towards the mountains. The crossing
was not really difficult, and was lower than we had dared

to hope – scarcely above seven thousand feet according to our estimate. The worst part came when the mountain had been crossed and we had to follow a rough, stony riverbed down to Ewok. My bare feet were pretty much cut about, and Les, who put on again the tattered remnants of his last pair of boots, did not fare much better.

The country as we approached Ewok was more like the Wain – country of luxuriant growth and heavy rainfall. It was a change from the arid grasslands we had left behind, and, moreover, we would probably secure much better food. We were sick of the taro and hard cooking-bananas which seemed to be all the Uruwa country had to offer. Boiled bananas are the most unpalatable and uninteresting food one could have – looking and tasting like a piece of grey stodgy clay. The only result of eating them, as far as I was concerned, was an unsatisfied hunger and a bellyful of wind.

Ewok, to all appearances, was a model village, set on a lofty, narrow ridge. It was clean, well laid out, and abounded with neatly arranged trees and shrubs, some decorative and some useful. The mission seemed well entrenched, to judge by the excellent state of the church and school. Although the mission teachers hurriedly vacated their houses and disappeared, the other natives greeted us in tolerably friendly fashion, answered our questions, and brought us food – including a dozen eggs which we ate at a sitting.

Being well into wild mountain country we were surprised and disappointed to hear that the Japanese had twice visited this village. While there, they had been informed of the easy route to the north coast over which we had just come, and their leader had announced that another patrol would soon come to investigate it.

'I don't like the sound of that,' said Les. 'It seems we might be chased all round the Leron country now.'

'I don't think I could take much of that,' I replied. 'If there's going to be any rough stuff, I think I'll look for a quiet, out-of-the-way spot, and hole up there till the bloody war is over – for years, if need be. The war can't go on for ever – or can it?'

Les smiled wearily. I could see he felt much the same as I did. All sense of adventure and excitement had long since vanished from this patrol, leaving behind an empty flatness that was only one degree removed from despair. We were just plodding on, in spite of frightful weariness, in an attempt to save our skins. More and more frequently we were coming to doubt whether those skins were worth the agony of sweat and sobbing breath and aching bodies and bleeding feet.

It was more to preserve the illusion that we still functioned as an intelligence patrol than in the hope of getting useful information that we sent for the few Ewok men who spoke pidgin and began to question them. Strangely, they had no aversion to talking freely, and we discovered a number of useful facts about enemy patrols in the area. They were much more extensive than we would ever have suspected, and everything seemed to point to the establishment of a strong overland line of communication between Madang and Lae. The Japanese had told the natives to be ready at any time to carry machine-guns, food, ammunition, and other stores, and to feed and guide other enemy parties.

Their propaganda, moreover, was cunning. In addition to the obvious line about all the white men having run away, they pitched the natives a story that won them a lot of service. Briefly, it ran somewhat along these lines: 'When you native people die your spirits go to live in Japan, our homeland. The spirits of your ancestral dead are living in Japan now. Unless you look after us Japanese well we will see to it that the spirits of your dead get a bad time.'

One could ridicule this, of course, but it was very difficult to counter effectively, and many natives believed it implicitly.

After we had sent off a long message to Port Moresby, incorporating all the information we had gathered about enemy patrols in this area, we felt that perhaps, after all, we were still of some use, and not merely a ragged crowd of fugitives.

Late that night a boy from a nearby village brought us news of another European at Wantoat, not far away. This, we surmised, was Fairfax-Ross, the man being withdrawn from the north coast. He had been expecting cargo to be dropped by plane to him at Wantoat about 17th June, but the cargo had not arrived. As it was now 18th June, and Wantoat was a good two days' walk away, we felt we had small hope of overtaking him. In any case, his chances of escape were probably better while he was alone. The natives said – though afterwards I was not able to confirm the point – that he was even worse off than ourselves, for he had neither boots nor clothes. We still had rags of some sort. It was strange to sit in Ewok and know that just a few days' walk, a few valleys away there was another white man struggling on to safety. He did not know it, but our thoughts followed him on his long, lonely walk to the Central Highlands, where he was eventually picked up by aeroplane.

It was nearly twelve o'clock that night before we finished laying our plans for the next few crucial days. The Japanese seemed to be everywhere, so our only hope was to move with all possible speed. Three rivers flow into the Markham from the north side – the Leron, the Irumu, and the Erap. To have followed the Leron down would have taken us within range of enemy patrols near Kaiapit, the district where Harry Lumb had been killed. The Erap would have led us down close to Lae, and, after my frequent trips on the river the previous year, the enemy would be almost certain to be watching it. Between the two lay the Irumu, flowing into the Markham not far from Chivasing, where we had begun our patrol a couple of months earlier. We decided to move as quickly as possible down this river, travelling mainly at night and avoiding, if possible, all contact with the natives.

We left Ewok at three in the morning, our immediate object being to get over the divide between the Leron and the Irumu rivers to Bogeba village. We arrived in Bogeba almost exactly twenty-eight hours later, having neither eaten nor slept in that time. When I came to write the official report of the patrol I found that I had no real rec- ollection of this part of the journey, but only a succession of impressions, unrelated in time or space: impressions of villages where we sneaked around in the dark, not waking the inhabitants, of rivers which almost swept us away, of legs which stumbled on, unknowing and uncaring, all feeling gone. I am sure that half the time we walked with our eyes shut from exhaustion.

At Bogeba we rested for a day and a night and made several good meals on native foods. The kanakas seemed friendly, and said that though the Japanese had never been to the village they knew there were many of them moving about the country. They introduced us to a native of Siang village, farther down the river, who said he could guide us along the Irumu to the Markham, avoiding all the tracks. This seemed a good plan, and we moved to a hamlet a few miles downstream to wait for nightfall. We set up the radio here for what was to prove the last time, asking Port Moresby to inform our forward posts along the Markham that we could be expected either next day or the day after. After a journey such as this had been, we wanted to run no risk of being shot by our own men, which could easily have happened, particularly if we crossed at night.

Just at sunset we moved off, leaving behind everything but light packs and our arms. We followed the Irumu, walking in the water for the most part, for though very swift it was not deep. The valley was a very shallow one in the Markham plain, about a thousand yards wide, and the stream wandered haphazardly from one side to the other, in several channels. As there was a bright moon, we had no difficulty in seeing our way. The country was as flat as a table, and covered with kunai- and cane-grass. Dotted here and there were weird black sentinel-like stumps, the remains of dead palms.

We were so tense and keyed up with the strain of this final stage that the slightest movement or noise in the shadows made us start, but we felt no weariness, though we walked without rest all night.

About three o'clock in the morning, as we splashed through the muddy water, we heard a rooster crowing, and then the howl of a dog. The sounds came from the bush on the right-hand side of the river, and we knew we must have passed Teraran village. So far, everything was going smoothly, and another eight or nine miles should find us at the Markham. However, the Irumu started to subdivide into numberless tiny streams, and finally petered out altogether in a tangled swamp of cane-grass, sago-palms, and cruel-thorned vines. Our native from Siang announced himself baffled too. It had not been like this years before, he said nervously, and then, afraid we would vent our concealed wrath on his person, he took to his heels and vanished into the night.

For a while we tried to cut our way through, moving on a rough compass-bearing. It was a scene I shall never forget: a dozen or so natives and two white men hacking like fury in the moonlight at the wall of jungle ahead of them, knee-deep in the slime, swearing, grunting, whimpering occasionally as bare feet encountered the savage thorns of the sago-palms.

When dawn broke we found that our progress had been disappointingly slow. Given time, we could have cut a pathway to the Markham, but we had no food and were near exhaustion. We felt our strength would never be enough to carry us through. After consultation with Kari and Watute we retraced our steps to the main Markham road, which we had crossed a couple of hours earlier. There were a number of prints of the enemy's well-known black rubber boots, but none seemed to be of recent origin. We followed the road, scouts well out ahead, as far as the old Wawin rest-house, and then turned south down the track up which we had come on our way out – two months ago to the day.

The track showed no footprints, and to judge by the way the grass was growing on it had not been used for some time. All the way to Chivasing we saw no people, and the hamlet half-way was deserted. We were weary, sore-footed and aching all over, but we kept kidding ourselves along with the thought of the cup of tea we would soon be drinking at Kirkland's, and of the European foods we would eat there. 'Not far now,' we would murmur each time we crossed a creek.

The hot Markham sun blazed down on us and the sweat squirted from our bodies. The dust from the dry track rose slowly round our feet, sticking to our wet skins. We did not care. The end was in sight. By about three o'clock we had reached the large coconut-grove at the edge of the village, and looked up longingly at the cool green nuts. A crowd of Chivasing natives, with the tultul and doctor-boy, appeared suddenly at the other end of the grove and advanced to meet us. Some of them climbed the palms to get green coconuts for us to drink. We sat in the shade and let the cool fluid trickle down our dust-filled throats.

'Are there any Japanese about?' we asked at length,

our inevitable question, which we hoped would be for the last time.

There was a silence. The steaming quietness of the Markham afternoon descended.

'Are there any Japanese about?' we repeated sharply.

'No-got, master! Me-fella no lookim some-fella Japan!' The answer came readily enough this time.

'Better make sure,' Les said. 'We'll send Arong into the village to have a look round.'

We called to Arong, who had had a drink, to move into the village. He was wearing no uniform, and there was nothing to mark him out from the Chivasing kanakas, so he would be safe enough even if there were Japanese there.

While he was away we tried to make conversation with the natives. They seemed strangely uneasy, but they said they had expected us and had the canoes all ready to take us down to Kirkland's. We wondered whether we imagined the tension in the atmosphere – whether the long strain now ending had made us over-suspicious. We were cheered when Arong came back a few minutes later with a smile on his face, to say that he had taken a look round the village and that all was as it should be. Then, Arong leading the way, and Les behind him, a few paces ahead of me, we walked into the village. Most of our boys stayed in the grove, still drinking coconut milk.

As we neared the clear space at the centre of the village there was a sudden burst of machine-gun fire and a volley of rifle-shots from one of the houses. Bullets kicked up the dirt all round us. We both made a dash for the creek that runs through the village, and as I jumped down into it there was another burst of fire from the house. Les gave a cry, fell, and lay still. Japanese – there seemed to be dozens of them – then jumped down from the houses and rushed over towards me. I lost my footing and fell into the water, got my clothes and Owen gun tangled in a submerged branch, and finally struggled across the creek and into the bush minus Owen gun and most of my shirt. Bullets were clipping the leaves all round me. I did not go far, but buried myself deep in the mud of a place where the pigs used to wallow, with only my nose showing, and stayed put.

For a few minutes all was quiet, but soon I heard the Japanese calling out to each other, and their feet sucking and squelching in the mud as they searched. I could not see, so I did not know exactly how close they were, but I could feel in my ears the pressure of their feet as they squeezed through the mud. It occurred to me that this was probably an occasion on which one might pray, and indeed was about to start a prayer. Then something stopped me. I said to myself so fiercely that I seemed to be shouting under the mud, 'To hell with God! If I get out of this bloody mess, I'll do it by myself!' It was no doubt a childish sort of pride, but I experienced a rather weary exhilaration that, terrified and abject, lying literally like a pig in the mud, I had not sufficiently abandoned personal integrity to pray for my skin to a God I didn't really believe in.

I lay there motionless, buried alive in mud and pig-filth, feeling, or imagining, creatures of unspeakable loathsomeness crawling over me in the slime. The voices became fainter and the squelching footsteps died away. I eased my face out, blinked the mud away from my eyes, and carefully pulled some leaves over my head in case the searchers returned.

For half an hour or so there was no sound. Then several natives walked round the outskirts of the village calling out to me. I heard their voices clearly, just a few yards away through the bushes:

'Master, you come! Japan all 'e go finish!'

I did not move. They continued to call out to me encouragingly for a quarter of an hour. Then one of them said apparently to someone nearby, ' 'Em 'e no hearim talk belong me-fella. I think 'em 'e go finish long bush.'

The Japanese started talking to each other again after that, having given up hope of capturing me, it seemed, now that the trick had failed.

I stayed in the same place until it was nearly dark. The mosquitoes were swarming on my head so thickly, and buzzing so loudly, that I thought they would give away my position. Then I crept out of the mud, wiped the mud off pistol and compass, and began to break bush, moving on a line south and west, which, as I remembered the map, should at last bring me to the bank of the Markham, some distance upstream from Chivasing, more or less opposite the mouth of the Watut River.

In a couple of years packed with bad journeys, that night's travel is the worst I can remember. Near the village it was essential to move with absolute quietness, no easy matter when the rows of hooked thorns on the vines caught at me continually and one hand was always occupied holding the compass. It was no use trying to free myself from the vines – as fast as one row of barbs was detached another took hold. It was easier, if more painful, to let them tear straight through the flesh. After the bush came the pit-pit – cane-grass eight or nine feet high, growing so thickly as to make a solid wall. It was impossible to part it and walk through it, and I was forced to push it over by leaning on it, and crawl over the top on all fours. It had leaves like razor-blades, which hurt terribly on bare legs; mine were soon dripping with blood from the cuts. Worse, the flattened grass left a trail a blind man could have followed. Though I had my compass handy the grass blocked all view of any object to sight on, and there were no stars, for it was a cloudy night. The two luminous points on the instrument danced and swung before my eyes. Sometimes I had to pause, close my eyes, and force my nerves to calmness before I could see properly. Every time I tried to march by sense alone, I found myself going wrong.

Hours later, during one of these pauses, I heard the dull swish of swiftly flowing water. The Markham! I had got there sooner than I expected. It would take every scrap of my energy to swim it, and I removed my clothes, such as they were, and buckled on again the belt which carried revolver, compass, and sheath-knife. Then I stumbled forward, heading for the sound of the water. When I reached it I found it was nothing but a small creek flowing down to the river. I nearly cried with rage and disappointment, and decided to go no farther that night, but lay down naked where I was. The mosquitoes were terrible, setting all over my body in swarms, and their bites nearly closed both my eyes. Finally, to escape them, I dragged myself into a shallow puddle of mud at the edge of the stream, and slept there.

Shortly before daylight I moved on, weak and stumbling, my heart jumping in the frightening way I had noticed in the mountains. The last few miles were easier, for the pit-pit gave place to kunai, through which one could at least walk upright. At any moment I expected a volley of shots, for the country was flat, and if, after sunrise, the Japs had taken the trouble to post a few men in trees, they could not have failed to see me. I crossed one new track through the grass, which showed many enemy footprints, and reached the Markham about mid-morning. As I looked across its swift brown streams I knew that I was too tired to swim it before I had had a rest, so I crawled into a patch of bush and dozed until about midday. Then I swam as silently as possible from one island to the next, resting for a short while on each one. Every time I touched a log or floating piece of rubbish I was terrified it was a crocodile, and struck out with renewed vigour. I really believe it was this fear, coupled with the expectation of a burst of machine-gun fire from the north bank, that enabled me to make the distance.

On the south bank at last, I lay breathless in a patch of grass. Voices came from not far away. I eased my pistol out of its holster and peered through the grass. Two Chivasing natives, with their women, were walking straight towards me, chattering happily, quite unaware of any alien presence. As soon as they drew level I jumped from cover, shoving the pistol into the ribs of the nearest one. The men trembled, but made no sound, and the women moaned faintly. They were too terrified to shout – apparently they thought I was going to shoot them out of hand.

'You-fella got canoe? 'Em 'e stop where?'

They nodded, and pointed to a spot on the bank nearby. I made them lead me to it and ordered them to take me to Kirkland's. They were so terrified that I was afraid they would faint, but I jabbed them in the ribs with the pistol and forced them to get aboard.

Although I felt certain in my mind that Les was dead, I did not have positive evidence. I did not want to ask the Chivasing people directly, so I phrased the question in a way which did not reveal my ignorance.

'What are you going to do with the other white man?'

Their reply snuffed out the lingering spark of hope that Les might be alive.

'We will bury him in the cemetery at Chivasing,' one said in pidgin.

'We will see that he gets a proper funeral,' added the other man ingratiatingly, as if that would atone in some way for his people's treacherous share in Les's death.

The rapid muddy stream was sweeping us down towards Kirkland's, and I made the natives hug the south bank closely, to keep out of the range of Japanese who might be on the north side. When Kirkland's came in sight

I stood up, waving my arms above my head and cooeeing, and I was shortly answered by a hail from the low kunai hill behind the camp. As the canoe nosed in under the foliage to touch at the landing-place, several Australian soldiers stepped out of the bushes and helped me ashore. Half carried, half supported, I made my way with them to the wretched little huts, and sat down in the mosquito-proof room while they brought me tea and some army biscuits.

Nobody said anything much, and I sat there dully, staring at the swamp. I had no sensation of joy or relief, though I knew in a remote and abstract way that I was now safe. I had no thoughts, no feelings whatsoever. I felt neither grief on account of Les nor anger at the Japanese or Chivasings. Nor did I feel any sense of warmth or companionship towards the soldiers who were now preparing water for me to wash, and giving me articles from their own scanty clothing to cover my nakedness. I was too spent, emotionally, to feel or think or care, and I know now that such a state is the nearest one can come to death – an emptiness of spirit much more deadly than a grievous wound.

After I had been sitting there for a little while, Kari, Watute, Dinkila, Pato, and all the other boys limped up to see me. They managed a salute, but I could see they felt as dispirited and weary as I did. They were cut about and tattered, and caked with grey Markham mud that cracked and dropped off in little flakes as the skin stretched beneath it. I shook hands with each one, and they shuffled back to the little hut, where they were crowded together. Kari and Watute remained for a few moments to talk. They had stayed across the river looking for me, they said, and when they found my tracks leading to the river, con-cluded I would be all right, and floated themselves down to Kirkland's on logs. Arong, the boy who had entered the village with Les and me, had been captured by the Japs and taken to Lae, Watute added.

Next day a horse was sent down for me, and I rode to Wampit. Here I had a proper hot shower, and willing helpers gathered round with needles and dug dozens of thorns out of my limbs and body. There was no skin at all on my legs, and my feet were so enormously swollen that I thought boots would never fit on them again. Months later, I was still digging out odd thorns that had been overlooked at Wampit.

The following morning I set out on horseback for Bulolo township, which had replaced Wau as the military headquarters of the area. The police and other natives followed on foot, and during the several days which for me were occupied in writing the long report of the patrol they straggled in by twos and threes, still very weary.

After a few days I went to the store to get new clothes. I was wearing a woollen shirt, a pair of ragged green shorts, and some old sandshoes, but no hat or socks. All of these had been given me either at Kirklands or Wampit.

'Where's your paybook and your other papers?' demanded the quartermaster.

I explained the fate of my clothes and papers and other possessions.

'Good God, man, that's no excuse!' he snapped. 'Don't you realize it's a crime in the Army to lose your paybook? You can't be issued with any equipment here without a paybook.'

I didn't argue, but let the district officer arrange a new issue of clothing for me. But I started to wonder all over again if wars were really worth the trouble.

IX

EXCEPT FOR sitting up to write the patrol report, I spent most of the time for the next week lying on my bed-sail smoking, reading, and dozing. The police and other boys were doing much the same, and I hardly saw them.

At the end of that time, however, my feet had shrunk to their normal size and I could get them into boots again. I wandered about, gossiping to anyone who had time to talk, and performing various duties in the district office.

Jock McLeod came in one day. He was in charge of the lines of native carriers supplying our troops as they advanced on Salamaua, through the Buang mountains, and was as usual engaged in a bitter feud with the Army.

'The rotten bludgers!' he exploded with characteristic vigour. 'I can't even be bothered talking to them any longer! I've got these coons slaving their guts out; they aren't properly housed, and they're on about half rations, and I've been telling the Army so for weeks. Now the boys are all going down sick and the Army is demanding explanations. When I tried to tell them the boys are only human, some bloody jumped-up snotty-nosed staff officer told me I had the wrong slant on the job. "You must regard the natives merely as so many units of energy, Mr McLeod," he said, "like motorcars" '

Jock's fulminations and Vertigan's more temperate representations had some effect, and arrangements were made for better rations for the carrier lines.

He was interested to hear of the situation north of the Markham, and had the last laugh when he remarked with a quiet grin, 'I said you'd find the Nips all round Boana by the time you got back there.'

After a couple of weeks, as soon as their raw feet and aching limbs were better, the boys wanted to return to the bush. Kari and Watute approached me as a delegation:

'Master, me-fella man belong work bush. Me-fella no like sit down long arse long station.'

I confessed to them that I was finding station life pretty tedious too – a dull routine of sending signals inspecting labourers, and writing letters and lists. I promised I would do my best to get us back to more congenial work in the bush.

In July luck changed for me: I was posted back to the bush. But I learnt with bitter astonishment that I was to have a new squad of police. They were smart recruits from the depot, faultless on parade, but utterly inexperienced in bush work. Mighty Kari, shrewd Watute, crackshot Nabura, and all the other policemen were posted elsewhere. We gathered in my hut for the last time, while Dinkila packed my gear. I gave Kari an old pipe, Watute a sheath-knife, and the others any odds and ends I could scrounge.

It was a sad parting when we shook hands. I never saw any of them again, though I heard that Kari was made a sergeant-major, the highest rank to which he could rise. But they are never far from my memory, and I hope that, back in their grass-thatched villages, they sometimes think of me.

I still had Dinkila and Pato, and all the other non-police natives who had been with me on the Huon Peninsula patrol, and we set out in July for the Lower Watut River – to Tsilitsili. Our errand was as follows:

The Allies were now firmly on the offensive, and the Americans wished to establish a forward fighter aerodrome in the Lower Watut area. This would enable our fighters to range as far as Wewak, which was not possible from the existing dromes in Port Moresby. It would also serve as a partial jumping-off place for our impending assault on Lae. A few Americans and Australians had already moved to Tsilitsili and begun work on a landing-strip.

Although our patrols, some of them native troops of the Papuan Infantry Battalion, were watching the Markham from the mouth of the Watut down to Kirkland's, there was a twenty-mile stretch of the Markham upstream from the Watut mouth which was quite unguarded. In this sector the enemy could easily cross the river and attack the aerodrome construction at Tsilitsili. Kaiapit lay just across the river from this stretch, and it was known that the Japanese were there in force, but since Harry Lumb's death information from the area had been irregular and uncertain.

Our job was to watch this twenty-mile stretch of river, find out all we could of enemy activity on the other side, and warn Tsilitsili if the Japs made any attempt to cross and attack the drome.

The four-day journey down the Watut was uneventful. One night we slept in a big comfortable house of native material overlooking the lovely valley. Fully equipped, the house looked as if it were awaiting the return of its owner, which would never happen, for the house was Harry Lumb's. It was from here that he had worked his gold mine in peacetime.

One of my new police-boys told me the story of how Harry was supposed to have died. He was in a village called Ofofragen, near Kaiapit, and the natives had assured him that there were no Japanese about. Then they betrayed him to the very same band of Japs who had so nearly caught Watute and Pato near Boana a few days earlier. He was shaving, and in the mirror caught a glimpse of the enemy advancing on the house. According to this boy they shot Harry down as he made a grab for his Owen gun. He had always said that the Japanese would never take him alive.

At Tsilitsili (pronounced, by the way, 'silly-silly') I found a mushroom metropolis. Where a week ago had been a sleepy native village, a tent town straggled through the fringes of the jungle, inhabited by American troops and airmen, both white and negro, Australian soldiers and airmen, Papuan infantrymen, native policemen, carriers, and labourers. On the rough earth airstrip, hastily cleared, DC-3 transports roared in and out, unloading troops, stores, and construction equipment. A major operational base had sprung from the earth just at the back door of Lae, the enemy's main stronghold.

By lamplight in their tent that night I met the local Australian and American commanders and discussed the details of my assignment. They were acutely conscious of the danger from that exposed twenty-mile stretch of the Markham, but were sceptical about its chances of being effectively patrolled by one white man and a few natives.

I told them it was my intention, if at all possible, to use the inhabitants of the villages as additional scouts, and by that means develop a fairly efficient watching system, to warn them of any attack. It was agreed that I should set out next day, and I was immediately supplied with an abundance of stores and enough carriers to transport them.

An American officer of engineers spoke for the first time just as I was about to leave the tent.

'I was wondering,' he began diffidently, in a soft, drawling voice, 'if you'd have me along on this trip? Must be kinda lonesome on your own.'

He was about thirty, with red hair, and a face brick-red from sunburn. Blue eyes smiled a little nervously from behind gold rimless glasses.

'My name's Tex Frazier, and I come from Texas,' he went on. 'I'm kinda interested in maybe putting some airstrips up that Markham River. I guess I'll see I don't get in your hair too much.'

I usually preferred to patrol alone, but I had been sick a great deal from fever, and weak from the hookworms which had invaded my system during the barefoot patrolling of earlier months. It would be an advantage to have someone along, and he had such a frank, engaging presence that I agreed at once, and we arranged to leave before first light next morning.

X

I HAD PICKED the village of Amamai for our headquarters. It took us four days to get there, of which two were spent on the banks of the Wafa River waiting for its floodwaters to subside so that we could cross.

Pato distinguished himself during those two days. He made a fishhook out of the brass clip that held the Rising Sun badge in my hat, a fishing-line from odd bits of twine, split a log open for grubs for bait, and in less than half an hour had landed a monster cod from the muddy waters of the Wafa.

A large part of the walk to Amamai was through dense sago-swamp. We squelched through it as cautiously as we could, scouts out ahead, for no one knew whether the Japanese were there or not. In the early stages I had great trouble with Tex. When silently reconnoitring a stretch of track he would suddenly think himself back in the Lone Star State and burst loudly into a spirited version of a Moody and Sankey hymn. He found it so hard to stop this that I detailed a policeman to walk nearby and silence any outburst before it gave us away.

By the end of the second day Tex had mastered the need for silence. That night, over our meal, he said sheepishly, 'By golly, it sure must have given you the shivers when I lifted up my voice a mite too high! But I'm all well controlled now.'

The people at Amamai were friendly. Most of the able-bodied men had been taken away by Harry Lumb to work as carriers on our supply lines. But the older men, and the women and children, built me a house on a knoll from which, with binoculars, I could sweep a vast extent of the Markham Valley, on both sides of the river.

Tex and I quickly patrolled every village for several days' walk around, distributing trade goods to establish ourselves in favour. The people were all fairly friendly, but wary. They knew the Japanese were just across the river; sometimes they saw parties of them on the opposite bank; sometimes the enemy sent natives across, seeking information.

I sent a police-boy back to Tsilitsili with a report on the situation, and Tex and I continued our patrolling.

During one of our walks Tex was unusually silent for a long period. When we sat down in a little village to drink coconut milk he told me what he had been pondering.

'This is the way I figure it, Peter,' he began. 'If we have to keep sending messages back by police-boy, it'll take him two or three days to get there, and another two or three days to get back – maybe six days he's missing. Now, if we have to send a lot of messages, we're mighty quick going to run clean out of police-boys. Yes, sir! What we need is an airplane.'

'Sure, we need one. But where will we get it?'

'People find it mighty hard to refuse a Texan when he's real set on something,' Tex drawled with deadly seriousness.

Next morning, with the aid of every man, woman, and child in Amamai, he set to work on an airstrip.

'Just a little one for a start,' he said. 'Enough to put a Piper Cub down on. If we want heavy aircraft later, we'll extend our strip.'

I could hardly believe he was serious, but he assured me that he was.

The following day, patrolling by the Markham, we pounced on a native who was doing his best to slip away from us into the river. He did not belong to any local village, and the police frog-marched him up to the house for interrogation. It was here that I missed Watute. In half the time, and with twice the accuracy, he would have uncovered the information for which I now had to work all day and night.

I got out of the man that he was a native of Orori village, across the Markham, and had been sent to spy by the Japs. He told me that a strong force of the enemy was starting to move forward from Madang, through Marawasa, to Kaiapit, and perhaps on to Lae. Some of the enemy patrols Les Howlett and I had encountered were partly engaged in surveying a route for this movement.

This was information of first-rate importance, for, as it turned out, the Japanese formation the native referred to was a strong group commanded by General Nakai, with which the Australians were to fight heavy battles in the months to come.

I wrote down what the man told me, and sent a report back to Tsilitsili with a police-boy. Tex went with him.

'This is the last time either you or I walk through that terrible messy swamp,' he said. 'When I come back, I'll be flying. You keep that airstrip clear!'

I was still doubtful, but I had grown so fond of Tex that I begged him to return, by whatever means he could.

Two days after he had gone we saw an American fighter aircraft limping back from an attack on Madang or Wewak. It was on fire, and crashed some miles away across the Markham. We saw the pilot jump and float down on his parachute, but we could not find him. Then, when we had almost given him up, two natives helped him into the camp, dirty, cut about, ragged, and exhausted.

We fed him and cleaned him up, and he told us about his struggles through the rivers and swamps.

'I never knew there was bears in this country,' he remarked.

When I told him that the bear tracks he described were in fact crocodile marks, he nearly passed out.

'Oh goddam!' he muttered. 'And to think I swam that river in three places!'

He stayed with me for a few days in the hope that Tex would come in with a plane. One morning at breakfast he held up his hand excitedly. 'Listen! That's a Piper Cub!'

The noise sounded more like a motorbike than an aeroplane but I rushed down to the little strip and set fire to a pile of dry grass. The smoke would give the pilot the wind direction, if it should turn out to be Tex.

Just at treetop height the little plane soared over and circled the camp. Tex's red face beamed down on us as he waved. Then – a perfect landing on the strip.

Tex grinned as he and the pilot stepped out.

'Plane's at our disposal,' he said proudly. 'I had quite a struggle to get it – had to go over to Port Moresby in the end. It'll be kept at Tsilitsili, and come out here every day or so.'

The Cub pilot and the fighter pilot were discussing the length of the strip. They didn't fancy their chances of a safe takeoff. They wanted it made longer for future flights, but told us what to do to help them off the ground on this occasion.

With the help of all the Amamai people we fastened strong vine ropes to the tail of the Cub, and then the two Americans climbed in. The pilot revved his engine as hard as he could, and while the tail of the plane lifted and bucked we held it back grimly with the ropes. Then, at a signal from the pilot, we let go, and the little craft shot forward and into the air, almost as if it had been catapulted.

'Well, I guess that's one way of getting that machine off the ground,' said Tex. 'But we better lengthen that strip and cut down that line of trees at the end.'

The days passed pleasantly enough. Tex moved to and fro, and extended the drome so that we even had visits from DC-3 planes. Troops moved up – native infantry, and then Australians. They were followed by an American radar unit. All this relieved me of the necessity for patrolling, and I concentrated on collecting native intelligence among the villages, which sometimes yielded information of value from across the river.

Most of the walking was over flat country, but my health was getting worse, with bouts of fever every few days. I could cover only short distances at a time, and had to rely more and more on the police.

One day, after a few days' absence, Tex flew in and casually handed me a parcel.

'Many happy returns of the other day,' he drawled. 'Just seen your folks in Melbourne, and they said it was your birthday.'

My twentieth birthday had passed the same way as my nineteenth – in the bush and forgotten. But Tex, in the nonchalant way I was now accustomed to, had drifted the several thousand miles down to Melbourne, just for the day, and had called on my family. I had not seen them for nearly two years.

When we heard the news of the fall of Salamaua we issued double rations all round and turned on a party for the local kanakas.

Then the assault on Lae began. Downriver we could hear the bombardment.

A few days later a R.A.A.F. Moth plane landed on the strip. We ran down and the pilot handed me a letter.

'Hurry,' he said. 'You're wanted pronto down near Lae.'

He would not even turn his engine off, and I had only time to get personal gear, climb into the passenger's cockpit, and we were in the air.

We landed at Nadzab, a few miles up the river from Lae. I had known the place in the early days of the war when, with Bill Chaffey and others of the 5th Independent Company, I had slunk furtively round its hot grass plain looking for Japanese. Now, from a parachute landing a few days earlier, it had grown to a mighty base, bigger than Tsilitsili. From it the assault on Lae was even now approaching success.

I was rushed at once to headquarters for consultations on the various tracks through the Wain and Naba, paths to Boana and Bungalamba, over the Saruwageds, and also up the Leron.

Lae was found nearly empty when our forces stormed the place. Many Japanese had been drawn off to reinforce Salamaua, and the others had made good use of their prepared escape-routes through the mountains. This was final proof that Watute and Pato had correctly interpreted enemy activity in the Wain. Yet, in spite of the information Les and I had sent from Orin, on 9th June 1943, New Guinea Force had said:

> In spite of recent native rumours, there seems to be no good reason, tactical or otherwise, why the Japanese should try to open up a track across the Saruwaged or Finisterre ranges, which are over 11,000 feet high!*

It was not until 15th September that Lieutenant-General Herring said in a signal to Major-Generals Wootten and Vasey:

> Indications support your view that enemy may be aiming

to withdraw northward from Lae to Sio by routes leading through Musom and Boana.*

Now, if only Jock and I had been equipped with radio and allowed to remain without interruption in the mountains, we could have been of some use, pinpointing for our forces every move the enemy made. As it was, our troops, unfamiliar with the fantastic terrain, had to chase and harry the retreating enemy as best they could manage.

The next day I wandered round among our troops as Lae finally fell to us after nearly two years in enemy hands.

Australians were doing a brisk trade in counterfeit Japanese flags, made by painting a bright red disc on a piece of parachute silk. Some copied characters from Chinese Epsom-salt bottles, and we frequently saw an American proudly displaying his 'Japanese' flag, which bore the words, had he known it, 'Two teaspoonfuls in warm water, followed by a cup of warm tea.'

The next step was at hand in our rapidly developing campaign to push the Japs right out of New Guinea. Kaiapit was our objective. It was to be taken and held, as one move forward on the important coastal town of Madang, which for long had been in Japanese hands. It was also intended to deny Kaiapit to General Nakai, in case he sought to use it as a base for a counter-attack on Lae.

The 6th Independent Company, one of our crack commando units, was to perform this task. I was to go in with them, organize a native labour force from the local inhabitants for carrying supplies and for aerodrome construction, and assist with reconnaissance and native intelligence.

---

* I am indebted to Mr Gavin Long, General Editor of the Official War History, for making known to me the existence of the two extracts quoted above, and for allowing me to see the text of a volume of the Official War History—David Dexter's The New Guinea Offensives.

An American flew me up the Markham in a Piper Cub. A high wind was tearing down the valley, and we made such slow progress that at times we seemed to be hanging motionless above the jungle. When we reached the rendezvous beside the Leron River a crashed DC-3, flat on the kunai, showed where the 6th Company had already landed.

The pilot found it difficult to put the light craft down in the gusty wind, and a driving rain made visibility bad. When at last we touched down, after many attempts, there was less than an hour to dark.

'Good luck, buddy!' bawled the pilot, and he took off again, back to Nadzab, whisked out of sight in a moment by the powerful wind behind him.

The 6th Company men were huddled under groundsheets and one-man tents dotted all over the kunai. Their stores and ammunition were also scattered in heaps among the grass. Portion of the unit had already moved forward a few miles to Sangan, on the road to Kaiapit. I ran after them, across the flat country, and managed to collect enough Sangan kanakas to bring to the Leron to carry the ammunition and stores forward. We made several furtive trips by torchlight, and had all the cargo in Sangan before dawn.

I collapsed with fever in Sangan, and remember nothing until the following night. I had made my bed under a native house, and one of the 6th Company men shone a torch under the mosquito-net.

'Sorry to wake you up, mate,' he whispered, 'but there's a Yank called Tex blown in. Says he wants to see you. Do you know him?'

There behind him was Tex, a grin all over his red face.

'Looks like they're going to need us,' he said. 'Going to be a powerful lot of airstrips needed between here and Madang. I'll find the drome sites, you work the natives.'

I shook hands with him, but it was hard to find anything to say. Dinkila, who had accompanied him, told me severely to get back to bed. His expression said clearly enough: See what a mess you get yourself in when I'm not there to look after you!

Kaiapit was taken in the next two days, after a fierce and bitter battle by the 6th Independent Company assisted by some troops of the Papuan Infantry. For the loss of ten men they killed about two hundred of the enemy. In the end they sent him reeling back with a bayonet-charge when their ammunition was almost spent. Tex went into action with them.

I lay under the house while the battle raged, too weak to move, whether forward with our troops, or backwards to escape the Japs had they won the day. While I shivered, the sweat ran out the end of the bed-sail, drip, drip, drip upon the ground.

It took me nearly two days more to hobble yard by yard to Kaiapit, leaning on a stick like an old man, and sometimes holding on to Dinkila. We had to pick our way between the Japanese dead, who still littered the ground. Bloated by the tropical sun, some of the corpses had burst right out of their uniforms. Near Kaiapit some of them had been hastily buried. From one of the shallow graves, at the side of the track, a stiffened hand and forearm reached over the path.

I watched, propped with my stick against the trunk of a palm-tree, as a number of soldiers passed. With macabre, unsmiling humour, which some say is typical of the A.I.F., they bent down one by one and shook the hand of death. 'Good on you, sport,' each one said gravely to the hand as he moved on towards…perhaps just as rough a grave of his own.

Kaiapit Mission House, on an eminence above the kunai plain, looked to me just like Boana Mission. Tex helped me onto its wide veranda, and got some food, but any attempt to swallow even a mouthful made me vomit.

Later in the day a doctor came, who said that I must be evacuated to Nadzab in the morning.

'Nadzab nothing, doc!' Tex drawled. 'I'll have a special plane take him straight to Port Moresby.'

I dropped off to sleep on the floor of the veranda, Dinkila squatting on his heels nearby, watching.

Next day, with Tex's help, I walked down to the strip. On the way we passed a Japanese soldier lying mortally wounded beside the track on a stretcher. He had been revived by one of our medical people, and was now being badgered for information by an interpreter and some intelligence men. As far as I could see he was saying nothing.

As I looked at his face, wasted with fever and suffering, I suddenly felt more akin to him than to the Australians who would not let him die in peace. His eyes, wonderfully large and soft, met mine. In that brief second I hoped he could read the message in my face.

I realized then that I did not really hate the Japanese – that I did not hate anyone. I realized that war accomplishes nothing but the degradation of all engaged in it. I knew that Les Howlett's death had been in vain, that the loneliness of spirit and suffering of body I had forced myself to endure had been to no end, and that the selfless devotion of my native companions had been, in the final analysis, purposeless.

I said goodbye to Tex and Dinkila. The doors slammed shut between us, and the plane took off.

We turned up the valley of the Wampit River, flying very low. At Kirkland's the kunai was already silently covering the place. At Bob's the jungle creepers would, in a few months, drag the houses down and smother them with their weight.

In a year there would be nothing – no mark or vestige to show where they had been.

As we flew across the land which had soaked up the sweat of two years, I could drag one mouldy crust of comfort and of hope from the events of 1942 and 1943:

Man is very brave. His patience and endurance are truly wonderful. Perhaps he will learn, one day, that wars and calamities of nature are not the only occasions when such qualities are needed.

Text Classics

textclassics.com.au